I0700381

REIGN AND RUIN

Enchanted III

MALLORY WANLESS

Cover design by @AnjoleyDesigns

First edition

ISBN:

Paperback
979-8-9855733-4-3

Ebook
979-8-9855733-5-0

Also by Mallory Wanless

Enchanted series:

Storm and Flame: Enchanted I
Blood and Destiny: Enchanted II
Reign and Ruin: Enchanted III

Coming soon:

Enchanted IV
Enchanted V
Enchanted VI

For Lisa.

I'm sorry we never met in person, but you were an amazing human
and we are all luckier for having had you in our lives.

Pronunciation Guide

Characters

Elena: eh-LAY-nah
Agon: A-gone
Quinn: qu-IN
Lyra: LIE-rah
Madame LaBelle: ma-DAM la-BELL
Zied: ZED
Roska: ROSS-kah
Demoni: de-MON-ee
Aiden: a-DEN
Aleerah: ah-LEER-ah

Places

Andover: ann-DOVER
Nexton: NEX-ton
Cyra: sigh-RAH
Riverayn: river-INE
Rolam: ro-LUM
Slyvestris: sill-VES-tree

1
QUINN

Q UINN WOKE TO THE sound of blood-curdling screams and a distant roar of anguish. Their cries exacerbated the pounding in his head.

Someone was calling out Elena's name. Their voice echoed around Q, but they sounded far away.

He tried to sit upright, but the pounding in his head only intensified as he moved. Instead, he remained in an awkward—and rather painful—reclined position and slowly opened his eyes.

The world around him seemed to be falling to pieces.

He was still in the cavern in the Dragon's Teeth. Aiden lay unconscious across the chasm with Aleerah. Lyra was slowly rising and shaking her head, struggling to remain steady on her feet. Roska lay beside him, blood pooling under his head. Demoni wasn't moving, coiled tightly around his neck.

Where was Elena? She had been with him when he'd been fighting the *turmio*.

Oh, gods! Where was the *turmio*?

"Elena!" the voice cried out again. A man's voice. Filled with panic and heartbreaking sorrow. Quinn's eyes scanned the room for the source of the voice. A guy, not much older than Q, lay on the ground across the chasm. His head and arms were dangling into the pit, as though he was reaching for something. Someone.

Mother Goddess. No. Please no.

Quinn's heart shattered as he put the pieces together. He was supposed to be the one who died fighting that damned monster. Not Elena! She was innocent, safe, clean. She was supposed to survive and live a long, full life. She wasn't supposed to be the one prophesied to fall in this battle.

"No. No. No no no." Quinn couldn't catch his breath. The word slipped out over and over as he struggled to make sense of what had happened.

Where had she gone? How had she been the one to fall instead of him or Roska? What the mux happened?

2

BEATRICE

BEATRICE COLLAPSED TO THE floor, gripping her chest, feeling a frantic and unnerving sense of disconnection. She and Belladonna had been walking the newest section of the Wall that now fully protected Harbor Ridge when she'd been overcome. Tears sprang forth from her eyes, unprompted and devastating.

"Bea!" Belladonna rushed to her side, catching Beatrice just as her knees were about to make brutal contact with the stone walkway atop the Wall. "What happened? Are you hurt?"

Belladonna's firm grip was the only thing that kept Beatrice from coming apart entirely. Something was wrong. Something was *very* wrong.

"I... I can't feel her." Beatrice sputtered. "I can't feel Elena. Something has happened." Beatrice didn't have the mental capacity to explain how she felt. She didn't have the words to vocalize the sense of loss and brokenness that shattered her heart.

"What do you mean?" Belladonna looked confused. Her eyes searched Beatrice's face, trying to understand the nonsense that was spilling from her lips.

"There was a connection. A tether of sorts," Zied offered. "It was a small, magical bond that kept the children eternally connected to us. Something has severed that connection. Elena's tie to us is gone." Zied shook his snowy mane, as though he were trying to break free of the sudden emptiness that threatened to envelop Beatrice entirely.

"She's gone." No sooner had the words left her lips, Beatrice gave over to the darkness that beckoned her.

When she awoke, Beatrice found herself lying in the middle of her bed, surrounded by healers. Belladonna was pacing between her open bedroom door and the window. Castor sat on the windowsill, flapping his wings anxiously and twitching his head every which way. Zied, who lay stretched out beside her on the bed, turned his head as she tried to remember what had happened.

"Praise the Mother!" one of the healers shouted. The remaining healers began bustling around Beatrice, touching her arms, hands, face, and neck. It was overwhelming and entirely unnecessary. If she was going to die from the loss of her child, there was nothing these healers could do to stop it.

Zied raised his head, slowly baring his teeth in silent warning. The healers quickly got the message and departed from the room without another word. Calmly, he laid his head back down, this time across her lower abdomen. Directly above the spot that had once grown and protected her children.

Beatrice hadn't bothered moving. She knew she wouldn't die this day, at least not from the loss of Elena, but she desperately wished she would. Perhaps then the ache and burning pain that flooded her body would release her. Perhaps she would even be reunited with her daughter in the Fade and be able to tell her all the things she'd never bothered to vocalize before. Beatrice desperately wished to tell her daughter just how amazing she was. That despite her previous actions to the contrary, Beatrice truly loved and was forever in awe of Elena.

Belladonna gingerly sat down beside Beatrice on the bed, taking hold of the enchantress's limp hand and gently pressing her lips to Beatrice's knuckles. "I thought we'd lost you." Her voice was a harsh, broken whisper.

"I'm sorry, my love. I didn't mean to frighten you." Beatrice tried to pour love into her words, but she knew they fell flat. She couldn't suffuse her words with love because her heart had shattered the moment Elena's soul had left this world.

Belladonna, clearly not taking Beatrice at her word, lay down beside the enchantress and pulled her into a tight embrace. "Is she really gone?"

Beatrice couldn't answer. The words wouldn't come. Instead, she broke. Tears flooded her eyes, soaking Belladonna's dress as the witch held her tightly. Beatrice didn't bother trying to maintain her composure.

Her child was gone.

Ripped from the world.

Beatrice wasn't sure she would ever feel whole again.

3
ROSKA

ROSKA COULDN'T BELIEVE THE sights before him. The sun was shining brightly through the opening in the cavern ceiling. Snow fell peacefully through the gaping hole, covering the cavern floor with a fine layer of white, almost as though it were trying to cover the ugly scene before him.

He hadn't moved since he'd regained consciousness several moments before. His mind simply couldn't comprehend the fact that she was gone. How had this happened? He was the one who was supposed to go down with the beast. He'd accepted his future and his punishment for unleashing the damned thing in the first place. Why did Elena have to pay the price for him?

Roska watched disconnectedly as Quinn interrogated the dark-haired man whose screaming had first roused Roska from his unconscious state. Q seemed enraged at the guy's presence, although Roska didn't understand why.

Truthfully, Roska didn't understand the "why" of anything anymore.

"What the hells are you even doing here?" Q's rage-fueled question drew Roska's attention back to the interaction before him.

"Who the mux are you to talk to me that way?" the man raged back just as viciously.

"I'm the guy with the flaming hands asking the muxing questions." Q's palm filled with fire as he spoke, shocking the man into silence.

Roska wasn't sure exactly when Q had crossed the chasm to reach the stranger, but even from his spot, dazed on the floor of the cavern leaning against the cave wall, Roska could see the flames blazing in his brother's eyes. Roska struggled to stand, relying heavily on the wall to keep him upright as he tried to speak to Quinn. He couldn't let his brother murder this man without at least knowing who he was and why he'd been crying out for their sister.

"Quinn," Roska called out, his voice sounding raw and distant in his own ears. He coughed a few times, trying to clear his throat and reclaim his voice. "Quinn," he said again, more forcefully. "You can't kill him."

Quinn didn't take his eyes off the man, continuing his slow, predatory steps toward him, flames building in both hands. "Why not, Ros? Why shouldn't I kill the man that brought our sister to her death? The man that probably had her kidnapped in the first place and did unspeakable things to her until she managed to escape?"

"Your what?" the man asked, incredulously. To his credit, the stranger didn't back away as Quinn encroached on his personal space. Roska could see sweat starting to bead on his face, but the stranger didn't shrink away from Q's fiery rage.

"Our *sister*, you mux." Q spat the words at him, flames shooting higher in his palms. Roska could feel the cavern temperature rising.

Roska kept his hand on the cavern wall as he walked the edge of the space, making his way across the chasm to reach his brother before Q did something he'd regret.

"She didn't tell me she had brothers." The man seemed genuinely confused. Astounded even.

"Why the mux would she tell you anything?" Quinn snapped.

"I thought... well, clearly I misunderstood." The man looked from Quinn to Roska, then to Quinn's flaming hands. He raised his own in surrender and added, "I didn't know she had brothers. I didn't kidnap her either. That was my mother's doing. I'm the one who helped her escape. I'm the reason she made it here in time to save your sorry asses."

"Say that again, you son of a—"

"Quinn!" Roska shouted. He closed the distance between himself and Q in a matter of seconds, calling on his frost while positioning himself between the man and his enraged brother.

They all needed to take a step back, partly because they were far too close to the chasm for comfort, but also because setting a man on fire would only create more problems.

Quinn tore his eyes from the stranger, directing his fiery gaze at Roska. "Move." His voice was a harsh growl, carrying the weight of his grief and fury.

"No," Roska said flatly. "This won't help anything. We need to check on Aiden and Lyra. We need to get out of here. We need to get back to the school and make sure that magic is healing."

"Look at me," Q raged. His eyes flared an almost painfully bright orange. "Magic is muxing working."

"Killing him won't bring her back." Roska's voice was a broken whisper. He felt the loss of their sister as deeply as Q, and he knew his brother's reaction was spurred by the emptiness they both felt.

"He's right. But there might be something else we can do to bring her home." Aiden's voice carried across the tense space of the cavern. Both boys turned to face him in an instant, forgetting entirely about the stranger as their attention honed in on their father.

"What the hells are you talking about?" Quinn's fire faded almost immediately. The sudden loss of his heat was jarring but not nearly as unsettling as their father's words.

"She's not dead. She fell. Just as the prophecy foretold. She fell with the *turmio* into The Nothing. But we can pull her back." Aiden stood slowly; his arm looked as though it wasn't quite connected properly. Gingerly, Aiden grasped his upper arm, lifted it slightly, and pushed it firmly back, grunting at the effort. The sound of the joint popping back into place was sickening. "Probably," he added, raising his arm slowly, testing out its range of motion.

"What the mux is going on here? Who the hells are you?" The stranger spoke up from behind them, startling Roska. He'd completely forgotten the man was there. Hearing that they might be able to rescue Elena, that she wasn't dead, had captured all of his attention.

"My apologies, Your Highness," Aiden offered the stranger a dramatic bow.

Your Highness?

"I am Aiden, Elena's father and a demi-god. I believe you've already met my sons, Roska and Quinn," Aiden continued. "This majestic creature is Aleerah. Oh, no, don't worry, Your Highness. She won't harm you. She's actually quite friendly once you get to know her. Isn't she, boys?"

The stranger took several cautious steps backward until his back was pressed against the cave wall.

"Your *highness*?" Quinn asked incredulously. He didn't even try to hide the mocking tone in his voice.

"Yes," the stranger answered, although he didn't take his eyes off Aleerah. "I am Prince Niko."

"Wait," Roska spoke up. "You said your mother had Elena kidnapped. Your *mother*, as in The Queen? The wife of the man our mother has been having an affair with for nearly a decade?"

"Aye. Mum's a bit sore about that particular topic. That's why she had the *turmio* unleashed in the first place. She hoped to weaken your mother enough to send in the army and have her killed. She had Elena kidnapped when she heard you were on your way to stop the *turmio*." Niko shrugged, as though all of this was old news. "I imagine she'll be in quite a mood when she learns that you succeeded. She'll be none too happy with me for releasing Elena in the first place."

Roska and Quinn stared at The Prince in stunned silence. This man, the son of their enemy, had released their sister and returned her to them. Granted, she'd promptly been taken away, sucked into The Nothing with the *turmio*, but Roska knew that wasn't the Prince's fault. He also knew it might take a little convincing before Q saw it that way.

4

QUINN

*T*HIS GUY? THIS *GUY was the one who rescued Elena?* Quinn couldn't comprehend how such a pompous, arrogant, clearly self-indulgent ass could have gotten dressed without a team of servants to help him, much less freed their sister.

Maybe he's got some secret powers we don't know about yet. Lyra offered. She had been knocked out beside Aleerah, but quickly closed the distance between them when the argument had gotten heated.

"So... you were saying?" Niko prompted Aiden when the awkward silence had become unbearable. "About being able to save Elena?"

"Aye, well it's a bit complicated, but it is possible. You see, she's in another dimension. The Nothing isn't in our world. It's connected to ours, but only slightly." Aiden casually dusted off his pants, like he thought this convoluted nonsensical word vomit was actually an answer to the Prince's question.

"Father," Roska spoke calmly, almost as if he were addressing a child. "I don't understand what you're saying, and I'm pretty confident that I'm not the only one."

Q knew his face was broadcasting just how confused he was by their father's words. Another dimension? What the hells did that even mean?

"Think of it like this: our world is a bubble," Aiden waved his hand, and a bubble appeared in the air before him. "Our entire planetary system fits comfortably within this bubble, and we've never had need or cause to venture out. But ours isn't the only bubble." He waved his hand again and another bubble appeared, floating in the air. With a gentle touch, the bubbles kissed but didn't combine, like the suds in a bathtub. "This is how our dimension connects with others. You see how they touch but don't merge? That part where they make contact is where the veil between dimensions is thin. This chasm," he gestured to the gaping hole in the cavern floor, "is one such point of connection."

Quinn just stared at his father. *What the mux is this old fool talking about?* He shared an incredulous look with Roska before turning away from his father and trekking back across the chasm to the makeshift altar they'd used to cast the spells and ritual. He knocked over the empty containers of herbs that Roska had painstakingly cleaned and ground into a powder the night before. Q could feel his rage building again, but he didn't bother trying to contain it this time. He screamed at the top of his lungs, throwing his flaming fists into the sky and unleashing his power.

Elena was gone. Again. He'd seen her, fought with her, and lost her. *Again.* And all Aiden had to offer was some batshyt crazy nonsense about dimensions and bubbles and gods-only-knew what else. Quinn raged until his throat was too raw to utter another sound and his fire was diminished to nothing but a hint of an ember buried deep in his chest. She was *gone*. He'd failed to keep her safe. Again. He didn't deserve to be here. She did. Elena was the best of all of them, and she'd fallen into oblivion to save them.

He collapsed in a heap of despair on the cavern floor beside the now charred altar. Lyra hopped along the edge of the chasm and came to rest at his side. His hands fell uselessly into his lap as he hung his head in defeat. Tears silently leaked from his eyes, but he no longer cared. He'd failed her. Nothing mattered anymore.

Unexpectedly, he felt the icy touch of something coil into his upturned hands. Q opened his eyes to find Demoni curled into his palms. Her frosty breath soothed his frayed nerves as well as his scorched skin. Roska didn't say a word as his familiar helped to calm his brother. It was an unspoken rule amongst the magical community—according to Elena—that one didn't touch someone else's familiar. Not to mention, in Q's experience, it left an almost slimy feeling under the skin of everyone involved when such contact was made. Yet here Demoni was, deliberately touching him without any concern about the "ick factor" as Elena had called it. Quinn's tears fell in renewed fervor at the selfless act of kindness he surely didn't deserve.

"It's no one's fault that she fell," Aiden said softly. Q hadn't noticed his father crossing over to him, but he felt the man's hand on his shoulder as he wept. "It was predetermined by fate, but we *will* get her back."

"It should have been me." Q's voice was strained and raw. He wasn't sure they even heard him until Roska replied.

"Don't be an idiot. It was supposed to be me." Ros placed his hand on Q's other shoulder and shook him slightly. "I was supposed to be the one to pay the price since I was the one to set the damned beast free in the first place."

"You deserve a second shot at life. I was supposed to be the one to fall so the two of you could have the lives you were meant to have," Quinn countered.

"Oh mux this. You can all debate who *should* have fallen after we get her back." The Prince snapped, drawing Quinn's tearful eyes from his brother's face to the arrogant princeling's across the chasm. "She'd be pissed to know the three of you wasted precious time bickering over this shyt when you could have been bringing her back."

Quinn hated to agree with the pompous, self-righteous Royal, but he made a good point. They were wasting time. He offered a nod of thanks to Demoni before gently lifting her and placing her on Roska's shoulder. Q ruffled Lyra's fur and rose to stand before the Prince.

"How the hells would you know what she'd think or feel, *Your Highness*?" Quinn didn't bother hiding his contempt. If this Prince really thought he had a chance with Elena, he'd have to get through Q first.

"You get to know someone pretty well when you spend three days alone on a ship with them." The Prince smirked.

Before he could even think, Q punched the arrogant jerk in the face. Right in his princely eye. *Muxing ass.*

To his credit, the Prince didn't lash out. Q was expecting—and fully prepared for—an all-out brawl with the Prince. He'd never been in a fistfight with royalty before, but he couldn't imagine it would be any more challenging than man-handling the drunks out of Amelia's after the solstice festivals.

Instead of punching back, or reacting in any way really, the Prince just stared at Q. If he didn't know any better, Quinn might have confused the look on the Prince's face as awe or admiration.

I must've hit my head harder than I thought, Quinn pondered.

Well, you did fly into a wall, but I think you're right. He looks impressed. Maybe he's never been punched before. I can't imagine there are too many people in the world stupid enough to punch a prince in the face like that. Lyra didn't look at him as she thought, keeping her gaze locked on the Prince.

"Quinn!" Roska's voice carried a tone of condemnation, almost concealing the pride in his voice. Q could tell his brother didn't approve of his actions but was also rather impressed with him. Roska might not condone violence, but Q knew his brother recognized the Prince's offensive innuendo and quietly approved of how Q addressed the issue.

"It's fine," the Prince said, wiping the blood from the cut where Q had split his eyebrow. "I overstepped. I apologize. I shouldn't have implied anything improper. I swear to the Mother, nothing untoward occurred between your sister and me."

"Oh, we know," Quinn said simply. "She would have reduced you to a pile of ash if you'd tried anything. She can take care of herself."

He said it lightly, but the weight of that memory nearly brought Q to his knees. The first time he'd failed her. She'd nearly been raped by a group of violent bastards. That was the first time she'd ever channeled her lightning, and it had resulted in the quick—and entirely justified—death of those sons of bitches.

Roska seemed to realize where Q's mind had gone, grabbed his arm, and drew him back to the present situation.

The Prince, seemingly unaware, chuckled and nodded his agreement. At least he wasn't an idiot. Prince or no, he knew not to mux with Elena, and that was comforting. Or it would be, if she were with them now.

Q pushed away all the dark thoughts and memories that threatened to bombard him and turned to face Aiden. "What do we need to do? Can we just do Roska's ritual again and release her?"

"Not unless you want to unleash the *turmio* too. No, we'll need to handle this very carefully. And we'll need your mother's help," Aiden replied.

"Mother? Seriously? What makes you think that bitch will help us do anything? All she seems to want to do is lock us away." Quinn couldn't control his temper. Too many things had gone wrong since he'd regained consciousness. He was certain he'd be on fire again if he had any energy left.

"She was trying to protect you. Yes, I agree that she went about it in a very backward way, but in her mind, it was the best thing for you." Aiden tried to soothe Q's irritation, but he failed miserably.

"Whatever. Let's just get the mux out of here and get on with it. The sooner we get Elena back, the better." Quinn was fuming, but raging in the cavern wasn't going to get his sister back. Maybe a few fireballs—perfectly aimed to maim but not kill—would motivate their mother to be useful for once in her gods-forsaken life.

5

ROSKA

ROSKA TRIED NOT TO think about Elena as they hiked back through the tunnels to exit the cave the same way they'd come in the day before. Quinn had expressed concern that they might not be able to leave that way, since the cave had closed up behind them upon entry and they hadn't tried that exit when they'd left the cave the last time they were there. Aiden promised that if the cave entrance was still sealed shut, he'd blast their way out. Q had seemed bolstered by the potential for violence—even if it was directed at an inanimate object—and had readily agreed to it. Roska agreed because, if the cave was open, it was a much faster route back to the main road and Harbor Ridge. The Prince had even offered them the use of his longship, which would cut down on their travel time immensely.

The Prince. He was an interesting character. He had the air of someone not used to hearing the word "no." However, when Quinn punched him, he took it without fighting back or even acting offended. Hells, he seemed impressed. Roska started to wonder if the Prince had been baiting them, seeing how far he could push them about Elena before someone reacted. But that would be foolish. Wouldn't it?

He strikes me as someone who's trying to find his place. Maybe he's hoping to win you three over so that when we get Elena back, he'll have a better chance with her, Demoni offered.

Maybe, but that's a pretty idiotic plan. Elena has a mind of her own. She doesn't need or want our approval. She makes her own choices. Roska knew his sister wouldn't need their permission to find a mate. She was a strong-willed person. She didn't need anyone's permission to do anything in her life.

Yes, Demoni hissed, *I know that, and you know that, but he's a prince. They're used to having life negotiated for them. Matings are arranged by the fathers of the future bride and groom.*

Matings? Who's talking about matings? Roska stumbled over his own feet in the darkened tunnel. Quinn, who was directly in front of him, turned back to check on him. Roska nodded and waved him off. No need to wrap Q up in this startling conversation. His brother wouldn't take kindly to the idea of mating Elena off to the Prince.

We aren't talking about mating her off, you dolt, Demoni chastised him. *I'm simply making an observation about the Prince and his archaic ideas about mating and how those things get worked out. I know that Elena wouldn't go for that anyway. She will make her own choices, regardless of what anyone else has to say.*

Well, I would like to think she wouldn't bind herself to someone we don't like, Roska added, suddenly anxious and a little self-conscious.

Roska studied the back of the Prince's head. As they trekked out of the cave, Aiden led the way with Aleerah. Prince Niko followed behind him with Lyra quick on his heels. Clearly, she trusted the Prince as much as Quinn, who walked behind the Prince with a small flame resting in his palm. He said it was to light their way, but Roska knew it was more likely there in case the Prince tried something foolish.

Roska was fairly certain the Prince had pure intentions. He'd heard the anguish in the guy's voice when Elena had fallen. It carried the same pain that had shattered Roska's heart. The pain of losing a loved one. Roska wasn't sure if the Prince truly loved Elena, but he believed that the Prince cared for her and wanted to bring her home safely. They could determine the depth of his feelings for her when she was back in their realm, safe and unharmed.

Much to Roska's surprise, the cave opening sat before them, as though nothing had happened. Agape, with its stalactites and stalagmites creating the imposing image of teeth, their exit lay ahead of them, when just hours before it had vanished without a trace.

"Muxing magical cave," Quinn muttered under his breath. Roska shared his brother's sentiment. The cave, its cavern, and the entire mountain range were filled with mystical energy that had caused them indescribable pain. The Dragon's Teeth hadn't seemed fit to rest until it had taken something precious from them. Now that

Elena was gone, the mountains had released them from the prison of its caves.

Aiden and Aleerah led the way down the mountain, making quick work of the rocky slopes. Vultures circled ominously overhead; a foreboding sign of worse things yet to come.

They reached their stone circle in record time. And it was *their* stone circle at this point. It had provided them with shelter, witnessed the growing bond between siblings as well as their failure to escape their mother's investigators. Now the circle would house them once more before they sought out their mother in the hopes of using her power to rescue Elena.

The sun was setting beyond the trees as Roska lowered his pack and began to dig through it, pulling out a small pot and tossing a hard travel biscuit to Q.

"What are you doing?" the Prince asked—more like demanded. "Why have we stopped?"

"It's getting dark, Your Highness," Quinn snipped. It impressed Roska how his brother could make "highness" sound like such an insult.

"Aye, and...?" The Prince was either very slow or very stubborn.

"We can't very well hike through the snow and ice in the dark, Prince. We'd freeze to death. Or fall into the half-frozen river. Or become someone's dinner. Or get lost." Quinn listed off all the ways night travel was a bad idea, checking them off his fingers while glaring at the Prince. "I can go on, but I think you get it."

The Prince glared right back. "We can't stop here. We have to keep going and get her back. We can't just leave her in that hells-scape."

Roska jumped in before Q punched the Prince again. "We aren't going to leave her or abandon her, Your Highness." Roska kept his tone as even as possible, hoping to calm everyone and avoid another altercation. "But we can't safely hike in the dark. We will have to rest tonight and begin our journey at dawn."

"If we hike a bit farther, my longship is moored just over the rise." The Prince pointed vaguely to the south, beyond a small, snow-covered hill. "We can rest on my ship while we continue on our quest to seek out your mother's aid."

"Quest?" Quinn scoffed. "This isn't something from a fairytale, you idiot. We aren't on some gods-given mission to jump through muxing hoops and prove ourselves to get some fancy-ass prize. We are trying to save our *sister*."

Roska stared at his brother, gauging his mental state. Quinn didn't even feign respect for the Prince's royalty. Roska knew that Q wanted to rescue Elena as quickly as possible, but he was starting to worry that confining them all to a ship while they raced off to a mother who didn't want them might end *very* badly. Q seemed to read Roska's mind because they locked eyes for a moment before offering a subtle nod and hauling his pack back onto his shoulder.

"Lead on, Your Highness," Quinn said, shifting his gaze from Roska to the Prince. Q's tone didn't actually imply the level of respect his words should have elicited, but at least he'd dropped some of his hostility. Lyra leapt through the tall grass, lighting the tip of her tail to provide them with safer passage.

"Please, call me Niko." The Prince turned away, heading in the direction of his ship. "All this Your Highness nonsense gets so tiresome."

Quinn rolled his eyes so hard that Roska worried he might make himself dizzy. Thankfully, Q said nothing and followed behind the Prince.

Aiden, who had been standing quietly off to the side of their stone circle with Aleerah, struggled to hide the smile that tugged at his lips. Aleerah must have thought something to him because Aiden chuckled and nodded to her.

"Is there something we should know?" Roska asked, one eyebrow raised as he studied his father and the dire wolf.

"You'll find out soon enough, son. I can't go spoiling the future for you. I am glad to finally have a name to go with the face that's been popping up in my mind over the cycles." Aiden pushed off the stone he'd been leaning against, scooped up Roska's pack, and handed it to him before stalking off after the others.

What the hells does that mean? Demoni asked

I have no idea, Roska replied. He tossed his pack over his shoulder and headed off in the direction of his family, praying to the Mother that their mother would be more helpful this time.

6

BELLADONNA

Seeing Beatrice break down like that had nearly wrecked Belladonna as well. Bea was the strongest woman Belladonna had ever known. To see her shattered into a million pieces, unable or unwilling to eat or even sit up, was terrifying. Belladonna held the enchantress in her arms all night, praying to the Mother that they'd misinterpreted the prophecy. That Elena wasn't really gone. That she'd simply lost her power but was still alive and well.

Yes, losing her power would be devastating, but at least she'd still be alive.

Although, Belladonna couldn't help but feel like a life without her own magic would be worse than death. Perhaps an enchantress, especially one so young, would be able to acclimate to a magic-free life more smoothly.

Or perhaps she would wish for death.

Belladonna shook her head, trying to erase those thoughts from her mind. Beatrice didn't need her speculating on Elena's potential as a magept. Belladonna needed to be a rock for Bea. The support system she'd been lacking all these cycles. Belladonna needed to focus on the problems before them and not speculate on things that she couldn't change.

The royal soldiers were close now, according to the latest intel they'd received from the guards that morning. They'd reach the Wall by nightfall. Beatrice hadn't left her bed since she'd felt the loss of her daughter. Belladonna had held her until her tears dried and she finally fell into a restless sleep. She was comforted by Bea's slow, deep breathing as she sat at the Headmistress' vanity, internally debating their potential courses of action.

Bea would want to go on the offensive. At least, she would if she were in her right mind. Unfortunately for Belladonna, Beatrice wasn't in a state to make any major decisions, much less command an army of enchantresses against an invasion. Which meant it all fell to her. The guards hadn't even stuttered when they turned to Belladonna for commands and guidance. She'd sent Castor out the night before to find the commander's tent and intercept their plans. Ideally, he'd be able to assassinate the general or whoever was leading this group of warmongering assholes. However, if he wasn't able to do that, then she knew he would at least come back with more detailed information about their plans than the enchantresses had been able to piece together. Having a shape-shifting familiar was quite handy when one needed stealth and intel on one's enemy. Once he returned, she'd be able to make a more finite plan of action.

Bea would attack aggressively, creating devastation among the soldiers but also damaging the forest. Belladonna would take a different approach. Proactive and aggressive, but with more stealth and considerably less damage to the plants and animals inhabiting the Dark Woods.

Belladonna moved from the seat at the vanity to stand before the eastern-facing window. Closing her eyes, she sent her magic out into the woods. She could sense the repugnant presence of the soldiers in their campsite, wreaking havoc and murdering her beloved plants en masse. Belladonna's rage boiled just below the surface as she made her plans. She communicated with the great fir and birch trees that cried out in agony in her mind. Belladonna could feel their pain, and she channeled that anguish into her magics. She strengthened their roots and offered her most sincere condolences for the losses of their saplings. Belladonna would ease their suffering as best she could and use their anger to fuel her spells.

She reached out farther still, connecting with the creatures of the woods. Rabbits and mice would be her eyes and ears. Foxes and wolves would work as teams to pick off the weak or stupid soldiers who wandered off on their own. The men would creep into the woods to relieve themselves and never return to their troops. A group of hawks volunteered to take out the soldiers' communications. According to the birds, the commanders were using carrier pigeons to keep in contact with the capital. Belladonna redirected the hawks, thanking them for their offer, but asking them to instead steal the soldiers' food supplies.

Belladonna refocused her energies once she'd been certain the hawks weren't going to attack the innocent pigeons. It wasn't their fault they'd been enlisted in this mindless war. Instead, Belladonna reached out to the pigeons themselves. They were shocked by her communication at first but were happy to work with her when they realized that she was a friend. The soldiers weren't kind to their animals. Turning the pigeons against them had been simple. There would be no more reliable communication with the capital.

Lastly, Belladonna searched for the horses. She knew the soldiers had traveled with a large herd of well-trained battle horses. As confident as she was in her skills as a witch, convincing the horses to go against their training would not be easy. Presumably, the horses would have been well cared for and might choose to fight with their commanders.

Thankfully, the horses had a leader. Belladonna was intrigued to learn that the herd deferred to an older mare. The horse had been with the army since her birth, having been bred in the royal stables and trained to serve in the army since she was a young filly.

What should I call you? Belladonna asked the mare.

War horses do not have names, came her gruff reply.

I can't accept that. A powerhouse such as yourself must have a name. A title at least. How do the other horses address you? Belladonna's heart hurt for the mare. No name? It was needlessly harsh. Everyone deserved a name.

They typically refer to me as "Ma'am" or "Mistress", the horse replied, curtly.

Well, Ma'am, I desperately need your help. Is there anything you can do to slow down or hinder the advancement of your troops? Belladonna intentionally referred to them as *her* troops. It was meant in deference to the mare's authority over the other horses, but it also seamlessly implied the mare's control over the entire army. The soldiers would have a rough go of things if the horses turned against them.

Why would I want to do that? The mare's resistance to her thoughts was exhausting. After spending hours connecting with all the forest plants and animals, Belladonna was drained. She needed the mare's assistance, but she wasn't sure she'd be able to accomplish it at this rate.

Because you are a good soul, and you know we have done nothing to deserve the treatment your soldiers have planned for us. Belladonna tried to impress her fears into her thoughts, ensuring that the mare felt just how worried she was about the impending invasion. *We have children here. Innocent children. As a mother, you must feel compelled to protect the young and defenseless.*

It was a low blow and not entirely accurate, as the children were all enchantresses and therefore not completely defenseless. Belladonna was desperate though. She needed to protect the school and keep the children safe.

There was a long period of silence, in which Belladonna worried that she had either lost her connection with the mare, or the mare had chosen to simply ignore her pleas.

Finally, the mare responded. *I will see what I can do. But I won't promise anything.*

Thank you, Ma'am. I cannot express how deeply I appreciate this act of kindness.

Severing the connection, Belladonna collapsed onto the edge of the bed beside Beatrice. The headmistress was still asleep, thank the Mother. When she awoke, Belladonna would be able to offer her some good news. It wouldn't make up for the loss of her child—nothing ever would—but perhaps it would lighten the load on Bea's shoulders a bit. At this point, that was all Belladonna could hope to accomplish.

7

AIDEN

T HE PROBLEM WITH BEING all-knowing was that people expected him to have all the answers, and that simply wasn't the case. At least not in Aiden's experience. He knew that Elena was probably still alive, although he'd felt like his heart had been ripped from his chest when she'd fallen through the chasm. He'd seen her fall in his visions, although he'd intentionally kept that information to himself. Aiden knew his sons would be infuriated that he'd led them into a trap, knowing exactly how it would end up, but in his defense, he didn't actually *know* until moments before she fell. By then it was too late to do anything about it anyway.

Yes, Aiden had been essentially cursed with the "gift" of foresight by some very bitter fae, but that didn't mean he could properly interpret the visions. He was a demi-god, but he wasn't built for the fae's visions. An unfortunate fact he didn't learn until it was too late.

Being "too late" was a running theme throughout his life, which was especially noteworthy—in his not-so-humble opinion—since he was nearly a thousand solar cycles into this life with no end in sight.

You sound pathetic, Aleerah chided. *All this self-pity bullshyt won't help anyone.*

She was right, but Aiden didn't think he was wallowing in self-pity. He was merely taking stock of his faults, in a very thorough and lengthy list.

Elena doesn't need your list of faults. She needs your powers and her mother's to bring her home. Instead of dwelling on all the things you've muxed up over the cycles, perhaps you should start strategizing how you'll address Beatrice when we see her. Again, Aleerah made valid points. Again, Aiden wanted to ignore her.

Beatrice wouldn't be happy to see him, but he knew she'd understand and be willing to help. She would have felt the same heart-rending anguish that had ripped through him when Elena had fallen into The Nothing. She would want to bring their daughter home. As distant and closed off as she was, Beatrice wouldn't leave their daughter to that hells. She couldn't. Right?

Your confidence is overwhelming. Aleerah's dry tone chafed in his mind.

The Prince's longship was much nicer than Aiden had expected. He quickly reminded himself that it had been nearly a century since he'd been around royals. The craftsmanship of their boat makers had drastically improved over the cycles. The benches were considerably sturdier and more comfortable, unlike the hastily crafted longships of wartime during the Age of Fire. This ship was built for luxury, and it was fueled by magic.

Aiden could feel the power radiating off the longship. It was blood magic, unlike anything he'd seen.

"Who crafted this ship?" He tried to keep his voice casual as he surreptitiously studied the power pulsing throughout the planks of wood that made up the longship.

"We have a team of shipbuilders back in Riverayn. They make all of our ships, along with any repairs." Niko strode across the deck, heading toward the steering oar. Taking hold of it, he said, "Please take a seat, ladies and gentlemen." He gestured to the benches. "We will be moving as quickly as possible to reach the main road. We'll have to go by foot from there."

Quinn and Roska sat on either side of the longship, seeming to keep their eyes on the Prince while preparing for a quick escape if needed. Aiden couldn't help but smile. His boys were so defensive. They had every reason to be, but Aiden knew the Prince's feelings for Elena were genuine. He could literally see the aura of love and protection surrounding Niko whenever he spoke of Elena. The Prince might not realize it yet, but he was head over heels for her.

Aiden chuckled. Quinn was going to be livid when he figured it out. He would *not* be comfortable with Elena and a Royal. Quinn had his own history with the Royal family, although he wouldn't talk about it. Aiden had witnessed one particularly cruel interaction between his fiery son and the Queen back when she was just the King's Betrothed. She'd been needlessly callous, intentionally trying to trample him with her horse when he was in the streets of Andover. It was during their betrothal tour, as the King was escorting his intended throughout his kingdom, showing her off while also convincing her that theirs was a worthy match.

The King had been too busy flirting with the baker's daughter to notice the malicious actions of his bride-to-be. Not that it would have made a difference. The King would have married her regardless. The Queen's father had promised half his army in a war that had yet to come to pass. Aiden suspected Beatrice had talked him out of invading Rolam, Waverly's neighbors to the east and their closest access to open sea trade. Not only would it have been an expensive and bloody endeavor, but it also wouldn't have ended well for the King. Aiden had foreseen that course of action and knew that Waverly would have paid dearly for the King's greed.

Quinn hadn't been seriously injured, thank the Gods, but he'd been bloodied, and his pride had taken a huge hit. He'd been living on the street at the time, surviving on trash and what little he'd been able to steal. Aiden had seen the resentment build in Q, watched the fire flicker in his eyes. For a few seconds, Aiden had expected that to be the moment that Quinn learned about his fiery talents. Aiden also knew that if Quinn had turned his powers on the Queen-to-be, it would have meant the death of his son. The people of Waverly tolerated the enchantresses because they didn't have any other options. But a street rat with fire magic? He would have been attacked by a mob of angry and scared townsfolk and met his end in the muddy gutters of the small hamlet.

Aiden studied Quinn, watching his hands trail across the smooth surface of the longship railing. The heat danced in his fingertips, burning a light path where his skin touched the wood. Aiden imagined it was intentional. Q had made it very clear that he wasn't happy about accepting the Prince's help under any circumstances.

He would have to get over that quickly. Now that the Prince was in their lives, Aiden knew that he wouldn't be going anywhere until they got Elena back. And even then, the Prince would likely become a permanent fixture in Elena's life, therefore making him a regular in the lives of her family.

"How long will it take to get to the main road on this thing?" Quinn's voice shook Aiden out of his musings.

"No more than a couple of days, I'd imagine." The Prince began maneuvering the longship off the riverbank and into the middle of the icy river. "This ice will slow us down, but we should still make good time."

"If we take the river past Andover, we can try to drive her upstream. One of the tributaries of the river is fed by the mountains behind Harbor Ridge. It's not a clear path, but the enchantresses have a port to their fancy school. It's not exactly public knowledge. I assume they didn't want to make it easier for the magept to access them." Quinn eyed the Prince, watching the way he drove the longship. Aiden thought Q might have been trying to learn how the ship worked so that he could captain it himself and cut out their need for the Prince.

"Aye," Aiden spoke, placing a firm hand on Q's shoulder, trying to discourage his thief tendencies. "I believe this longship is powered by blood magic, is that right, Your Majesty?"

The Prince grinned widely. "You are correct, sir!" He practically glowed with pride as he stroked the steering oar. "This is one of my family's fleet of longships. They are all equipped with enough oars for a small military force, *but* they can also be powered by the touch of a member of the Royal Family."

Aiden felt Quinn deflate at the Prince's words. He wouldn't be able to captain this ship alone. Aiden knew Q wanted to be free of the Prince, but he also knew his son was no fool. Quinn recognized that he wouldn't be able to manage the longship without the Prince unless he found a crew of oarsmen. While Aiden acknowledged that Q was a very resourceful young man, he was also a realist. He wouldn't try to kick the Prince off his own ship without a fool-proof plan to captain the craft.

The Prince was safe. For now.

8

BEATRICE

TIME PASSED IN A blur of movement and sound, but Beatrice barely registered the events around her. In the back of her mind, she knew there were things that she needed to be doing, duties that demanded her attention. She just couldn't bring herself to care. Her daughter was gone. Nothing mattered anymore.

"Bea, love, I need you to eat this." Belladonna appeared in Beatrice's field of view. She held a steaming bowl of something in one hand and a cup of tea in the other.

Numbly, Beatrice sat up in bed, where she'd spent most of her waking hours since the loss of Elena had shattered her soul. She only ventured out of the bed long enough to tend to her bodily functions, and then she would climb right back into it. Zied stayed by her side at all times. Beatrice knew he was likely dealing with his own grief, but she couldn't feel his pain. She was too busy drowning in her own.

Belladonna sat the cup and bowl down on the table beside their bed and repositioned the pillows behind Beatrice to help her remain upright.

"I asked the chef to make you some hearty stew. I know you aren't feeling up to much these days, love." Belladonna gently brushed

Bea's unruly hair from her face. "But you need your sustenance. There's a horde of soldiers making camp outside your walls. I managed to befriend the leader of their warhorses. She was able to slow their arrival, but they're here now. Settled in last night. Not to mention, I imagine your sons will be coming here at some point."

Her sons.

They would be coming for her, probably to end her miserable existence, since it was her fault that they'd lost their sister. She deserved their wrath. She deserved every vile and hateful thing they planned for her. Beatrice knew she didn't deserve to draw breath when Elena was unable to do the same.

Belladonna said nothing as she joined Beatrice on the bed and slowly started spooning the stew into her mouth when it became clear that Beatrice had no intention of feeding herself.

She didn't deserve to eat. She didn't deserve to live.

She had failed them all. Her children deserved so much better than she could possibly dream to be. They suffered as a direct result of her arrogance and hubris. Beatrice had done nothing but hurt her children since their birth.

When they'd been born, Beatrice had sent the boys away without even a glance. She'd entrusted Quinn to her former headmistress, who promised to find him a good home in a nearby town. She'd sent Roska away with one of her private guards. The guard took the babe to a woman Beatrice had once considered a dear friend, Rosalina. In her letter to Rosalina, Beatrice had pleaded that she welcome the child into her home, adopt him as her own, and raise him with her own young son. Rosalina had not responded to the missive.

That should have been her first clue.

Rosalina had once been one of Beatrice's best friends, as close as two girls could be when one was magical and one was magept. Beatrice hadn't thought that their differences would matter, but she'd been naive. Rosalina's parents had been suspicious of the magical community. They distrusted the enchantresses of Harbor Ridge and that distrust ultimately killed their friendship.

Beatrice had hoped Rosalina would take pity on Roska and love him as if he were her own. She couldn't have been more wrong.

Rosalina. The Rose Queen had sent the boy to live with the Brotherhood of the Healing Light, sentencing him to a life of torture, torment, and abuse. Beatrice was still amazed that he'd grown into such an amazingly compassionate young man.

That betrayal was what had initially driven Beatrice to bed the King. The power he wielded was an added bonus, but Beatrice had been primarily motivated by the desire to destroy the woman who violated her trust so completely. Punishing a child for his mere existence and using him to destroy the world. It was unthinkable.

Beatrice had agonized for so many solar cycles. Sending team after team of investigators to try and uncover the whereabouts of the Brotherhood's compound. The triplets had been nearly twelve cycles old when she'd finally located the compound, but she'd been unable to infiltrate it. With the Brotherhood being exclusively male, and all of her enchantresses being female, Beatrice had been unable to get any spies inside. Covert operations were her only option. She couldn't let on that she was trying to save her *son*. It couldn't be known that it was even possible for enchantresses to have sons. That information was too sensitive, too volatile, to be public knowledge.

In the end, she'd been unable to save him. Just as she'd been unable to save Quinn. He'd been forced to save himself. Beatrice hadn't even known that he'd been in a dangerous situation. She'd learned in a missive from Amelia that he'd burned his foster parents and rescued the other children who had been trapped in that hells with him.

Beatrice had continued to fail all of her children. Over and over. At every opportunity, she'd made the wrong choice. Even the child she'd kept with her had resented her. Elena deserved so much better than Beatrice ever gave. She deserved a mother's love, support, and affection. Instead, Beatrice had taken out her bitterness at the loss of her sons on the only child she had left.

"Bea, I can feel you spiraling. You aren't to blame for any of this." Belladonna put down the spoon and gently lifted Beatrice's face to lock eyes with her.

"We both know that's not true." Beatrice didn't even recognize her own voice. It was so harsh and gravelly from lack of use. "I abandoned them all. I'm the reason they've suffered all these cycles. I'm the reason she's gone." Her voice broke, barely able to finish the sentence.

"Oh, love, you couldn't have known things would work out the way they did. You were trying to protect them." The witch placed the bowl back on the table, scooting back beside Beatrice on the bed and taking her in her arms.

"I should never have let them out of my sight," Beatrice whispered between silent sobs.

"You were doing what you thought was best. That's all any of us can do." Belladonna rubbed her back soothingly.

Beatrice desperately wanted to believe her, but she knew her sons wouldn't see it that way. She couldn't help but think they were right. She'd abandoned them because she'd been worried about exposing her own weakness. She'd been selfish and her sons had paid the price for it.

And now they were coming to seek their revenge.

9

QUINN

QUINN HATED RELYING ON the Prince for help. But he hated even more that he was actually starting to like the guy. Kinda.

A little.

You're getting soft. Lyra glared at him from where she lay on one of the benches of the Prince's longship.

The hells I am! Quinn glared right back. He was trying to give the Prince a chance like Aiden had said. The Prince seemed to really care about Elena, which at least meant he had decent taste. If it turned out that Elena cared for the Prince too, then it would be better for Quinn to learn to live with the guy now.

Since when do you listen to Aiden? Lyra didn't break their stare, but her ears twitched ever-so-slightly. She was surprised. He'd actually managed to surprise her.

I'm not really listening to him, but Roska trusts him, and I'm trying to do the same. Quinn shrugged, hoping it came off more casual and less awkward than he felt. *Besides, he is our dad. Might be worth it to get to know him. Even if it's just to figure out more about our powers and this "hard to kill" thing he mentioned before.*

Lyra smirked. Q knew she didn't entirely believe him, but she was dropping the subject—for now— and that was enough.

Quinn wondered if he was getting too attached to these people. Aiden. Roska. Elena. Maybe it wasn't smart to get so invested in them. History had taught him that he couldn't rely on anyone. People always left. Always disappointed.

Except Amelia, Lyra chimed in again.

Yes, fine, but she's the exception, Quinn argued.

Elena was the exception after that. I think Roska is a good exception too. Aiden is flakey and probably insane, but I think we can at least rely on Aleerah. Lyra looked over Q's shoulder to where the dire wolf sat at the prow of the ship.

Quinn turned on his bench. Aleerah cut an imposing form, leading their bedraggled crew on yet another seemingly doomed mission. No other ships would come near them on the river while they traveled at a surprisingly fast speed atop the freezing water. Not that there were many ships out during the frost season. Traders tended to stay closer to home as the temperatures dropped. Just like the farmers, traders stocked up for the colder weather and stayed in their respective homes once the snow began to settle on the ground.

Quinn's mind wandered back to his childhood. Not a trip he often allowed himself, since those memories were rarely happy. But he remembered one cycle, as the frost was coming in and the snow had begun to take up permanent residence on the roof that Quinn had precariously balanced on the top of their first forest home. It had served them well enough in the harvest season. Unfortunately for young Q, the snow was much heavier than his stopgap roof was able to bear. He woke with a start in the middle of the night when their roof finally gave in to the weight of the snow, collapsing on top of him and Lyra. Lyra had immediately jumped up, tail on fire, and accidentally set flame to their home.

I've told you a thousand times, Lyra interrupted his thoughts. *I didn't start that fire. It must've been you.*

Quinn smiled but didn't bother responding. This was an argument they had several times a cycle. No need to rehash the details while trapped on a boat with all those prying eyes and ears. He didn't need their input. Q knew what happened.

He also knew that that night was the first time he'd admitted defeat and returned to Amelia to seek refuge from the storm. She had taken in the other kids Quinn had liberated from the foster home, but he had initially refused her kindness. He didn't want to depend on anyone. She had understood but told him he was always welcome to stay if he ever needed a place.

Amelia had helped each of his foster siblings find safe, happy, warm homes to live and grow up in. Quinn learned to trust her, over time, and ultimately adopted her as his mother.

Do you think she recognized us? he asked Lyra suddenly.

What do you mean?

Do you think she recognized me like Belladonna did? Seeing our mother in my face and realizing whose child I was? Quinn hated to think that Amelia had only been kind to him because of who his mother was.

I doubt it, Lyra replied. She studied his face for a moment, then added, *She might have felt like your face was familiar, but no one had even known it was possible for an enchantress to have a son until our birth. From what I overheard when we were back in her school, those guards still didn't fully believe we were her children.*

Really? You never said anything before. Quinn was surprised to hear that their mother's guards had questioned her. He didn't think Madame LaBelle would tolerate that.

Well, it didn't really seem important, since we were all a bit preoccupied with trying to escape so we could stop the end of the world, Lyra replied flatly. Quinn couldn't help but chuckle at her dry tone.

Smart ass, he thought back to her, flicking a spark onto her nose.

She licked the ember off with a quick swipe of her tongue, completely unfazed.

"At this rate, we should make it to Harbor Ridge by sun up tomorrow." The Prince strode confidently across the deck of his ship, adjusting the sails. "If this wind holds, we might arrive sooner, although I don't want to put too much faith in the weather being kind. Those clouds look fairly ominous."

Quinn looked in the same direction the Prince had pointed to see thick, dark gray clouds pushing in from the north. They weren't going to make it through the night without getting buried in ankle-deep snow, at least.

"Mux everything," Quinn muttered under his breath.

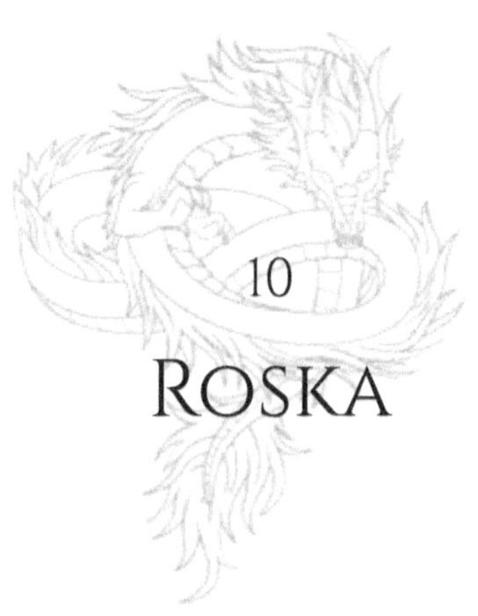

10

ROSKA

ROSKA STUDIED THE SAME oppressive clouds that held Niko and Quinn's attention, filling him with dread and worry. He couldn't ask Lyra or Quinn to use their powers to make a fire or even warm the floor for Demoni because the floor of the ship was wood. They'd burn the ship to ash trying to keep Roska and Demoni from freezing to death.

Quinn, seeming to sense Roska's trepidation, turned to Aiden and said, "Can you conjure something to keep us covered and warm? This is gonna be one hells of a storm."

"Aye, I can come up with something." Aiden stood from where he'd been lounging, half-asleep on one of the benches. Swirling his hands as though he were forming a ball of dough, purple smoke began to billow and twist around him.

Roska chanced a quick glance at the Prince, curious to see how the royal would react to such a dramatic show of magic. Much to his surprise, Niko watched their father with a look of pure awe. There was no hint of jealousy or desire. Roska caught Q's eye and directed his attention to the Prince, whose focus was still hyper-fixated on their father. Quinn's face broke into a huge grin, clearly amused by the Prince's curiosity. Roska's own smile was one of relief. If the Prince was this enthralled with their father's conjurings, then he would likely be interested in Elena's magic as well. Interested in it without being covetous of it.

Roska had been so focused on watching the Prince that he'd missed when their father had unleashed his spell. They were all standing inside the warmth of a small cabin, complete with a stone chiminea and four beds. The chiminea was encircled by a stone hearth, upon which there appeared to be freshly baked bread and fish wrapped in leaves, similar to what they'd eaten at Belladonna's several moons ago. There were two beds on each side of the cabin and windows on all four walls, along with a thick, windowed door that led out to the remainder of the ship.

Niko exhaled a sound of amazement, carefully walking up to one of the walls and gently placing his hand on the wood.

"It... it feels so real," he whispered.

"That's because it is real, Your Highness." Quinn always managed to make the title sound like an insult. It was a talent really, but one Roska was content to let his brother keep.

Demoni slithered from Roska's neck, down his arm, and jumped happily from a bed to the floor until she reached the chiminea in the center of the room. She promptly curled up underneath their freshly-conjured heater and exhaled a fine mist of ice to express her gratitude. Roska's own body temperature began to rise instantly. He hadn't even realized how cold he'd gotten. He was going to have to start paying more attention.

"Hey, bro. You good?" Quinn nudged him with his shoulder.

Roska thought for a moment before answering. Was he good? He'd unleashed a deadly evil that had likely already killed dozens before they'd been able to recapture it. In their attempt to lock the *turmio* away, they'd lost their sister to an endless Nothing. She'd been sucked in with the *turmio* when Roska had intended to sacrifice himself. He was the reason she was gone.

"It's not your fault," Quinn said before Roska even had a chance to voice his guilt. "You didn't push her in. She did what she could to protect us. To save the world. You know she'd be pissed if she learned you were feeling any kind of guilt over *her* actions." Quinn put a firm hand on Roska's shoulder. "Besides, our new favorite royal is whisking us away on his daddy's boat. We're sailing at record-setting speed with Daddy Aiden to see Mommy Beatrice and Witch Mommy to bring Elena home."

Roska couldn't help but chuckle at Q's ridiculous names for the adults in their lives. It was just so outlandish that it worked.

"Daddy Aiden? Is that really what you're calling me now?" Aiden asked, a single eyebrow raised so high it disappeared behind the hair brushing across his brow.

"Until I come up with something even more entertaining? Hells yes." Quinn gently clapped his hand on Roska's shoulder. "So, what's for dinner? Smells delicious!"

Dinner was perfect. They finished their meal of fresh bread, salmon, green beans, corn, and tea just as the snow began to fall in earnest. Niko explained that as long as he was on the ship and alive—he'd locked eyes with Quinn when he'd said that—the ship would keep moving wherever they directed it. Meaning he didn't have to be the one steering the longship in order for it to keep going. They agreed to take shifts throughout the night, guiding the ship through the icy river, until they reached the tributary that would take them to Harbor Ridge.

Niko took the first shift, as the sun was still up and he was still able to see the front of the longship from the rear—where the steering oar was located. Roska and Demoni had volunteered to take the second shift before the night fully took hold and the temperatures dropped even lower. Demoni coiled herself around the figurehead at the prow, informing him when he needed to steer around floating hazards like logs or chunks of ice.

Unfortunately for Roska, there wasn't much else to do while they guided the ship, so he was left to stew in his thoughts. He gazed off, into the woods beyond the river as his mind wandered. He wondered if Elena was ok. What would she be like when they finally got her back? Would she even be Elena anymore, or would The Nothing have drained her of everything that made her who she was? He didn't know much about The Nothing; no one had ever been there and lived to tell about it, so he had no way of knowing what she was going through.

It should have been me, he thought glumly.

Whether or not that's true, it doesn't matter. Demoni interrupted his self-pity. *She is there now, and we will do everything we can to bring her and Agon back as quickly as possible. Aiden seems to have a plan, or at least the beginning of one. We will see her again soon.*

I hope you're right, Roska thought. He couldn't bear the thought of her being stuck in that hells any longer.

Something stirred in the woods, just beyond the river banks. The flash of the creature's eyes caught his attention for a moment, but he couldn't make out what it was as the ship sailed quickly passed. It looked large.

Maybe once we get her back, we can take her to Nexton and introduce her to Brigit, Demoni offered, bringing his attention back to their conversation as he lost sight of the creature along the riverbanks. Roska could feel the humor in her words. She was teasing him. Still, Roska didn't hate the idea of his sister meeting his goddess.

11

AIDEN

QUINN HAD TAKEN THE third shift, leaving Aiden with the final shift, guiding the ship up the small, icy, and rather treacherous creek that began somewhere in the mountains behind Harbor Ridge and led to the River.

Aleerah sat at the stern, keeping watch for floating chunks of ice. Aiden wasn't putting much thought or effort into steering the ship. He'd direct the vessel whichever way Aleerah told him, but otherwise, he was stewing in dread at the impending reunion he'd be walking into with his ex-lover and mother of his children. And Belladonna. The witch that would happily burn the flesh from his bones in a heartbeat. He was hoping Belladonna's love for the triplets would stay her hand long enough for him to win her over.

Ha! You truly are the most arrogant being on the planet if you think you'll be able to "win over" either of those women, Aleerah scoffed. *You'll be lucky to make it out of that school with all of your body parts intact. I hear Beatrice likes to castrate the men in her employ.*

Well, then, it's a good thing I'm not looking for a job, Aiden shot back. He wasn't really worried about losing his manhood. He was more concerned that the witch and enchantress would combine their magics and hurl him into the sun. Or throw him into the Southern Sea. Maybe into a volcano. Or Belladonna might use her trees to trap him, rooting him in one place for eternity. He was basically unkillable, but Aiden had no doubt that Beatrice and Belladonna would want to push that to see just how close to death they could bring him.

You really have a bleak outlook of these women, Aleerah noted.

It feels appropriate since at least one of them—more likely both—blame me for the way their lives have turned out. If not for me, they might have stayed together in the woods all those cycles ago. Aiden was stewing in self-pity. It was something he'd come to do often over the last seventeen cycles. Ever since he'd assisted in the conception of the triplets. He felt responsible for the kids—as he should—but he also felt responsible for wrecking the happy home that Belladonna and Beatrice had built. Aiden put on a brave face for the boys, projecting an optimism he didn't feel about reuniting with the women.

Inside, he was overflowing with an icy dread that wouldn't release him.

The first few rays of sunlight were filling the sky, driving the darkness away as their ship rounded the final bend and the harbor of Harbor Ridge came into view.

"Whoa." Quinn's voice was a harsh whisper as he stepped out onto the deck. "Looks like she's made some changes."

Indeed, Harbor Ridge was surrounded by quite a few more fortifications, including well-staffed guard towers whose flaming arrows were trained on their longship. Aiden had known his arrival wouldn't be welcomed, but he hadn't expected Beatrice to have made such dramatic fortifications to keep him out.

"I guess Belladonna was able to warn Mother about the soldiers after all," Roska observed, studying the looming towers as their ship sailed ever closer.

Right. Soldiers. Beatrice had built up protections around the school to defend it from invaders. She wasn't trying to keep him out.

Well, now, I wouldn't go that far. Aleerah offered him a wolfish grin.

Once they were within range, a single flaming arrow was fired at their vessel.

"Oy, hang on a minute!" Niko cried out. The arrow had pierced the deck, leaving a scorched scar on the otherwise flawless planks. "Don't they recognize my flags? I'm royalty, damn it. Why are they firing at my ship?"

"Likely *because* this is one of the King's ships, and the King's soldiers are currently trying to invade and murder them all," Quinn answered flatly. He clearly hadn't softened to the Prince during their journey.

Niko scowled at him, but didn't respond. Instead, he lowered the sails and raised a single white flag.

"Gods, I hope that works," Aiden muttered. He didn't like the idea of being charred to a crisp before even getting to see the face of the woman who had birthed—and abandoned—his children.

Thankfully, the archers in the twin towers guarding the entrance to the harbor lowered their weapons and allowed the longship safe passage into the docks.

Unfortunately, that was where their hospitality seemed to end.

As soon as the men had safely tethered the longship, the guards rushed in and grabbed hold of them.

Aiden prayed to whatever gods might be listening that his boys—mostly Quinn—would contain their powers long enough to reach their mother.

12

QUINN

THE INSTANT THE GUARD'S hands latched on to his upper arms, Quinn forced himself to use every ounce of strength he had to maintain control of his powers. The rest of his energy was put into a mental argument with Lyra to convince her that roasting these guards wouldn't be helpful.

Although it did sound like it would be more fun than being forcibly dragged into a cell. It probably would have motivated their damned mother to come free them faster. The guards had separated them all. Lyra lay trapped in a smaller cage-like cell with Demoni. Aleerah had been much too big to fit in the cages clearly meant for familiars, which meant she had her own cell. Roska and Aiden were locked in the cell directly across from Quinn, which he shared with the Prince.

Being trapped in such close quarters with the Princeling had only added to Quinn's irritation. The Prince seemed to pick up on Q's mood and thankfully hadn't spoken since they'd been captured. He'd simply sat quietly on the small cot on the far side of the cell. Likely biding his time until he could use his pompous princely "charms" to talk his way out of the shyt-show they'd walked into.

It was well past lunch before the Headmistress deigned to show up.

If Quinn hadn't been so pissed off at having to spend the better part of the day in a drafty stone jail cell, he might have noticed how tired and defeated their mother looked. Like she hadn't slept in days, and yet also like she'd just rolled out of bed. Disheveled. Disheartened. Beaten down.

If he hadn't been so irritated and worried about Elena, he would have thought their mother looked a lot like how he'd felt when he'd finally turned to Amelia for help. Like someone who desperately needed to be saved. Protected. Taken care of.

But he didn't care. He wouldn't let himself care for the woman who had abandoned him to the hells of that foster home when he was just a defenseless babe.

Sounds a lot like caring to me, Lyra pointed out coolly.

Their mother didn't say a word to them. She merely motioned for the guards to unlock the cells, then she turned to walk away, as though their presence meant nothing.

Quinn couldn't take it.

"That's it?" he fumed. "No 'Hello, kids. Thanks for saving the world'? No 'Sorry I abandoned you for cycles and then locked you up for merely existing'? What about Elena? You aren't even going to ask about her?"

Flames danced along his arms, and he was sure his eyes were glowing, but Q didn't care. That heartless woman wasn't going to turn her back on them. Not again.

"Quinn," Roska started, placing an icy hand on Q's shoulder. Q wouldn't be cooled down this time, though. He shook free of Roska's grasp and took a few aggressive steps toward their mother until her guards stepped in to block his path. They at least had the good sense not to touch him. Quinn wasn't sure he would have been able to stop himself from burning them if they tried to physically hold him back.

Slowly, Beatrice stopped and turned to face him. Her eyes were empty: a dark, endless abyss. It reminded Q of the cavern in the Dragon's Teeth. He shuddered thinking about that bottomless chasm.

"I know what happened to Elena." Her voice was rough, as though she hadn't used it in a while. "I felt it the moment she fell. She's gone." Her words faded as she spoke. It almost seemed like the act of speaking was draining all of her energy. Quinn thought it looked like she was deflating as she stood before them.

"We can get her back." It was the first time Aiden had spoken since they'd laid eyes on the damn school.

Beatrice seemed to flare back to life at his voice. Quinn was shocked to see her body instantly straighten as she recognized who'd spoken. The force of the glare she leveled at their father would have demolished any other being. The fire and rage that burned in her eyes were almost as frightening as the sudden drop in the already-cold temperature of the jail.

13

BEATRICE

"**Y**ou." Beatrice took a step toward the demi-god. The monster who turned her world upside down all those cycles ago. "How *dare* you come here. Who the hells do you think you are?" Rage poured off of her in waves, flooding the tower with the raw energy that filled her voice.

In the back of her mind, Beatrice noted that this expulsion of emotion was the first thing she'd felt since Elena had left the world. It was a revelation to feel this strongly about anything after having lost the one thing she'd always assumed she'd never be without. Even when she'd kicked Elena out of Harbor Ridge, Beatrice had always assumed Elena wouldn't go far.

She'd never hated being wrong more in her life.

"Love, I'm—" he tried again, but she silenced him with a single look.

"Don't you muxing dare. You will not address me as 'love'. You will not address me at all. You will not apologize. You will *not* try and justify yourself to me. Not now. Not ever." Beatrice was seething. That arrogant, stupid *man* had the audacity to try and placate her?

The guards who had stepped up to block Quinn's path to her seemed to cower at their Headmistress's commanding tone. Beatrice gave the guards a subtle nod, and the women fled the room, closing the door firmly behind them. Her enchantresses knew she could hold her own against any foe. She didn't need them to protect her, and it was dangerous for them to stand between her and the focus of her ire.

Movement in the corner of her eye caught her attention, causing Beatrice to flick her eyes to investigate and take her gaze off the trickster before her. It was the dire wolf who had bound into their clearing so long ago. His *familiar*. Beatrice felt the blast of her spell before she even realized she'd been casting. The wave of power threw Aiden and his wolf against the walls of their respective cells, knocking them both unconscious.

"Mother, no!" Roska cried out, rushing to the side of their deadbeat father.

Zied burst into the room behind her, panting, clearly having rushed to her aid the moment he'd felt something amiss.

Why didn't you wake me when you left our room? he questioned accusingly.

It honestly hadn't occurred to her that she would need backup. They'd both had such a restless time of late, she'd hoped that letting him sleep might mean that they would both feel slightly less numb to the world. It turned out all she needed to awaken her spirit was to face off with the man that had torn her world apart.

She didn't respond to Zied, nor did she allow herself to react to Roska's exclamation and concern for Aiden. Instead, she turned her focus on Quinn. The boy was a bottle of barely contained fiery rage, and, oddly enough, she understood exactly how he was feeling.

His rage was completely warranted, and she hated herself almost as much as Quinn clearly hated her.

Beatrice held his stare, watching the flames dance in his eyes, as she took several deep breaths. The temperature of the tower returned to normal as she carefully recaptured her fury.

Once she was certain she had control of her magic again, she spoke to her sons.

"I'm sorry for the way that I treated you. I truly am. I understand that may be hard for you to hear and likely harder for you to believe, but I thought I was doing what was best for you." She never dropped her eyes from Quinn's as she spoke, but she could sense Roska's gaze on her. "Nothing I can say will ever make up for the way the world has treated you. For how *I* treated you when you were brought back by my investigators with Elena." Quinn's glare hardened at his sister's name, but he didn't speak or move to interrupt her, so Beatrice continued. "I was told that your mere existence would make you a target. Magical boys were meant to be impossible, and so you would be hunted. I thought by sending you away and hiding you, you would be safer. I shouldn't have. I trusted the wrong people. I was young and impressionable. I should have trusted myself and my intuition more. All of this could have been avoided." She tore her gaze from Quinn's for a moment to ensure that she had Roska's full attention as well. "I am truly sorry for all that befell the two of you. I should never have let you out of my sight."

Beatrice left the guards with Aiden and his dire wolf in their separate cells in the tower, and she escorted the boys—her sons and the King's only child—into the school. No one spoke. She didn't understand why the Prince was traveling with her children, but she didn't want to get into any of that with them until they'd reached the privacy of her office.

At Zied's silent insistence, Beatrice had taken them through the dining hall and allowed the boys to fill their stomachs with the rest of her charges. Between her students, employees, and guards, her children seemed quite out of place. The only men in the entire school were the eunuchs, and they weren't allowed to eat with the students. Naturally, the students were very curious about the boys the Headmistress had brought into the school. Many of the older girls strained to catch a glimpse of the Prince.

Beatrice noted that the Prince made no effort to meet the eyes of the girls. He wasn't rude to them, but he didn't return their obvious advances either. Begrudgingly, Beatrice noted that he was a perfect gentleman.

Roska seemed thoroughly uncomfortable: constantly surveying the room, watching the girls and guards all around him as though he expected them to jump and attack him at any moment. He likely believed that they would.

Damn the Brotherhood. Damn Rosalina and her ignorant, bigoted beliefs.

We never should have trusted her. Zied's anger seeped into her mind, blending with her own and making it nearly impossible to quell her powers. She was going to have to take time outside, alone, to release some of her pent-up energy.

We didn't know. She turned out to be quite the impressive actress, Beatrice argued.

Belladonna would have known. She would have warned us if she'd been given the opportunity, Zied countered.

Beatrice sighed, exhausted. She'd hoped that reconciling with Bells and Castor meant that Zied had forgiven her. Clearly, that was not the case.

We can't know that. You are making grand assumptions, based on nothing. Not to mention we have no way of knowing if you're right. Beatrice turned from the table, taking Zied's head in her hands and forcing his attention to solely focus on her. *I'm sorry. I can say it a hundred thousand times. I can say it every day for the rest of our life. It won't change the past. But holding this grudge against me will make our future very hard. Not to mention tiresome.*

Zied held her stare for several long moments. Beatrice was starting to think that he might choose to hold this grudge forever, regardless. Then he blinked. She felt his emotions shifting from a place of anger to a place of quiet annoyance. It wasn't ideal, but it was still better than being hated by her familiar. Beatrice hoped that he would grow to forgive her soon. She hated being at odds with him.

When she turned back to the table, Beatrice noticed that Quinn had been watching her interaction with Zied. He couldn't have known what they were talking about, and yet he seemed to share a knowing look with his fox before taking another bite of his shepherd's pie. Quinn seemed to be more intuitive than Elena, which was unsettling to think about.

Elena had always been very good at reading people. To the point that Beatrice had started spending less and less time with her daughter for fear that the girl might pick up on all the secrets Beatrice had been keeping. She couldn't risk her daughter learning about her brothers. It would have been too dangerous. Although, as it turned out, her sons hadn't been as safe and protected as she had assumed when she'd sent them away.

Beatrice couldn't help but wonder if they'd all inherited a bit of their father's prophetic abilities.

She prayed to the gods that they hadn't.

They finished their meal quickly, and Beatrice escorted them to her office. Before they'd left the dining hall, she'd sent one of her guards to fetch Belladonna. The Headmistress wouldn't admit it out loud, but she needed Bells. The witch had a knack for understanding what Beatrice was feeling and putting it into words when Beatrice herself struggled to vocalize her emotions.

To her great relief, the witch was waiting in her office when Beatrice arrived with the boys.

To her annoyance, the witch was sitting in the *headmistress's* chair, her feet on the *headmistress's* desk, looking irate.

14

BELLADONNA

"**B**EA, YOU MIGHT BE the boss of this school, but you don't get to summon me whenever you—" Belladonna froze mid-rant when she saw the boys trail into the office behind Beatrice.

Jumping to her feet, she raced to Roska and Quinn, wrapping them in a hug that neither of them seemed to have been expecting or prepared for. Quinn tried to pull away, but Belladonna held tight. Roska looked as though he'd been frozen in place. The third man who had come in with Bea closed the door behind them, then leaned against it, propping one foot on the wood as he failed to contain a look of glee.

Belladonna finally released the boys from her hug, holding them at arm's length while she inspected them. "I'm so happy you're alive. I feared the worst when I heard the soldiers talking about capturing Elena. Then when Beatrice collapsed and we lost Elena, I worried that you two might not make it."

"I'm sorry, you were what?" Quinn looked shocked and utterly confused.

Belladonna realized—a little too late—that this was more affection than she'd ever allowed herself to show Bea's children. She'd worked so hard to keep her distance, emotionally at least, from the triplets. They weren't her kids, after all. Bea had left her to conceive these magical babies with that son-of-a—

Be nice, Castor cut into her thoughts. *You might not like him, but he fought beside them to save the world. He knows how to bring Elena back.*

"He what?" Belladonna hadn't meant to shout the words, and yet they'd spilled out before she could stop herself.

Quinn stared at her, even more confused than when she'd forced him into a group hug with her and Roska. Roska, on the other hand, cocked his head as he studied her.

Castor picked that moment to fly through the open window, shifting into his man form and landing silently beside her.

Belladonna quickly released the boys and turned on her familiar. "What the mux are you talking about? How can you possibly know that?"

"Know what, Bells? What's going on?" Beatrice stepped up and placed a firm, but gentle, hand on the witch's shoulder. Her touch had a grounding effect that calmed some of Belladonna's heightened emotions.

Castor spoke before Belladonna could formulate a coherent thought. "I've just been speaking with Aiden." At his words, every pair of eyes in the room, including Demoni from her perch around Roska's neck, and Lyra where she stood before the hearth, turned sharply to him. Some of those eyes were filled with fire. Others with nothing but curiosity.

"What the hells do you mean you were speaking with him?" Beatrice ground out through gritted teeth. "You have no right to question my prisoners." Beatrice's fingers tightened on Belladonna's shoulder to the point of pain. Belladonna placed her hand atop her lover's and squeezed.

Bea seemed to realize she was hurting her and released her grip.

"I wasn't questioning your prisoner," Castor countered casually. "I was speaking with my friend. It's not my fault you locked him up." Castor did nothing to hide his disdain for Beatrice's treatment of the demi-god.

Belladonna had never felt such internal conflict before. She hated Aiden for tearing their lives apart all those cycles ago, and then again for impregnating Beatrice and driving the wedge between them even deeper. Yet she couldn't help but feel a loyalty to her familiar. Despite his sneaky behavior, he was her soul mate. He deserved to have her fight for him, even if he'd lied to her and kept so many things from her for so long.

Beatrice's fingers worked feverishly, building a spell that looked to be rather painful to its recipient. Belladonna acted quickly, placing herself between her lover and her familiar. "Bea, wait," she said quietly. She tried to infuse as much calm into her words as she could, despite not feeling calm at all herself.

"Move." Beatrice glared over the witch's shoulder, eyes locked on Castor: the target of her rather malevolent-looking spell.

Belladonna held her hands up in defense. "I'm sorry. You know I can't do that, if for no other reason than because if you hurt him, it will hurt me too."

Her words seemed to knock Beatrice out of her vengeful trance. She instantly dropped her gaze to her hands, a look of fear crossing her face. Just as quickly as it appeared, the rage and her spell vanished.

"Shyt. I'm sorry, Bells. I wasn't thinking." Beatrice kept her eyes downcast.

Belladonna reached for the enchantress, placing her hands on the woman's face and guiding it up until she held Bea's gaze.

"It's ok, love," Belladonna comforted quietly. She stroked her thumbs back and forth across Bea's cheeks for a moment before offering her a small smile and a kiss on her forehead.

When Bea returned her smile, Belladonna released her face and turned back to deal with Castor.

"You might not approve of her actions, but you will respect her decisions or so help me, Castor, I will banish you from this school." Her words left no room for argument. It wasn't something witches liked to do, but it was possible for her to create a boundary around the school that would block Castor from entering the space. It wasn't something she threatened lightly. The act of creating such a barrier was only used as a last resort, typically when a witch had been imprisoned by her own kind for violating the rights of other living beings. The familiar would be banished from the prison grounds, forcing the witch to suffer alone in her cell, while her familiar was compelled to wander the world without her. It was an unimaginable punishment for both the witch and her familiar. It didn't kill them, but it often resulted in the witch going mad and the familiar devolving into a literal animal for the remainder of their lives.

Death by fire would be preferable. Castor's dark thought invaded her mind.

Then stop being an ass. Belladonna didn't want to banish him, but she couldn't keep breaking up fights between Castor and Bea.

Granted, her banishment of him wouldn't be nearly as detrimental as it was for those imprisoned witches. She could leave the school any time and join him out in the forest. He simply wouldn't be allowed on the school's grounds. Or in the school's air space. Or the school's harbor and docks.

Still sounds like a muxed up death sentence to me, Castor grumbled. Thankfully, when he addressed Beatrice, he did so with a modicum of respect. "I apologize. I crossed a line. I'll be more respectful next time."

Belladonna thought she heard a hint of sarcasm in his use of the word "respectful" but she let it slide. If Beatrice noticed it, she said nothing. Nodding to him, Bea signaled for Castor to continue.

"As I was saying," the moonbird went on, pacing the room as he spoke. "Aiden says he has a way to bring Elena back." He turned to face Beatrice, trapping her in his near-hypnotic stare. "He needs your help." Flicking his eyes to meet Belladonna's. "Both of you."

"Why? What could he possibly need from me?" Belladonna asked. She didn't want to be a part of anything that demi-god had planned. She didn't trust him, and she couldn't comprehend why Castor did.

"He needs your combined powers to work a spell to draw Elena out of The Nothing without bringing the *turmio* with her."

Belladonna's hands tightened into anxious fists at the same time that Bea nearly collapsed. Thankfully, Zied and Castor were there to catch her.

It was generally frowned upon for one magical being to touch another's familiar, but it never seemed to bother them. Beatrice had always been able to touch Castor without feeling any sort of nausea or queasiness that usually accompanied physical contact with someone else's familiar. And vice versa. Hells, back when they still lived together in the woods, Belladonna and Zied would lay in the grass, her head on his back, or his on her belly, and gaze up at the stars. Belladonna wondered if that was something unique to the pair of them, or if it was the case for all fated loves.

"She's in The Nothing?" Beatrice asked, her voice a strained whisper.

"Yeah, the *turmio* sapped our powers. Then it threw us against the walls of the cave, knocking me and Aiden out and nearly breaking Roska's back. Elena was the only one left, powerless. The *turmio* dragged her down into the chasm with it while she was busy stabbing that damned thing with her dagger." Quinn smiled a little at the memory. Belladonna shared his pride at Elena's ferocity. Of course, she would be the one to stab the *turmio*. Elena was fierce, with or without her powers.

Beatrice seemed to be struggling to keep her emotions at bay. Belladonna forced herself to relax her fists and grasped one of Bea's hands. The enchantress squeezed her hand as though it was the only thing keeping her from falling to pieces.

"She is quite the brave girl," Belladonna said to Bea. "A trait she certainly inherited from her mother."

Quinn scoffed but had the decency to keep any comments to himself. Roska shifted on his feet but said nothing as well.

Castor pulled a chair around the desk for Beatrice. She didn't sit, but Belladonna watched as Beatrice slowly allowed her free hand to grasp the back of the chair for support, almost as though she were trying to hide any weakness.

"If I may?" It was the first time the Prince had spoken, and Belladonna wanted to shut him down, but Bea responded first, with a subtle nod encouraging the Royal to continue. "Thank you, Headmistress," he said with a quick bow as he pushed off from the wall he'd been so casually lounging against. "I realize you might recognize me, but you don't know me. I'm the one who helped Elena escape from my mother's evil—and, might I add, poorly concocted—plan to start a war with you." He directed his words at Beatrice, but Belladonna could tell he was speaking to the room, making his case for why he was there with them all. "Elena is the most amazing being I've ever met, and I'd hate to think of her lost in The Nothing with a demon. From what little I understood of Aiden's plan, he thinks he can use your blood, Headmistress, mixed with his own blood as Elena's father, to call to her, drawing her to the edge of the veil between this world and The Nothing. Then, Mistress, he would need you to cast a spell to keep the three of them in a secure bubble of sorts while they pulled her through. Just in case the *turmio* tries to attach itself to her like the vile leech that it is."

The room fell to utter silence. Belladonna was fairly certain that she could hear the snow as it landed on the windowsill.

"What? Did I misunderstand the plan?" the Prince asked Roska and Quinn.

The boys said nothing. It seemed as though their jaws had become fully unhinged and they were incapable of forming words.

Castor's guffaw caught them all off guard. "Well, damn, Princeling."

The Prince studied Castor, probably trying to determine if the shifter was making fun of him or not. Honestly, Belladonna wasn't sure either way.

"You... you were listening to our plans?" Roska asked incredulously.

"Well, it's not really eavesdropping when we're all in the same tiny cabin on my ship," the Prince countered with a smug grin.

Belladonna thought she saw Quinn smile, but he quickly hid it behind a cough.

He'd better get comfortable with the Prince quickly, Castor said in her mind. *According to Aiden, the poor, conflicted Royal is already in love with Elena.*

At that, Belladonna felt herself fall roughly into the chair Castor had brought Bea.

Mux. Everything.

15

ROSKA

ROSKA WAS SURPRISED THAT the Prince had so succinctly summarized their plans to free Elena. He was torn between being impressed that the Prince had understood their plan—Aiden had been incredibly technical when he'd explained it to Roska—and betrayed that the Prince had been listening in on their private conversation.

He supposed ultimately, it didn't matter how he felt, as things would still have to progress and they needed to focus on preparing for the rites and rituals they'd need to perform in order to bring Elena home.

Their mother hadn't uttered a single word since the Prince informed her of Elena's current predicament. Belladonna, however, had eventually recovered herself and peppered him and Castor with dozens of questions about the rituals and magics involved in summoning Elena and pulling her back from The Nothing. When she got frustrated with their lack of detailed information, she threw up her hands and strode from the office. Their mother, still stunned and seemingly catatonic, stood frozen behind the chair Belladonna had vacated. Zied called for the guards to escort the brothers to an empty bedroom, and Niko was given the room across the hall.

The rooms were bare. Roska got the sense that the school was running out of rooms, or perhaps they'd already filled up all their regular rooms. Regardless, the brothers were stuck in a room not much larger than a pantry at the Brotherhood's compound. Two cots lined the walls, with a small window near the ceiling of the wall across from the thick, wooden door.

"Well, this is going better than I expected." Quinn flopped onto one of the cots, propping his head up on his arms and crossing his legs casually at the ankles.

"Seriously?" Roska couldn't believe that. Since they'd arrived, they'd been imprisoned, interrogated, Q had nearly set fire to the tower, then their mother had looked prepared to murder their father in cold blood. Oh, then there was the incredibly awkward—although quite delicious—meal in the hall with a couple hundred enchantresses studying them like they were from another planet. Their mother nearly came to blows with Castor. Castor dropped multiple life-altering facts as though they were nothing. And Belladonna seemed like she might actually explode before she stormed out of their mother's office. Not to mention Aiden and Aleerah were still locked up, and Elena was trapped in a demon dimension.

"Sure," Quinn said. "No one got murdered."

His brother offered him a rueful grin.

Roska sighed and sat down on the empty cot. "Yes, I suppose that's true. Although it seemed pretty touch-and-go there for a while. I fully expected you to set something—or someone—on fire a few times."

Q shrugged. "Guess I'm more emotionally evolved than you thought."

"That's hilarious." Lyra laughed mockingly at her human counterpart. Roska couldn't help joining in.

He knew things were a mess, and would likely get worse before they could bring Elena back, but he was grateful for the relative peace in the quiet room he now shared with his brother.

They spent the rest of the day alone in their room. Neither bothered to try the door; although Roska hadn't heard a lock click when the guards had closed the door, he felt confident that their mother wouldn't want them wandering around the school. At least not unsupervised. He assumed it was likely she had guards stationed outside their room.

Instead, they passed the time practicing—*more like playing with,* Demoni interjected—their powers. Roska made ice blocks and passed them to Quinn, who channeled his powers into a single fingertip and shaped the ice into various creatures. Roska's favorite so far was a creature Q identified as a hippokampos. It had the head and forelegs of a horse and the tail of a massive fish. In his ice sculpture, Q had the creature riding a wave, its forelegs seeming to run across the top of the water. It was magnificent.

The sun disappeared from the view of their tiny window. Roska could see the faint pink light quickly fading to deep lavender. Quinn pulled a dry log from his pack—which the guards had returned to him upon their release from the jail cells—wrapped some cloth around the end, and set it aflame. He placed the torch on the windowsill to avoid setting fire to their cots.

"Do you think they'll let us out for dinner?" Quinn asked, absentmindedly rubbing his stomach.

Despite their large lunch, Roska was famished.

Probably because we've been living on scraps our whole life, and now we know what full actually feels like, Demoni suggested. Roska couldn't help but agree.

"Hopefully, they'll at least bring us something to eat. If not, we still have supplies in your pack, don't we?" Roska didn't *want* to eat more travel bread, hard cheese, and dried meat, but it was better than nothing.

"I wonder if Elena is hungry." Quinn stared blankly at the stones of their ceiling. Roska wasn't sure he'd meant to say the words aloud.

"I don't think she is," Roska answered. "From what Father told me of The Nothing, she doesn't feel anything. Time stands still. It's possible, when we bring her back, she won't even realize that any time has passed at all."

"I guess that makes her the lucky one then," Quinn mused bleakly. "She doesn't have to deal with the stress or worry that we're stuck feeling."

"I doubt she'll see it that way," Lyra countered.

"Well, she can yell at me for being insensitive when we get her back." Quinn crossed his arms over his chest and continued to glare at the ceiling.

Roska knew Quinn was worried. He was too, but they couldn't dwell on their fear. They needed to put their energy into useful things, like pinpointing the exact date that would be ideal for the ritual. Aiden had said it needed to be the first Black Moon in the planting season. Something about the cosmic energies surrounding the time of rebirth and the new beginnings symbolized in the Black Moon. He'd said because they were basically giving birth to Elena for the second time, the time of rebirth would be the most effective.

The frost season would be ending soon, although the snow didn't seem to know or care about that fact. The first day of the planting season was coming. They needed to prepare. Gather supplies. And convince the adults in their lives to get along long enough to bring their sister back.

Gods, help us.

16

AIDEN

I T WASN'T THE WORST prison cell Aiden had been locked up in, but it was easily in the top five. The most frustrating part was the magic built into the walls that prohibited him from conjuring anything. He was stuck, like a human, in the tiny, hard, cold cell with nothing to entertain him or make him more comfortable.

That's the idea, idiot, Aleerah grumbled. She wasn't thrilled about being locked up either. *You turned her life upside-down. Twice! She blames you—and me by extension—for all the shyt things that have happened in her life over the last twenty cycles.* Aleerah flicked her tail in annoyance.

Aiden knew Aleerah was right, but he'd foolishly held out hope that Beatrice would have accepted his predestined role in her life by now. That she would have seen that all of Aiden's actions were either while he was under the influence of various substances—he had a bit of an issue with mind-altering plants when he'd first been burdened with foresight—or driven by prophecy and therefore equally out of his control.

"You self-centered, immature, arrogant prick." Hearing Aleerah's voice echo in the prison was startling. Aiden rose from where he'd been sitting uncomfortably on the stone floor of his cell to face her.

"What are you talking about?" Aiden challenged.

"You can't take responsibility for *anything*, can you?" Aleerah got to her feet as well, pinning him with a violent glare and baring her fangs at him.

Aiden was suddenly quite grateful for the bars separating them. He was sure that if she'd been able, Aleerah would be digging those vicious claws of hers into his flesh.

"I thought," she continued, "you were finally stepping up after everything that happened with the kids, and losing Elena. I stupidly believed that you would *finally* mature and be the man I know you're capable of. A man who your mother would be *proud* of." Aleerah looked down her fierce snout at him. "I hate being wrong."

"Wow, Alee. That's low, even for you." Aiden looked away from the direwolf. He didn't want her to see the pain her words inflicted on him, even though he knew she would feel the effect she had.

"You have the power of a *god*. You are hundreds of cycles old. You should be one of the wisest beings on this planet, and yet you still act as though you don't understand the simplest concepts." Aleerah's claws clicked on the stone floor as she began pacing her cell. "Beatrice is hurting. She's suffered immensely as a direct result of your choices. Yes, it might have all been a part of that damned prophecy, but you could have handled things differently. You could have been at least a *little* more transparent with her."

Aiden didn't respond. He sat on the rough, highly uncomfortable cot against the far wall of his cell and ruminated on her words. Perhaps Aleerah was right. Perhaps he should have been more forthcoming with Beatrice when he reconnected with her at that tavern the night the children were conceived. But telling her everything might have changed the course of events. Yes, the events took a very negative turn, and they were all still trying to recover from those actions. But that was prophecy. That's how those things were meant to turn out. Being upfront with Beatrice wouldn't have changed the fate of their world, it would have just created a heavier burden for Beatrice to have to carry. He never meant to make things harder for her. He just wanted to keep everyone safe.

They didn't speak to each other the rest of the night. Aiden was worried that Aleerah might have been right about him, but there was no way in hells he'd admit that to her. And she was still too pissed to even look at him.

Just as the sun was beginning to shine through his cell's barred window, Belladonna burst through the thick wooden prison door. The door flew open with such force that Aiden heard the wood splinter and crack down the middle.

"What the hells is wrong with you?" the witch shrieked. Her green locks swirled behind her as she turned the full force of her rage on him. The flowers that grew in her hair seemed to wilt at the heat of her anger.

Wow. Shrieked? That sounds a little offensive. A little sexist. If a man came in with this level of rage, would you refer to his tone as shrieking? Aleerah chastised, but he could hear the amusement in her tone. She was thrilled that someone else was going to yell at him some more.

Aiden ignored Aleerah's question and decided to respond to Belladonna's instead.

"You know, people keep asking me that. I'm fairly certain there's nothing wrong with me, but I'm sure you'll have something to the contrary to say." Aiden didn't bother getting up from the cot he'd spent the night attempting to sleep on. There was no point in getting up. It was clear Belladonna had no intention of letting him out of the cell. Might as well stay in the uncomfortable bed. He'd finally found an *almost* comfortable way to position his body, no reason to change that now.

"You son of a bitch." The irises of Belladonna's eyes had turned white with rage.

Aiden fixed her with his own fiery glare. "You will not speak of my mother in that way," he bit out. He could take all the tongue lashings they wished to give him, but no one would speak a word against his mother.

"You're right," Belladonna continued. "She's been gone for ages. It's not her fault you turned out to be such a self-righteous disappointment."

Aiden looked away. He knew his mother wouldn't have been happy with his choices of late—putting his children at risk—but he didn't have any other options. The entire world had been hanging in the balance. Aiden would never describe himself as a good father; hells, he wasn't even a decent one. But he did what was necessary to keep the world from falling into the hands of the *turmio*. His mother would have understood that.

Is that what you're telling yourself now? Aleerah eyed him incredulously.

"You were supposed to be gone from our lives. *Forever*. You were never supposed to show back up and throw Elena into The Nothing!" Belladonna raged.

"Now, hang on. I didn't throw anyone," Aiden corrected. "Hells, I was the first one to get thrown, and I lost consciousness as a result. Not to mention, Elena is my daughter too. I would never have knowingly hurt her."

No, you'd just lead the three of them into a trap and wait to see which one fell.

Mux off, Alee. You knew too, and you didn't stop them. Aiden could take a great deal of punishment, but he refused to take all the blame for what happened to Elena.

Belladonna didn't take her rage-filled eyes off him as she paced back and forth before his cell. Wringing her hands, Aiden watched as her white eyes shifted to an icy blue-green. From what little Aiden knew of witches, he assumed this color change meant that her mood was shifting from enraged to either anxious or nauseated. Possibly both.

She stopped pacing and studied him for a moment.

"Can you really bring her back?" she asked quietly.

Aiden could feel the trepidation in her words. He made a mental note that the icy teal color of her eyes meant fear and rose to join her at the wall of his cell.

"Yes," he said confidently. "I really can bring her back. With your help. And Beatrice's. Roska has been helping me plan the ritual. It will take some time to prepare and set up. And we need to do it on the equinox. It's the most powerful time for rebirth, as I'm sure you know. You'll be channeling your magic to serve as a sort of magnet, drawing Elena to you. Then her mother and I will essentially give birth to her, pulling her through the small opening we carve into the dimension. It will be painful, for all of us, but it will work. I promise."

Aiden spoke with so much confidence and conviction, he almost believed it was a fool-proof plan, as he implied. There were still many variables outside their control that could mux everything up, but there was no need to burden Belladonna with such things yet.

Maybe ever.

Self-righteous ass.

17

QUINN

THE NEXT MORNING, MADAME LaBelle relocated Quinn and Roska to a different wing of the school. It was *much* nicer, and Niko told them that these rooms were similar to the guest suites they had at the castle in Riverayn. Quinn decided this was probably where their mother's "special guests" stayed when they came to visit.

Quinn had his own bedroom, but he and Roska shared an adjoining sitting room. All three rooms—their bedrooms and the sitting room—had massive, decorative, and honestly extravagant fireplaces along the external wall. Each fireplace was framed by floor-to-ceiling windows, but the sitting room windows opened like doors, leading out to a balcony overlooking the tributary they'd sailed in on.

Quinn stood out on the balcony, staring unseeingly at the mountains that seemed to rise directly from the river. He had no idea how long he'd been staring out there, looking at nothing, when he noticed subtle movement along the water's edge, across the river from the school's harbor.

Instantly, he dropped to his knees, peering out between the balustrades, trying to see what was creeping up on them.

A hawk cried ominously as it soared overhead.

Lyra, who had been lounging against the back of the chimney enjoying the warmth of the stones, stealthily joined him at the edge of the balcony. She had considerably better eyesight than he did, so Q stepped aside to give his familiar a better vantage point.

Soldiers, she observed. *At least twenty, based on the movement I can see from here. Probably more.*

Do you think they can make it across the river without being noticed? Quinn needed to determine how much of a threat these soldiers were before running off to fetch their mother's guards.

Probably not, but it looks like a few of them have bows, so they may not be planning to cross at all.

As if on cue, the archers at the edge of the river, barely hidden among the young saplings, raised their bows, nocking them with flaming arrows.

"Roska!" Quinn cried out, jumping to his feet. He took aim and blasted his fire across the river at the soldiers. He had no hope of reaching the archers, but Q prayed his fire would distract them enough to miss their shots and get the attention of the guards at the harbor.

Just as he fired his second blast, Roska came rushing out onto the balcony beside him.

"What's going on?" he shouted over the din of orders being called out below.

"Soldiers," Quinn answered briskly before firing yet another blast at the archers.

Roska's gaze followed the stream of Q's fire to spy the would-be invaders. Not needing any further instruction, Roska began blasting snowballs of various sizes at the flaming archers. His aim was impeccable, and Quinn made a mental note to compliment his brother on his skill when this was all over.

The guards, using Q and Roska's assault as cover, climbed into rowboats and crossed the small river in moments. As soon as the boats were into the shallows, the guards began jumping out and waging their own assaults.

From his vantage point, Q couldn't see past the trees lining the riverside, but he continued blasting his fire at any arrows that managed to launch across the river, turning them to ash before they could do any damage.

Roska switched from snowballs to ice spears, the same ones he'd used to fight the *turmio*. Quinn noticed that Roska wasn't aiming to kill any of the soldiers. He admired his brother's precision as he fired ice spears, taking out knees and thighs without inflicting any mortal wounds. Quinn brimmed with pride. His brother was an *amazing* shot, but he wasn't a killer. Roska could have easily killed any guard within range, but he chose only to incapacitate.

When the arrows finally stopped flying, Quinn lowered his hands and stared into the trees, trying to see what was going on. He didn't see any more soldiers, but he could still hear the battle raging deep in the trees.

"Lyra, can you see anything?"

"Not much. The enchantresses have pushed the soldiers back. Looks like they're trying to retreat, but the guards aren't letting them get away. Killing or capturing anyone they get their hands on."

"Have we had any injuries?" Roska lowered his hands, halting his assault as the final archer fell, grabbing his thigh where an ice spear pierced clear through the meat of it.

"Looks like a few of the enchantresses were struck by arrows, and one seems to be bleeding pretty profusely. I can't tell what's causing the bleeding from here, though." Lyra relayed the information with a confident, almost careless, air. Quinn wasn't sure if she was actively trying to distance herself from the carnage below, or if she truly didn't care. He was pretty sure it was the former. Lyra wouldn't admit it, but she couldn't stand the sight of blood. It had always seemed amusing to Q—growing up with a fox who hated blood—but seeing the blood staining the snow across the river, he completely understood it.

"Thank you for warning us," one of the guards said with a bow as Quinn and Roska walked between the beds of the injured enchantresses in the infirmary.

"Yeah, um, no problem," Quinn said for the fiftieth time. He didn't know how to respond when the women thanked him, but they kept doing it. He hadn't done anything special; he didn't understand why they kept expressing their gratitude. It was ridiculous and unnecessary.

Roska nudged his shoulder. "If you hadn't seen the soldiers, this infirmary would be filled with far more bodies, both injured and deceased."

"It's not like I'm some kinda hero, though. I just happened to be on the balcony at the right time." Quinn shrugged. He tried to brush off the praise others continued to heap on him. He didn't deserve their praise. He simply did what anyone else in that position would have done.

The brothers had insisted on walking the infirmary to check on the guards who'd been injured. Q felt compelled to apologize to each and every one of them for not acting faster and not keeping them from harm. Lyra chided him for his "bullshyt attitude" and was quick to reiterate Roska's comments that there would have been a lot more injuries if he hadn't been there in the first place.

Q chose to ignore her.

Madame LaBelle hadn't informed her guards or her students about the existence of her sons, so it had been quite the shock for them all to realize that the fire and ice raining down on the soldiers was from the hands—literally—of two teenage boys.

Their mother still hadn't addressed their existence as she walked the infirmary ahead of them, but she'd made a quick announcement that she would explain everything to the whole school at dinner in the Great Hall.

Quinn couldn't wait to hear what she had to say about them.

18

BEATRICE

A s Headmistress, Beatrice rarely had to answer to anyone. There was the council, of course, but they were old and mostly let her run the school as she saw fit. Still, they wouldn't be happy to learn there were boys staying at Harbor Ridge. Even less so when they learned that those boys were, in fact, magical. And her children.

Every time she thought things couldn't possibly get any worse...

She sat at the head table on the dais in the Great Hall, presiding over dinner with Belladonna by her side. It had been a rough day, but, thankfully, Harbor Ridge hadn't suffered any death or even serious injuries at the hands of those damned soldiers. Beatrice didn't know how they would have survived such an attack if it hadn't been for Quinn's quick action. His fire not only burned through the arrows intent on killing her guards, but it served as a flaming beacon, revealing the would-be invaders. The soldiers thought they could outsmart her enchantresses—and loath as she was to admit it—it had almost worked.

Looking down from her seat at the table, Beatrice couldn't fight the feeling of utter helplessness that rolled over her. All of these girls—the students, the instructors, the guards—were her responsibility, and she'd nearly failed them today. How many would have died if Quinn hadn't been out on that balcony at just the right time? How many more children would die before Rosalina gave up her crusade against magic?

Beatrice was stewing in her thoughts, barely eating, when Belladonna reached over and took her hand. "Bea, you need to talk to them. Explain what happened and how we're going to protect them." Her voice was quiet, so as to not be overheard, but as firm as her grasp on Beatrice's hand.

"I know," she responded, desperately wishing she had the magic words to take away the fear she'd seen in the eyes of her students. "I just don't know what to say. I don't know how to protect them. We've used all the wards and spells we have, but I can't exactly put a wall in the river. I'll double the guard, but that's really all we can afford. We're spread thin as it is."

Belladonna's jaw twitched as she flexed her fingers around Bea's hand. "You know... and I know I'm going to regret suggesting this, but we could ask—" she ground her teeth, as though speaking was becoming quite difficult. "We could ask Aiden for help."

Beatrice sat in stunned silence. She never thought a day would come that Belladonna would suggest asking Aiden for anything, especially not with something as important as protecting the children of the school. He'd already established long ago that he had no regard for anyone else's well-being.

"I can't believe you actually said that." Beatrice couldn't help the smile that crossed her lips. It felt wrong to smile after such a traumatic day, but the idea of Bella suggesting turning to Aiden was damn near laughable.

"I know, but think about it," Belladonna began.

"Oh no, I understand. He has access to powers and magics that we couldn't even dream of. It's just such a hilarious notion. Turning to that fool for help." Beatrice chuckled at the ridiculousness of it all. "It's not a bad idea though. A crazy idea, without a doubt, but it can't possibly hurt to ask him. Not after the hells we barely avoided today."

"So, it's decided? We'll talk that selfish demi-god into helping to protect a bunch of strangers he has no reason to care for?" Belladonna seemed just as amused by the outlandishness of their plan, but they were out of options.

"Yes. He'll help us," Beatrice stated with annoyance, "if it means he'll be let out of that cell. But he's not staying in any of the nice rooms here in the school. He and that dire wolf of his can have the tower I put the triplets in before."

Beatrice rose stiffly. She still didn't know what to say, but the meal was coming to a close and she needed to address the events of the day, as well as the presence of the magical boys in their midst. Within moments, a tense silence had settled throughout the Great Hall.

Beatrice felt the weight of hundreds of eyes as they settled on her.

Just be honest with them. Zied's voice was strong and calm in her mind. She allowed his confidence to strengthen her resolve as she spoke.

"As you are all aware, this morning we were assaulted by the royal soldiers." A wave of hushed voices rolled through the hall, interrupting her words as she confirmed what some had likely hoped was only school rumor. "I'm pleased to inform you all," Beatrice continued as though she hadn't noticed the sudden whispers echoing in the expansive space, "thanks to the help of some unlikely men, we managed to defend our school, capture several soldiers, chase the rest away, and avoid any serious casualties."

Cheers burst through the hall, bouncing off the walls and magnifying the sounds of the triumphant students. Beatrice smiled down at them, sharing in their pride and sense of victory. She wanted to sit down and let that be the end of things. Unfortunately, she still had much to say. Calmly, she raised her hand, waited for silence to reign again, and continued.

"Most of you know my daughter Elena." Beatrice's voice cut out as she spoke her child's name. Clearing her voice, she went on. "You all also know that it is said to be impossible for magical males to exist. The male body is supposedly too weak to handle the powers of magic. It's what we have all been taught for as long as anyone can remember. It is known." Beatrice's eyes found her sons in the crowd. Seated beside the Prince, Quinn's face was filled with annoyance while Roska's was a passive mask of indifference. Beatrice knew better than to trust that mask. She had one of her own. All enchantresses did. "Sixteen solar cycles ago, that known fact was demolished by the birth of my sons."

For several long seconds, no one made a sound. No one moved. Beatrice wasn't even sure anyone blinked. She worried that perhaps they didn't hear her, or they thought she'd lost her mind. Then, all at once, the room exploded with hundreds of voices asking questions, shouting, and talking over each other. The room went from proud—bordering on celebratory—to tense, filled with doubt and uncertainty.

Beatrice remained standing, her hands clasped tightly before her in an attempt to project calm confidence. She let the students and staff voice their concerns for a few moments before raising her hands once again, calling them to take their seats and restore silence so she might continue. It took considerably longer than normal to restore order to the hall, but once everyone had returned to their seats, Beatrice turned her focus back to her sons.

"Quinn, Roska, will you two please join me up here?"

She could tell by the stiffness of his spine and the literal fire in his eyes that Quinn didn't appreciate her calling attention to him in this way. Roska was equally uncomfortable, although for him, it resulted in shutting down. He looked defeated and despondent as he followed his brother up the steps to join her on the dais. Beatrice walked around the table and met them at the top of the stairs. Turning them around to face the assembly, she positioned herself between them.

Lyra sat proudly at Quinn's feet, fire blazing on the tip of her tail almost in challenge. In further contrast, Beatrice noticed Demoni curled protectively around Roska's neck, as though she expected a fight and was prepared to defend her companion, shielding him with her own scaly body.

Beatrice placed a hand on each boy's shoulder and spoke again to the enchantresses.

"These are my sons. Quinn, the prophesized FlameBorn, identified and warned us of the invading soldiers. His keen senses and quick action saved countless lives today." Beatrice caught Quinn's stare for a moment. She couldn't help but notice the look of confusion in his eyes at her praise. That look told her that he either couldn't comprehend the pride in her voice, or he felt undeserving of it. She broke eye contact. She couldn't allow herself to dwell on his feelings right now. They could talk later.

"Roska," she continued, turning her gaze to her youngest child, "is the prophesized FrostBorn. His flawless aim helped to take down many of our enemies and protected our guards as they chased the soldiers back into the woods." Beatrice spoke the words to the enchantresses, but her eyes never left Roska's face. Roska, however, didn't make eye contact with her. He didn't even turn to face her. Instead, he held his mask in place as she studied his profile. He looked so much like Aiden. It was devastating. Almost as devastating as the look of concern that passed across his dragon's face as she returned the Headmistress's gaze.

Beatrice thought she saw tears gathering in Roska's eyes, but they were gone the moment she looked back at his face from Demoni's.

Clearing her throat once more, she added, "My children are the product of prophecy and are more magical than any other beings born in the last one hundred cycles. They will be staying here, indefinitely, along with Prince Niko." Cries of outrage filled the room at her last statement. Beatrice raised her arms to try and restore order, but the crowd was too busy raging at this new development to pay attention to her. Zied rose from where he'd been lounging behind her seat, jumped over the table, and let loose a resounding roar.

Silence fell instantly.

With a grateful nod to her lion, Beatrice spoke once more. "I am the headmistress of this school. You do not have to like or agree with my decisions, but you will all respect them. I have granted the Prince asylum within these walls, and I expect each and every one of you to treat him as an honored guest. He will be vital in bringing this foolish attempt at war to an end quickly and with as little bloodshed as possible."

Niko, who had been wise enough to not make a show of himself before now, chose this moment of tension to rise from his seat at the back of the hall and address the crowd himself.

"My mother does not speak for the realm," he said loudly and with a fierceness she hadn't expected. "She has allowed her own ignorance to drive her to make dangerous and violent decisions. I intend to put a stop to her aggression as quickly as possible." He offered a curt bow and returned to his seat.

The hall filled with more arguments. Beatrice couldn't understand much of what the enchantresses were saying, but she could assume, based on the growing tension in the air, that they weren't thrilled about the paradigm-shifting information she'd revealed to them.

Better that they know now than for them to find out later and think you hid it from them, Zied offered.

Better for whom, I wonder.

Despite Belladonna's reassurance that Aiden would be helpful, Beatrice was still surprised by his eagerness to be useful. It almost seemed as though he was assisting the school as penance for past transgressions.

He certainly has plenty to apologize for, Beatrice mused while she oversaw his castings. Although she didn't have access to the types of power he could tap into, Beatrice understood the spells he was using and the godlike power he was infusing into his wards. His spells weren't that different from her own, but his deity parentage granted Aiden access to magic that Beatrice could only ever read about.

"How's it going up here?" Belladonna spoke quietly, presumably so as to not disrupt Aiden's concentration. Or perhaps she was hoping to avoid his attention. From what Beatrice had been told by her guards, Belladonna had had quite the explosive reunion with Aiden when he was still locked away in the prison.

"Good, I think. He's essentially making a bubble around the whole school that is impenetrable to those without magic. The magept already within the confines of the barrier will be fine, but if they leave, they won't be able to regain entry until he takes this barrier down." Beatrice had been very clear on that part. She employed plenty of magept in her housekeeping and cooking staff. Not to mention, the Prince, who was still residing in the royal suites. Beatrice might not care for his parents, but there was no need to take her anger out on their child. That would make her no better than Rosalina.

19

ROSKA

THE BLACK MOON WAS quickly approaching, and Roska's anxiety had reached new peaks. Since their mother's announcement—proclamation—of her relationship to him and Q, and her near-bragging about his skillful use of his frost to defend the school, several of the students had taken to watching him. Some had even gotten so bold as to start following him around and whispering about him. None had attempted to speak to him directly, but he could sense their confidence growing with each passing day.

Soon, one of the girls would get up the nerve to speak to him. Then he'd have to respond. He couldn't be rude, but he also couldn't fathom speaking to any of these girls. Roska wouldn't go so far as to say he was *afraid* of the enchantresses, but he was highly aware of their magical skills. He didn't want to offend anyone or upset their mother by being rude, but he also had no interest in any of these girls.

Whenever he wasn't working with Aiden, collecting ingredients, or prepping the tower they were using for the ritual to bring Elena home, Roska's mind often wandered back to Brigit.

Did she miss him? Hells, did she even remember him?

Stop that. Don't think like that. Of course she remembers you. She was as smitten with you as you were with her. Demoni's voice interrupted Roska's self-doubt spiral.

It's been several moons since we left her. I doubt she even thinks of me. Roska hated that she might have forgotten him, but he worried even more that she could be worried about him. Better for her to have forgotten him than for her to feel the anxious, crippling worry he felt whenever he thought about Elena trapped in The Nothing.

The Black Moon is in three nights. We'll bring Elena home, then we can go back to Nexton and find Brigit, Demoni offered, as though the process of bringing Elena back was simple, like picking her up at the harbor. As though she'd been on a trip to visit distant relatives. Not trapped in a hells dimension with a monster who wanted to essentially eat all the magic in the world.

Roska flopped disheartened on the couch across from the blazing fire in their hearth. Demoni unwrapped herself from his neck, climbing across the back of the couch to stretch out along the arm.

It's not that simple and you know it, he argued.

It doesn't have to be as complicated as you're making it though, she countered.

Roska sighed but didn't respond. It was the same circular argument they'd been having for days. Demoni was convinced that Brigit would be waiting for them at that inn in Nexton. Roska was considerably less confident. Sure, she seemed to enjoy his company when he was right in front of her, but maybe it was all an act. Or maybe she'd lost interest over time while he'd been away.

Or perhaps she believed he'd died.

Roska hadn't told her exactly where they were going or why, but he knew Brigit was worried. She'd been able to tell that *something* was wrong, even if she didn't know the extent of what it was or how bad it truly could have been.

Hells, he *had* nearly died. If it hadn't been for Elena, he likely would have.

Roska opted for changing the subject, rather than having the same fight again. *Let's just focus on bringing Elena home. Aiden and Mother will do the bulk of the ritual, but I think we should be there too. Calling to Elena and helping to pull her back. It will strengthen the pull of the spell if all the people who love her are in that tower.*

Will the Prince be there too, then? Demoni asked pointedly.

What are you talking about? Roska looked at her, stunned by her implication.

You can't tell me you haven't noticed how committed he is to bringing her home. The desperation in his eyes when we woke up in that cave. How quickly he offered to help bring us here, and his eagerness to do anything he can to help bring her home. Demoni flicked her tongue at him, almost condescendingly.

Well, yes. I have noticed his eagerness to help. But that's just because he knows his mother is wrong about magic and he's trying to right her wrongs. Roska ran a nervous hand through his white blonde hair. *You don't think he... he's not in* love *with her. Right? How could he be? They barely know each other.*

Love can be instantaneous. Demoni held his stare meaningfully. *One doesn't need to spend an excessive amount of time with someone to know love is there.*

Roska broke eye contact, shifting his focus from his familiar to the flames dancing on the logs in their hearth.

He knew she was trying to make a point. Niko could in fact be in love with Elena.

Roska might also be in love with Brigit.

Roska woke with a start at the sound of a slamming door.

"Oh, shyt. Sorry, Ros. I didn't mean to wake you. I didn't realize you were even in here." Quinn removed his coat and hung it on the rack by their suite door. Lyra bounded into the room, straight to the hearth. She mouthed a couple of logs from the cast iron log holder beside the fireplace and gently placed them on the slowly-dying embers of their fire. Flicking her tail at the fresh wood, she reignited the fire.

Roska rubbed the sleep from his eyes. He hadn't intended to fall asleep on their couch. His late nights with Aiden must have been catching up to him.

"It's no problem. I shouldn't be sleeping here anyway. We still have a few more things to prepare before we can begin the ritual."

"Three more days." Q clapped his hands, rubbing his palms together and glowing with a gleefulness Roska had never seen in his brother. "Three more days and we can *finally* bring our sister home and get the hells out of this place for good."

"Q," Roska began. He loved seeing how hopeful Quinn was, but he needed to manage expectations. "There's no telling how Elena will be feeling when she first comes back. She's been in a hells dimension. She might not be," Roska paused, struggling to find the right words. "She might not be up for traveling right away."

"I know," Quinn answered, scraping his hand roughly on his chin. It was a nervous habit Roska had noticed his brother do whenever he was worried. "But she'll be *home*. It feels like it's been ages since we've seen her. Touched her. Hugged her. Listened to her chastise my 'foul language' and your 'negative self-talk.' I miss her. We need her back."

Quinn sat hard on the couch beside Roska, leaning forward and holding his head in his hands.

"I know. I miss her too. We will bring her home." Roska laid a cool, firm hand on his brother's back. Feeling the fire raging beneath his brother's shirt, Roska poured some of his frost into his hand in an attempt to quell the heat racing through Q.

"Three more days," Quinn said with a sigh.

Roska felt the heat in his brother slowly dissipate as he took several deep breaths.

"This will work, won't it?" Q didn't look up as he asked the question. Roska thought perhaps his brother was afraid of the answer.

"I believe it will." He infused as much confidence as he dared into his words.

20

QUINN

THE CLOCK IN THEIR room ticked quietly on the mantle, counting down the seconds until it was exactly midnight. Time for the ritual to begin. Roska and Aiden had been up in the tower all day, setting up all the ingredients, and positioning all the tools including a collection of large mirrors. Roska had explained the point of the mirrors to him at one point, but Quinn hadn't really been listening. He didn't really care *how* the ritual worked. He just needed to be sure that it would in fact work.

We should head up there. They're going to start soon. Lyra dropped his boots dangerously close to his sock-clad toes.

"Watch it!" He jumped back, curling his toes in protectively.

Lyra didn't respond, flicking her ember-filled tail at him to express her annoyance and impatience. He could understand and even relate to her anxious feelings, but taking his toes off wouldn't make him move any faster.

Q shoved his feet into the boots, scooped up the blanket Roska asked him to bring, and strode from their suites. He suspected that Roska only asked him to bring a blanket so that Q had a job to do, something to contribute because he'd been an anxious—*and annoying*, Lyra chimed in—mess all week. Roska gave him a job, just to give him something to focus his nervous energy on.

Still, it had worked. Quinn spent the week finding the thickest, softest blanket in the entire school to wrap Elena up in as soon as she came back. She would feel warm and safe, dammit. He would make sure of it.

The tower was surprisingly well light, considering there wasn't a hint of moonlight in the sky, and the clouds blocked out the majority of the stars that stood watch over them on the equinox night. Roska and Aiden had filled the room with dozens, possibly hundreds, of candles, ranging from brand-new tapers to short, squatty candles likely stolen from empty classrooms. Eight mirrors lined the walls, at the cardinal and intercardinal points, all facing the center of the room. Slightly off-center, Roska and Aiden stood at a worn wooden table covered in grinding bowls of herbs, some sort of stone tablet with odd-looking lines crisscrossing all over it, a dagger, some vials of vibrantly colored liquids, and even more candles. Belladonna and Beatrice stood across from them, leaving a decent space in the middle. Supposedly, that was where the portal was meant to open.

"Oh good! You're here!" Aiden cheered as Quinn set the blanket down by the door, taking in the scene before him. "Here, take this and pour it in the center of the room. Make a circle. About the size of this table." He thrust a large canvas bag into Q's hands and turned back to the table.

Quinn eyed the bag suspiciously. It smelled oddly floral but stale.

"It's a concoction of herbs meant to draw her to us and give her a target for where to land. You're marking the portal location with the herbs," Beatrice explained. She motioned for Q to step into the mirror circle and showed him how to pour the herbs. Not too heavy that there wouldn't be enough to complete the circle, but not so thin that the wind could blow through and wreck their ritual either.

Once the circle was complete, Beatrice and Belladonna relocated four candles on stands from the corners of the room to directly in front of the mirrors at the cardinal points. Quinn stepped back, outside of the mirror circle, to avoid being in the way.

Niko entered the room, the look of grim determination on his face replaced by one of confusion for a moment. "What the..." he whispered, barely audible over Roska and Aiden's chanting.

Quinn moved to stand beside the Prince. Best to keep close to the Prince, so he doesn't do something stupid like try to "help" and end up wrecking the whole thing.

You mean like you did when you tried to help Roska collect herbs and nearly started a wild fire—again? Lyra stood between Q and the mirror circle, keeping a watchful eye on the herb circle in the middle while still managing to berate him.

For the last time, I didn't start that fire. You *did.*

Lyra flicked her tail at him, sending a few harmless embers across the bare stone floor, but didn't continue the never-ending argument.

The air in the room felt charged, not unlike when Elena would lose her temper while they were being held captive in that damned tower. The air within the herb circle began to shift, warping like heat raising from the cobblestone streets of Andover in the height of the growing season.

Something was happening.

21

ELENA

T HE DARKNESS SURROUNDING ELENA was impermeable. Despite her best efforts, even her own lightning couldn't light up the space she floated in. Floated. Her feet weren't on any solid surface. Elena had a cursory thought that this must be how the fruit in Nikki's gelatin dessert must feel. Suspended in nothingness, unable to move. Encased in an endless black abyss. A silent, endless black abyss. Not a single sound. That was the first thing she tested when they'd been unceremoniously dumped here however long ago. Yelling. Talking. Screaming. Crying. No sound existed. Either her ears were fully clogged or her voice had vanished along with the light.

Her only saving grace was Agon. He was still with her. Elena could feel the weight of him on her shoulders and catch snippets of his thoughts in her mind. She couldn't hear him properly though. It was like they were trying to have a conversation underwater. Yelling at each other as the bubbles poured from their lips but their words were barely coherent.

Elena had no idea how long they'd been stuck in this hellscape. She could sense that they weren't alone, but they hadn't physically encountered anyone. She assumed the *turmio* was with them some-where, but she had no way of knowing for certain.

Elena prayed to the Mother that the *turmio* had fallen through with her and hadn't managed to escape and remain in their world. The idea of that demon being trapped here was the only solace she had. She couldn't let her mind wander or consider for even a moment that the *turmio* was still wreaking havoc in her world. If it were still on the loose, it would murder her family. Assuming it hadn't already.

Don't think like that, she chided herself. *They are all fine. You dragged that demon down with you. Quinn and Roska are perfectly safe and living happy lives in Waverly.* She refused to let herself think too hard about them moving on without her.

Elena had no idea how long she'd been trapped here, but she had to assume at least *some* time had passed. Days? Weeks? Moons? She had no way of knowing. Perhaps it had been dozens of solar cycles. Perhaps her brothers had found love, mated, and even had children. It broke Elena's heart to think she'd never meet her brothers' mates or their children.

Niko.

Niko would certainly have moved on. Mated some Royal from another land. Had a full brood of Royals to carry on his family name and royal line. He certainly wouldn't have spent his days waiting around for her to reappear.

Thinking that he might was just foolish. Childish. Unreasonable and irrational.

Even if he had truly cared for her, he had a duty to crown and country. He had no such loyalty to her.

Ages floated by around her. Elena was slowly accepting that this was how she'd spend the rest of her days. Never feeling the wind on her face. Never knowing the touch of another human. Never hearing the sound of birds chirping in the leafy canopy of the Dark Woods. Never feeling the rush of the River as it flowed between her fingers when she dangled her hand from the side of Niko's longship.

Why then did she suddenly feel different? If she didn't know any better, she might have thought she was *moving*.

But that was impossible.

Wasn't it?

And yet...

What is going on? she wondered, feeling a sudden warmth pass over her skin.

I have no idea. Agon's voice was clear for the first time in what felt like ages.

Agon! Elena cheered. Relief washed over her. Whatever it was that was causing this change, she was unfathomably grateful for it. She felt as though the world were swallowing her up. Or perhaps forcing her out.

Without warning, the darkness began to push in around her. It felt as though the nonexistent walls were closing in. Squishing her. Forcing all the air from her lungs. A blinding light filled her vision. Incoherent shouts invaded the space.

Elena squeezed her eyes closed as tightly as possible while covering her ears to protect her from the deafening noise.

Something was pulling her. Forcing her to leave the quiet solitude of the abyss. Elena tried to lash out, protect herself from the violent grip that had taken hold of her shoulders and legs, but her magic failed her.

Elena felt Agon slip from her shoulders, severing the only physical connection she'd had to another living being in ages.

"No!" Elena's voice reverberated through her throat, bouncing off the stone walls that now surrounded her.

Squinting, Elena could make out the shapes of several people and a few large, furry creatures.

The sights, sounds, scents, and feelings of everything around her were too much to bear. Elena stumbled away from the people, tripping over something on her weak legs, and collapsed, embracing the darkness that clouded her vision yet again.

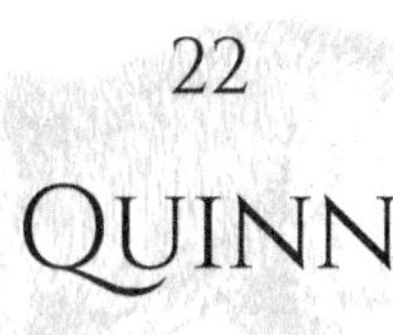

22

QUINN

I T HAD WORKED. It had really muxing worked! Elena was back, and Quinn couldn't believe his eyes. In a matter of seconds, he'd gone from anxious, to exhilarated, to terrified.

Elena was back, but she didn't seem like herself. Hells, she'd collapsed almost instantly. If the Prince hadn't been there to catch her, she likely would have smacked her head on the rough stone floor of the tower and possibly never awoken again.

Q should have caught her.

He'd been too stunned by her reappearance to move.

Quinn didn't like being grateful for the Prince, but Niko had saved his sister from a potentially grievous injury. Q would be an idiot *not* to be grateful for that.

Seeing the Prince holding his sister had left Q frozen for a second longer before he rushed over and helped carry an unconscious Elena to the nearest secure bedroom. Much to his disdain, that room had turned out to be one of the royal suites. But not just any royal suite. No. It was the Prince's.

Carefully, they laid Elena out on his bed, tucking her in snugly under an inordinate number of quilts. Her skin was like ice, and she looked like a corpse. Around her pale white face, dark hair spread out across the pillows.

Roska came in behind Q and laid Agon beside Elena, wrapping him in another quilt all his own. Lyra quickly jumped onto the bed and wrapped her tail around the blanket encasing Agon. Quinn could feel her heat spreading from her tail to the weasel's quilt. Both Agon and Elena would be warm and comfortable very soon.

If he hadn't seen the subtle rise and fall of her chest, Q would have been worried that she was dead. He sat on the edge of the bed, staring at her. He couldn't take his eyes off of her. Quinn was convinced that if he looked away, even for a second, she'd be taken away from him again. He couldn't lose her. Not again.

"I'm staying with her," he announced to the room. Not that he really expected anyone to leave her alone any time soon. Still, he wanted it to be perfectly clear.

"As am I," Roska chimed in, taking a seat at the foot of the bed and leaning back against the bedpost, making himself comfortable.

"Of course," Aiden nodded. He pulled chairs from the table by the window for himself, Belladonna, and Beatrice, motioning for the women to sit before he joined them and conjured two steaming pots— one filled with coffee, the other with some type of tea—as well as a plate of biscuits.

"Ah, well, all right. I guess just make yourselves at home." Niko smiled ruefully. He didn't seem bothered by his space being suddenly invaded by their entire family.

Their *family*.

Mux. Quinn would never have thought he'd be sitting in a royal suite, surrounded by his blooded family, ever. And yet, he couldn't imagine anywhere he'd rather be. Sitting with these magical beings, all waiting anxiously for Elena to open her eyes.

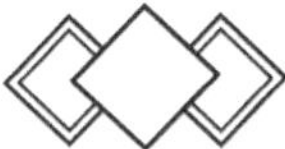

As he stared off into the dark night sky, Quinn's mind drifted back to just a few hours before. The tower had been empty—minus the altar and ritual supplies—when Quinn had first entered. The ritual required the first Black Moon of the planting season. Luckily for them—or it was divine intervention, if Quinn listened to Aiden's logic—the first Black Moon was also the equinox, the very first day of the planting season. Belladonna had said it was a very auspicious sign and the most powerful night they could have hoped for to try and bring El home. As such, they'd had to wait until near midnight to perform the ritual, when the Black Moon was at its peak.

Quinn hadn't put much thought into all their timing, planning, and ritualizing. He'd just wanted his sister back. He'd spent far too many cycles not knowing he had a family. Then he'd found her and latched on tightly. He hadn't known who she was to him in the beginning, of course, but there had always been a tie between them that he couldn't shake or ignore. When she'd been kidnapped just a few moons after discovering the truth, it had been devastating. When she'd shown up to help fight the *turmio* back in the cavern, Quinn had been so sure that she was there to stay. He'd been equally confident that he'd be leaving both her and Roska, sacrificing himself to complete the ritual and trap the *turmio* once and for all. But fate had intervened yet again, and he'd been knocked out while she'd been sucked into The Nothing with that damned demon. The last few lunar cycles without her—not knowing if she was ok, not knowing if she was even alive—had been unbearable.

Lyra snapped her sharp teeth at him, shocking him out of his memories and bringing him back to the present.

Elena is back, she thought to him. *Back home, safe and sound.*

First of all, this place is not *her home,* Q mentally muttered, glaring around the room filled with sofas and more feather pillows than was decent. *Her home is with us at Amelia's. This is just a resting place until we can get back to our real home. Secondly, we have no idea how "sound" she is. I don't know if you noticed, but she just muxing collapsed. We have no way of knowing if she'll be ok. And third, none of us are "safe" until we stop that damned Queen and her anti-magic army.*

Fine, Lyra conceded. *You make a few good points, but can we just take a moment to celebrate the win here? Elena and Agon are back. A week ago, we weren't even sure* that *was possible.* Her ears twitched, tracking the movements of mice or rats that lived in the castle walls.

Quinn nodded. She was right. They hadn't been positive that the ritual would work. It had been a huge risk and—according to Roska's slightly intoxicated midnight confession—the chances were "decent, at best." Yet here she was.

It was a miracle in itself. They'd just have to wait and see how she was doing when she woke up.

If she woke up.

23
BELLADONNA

"WOULD YOU SIT STILL?" Belladonna snapped at Quinn. He was just so damned fidgety. Like he expected her to dump a bucket of roaches over his head at any minute. "This won't hurt unless you continue squirming. Then I won't be held responsible for any injuries you receive." She added a quick flick to the back of his ear to enforce her words.

"I don't understand why we're even doing this." Quinn squirmed a moment longer, then stretched out on the lounge before her, resting his head on the arm of the chair.

Belladonna placed her hands on either side of his head, hovering next to his ears, without actually making contact. "I want to see the fire."

"Well, if that's all you want," Quinn raised a flaming palm confidently, "all you had to do was ask."

"Not *that* fire, you troublesome boy," Belladonna knocked his hand away when he raised it too close to her flowering hair. "I want to see *the* fire. The first fire you ever set, in that hells of an orphanage."

The fire on Q's hand flared quickly before he grimaced and recalled his power completely. "Why the mux would you want to see that shyt? And how are you planning on *seeing* anything? That was nearly ten cycles ago."

"Magic, boy. Magic." Belladonna placed her hands back at the sides of his head, closed her eyes, and focused on the memories she wished to visit. The faint scent of wood smoke drew her into his past.

Smoke clouded her vision. Belladonna tried to blink through the haze that was rapidly filling the room. She'd arrived in his memory later than she had intended. She'd wanted to see the start of the fire, but based on the smoldering corpses in the corner of what used to be a kitchen, Belladonna could pinpoint exactly where the flames had begun.

In the middle of the smoky room stood a gaunt young boy with light blonde hair, green eyes, and a bundle of orange fur cradled in his arms. Quinn. He couldn't have been more than seven cycles old. Younger than she'd expected. Flames danced in his eyes and around the room.

The fire in the house behaved quite unusually. Instead of spreading smoothly around the room, it seemed to jump around without logic. The flames had clearly started with the corpses of Q's foster parents, then shot to the dining room table across the room before jumping to a cupboard beside the stove. It seemed entirely illogical until Belladonna turned her attention to young Q. Everywhere his eyes flicked, the fire followed. When his gaze left the cupboard and focused on a collection of wooden spoons that hung above the kitchen sink, the fire followed his view, reducing the spoons to ash.

When it seemed as though young Quinn had eliminated everything he'd had specific resentment toward, he blinked several times. The fire in his eyes faded, and the flames in the room quickly shifted from seemingly having a mind of their own to a more natural fire, burning everything in its path.

Young Quinn looked down at the charred remains of his abusers—as though making sure they were truly gone—then he shifted Lyra's furry weight in his arms, opened the kitchen door, and left. He walked away so calmly and confidently, as though the house wasn't ablaze behind him.

When Belladonna opened her eyes again, she was only mildly surprised to find Lyra curled protectively on Quinn's chest, heat dancing beneath the surface of his skin, and a faint orange glow emanating from his eyes.

Belladonna moved from behind his head and took the empty armchair beside him. "You controlled the fire."

"No shyt," he said snarkily, lighting the tip of his index finger and waving the flame at her mockingly.

"No, Quinn, I mean you *controlled* the flames. You directed them where to go. You didn't just burn down the house, it started out very targeted. All you had to do was look at something, focus your attention, and it caught fire instantly. I've never seen anything like it." Belladonna didn't bother keeping the admiration from her voice. Quinn needed to know that what he'd done had been amazing, impressive, and entirely warranted. He rained justice down on those wretched humans.

He blinked at her, stunned. "You called me by my name." His voice was raw with emotion. Likely a result of having relived those memories with her.

It could also be because you've literally never called him by his name before, Castor noted, stretching his wings from his perch on the mantle.

Belladonna cocked her head, trying to remember if that was actually true. Had she really never called the boy by his name before?

It's true. You call him boy, *if you bother to address him directly at all.*

Belladonna flinched internally at Castor's words. She'd been so cruel and needlessly harsh to Quinn. She needed to take steps and rectify the situation.

"Yes, I did." Belladonna nodded, attempting to project confidence. She couldn't understand why she felt such awkwardness around him. She'd never felt this way about Elena or Roska. Quinn looked so much like the woman she loved. Seeing him shouldn't make her awkward. If anything, she should be more comfortable with him, simply because looking at him was like looking at the masculine version of the face she loved more than life itself.

Quinn shook his head, shifted Lyra off his chest, and pulled her into his lap as he sat up on the couch. "So, I can control the fire even after it's left my hands?"

Belladonna nodded again, grateful to be back on point. "It seems that way. When you were shooting flames at the soldiers the other morning, you were aiming. Didn't you notice? Your flames never followed a straight route, as a typical firestarter's would. The fire would leave your hands, cross the river, and curve, setting fire to any soldiers within eyesight."

"I guess I was so focused on stopping them that I didn't think too much about where the fire was going, just where I needed it to end up." Quinn shrugged awkwardly.

Awkward seems to be a thing for you both, Castor teased.

Belladonna shot him a vicious glare and turned back to Quinn. "If this is something you can hone and do deliberately, it would be incredibly useful in our fight against the Queen." She placed subtle emphasis on the word *our*. It was every magical being's duty to fight back against the oppression the Queen was attempting to enforce.

"You make it sound so simple. I didn't even know I was doing it. How the hells am I supposed to start doing it on purpose now?"

Belladonna smiled widely. "Practice, my dear boy. Lots and lots of practice."

24

ELENA

S UNLIGHT FLOODED THE ROOM, warming her skin and drawing her out of the sleep that had so readily enveloped her. Slowly, Elena blinked her eyes open, taking in the room around her. She lay in a large, plush bed, covered in at least a dozen quilts. Agon was curled up on the pillow beside her, his back to her as he faced the door. To her left, the sun was blazing in the bright, clear blue sky behind the iron and glass windows. A fire roared in the hearth across the room with a chaise lounge stretched out before it.

It took her eyes several moments to adjust before she noticed the head of curly dark hair that rested—at a rather uncomfortable looking angle—on the back of the chaise.

Elena shook her head. She must be in shock. She couldn't possibly be where she thought she was. And there was no way that head belonged to who she thought.

Gingerly and as silently as possible, Elena shifted into a seated position in the middle of the massive bed. Blinking and rubbing her eyes, she tried to comprehend what had happened. She'd been trapped in the darkness for so long that now—being surrounded by lights and sounds—her senses were overwhelmed.

Or perhaps she'd finally gone insane.

She wasn't in a royal suite at Harbor Ridge.

She was merely hallucinating. Imagining a place that felt like home, with the Prince.

Seems like an odd thing to imagine, Agon's voice cut in.

What? Elena's thoughts were muddled. She was in shock. She had to be.

Shock, sure. But of all the places you could imagine—of all the places your mind might conjure to give you a sense of home and safety—do you really think Harbor Ridge would be your go-to place? Do you truly feel safe and at home in your mother's school?

Agon made a valid point. If she were going to hallucinate a place where she felt most at home, it would likely have been Amelia's inn. Or Q's home in the Dark Woods.

She'd never spent any real time in the royal suites at Harbor Ridge. Elena had vague memories of exploring the rooms as a child, playing hide-and-seek with Nanny Maureen.

Not to mention, the Prince? That's who you think you'd dream up as the first person to see after escaping hells? Agon's voice had a slightly pointed, teasing air to it.

She wouldn't have voiced it, but Elena wouldn't have been surprised if her mind *had* conjured Niko. She'd been thinking about him more often than not since she had been forced to leave him in the cave when the tunnel had collapsed.

"You're awake." Niko's voice was rough. He rose from the chaise and came to sit at the foot of the bed.

"I..." Elena began, but her voice cracked, weak from lack of use.

Niko rose and reached for the pitcher that sat on the bedside table. "Here," he said as he filled a glass with water. "Drink this."

Elena attempted to take the glass, nearly dropping it and splashing water all over the bed. She stared at her hands in confusion. They looked the same, but for some reason, they didn't follow her commands.

"No worries, Firefly," Niko said with a gentle smile. He refilled the glass and climbed into the bed beside her. "I'll help you. It looks like your body isn't quite ready to cater to your needs just yet. Lucky for you, I'm more than eager to fulfill your every need." Niko's eyes sparkled at the innuendo implicit in his words, but he didn't say any more.

"That's really not necessary," Elena replied hoarsely, but she let him lift the cup to her lips anyway, tilting her head back and nearly fainting at the glorious taste of the cold water. She moaned as the cool liquid bathed her parched tongue. In seconds, Elena had drained the glass. "More, please," she gasped as the last drops of water slid down her throat.

Niko refilled the glass and returned it to her lips. As desperately as she needed the water, Niko maintained a slow-and-steady pace. If she'd been able, Elena would have ripped the glass from his hands, downed the water, and then drunk the rest straight from the pitcher. In the back of her mind, Elena was grateful for her weakened state and Niko's careful movements. She'd likely drown in the pitcher of water if she tried to do it all herself.

Niko's eyes never left hers as she inhaled the water he offered. Elena finished the pitcher, sitting back to inspect him as he'd been studying her.

He looked the same, and yet less than himself. Paler, with several days' worth of stubble on his face. His hazel eyes seemed dull and the heavy bags under his eyes hadn't been there before.

"How long was I gone?" Elena whispered.

The Prince set the empty glass back on the bedside table, ran his hands roughly through the mess of curls on his head, and stared into the fire.

When it seemed clear that he wasn't going to answer, Elena clumsily reached for his hand where it rested on his thigh. Her grip was weak, but she managed to grasp his fingers with her own and force his attention back to her.

"Please, Niko. How long?"

"Moons," he said roughly. "You've been gone for several moons. The frost season is over. The planting season began last week. You've been unconscious in my bed since your family brought you back on the equinox."

Elena blanched. In the darkness, it had felt like time stood still. She didn't know how to handle the idea that she'd been gone for nearly the entire season, or that she'd been asleep for a week.

"Where are my brothers?" Elena couldn't even imagine how they were feeling. If she'd lost one of them for moons, she would have likely gone mad with worry.

"They're here. Your mother kicked them out of my suite after a few days, when it was clear you weren't going to wake up right away."

Niko repositioned his hand, interlocking their fingers. "We've been taking shifts, so you'd never be alone. Q has started training the fire starters in the courtyard. If he's down there now, you can probably see them from the window." He nodded toward the large window beside the hearth.

"Wait, what?" Elena must have misheard him. There was no possible way that Quinn would be working with the enchantresses. Much less *training* them? Even if her mother would have allowed it, Quinn hated enchantresses and everything Harbor Ridge represented.

"Aye, it was a bit of a shock to everyone," Niko chuckled. "But after my mother's attack on the school a few weeks ago, Q and Ros swooped in and saved the school. Your mum introduced them over dinner and recruited them both to help train the girls to defend themselves in battle."

Elena couldn't believe what she was hearing. There was too much information in those two sentences. She couldn't wrap her mind around it.

"As for Ros, he's been more interested in working with Aiden. He helped prepare the ritual that brought you back to us." Niko's eyes searched her face, as though he was worried she might vanish into thin air. His grip on her hand was tight. Not painful, but it was clear he didn't want to let go for fear of losing her again.

Elena gave him a small smile. A warmth spread from their joined hands, heating the rest of her body.

Seems like he missed you, Agon whispered in her mind. That teasing note still present in his words. It didn't bother her, though.

Elena was glowing from the idea that he'd been as worried about her as she'd been about him.

You're literally glowing. You might wanna let go of your prince before you electrocute him. If a weasel could smirk, Elena was certain Agon's face would be lit up with an implicitly superior grin.

Elena ignored his snark and tried to pull her hand back from Niko. She didn't want to hurt him, but the second she moved to take her hand away, the Prince tightened his grip. His expression didn't change, and Elena wondered if he even noticed what he'd done. Regardless, Elena shifted her focus from his eyes to her power, trying to reel it back in before it could cause any harm.

Without warning, Elena's stomach let loose the loudest—and most mortifying—grumble she'd ever heard. Heat instantly flushed her face, and Elena knew there would be no hiding the red that flooded her cheeks.

"Hungry, Firefly?" Niko asked with a grin.

"Well, it's been a little while since I last ate." Elena tried to sound cool and collected, but she wasn't quite sure it came out that way, as her stomach grumbled a second time.

"We can fix that." Niko released her hand and jumped from the bed. He strode to the door, opened it a crack, and spoke to someone on the other side. Most likely one of her mother's guards. They were always stationed outside occupied royal suites. It was as much for the guest's convenience and comfort as it was for the security of the school. Madame LaBelle couldn't let the royals roam around the school unsupervised. It would simply be out of the question.

Niko closed the door gently and returned to her bedside, stretching out beside her and propping his head up on his hand. Casually. Like lying in bed with her was the most natural thing in the world.

Oh, he's gonna be in so much trouble, Agon scoffed with a weaselly chuckle.

Elena didn't quite understand his meaning until Quinn and Roska burst through the door.

"We heard she was—"

"Elena! Are you—"

They both spoke at the same time as her brothers rushed into the suite, only to freeze and choke on their words.

"Hello, boys. Your sister and I were just reminiscing about our wonderful time together. Recalling all the fun we had on my ship while we were off to rescue you lot." Niko grinned arrogantly, reaching over to take her hand in his again.

Quinn's glare could have set the room on fire, if not for the balance of ice pouring from Roska's hands. Lyra bared her sharp teeth, a growl rumbling in her chest.

"Stop that, you ass!" Elena snapped, jerking her hand back from Niko and forcing herself into a more upright position. "He's joking. Badly." Elena searched Q and Roska's faces, trying to pull their attention back to her. Gods, she'd missed them so much.

"Oh, we know," Roska said calmly, flinging a few harmless snowflakes at the Prince's head.

"Doesn't mean we have to laugh." Q shot a blast of heat at Niko, instantly melting Roska's snowflakes and leaving the Prince's face dripping.

As her brothers strode across the room, Roska picked up a cloth napkin from the small dining table and tossed it to Niko, who caught it easily. The Prince chuckled as he dried his face and removed himself from the bed. Quinn immediately claimed the space. Roska joined them both on the bed as well.

Elena's eyes quickly flitted from Q's forest green eyes to Roska's icy blue gaze. They both held strong expressions of love, concern, and apprehensive excitement as they watched her.

"You're really back." Quinn's voice was a reverent whisper.

"I thought we'd never see you again," Roska mumbled, emotion clogging his words.

"Wait, what?" Quinn snapped at Roska. "You said we had a decent chance!"

Roska looked away sheepishly, his cheeks turning a brilliant shade of pink as he tried to avoid their stares. "Well, yes, I did say that..."

"He lied," Demoni stated plainly.

"Come again?" Niko asked, inserting himself back into the conversation as he leaned against the bedpost at the foot of the bed.

"All right, fine," Roska sighed. "I *lied*, ok? I had no idea if the rituals would really work. I was hopeful, but there was no guarantee." He grabbed Elena's hand and squeezed tightly. "I prayed to the Mother every single night, asking her for guidance and assistance." He looked at Quinn, eyes suddenly fierce, as though he was daring Q to argue with him. "Would you have rather I'd been honest? That it was far more likely we'd never lay eyes on her again?"

It was Quinn's turn to look sheepish now. "No, of course not."

"So I lied. It was the best option. I didn't see the point in adding to your stress," Roska continued. "For the last few moons, you've been one crisis away from total combustion. I was just trying to give you hope." His voice trailed off as he spoke.

Elena tightened her grip on Roska's hand and reached her other out to grab hold of Quinn. They'd been through their own kind of hells while she'd been gone. But she was back now, and she would never leave them again.

25

ROSKA

W HEN HE'D SEEN ELENA come through the portal he'd help create, Roska had feared that it was too good to be true. Then she'd instantly collapsed, and he knew it had been. No one could survive moons in The Nothing and come out unfazed. Elena was impressive, but she was still human.

Once she'd been settled in Niko's suite, Roska and Quinn had taken shifts, making sure one of them was with her at all times. After the third day, the Prince showed his royal breeding—also known as his superiority complex, according to Q—and kicked them out. Niko argued that none of them were getting any decent sleep and hovering over Elena wouldn't make her wake any sooner.

He was right, of course, but after losing her so suddenly, *twice*, it was hard for Roska to leave her. Niko agreed to stay with her, so she wouldn't be alone.

Roska couldn't help but feel a little miffed that Elena had woken during the Prince's shift, rather than his or even Q's. Rationally, of course, she hadn't had any control over when she'd regained consciousness, but Roska couldn't help but feel a bit jealous that the Prince had been with her first.

As promised, Niko had notified the guards, and they'd sent up a magical flare that had brought Roska and Quinn running from their suite farther down the hall in the Royal Wing of Harbor Ridge.

Mother strode in just as Elena was tucking into the massive lunch the kitchen staff had brought up. Roska rose from the bed and pulled a seat from the small breakfast nook over to the bedside for her. Quinn gave him a disapproving frown, but Roska just shrugged. She might not have been a good—or even decent—mother to them, but she was still their mother, and he couldn't ignore that fact.

"Thank you, Roska," Mother said quietly as she perched on the edge of the seat.

Roska had never seen her like this before. Her fingers were intertwined so tightly that her knuckles were white, and her spine seemed to be strapped to an invisible board. If he didn't know any better, Roska might have suspected their mother was actually nervous to see Elena. But that couldn't be right, could it?

"Hello, Mother." Elena's voice was cool, distant. She barely looked up from the plate of biscuits and honey Niko had placed on a tray across her lap. Roska studied her face, trying to read his sister's expression, but she seemed to be wearing a mask that hid all emotions. Their mother often wore a similar shielded expression. Roska started to wonder if that was a skill they taught at Harbor Ridge. How to Hide Your Emotions. Facial Masking 101.

"How are you feeling, Elena?" Their mother casually picked nonexistent lint from the skirt of her black dress.

"I'm well, thank you, Mother." Elena didn't make eye contact with Beatrice when she answered. Instead, she picked up a small piece of bread and dipped it in the lavender honey.

"Oh, for mux sake." Quinn's exasperation shattered the mock serenity in the room. "You two can't possibly think this shytty small talk is going to be even remotely productive."

Elena nearly choked on her tiny piece of bread, and Roska struggled to hide the chuckle that bubbled up the back of his throat.

"Excuse me?" Mother's single raised eyebrow was probably meant to convey annoyance and—in any other situation—correct rude behavior, but Q had been immune to her facial expressions since they'd first arrived here so many moons ago.

"You with the 'How are you feeling?' dumbass question," Quinn mocked with a very bad impression of their mother's posh tone. "And you," he turned to Elena, raising a single eyebrow of his own. "You're well, are you?" His mocking laugh echoed in the large room. "You haven't been *well* in moons. Possibly ever. Between being raised in this sheltered enchantress factory, then living with me at Amelia's, getting attacked, unleashing the *turmio*, going on the run from her," he jutted his chin indicating their mother, who leaned back in her chair, crossing her arms over her chest and narrowing her eyes at Quinn. "*Then*, after escaping this place, you got kidnapped by his mother's muxing soldiers." Q turned his annoyed glare on the Prince, who had been casually lounging on the chaise trying to look as though he wasn't eavesdropping. The Prince looked as though he was about to argue when Quinn pinned him with a more pointed glare. "Don't. Yes, you set her free, but it doesn't undo the fact that she was *kidnapped*."

Quinn took a seat back on the bed next to Elena, took her face in his hands, and forced her to focus on him. "You are *not* well. You're barely upright, and based on how much food you requested from the kitchens, your dainty ass bullshyt eating is just posturing to try and convince her otherwise." Roska watched as Elena seemed to melt a bit at their brother's words. "Stop trying to be brave for everyone." His words were a comforting whisper as his eyes began to glow. "We are all here to take care of you. Even her. Let us."

His words finally broke her. Tears quickly overflowed her lashes, streaming down her cheeks as sobs racked her body. Roska climbed into the bed beside her, pulling her into a tight embrace while Q shifted his grip from her face to her hands. Roska rubbed his hand gently up and down her spine, pouring a hint of his power into his hand to help cool her off as her body overheated with emotion. The fire quickly faded from Q's eyes as tears fell from Elena's.

Roska glanced over his shoulder to see their mother staring at the three of them. She looked confused, as though she didn't understand where she belonged with her children. It was an understandable predicament, but Roska couldn't waste time trying to convince her that she was still important to them. Yes, they had a lot of justifiable resentment toward her, but right now, Elena needed her family. He released Elena with one hand and reached out to Mother, offering her a chance to be a part of this moment. An olive branch in a moment filled with strangled emotions and shattered hearts.

He was equally surprised and grateful when he felt her hand in his. Roska pulled her onto the bed with them, wrapping her arm around Elena, making room for their mother in the emotionally charged bed.

She wasn't a perfect mother, but in this moment, she was exactly who they needed her to be. That was all they could ask.

"Since when do you use words like 'posturing'?" Elena asked.

Once the tears had slowed, and her breathing had returned to normal—minus the occasional hiccup—the boys and their mother had moved off the bed, giving Elena space to eat. Lyra, Demoni, and Agon lay curled together at the foot of the bed—tails and noses overlapping in an interwoven mess of fur and scales.

"Since I started living at a school full of smart-ass enchantresses," Q teased. He picked a grape off her plate and tossed it confidently into his mouth.

Elena tossed a second grape at him, presumably hoping to catch him off guard, but Quinn caught it with practiced ease.

Roska rolled his eyes at Q's antics. It had been so long since the three of them had been together, and it seemed like they'd never really had a chance to relax. The *turmio* had always been looming in the background, weighing heavily on their minds.

Now that the threat of imminent death was vanquished, they were able to breathe easier and play like siblings normally would.

At least, how Roska assumed siblings played. He'd never actually met any siblings prior to encountering his own. If there had been any biological brothers within the Brotherhood, they hadn't been forthcoming about it.

"Yes, your brother has become a bit of a scholar since they arrived here." Mother offered Quinn a hopeful smile. He didn't shut her down like he might have a few weeks ago, but he didn't return her smile either.

Progress is still progress, Roska thought to himself.

"Oh! And I hear you've been training the fire starters? I need to know how that got started and how it's going." Elena seemed giddy at the idea of Q as an instructor.

"You called the guards as soon as she woke, huh?" Quinn speared Niko with a look of fake annoyance.

Niko shrugged unapologetically. "I might have given myself a few minutes with her before I notified the cavalry."

"So, tell me! I wanna hear all about how *you* of all people became an instructor. I thought you hated this school and everything it represented." Elena flushed at her words, catching herself just a bit too late. "I'm sorry, Mother. I didn't mean it like that."

"No, no. You're right. He hated it, and he had every right to." Mother shifted in her seat, not uncomfortably, but clearly not quite confident in her role as their parent. "He was very reluctant to come here, and he wasn't shy about voicing his opinions of this school, its inhabitants, and its leadership."

"I'm still not *thrilled* to be here, but teaching those girls to burn it to the ground has been fun." Quinn grinned shamelessly.

Elena laughed. "Yeah, I can picture you having a great time with that."

"I've been working with a handful of girls, and I think they're getting pretty good." To everyone's surprise, Quinn looked questioningly at their mother. Seeking out her approval? Her praise? Whatever he was looking for, he'd found it in the pride that shone in her eyes.

"I can't wait to sit in on a class." Elena hadn't missed the look that passed between their mother and their brother.

"Once you're up and walking around again, I'll escort you," Roska offered.

"I would love that." Elena beamed at him. "I also heard that you were instrumental in bringing me back."

Heat flushed Roska's face and neck. He was about to downplay his involvement when their mother spoke up.

"He truly was. Roska is immensely skilled in crafting and casting intense rituals. I'd like to get him into some of our more advanced classes, but he keeps refusing me." Mother looked up at him, pride gleaming in her eyes yet again. "Maybe now that Elena is home, you'll reconsider?"

Roska didn't think his skin could get any hotter. Under the venerated gaze of his mother, and then his sister, Roska thought he might actually catch fire. He didn't know what to say. He wasn't even sure his voice would work, the tightness of emotion that clogged his throat made him doubt it. Instead, he merely shrugged and studied his shoes.

26

BELLADONNA

"I SHOULD BE IN there too," Aiden grumbled. He slouched like a petulant child in an armchair, staring out the window of Beatrice's sitting room.

"You most certainly should not be," Belladonna chided. "You will make the whole thing about you when Bea needs to be learning to bond and connect with her children."

"They're my children too, you know," he muttered.

"Yes, I know that, but you have an annoying habit of shifting every conversation and situation to be about you. None of them need that right now." Belladonna toyed with the flowers blooming in her lush green locks. "Besides, Bea really muxed things up the last time the four of them were together. She needs time alone with them to build trust."

"But Niko gets to be there." Aiden seemed to have reverted back to a literal child. He'd done nothing but sigh dramatically and whine since Elena had woken up. Beatrice had been summoned immediately. It had been Belladonna's idea to keep the demi-god from the room for the time being. Bea wouldn't admit it, but she was desperately hoping to have some quiet time alone with her children.

If Bea wouldn't ask for it herself, then it was Belladonna's job to ensure that she got what she needed.

"Gods, you're annoying. Yes, Niko is there because it's *his* suite and—as you have told us time and again—he's in love with Elena. We couldn't really kick him out. Not to mention, if you'd seen the look on his face, you would have known: only an army would be able to take him from her side right now." Belladonna wasn't sure how she felt about the Prince, but she knew he could be trusted with Elena's safety. The look of pure violence she'd seen on his face when they'd initially suggested moving Elena to her brothers' suite... no one was getting near that girl without his expressed approval.

She admired Niko's commitment to Elena. He'd been in that room with her ever since he'd caught her and carried her to his bed. To his credit, he'd never once tried to sleep in the bed with her. And Belladonna had been checking. She and Castor both had been making irregular and uninvited visits to the Prince's suite at odd hours of the night since Elena's return. One false move and they would have relocated Elena, by force if necessary. But every single night, Niko was either passed out on the chaise, reading aloud to Elena from a chair at her bedside, or sleeping in a clearly uncomfortable position in that chair with a book flopped carelessly on the floor.

Belladonna thought he was quite sweet. Bea and Quinn weren't as convinced. Roska seemed to keep all of his opinions to himself. He was proving to be the quietest of the siblings.

"At some point, you will permit me to see my daughter, won't you, witch?" Aiden's voice held a threatening tone, but Belladonna wasn't worried. Demi-god or not, he wasn't stupid enough to challenge her. They were nearly equal in age, and *she* hadn't lost cycles of her life to a madness brought on by arrogance and muxing with the Fae.

"When Beatrice is back, you can go. But I think it's best that you both see the children separately for a while. You two are highly volatile, and Elena doesn't need the stress of another fight between you. We can't rely on Roska to constantly put out the fires you two seem to start every time you have a conversation." Belladonna looked pointedly at the charred stone and singed rug by the door. The last time Bea and Aiden had attempted to have a conversation, one of them had made some barbed comment at the other, and tempers had flared. Luckily Roska had been waiting in the hall for his father, and he was able to quell the fire before any serious damage was caused.

"It's not my fault she's a fiery lass." Aiden shrugged casually. "I bring out the passionate side of her, that's all." His rueful grin pushed Belladonna to near-murderous intent.

Bea wouldn't fault you for it. Hells, she'd probably approve. Castor's snark was a welcome relief. He flew in through the open window and seamlessly shifted into his human form. "Keep talking like that, old man, and she'll kill you before you ever get to see Elena."

Aiden gripped his chest in mock horror. "She would *never*."

"Oh, she definitely would. At this point, it's only a question of how and when." Castor flopped casually on the couch, putting his feet up on the low table.

"I wouldn't even feel bad about it, honestly." Belladonna walked across the room, knocked Castor's booted feet off the table, and took a seat in a chair across from him. "What have you learned?"

"About the soldiers? Same old shyt. They aren't attacking, but they aren't moving on either. It seems like they're still waiting for something. Aiden's shield has kept them from gathering any intelligence on our fortifications or movements." Castor flicked his sharp eyes to Aiden. "Aleerah is still walking the perimeter on the mountainside, but she hadn't seen, heard, or smelled anything indicating a second invasion attempt when I spoke with her on my sweep."

"Aye, she told me as much." Aiden tapped his temple. "Looks like we've scared them off, for now."

"Hopefully, it will last long enough for Prince Niko to negotiate with the generals in the field and convince them to go home."

Belladonna was cautiously optimistic. The Prince was the next in line for the throne, which meant his orders carried nearly as much weight as the King himself.

In the magept world, men ran things. Even if they were utter fools, men made the rules and women were meant to fall in line. No one had heard from the King in a few weeks. The Queen had taken advantage of her husband's absence and sent the soldiers on a mission of pointless violence to cater to her own bigotry. Niko had said it wasn't uncommon for his father to drop off without word for weeks at a time, but Belladonna couldn't help but think that the timing was suspicious. As soon as the Queen makes her move on Harbor Ridge and the magical community as a whole, the King goes missing?

Something was off. Belladonna prayed to the Mother that Niko would be able to quell this war before things got out of hand.

27

QUINN

QUINN STRODE PURPOSEFULLY ACROSS the courtyard to his class. *His* class. He still couldn't understand why anyone would defer to him on anything, but these kids really looked up to him. Today, he'd planned to teach them how to start a controlled brush fire. He'd asked the guards to create a makeshift grassland in the middle of the courtyard with all the dry brush they could find. Q knew that this particular technique would be really helpful if they had to fight the soldiers out in the open.

Despite Belladonna's insistence that it would take him moons to gain proper control of his powers, Q had managed to surpass all expectations of his skill in a matter of weeks. After he'd excelled at all the things the instructors at Harbor Ridge could teach, he'd taken to disappearing into the snow-covered fields and practicing on his own. Quinn had been going stir-crazy sitting around, waiting for the right moon in the right season. He'd been relieved when their mother had suggested the barren fields as his training ground. Eventually, the fields would be filled with new crops, but for the duration of the frost season, it had been his to burn as he liked. And he did. He melted the ice, scarring the earth and creating massive designs in the charred soil.

When it had been clear to the Headmistress that Quinn's skill with the flame was leaps and bounds beyond that of her fire starter instructors, she'd asked him—through Belladonna and Roska—if he'd be willing to teach. Q had been put off by the idea at first. He couldn't imagine *anyone* would want to put him in charge of the safety and well-being of children. Lyra had pointed out that he'd already taken it upon himself to care for kids once before, when he'd rescued them all from the foster house. She'd also made it clear that no one was asking him to *raise* the little enchantresses. Just teach them to burn stuff. And he was quite adept at burning stuff.

It had been awkward at first, but now it was the best part of his day. Watching these girls grow into their power, seeing them push their limits and become even stronger than they'd ever imagined—it was the best feeling in the world. He totally understood why some of the enchantresses chose to stay and teach rather than leave the school and venture out into the world.

"Professor Quinn!" A young girl came rushing up to him with a huge smile on her face.

"Minka, please, I've told you. Just call me Q." He hated being an authority figure. "Professor" carried way too much weight and responsibility. A professor should be older, maybe with some white hair and endless stories that served as valuable life lessons. Quinn was just a kid. According to Elena, they were nearly seventeen cycles old. He sure as shyt wasn't old enough to be a *professor*.

"I'm sorry, Professor Quinn. I'll try, but guess what I did!" Minka was one of Q's oldest students, around twelve, and by the looks of things, she'd been playing with fire outside of class.

Quinn knelt down in front of her, gently placing his hands on her shoulders and twisting her slightly to the right to see her face better in the sunlight. "What happened to your eyebrows and eyelashes, Minka?" He tried to remain calm, but he struggled to contain the laugh that was bubbling up his throat.

"Oh, that? Don't worry. They'll grow back," Minka said with a casual shrug. "They always do."

Always...?

"Professor, I shot a fireball and hit the bullseye at *thirty paces*!!" The young enchantress's face beamed with pride.

"Whoa. Seriously? That's amazing! Nice job." Quinn clapped her on the back and offered her a flaming-five. It was a gesture the class had accidentally started when one of the other girls had gone in for a traditional high-five, lost control of her fire for a moment, and hit her hand against Q's while it was on fire. Being FlameBorn, Quinn was essentially immune to fire. The class had been in shock at first but they quickly got over it and spent an uncomfortable amount of time throwing fire at him to see if he would burn. That was one of his earlier lessons. Ever since then, flaming-fives were the girls' favorite way to celebrate an accomplishment. Quinn really loved it too.

Minka's hand caught fire just as she made contact with Quinn's, an expression of pure joy on her face.

"Thirty paces is a huge accomplishment, kid. I hope you weren't practicing without an instructor, though. We can only control the fire so much. It still has a mind of its own."

"Yes, Professor. I was with a couple of the other firestarter instructors, and one of the tidal enchantresses was nearby, working on something with the well. I was being very safe, Professor. I promise. Not like last time." Minka's mischievous grin proved to Quinn that she still didn't actually feel bad about nearly grazing another student with a fireball a few weeks ago. Quinn suspected that the student—a bratty glamorist who seemed to think she was better than everyone else simply because she'd proven to be more adept at glamors—had been harassing Minka for weeks, and Minka's fireball had hit exactly where she'd intended. About a handbreadth from the brat's leg, singeing the fabric of her school robes.

Internally, Quinn had been really proud of Minka's control and aim, but publicly—as his mother had repeatedly told him—he had to maintain "an air of authority" and not laugh when one of his students scared the shyt out of a bully. Personally, Quinn was confident that the bratty little bully got *exactly* what she deserved.

Q had no tolerance for bullies. Regardless of their age, gender, or magical aptitude.

"No class today." The gruff announcement came from a guard who stalked purposefully into the courtyard. "The Headmistress needs you, Professor."

"What? She's canceling my class? She can't do that." Quinn stood quickly, keeping his hands on Minka's shoulders. His voice held a tight edge. He was pissed at the intrusion, but he didn't want to take it out on the messenger. It wasn't her fault she worked for a controlling bitch.

Lyra came bounding into the courtyard. *Something's wrong.*

What? Is Elena ok? Roska?

Yes, they're fine, but the soldiers are moving. Quickly. We need to meet Beatrice at the wall. Lyra didn't stop running. She looped around his legs and shot straight back out the way she'd come, expecting him to follow.

Quinn glanced quickly from the guard to Minka. He knelt back down in front of the girl and said, "I'm sorry, Minka. Can you let the rest of the class know we'll have to cancel class today?" The enchantress's eyes fell, clearly disappointed. "Don't worry, kiddo. I'll make it up to you all in our next lesson. I promise."

Minka smiled at his words and gave him a quick nod. He squeezed her shoulders gently, then rose and raced after Lyra.

Whatever was happening at the Wall, it wasn't going to be good.

28

BEATRICE

BEATRICE STOOD AT THE top of the tallest tower in the center
of the Wall, looking out at the mass of soldiers spreading out
and attempting to encircle their defenses. They violently hacked
their way through Bella's thorny barricade. Beatrice's beloved witch
felt every single slash of those careless swords, leaving Belladonna in
agony on their bed. Beatrice had rushed out to the Wall the second
they'd realized what was causing Bella so much pain.

The soldiers were making progress. It was slow going, but they
would reach their massive stone Wall by sunset. Beatrice couldn't
imagine that they would try to breach the Wall without the benefit
of light, but she hadn't expected them to spend hours hacking away
at Bella's plants either. The soldiers were highly motivated today.
They'd spent weeks in the Dark Woods. Why did they suddenly
decide that today was the day to attack?

"What's going on?" Quinn burst into the tower room, out of
breath with a look of panic on his face. Lyra bound across the room
and placed her front paws on the window ledge, trying to see outside.

Zied nudged a chair over to the window, and Lyra hopped quickly into the seat.

"Looks like they got tired of waiting," the firefox observed.

"Seems like it." Zied nodded.

"They started attacking Belladonna's thorns in earnest at first light." Beatrice flinched at the memory. She had awoken to Belladonna's cries before the sun had fully risen. Seeing her love in such unimaginable pain and being helpless to stop it had been devastating.

"Why now?" Quinn wondered aloud.

"I'm honestly not sure." Which was the most unsettling part of it all. Beatrice had no idea what had triggered the soldiers to attack now, after weeks of nothing.

"Have you tried asking?" Lyra looked at Zied, then Beatrice.

"Asking who what?" Zied replied, confused by her odd question.

"Asking the soldiers why they're attacking now? What changed? What do they want? They must know that the *turmio* failed. They aren't stupid. Attacking a compound filled with fully empowered enchantresses is a suicide mission." Lyra always seemed to make the most obvious points in times when everyone else was completely befuddled.

"We haven't asked," Beatrice answered flatly. "How would you suggest starting up a conversation with our would-be murderers?"

"How about 'hey, what are you doing?'"

Beatrice was certain there was a glint of humor in the fox's stare, but her prim posture betrayed nothing.

For several moments, Beatrice and Lyra locked eyes. A staring contest. A battle of wills. Who would be the most stubborn female in the tower? But then the memory of Belladonna's pain washed over her again, and Beatrice blinked.

Without a word, she left the room, following the spiral staircases down several levels until she was only two floors from the ground. She went to one of the archer's windows facing the Woods, spelled her voice to ensure she'd be heard over the ruckus the soldiers were making, and called out, "Hey! What are you doing?"

She hadn't really expected much of an answer, but anything would be better than nothing. A handful of soldiers in her immediate vicinity froze. They seemed just as confused by her query as she had been when Lyra suggested it. Then one of them step forward, boldly raised his sword in the direction of the tower—clearly, he wasn't sure where her voice had come from—and shouted back, "We are here to save the King!"

His words were followed by several cheers of agreement and renewed vicious hacking and slashing of the thorny wall.

Did he say they want to save the King? Save him from what? He isn't even here. Zied's confusion mingled seamlessly with her own.

Do you think they meant the Prince? They couldn't have confused the King for Niko, could they? An entire army couldn't be *that* dense... right?

"There's no King here." Her spelled voice echoed throughout the tower and out into the woods.

Cries of rage and accusations of lies were hurled back at her, as well as a few arrows. The latter bounced harmlessly off the stone wall. The former added to her growing confusion.

Releasing the spell from her voice, Beatrice turned to the guard. "Fetch the Prince," she commanded. Her voice was temporarily reduced to a harsh whisper, but thankfully the guard heard her just fine. The enchantress turned on her heel and ran from the tower.

Maybe if the Prince could explain to the soldiers that his father was in fact *not* here, they'd simply go home and she could avoid the whole bloody affair.

She'd never been one to back down from a fight before. However, now that Harbor Ridge was filled not only with her students and staff, but also her *children* and the love of her life, she would happily avoid any conflict.

She prayed to the Mother that the soldiers would listen to Niko as well as he thought they would. If not, they had some hard choices ahead.

29

ELENA

ELENA COULD HEAR SHOUTING from outside the bedroom window, but it was too far away to be coherent. Niko stood at the window, trying to see what all the fuss was about when a guard rushed into the suite.

"The Headmistress needs you at the Wall." The guard spoke quickly, but with surprising calm. If she'd truly just run here from the Wall, she should be out of breath.

Elena was forever impressed by the physical fitness of the guards. They were *never* winded. She, on the other hand, got winded walking from the bed to the couch by the fire. The healers had speculated that her physical weakness was a result of having spent moons in The Nothing, and her body would regain its strength eventually. Until then, Elena had been limited to Niko's suite. She wasn't allowed to leave the rooms without an escort, along with her regular guards.

She'd been surprised at first when she'd been relegated to Niko's rooms. It seemed unlikely that her brothers were truly comfortable with this arrangement. She'd asked Roska about it once, but he'd quickly changed the subject and steadfastly refused to answer her questions.

It wasn't until she overheard two of the guards discussing the Prince that she learned the truth of the situation.

"I heard," the younger guard had whispered conspiratorially to the other, "that the Prince threatened violence if anyone tried to move her."

"Where did you hear that nonsense?" the older guard had scoffed.

"I heard it from the healers who were there when he pulled a dagger on the Headmistress. They said he threatened to slit her throat if she tried to move Elena to another suite." The younger enchantress spoke louder, clearly incensed that the other guard would doubt her sources.

Elena had tried to imagine it taking place. Niko hovering over her like some sort of feral animal, dagger pointed angrily at her mother. She wondered where her brothers had been in that situation, but then she'd realized that it didn't really matter. Whatever Niko had said or done, he'd gotten his way. Elena had been living in his bed for nearly two weeks now. Granted, she'd been unconscious for the first week.

The guard coughed subtly in the doorway to their suite.

"Yes, sorry. Of course. Niko, can you help me up?" Elena shifted herself to the edge of the bed and reached a hand out to Niko when the guard spoke again.

"Apologies, Miss Elena. The Headmistress only requires the Prince at the moment."

Elena gaped at the guard. That couldn't be right. Why would her mother need the Prince at the Wall?

"Well, that's unfortunate," Elena replied sharply. She didn't want to be rude, but she refused to be excluded any longer. "I will be joining the Prince regardless."

It took much longer for the pair of them to reach the tower where her mother was waiting than if Niko had gone alone, but Elena refused to be left out of whatever hells was breaking loose at the Wall.

Elena moved slowly. Painfully slowly, on painfully weak legs. Her muscles felt like they hadn't been used in ages. At one point, Niko had picked her up—despite her vehement protests—and carried her through the empty halls and stairs that led outdoors. Once they were around others, he placed her back on the ground and allowed her to walk. She'd railed against him—in angry whispers, of course; she wouldn't cause a scene—and his chauvinistic behavior, but the second they were out of sight of others, he'd picked her right back up and carried her the rest of the way to the tower where her mother was waiting.

"Put me down," Elena snapped, punching Niko repeatedly in the chest.

Much to her annoyance, he just laughed. "Don't worry, Firefly, I'll put you down when I have a chair for you. Until then, could you hit a little to the left? I have an itch that's been bugging me for the last few minutes."

"Mux you. Jerk." She did shift her aim—as he so arrogantly requested—but instead of punching him, she sent a small bolt of lightning through his shirt, causing him to exhale sharply in pain and singe the fabric of his tunic.

"Chair, please," he grunted to the guard standing watch inside the room. The guard stepped quickly out of the room and returned in moments with a sturdy wooden chair. She placed the chair beside the Headmistress in the middle of the room and went back to her post. Niko dumped Elena unceremoniously on the chair and turned to her mother. "You requested my presence?"

"I did." Mother eyed him curiously. "But I'd intended for you to come alone."

"Aye, we got that message. Unfortunately, *someone*," he tossed a not-too-subtle look over his shoulder at Elena, "didn't want to be left out."

Elena huffed. She'd missed so much in the last few moons; she didn't think it was unreasonable to not want to miss anything else.

The door to the tower room opened, and Lyra vaulted into the room, Q quick on her heels. "You need to see what's happening." He addressed their mother, then seemed to notice he'd walked in on something. "Hey, El! Nice to see you out of bed and *his* fancy ass rooms. What are you doing here?"

Niko cut in before Elena had a chance to respond. "I was summoned, and she wanted to come along, so I carried her here."

Elena rolled her eyes so hard she gave herself a mild headache. "That's not exactly how it happened," she began, but Agon—who had been quietly warming her neck the whole time, took this opportunity to add his own commentary.

"Actually, that sums it up pretty succinctly."

Betrayer! Elena snapped at him, clenching her jaw at his inaccurate summation of events.

What part of what he said was untrue? Agon countered.

Well, none of it, technically, *but there's more to it than that!* Elena glared at Niko as she continued to bicker with Agon.

Maybe, but we don't have time to argue semantics right now. Listen.

Outside the window, there was a cacophony of noise. Grunting, shouting, the sound of metal on stone.

Metal on stone?

"The soldiers are through Belladonna's angry garden wall." Quinn pointed out the window for Mother and Niko to go see for themselves.

"What's going on?" Elena asked Q quietly.

He knelt down beside her, placing a hand on the back of her chair and studying her face intently.

"Q, I'm fine." Elena reached up and put her hand on his shoulder. "I promise. My muscles just aren't as strong as they used to be. Yet. Please, tell me what's happening out there."

Q studied her eyes for a second longer before nodding. "The soldiers think we have the King. They've chopped and hacked their way through Belladonna's thorn wall and are now trying to scale the Wall."

"I'm sorry. What?" Niko turned from the window and gave Quinn a speculative look. "They think my father is here? Why the hells would they think that? And if they believed that this whole time, why are they only now trying to rescue him?"

"Those are very good questions, and exactly why I summoned you." Mother's voice was rough, almost raw. Something else had happened—or was happening—that seemed to be causing her great pain.

"Mother, are you—" Elena began, but her mother quickly shut her down.

"I'm fine, Elena. I just need those damned fools to stop chopping up Bella's plants." Her mother's voice was decidedly *not* fine, but Elena opted not to push. She knew that Belladonna's nature magic physically bound her to a place. Elena wondered how the soldiers cutting up the plants might have affected the witch. She couldn't imagine it felt good to have her magic physically chopped and damaged.

"It doesn't make any sense." Niko continued. He was either oblivious to the tension between Elena and her mother, or he was simply ignoring it to focus on the bigger problem. "If they truly thought he was being held captive here, they should have attacked instantly, not spent weeks camped out in your woods."

"Can you stop them?" Elena asked. The Prince was next in line for the throne and the only Royal authority they had at their disposal at the moment. Not to mention, the patriarchal bullshyt that ruled over the magept of Waverly meant that Niko was the only one who could step in and give orders to the soldiers. They would have to follow his orders over his mother's. It was what their sexist laws required. However, Elena didn't know if Niko's authority would rank above the Queen's if she were, in fact, speaking for the King.

"I can try, but I doubt they'll be able to hear me over all that noise."

"I can help with that," Mother offered. "I will warn you though, the longer this spell is in effect, the longer you'll lose your voice once we remove the spell."

"Fantastic," Quinn cheered mockingly. "We'll finally get some use out of you *and then* you'll have to shut up for a while. I can't wait." His grin was so pure that Elena could almost forget the horde of violent men waiting on the other side of the stone wall.

"Must be your lucky day." Niko laughed dryly. "Well, let's get on with it."

Mother twisted her fingers into odd angles, chanting some foreign words under her breath, and gently touched the tips of her middle fingers to Niko's throat. He coughed several times, then spoke in a painfully loud voice.

"Did it work?" His eyes grew wide and his hand raced to grip his throat as his spelled voice reverberated off the stone walls at a painfully loud volume. "I guess so."

"Get on with it then." Mother practically pushed Niko to the window and shot a spark of bright light upwards, drawing the attention of every soldier in the vicinity.

"This is your Prince speaking. Put down your weapons at once." Niko's firm tone as he addressed his military sent unexpected tingles throughout Elena's body.

Seriously? Now?

What are you talking about? Elena's face heated with embarrassment.

We're under attack, and you're getting excited by his bossy voice? Agon flexed his tiny claws on her shoulders.

Shut up. Elena was certain her face was actually on fire now.

"How do we know it's really you?" came a hostile shout from below.

"Because, Jamieson, I was at your knighting ceremony, and I recall exactly how many women shot you down that night." Niko winked at Elena, and a soft chorus of laughter drifted through the archer's windows.

"Stand down, men!" The order was shouted once and echoed by different voices until all the banging, slashing, and scraping stopped.

"Why are you attacking?" Niko demanded once it was clear the order had been accepted and followed.

"The King has been taken," Jamieson answered. "We received intel this morning that he was being held by the Headmistress."

"Well, I'm sorry to tell you, your intel is wrong. I've been here for several moons—being treated with the utmost kindness and respect—and I haven't seen any signs of my father. You can ask the Headmistress yourself, if you'd like." Niko waved Mother over and she joined him at the window.

"With all due respect, Your Highness," this voice was considerably older and didn't seem all that respectful, "we aren't going to take that witch at her word."

"Commander Stanley." Niko clenched his fists as he addressed the man. "Firstly, Madame LaBelle is not a witch. She is an incredibly powerful enchantress and a dear friend of my family. You will treat her with the respect she is due. Secondly, I am removing you from this command."

This proclamation was met with gasps and shouts of disagreement.

Niko gave the men a moment, then raised his hand, demanding their silence. They quieted down immediately.

"Your bigotry has been boiling just below the surface for cycles, Stanley, and I will not stand for it. You are ordered to return to Riverayn immediately. Inform my mother that the King is elsewhere, and remind her that it is not her place to call for military action." Niko paused, flexing his hands and clearly waiting for any backlash from the former commander. When none came, he continued. "Jamieson, congratulations, you're the new Commander of this army. Men, you are ordered to clean up this mess, *gently and carefully*, as these are living things that you've been hacking away at. Then return to camp and await my orders. Jamieson, I want you—and *only* you—to join me within these walls to discuss next steps." Then he turned to Mother. "That is, if that's alright with you, Madame LaBelle."

Mother offered a curt nod and motioned for the guard to go out and retrieve Commander Jamieson. "We'll take him to my office. We can continue this conversation there."

"Excellent," Niko said. Unfortunately, his voice was still overly loud and sent a ringing in Elena's ears. "Shyt," he whispered. "Sorry, how do we undo this?"

Mother lifted her hands, crossed her index and middle fingers, touched both middle fingers to his throat, and uncrossed her fingers.

"Is that—" Niko coughed, rubbing his throat. His voice was barely a whisper, his vocal cords raw from such prolonged, extreme use.

"It will wear off in a few hours," Mother promised.

"Great. Now we have a Prince with no voice, an enchantress with no strength, and a brand new military commander coming to dinner." Sarcasm dripped from Lyra's words. "What could possibly go wrong?"

30
ROSKA

"**Y**OUR MOTHERS, SIBLINGS, AND the Prince are meeting some soldier in the Great Hall." Castor walked into the greenhouse where Roska was tending to his latest obsessions. After they'd brought Elena back, he'd been struggling to find his place in the school. He'd had a purpose when he was working with Aiden to figure out the rituals needed to return her to them. However, while she was back and unconscious, Roska had no idea what to do with himself. It had actually been Castor who'd suggested the greenhouse.

"Are you telling me this because you're a gossip or because I'm actually needed there?" Roska asked, not bothering to look up from the rosemary he was tending.

"No one sent me, if that's what you're asking. And I'm thoroughly offended that you think I'm a gossip." Castor sat on the bench beside Roska. "I'm not a gossip. I just like to know information and share it with people who might also be interested."

"That is the literal definition of a gossip," Demoni hissed from the spot of sun she'd been lounging in for hours.

Castor tutted, waving a dismissive hand at the frost dragon. "Agree to disagree, love. I'm sharing this information with *you* because it's relevant to your life."

"How so?" Roska trimmed a rather lengthy branch of rosemary and laid it in the small wicker basket on the table. This harvest was for the kitchens. In a few weeks, he would come through and trim the rosemary plants again, collecting for the potions classes. Normally, that would be too quick for the plant to recover, but in the magical greenhouse, if he didn't trim the rosemary plants at least twice a moon, they would get unruly and out of control.

"Well, aside from the fact that Niko *carried* your beloved sister across the school to address the soldiers, the Prince has demoted the commander who was attacking us this morning, promoted a new soldier, and invited that man to "have a conversation" in the Great Hall." Castor was always in the best mood when he had fresh news to share. He loved being the one to break new information.

It was exhausting.

"Seems like we missed a lot this morning, Demoni," Roska said casually. She flicked her tongue. Turning her head slightly, she flicked her tongue again, muttering some thought about rodents, and rested her head back on the sun-warmed table. Roska didn't want to let on that he was thrown by all this information. Quinn was the fiery hothead who was always quick to action, typically lashing out before thinking things through. Roska was inherently the opposite. The cool, calm, collected one. Outwardly, he knew it likely made him appear cold or indifferent, but he needed time to process things so he could make the best possible choice. Rushing in wasn't his style. It never had been.

"Understatement of the cycle," Castor exclaimed, dramatically throwing his hands in the air. "So let's get moving!"

Roska looked up from his plant, lowering the garden shears while simultaneously raising a single eyebrow. "Sorry, going where?"

"Gods, were you even listening?" Castor sighed powerfully. "To the Great Hall." He spoke slowly, and just a little too loudly, acting as though Roska might be hard of hearing.

"Why? It seems like they have it all handled." Roska wasn't entirely sure why he was avoiding being a part of this summit in the Great Hall, but he felt severely out of place in the school and preferred to keep to himself. Out of the way and out of sight.

"Roska, you are a part of this family," Castor gently took the shears from Roska's hand, turning to give Roska the full force of his black-as-night stare. "This muxed up collection of magical creatures who brought you into the world and came into it with you, are *your* people. You might not see it yet, but you belong with them. You belong in the rooms that are making all the big decisions."

He's not wrong, Demoni chimed in.

I have nothing of value to add to their conversation. I'm not a part of any royal family. I don't have ties to this school or the loyalty of anyone. I wouldn't be any help. Roska couldn't say those things aloud, but Demoni already knew his feelings. She knew the hells he'd been through and understood his desire to make himself as useful as possible without being in anyone's way.

"I understand that you don't feel like you belong here. Yet." Castor's eyes narrowed when he said "yet," emphasizing the word none too subtly. "But the best way to find your place among your family is to be surrounded by them. Not hiding out in here."

Roska looked away, trying to blink his tears away before the shifter could notice them. "Fine," he said in a rough voice. "I'll go, but I don't know what good it'll do."

"Splendid," Castor cheered, then he jumped into the air, seamlessly shifting into his moonbird form.

When Roska didn't immediately rise from the bench as well, Castor cawed grumpily. The large black bird swooped down, grabbed hold of Roska's collar, pulled him to his feet, and dragged him toward the door.

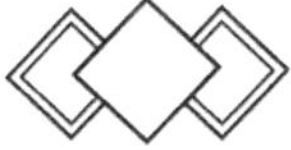

"What do you mean he's missing?" Niko's voice echoed through the empty Great Hall.

Roska slipped through the door, gently closing it behind him, and took quick, light steps across the room to join his siblings on the dais. Elena was carefully seated in the only chair with arms, Quinn directly to her right. Niko was pacing in front of the table on the dais, his hand nervously pushing his tight, black curls away from his face.

Roska took the seat on Elena's left, reached over to give her hand a gentle squeeze, and whispered, "What's going on?"

"What's going on?" Niko mimicked angrily. "Well apparently, my father's famed military has *lost him* and was attacking this school under the false belief that he was being held prisoner here."

Roska flinched at Niko's tone, but Elena held his hand. "Niko," she warned gently.

"Mux. I'm sorry. I didn't mean to snap at you, Roska." Niko raked his hand through his hair again.

Roska gave the Prince a quick nod, but chose not to speak again. He'd already screwed things up, and he'd just walked into the room. He shouldn't have come. He didn't belong here.

That's not true. Niko is on edge. It seems like they all are. Demoni gently pushed her cool, teal nose into his cheek, directing his gaze to their mother—who was gripping the edge of the table so tightly she would likely leave impressions of her fingers if she ever let go. Looking farther down the table, Belladonna seemed completely drained. Her normally glowing brown skin was as pale as ash and the flowers in her green locks had wilted to nothing. Roska wondered how she'd managed to walk into this room from their mother's suite in the far tower. She looked like she could barely sit upright.

"Apologies, Your Majesty." The soldier—the new commander—stared at his boots as he spoke. "I'm... uh, I'm not sure where the former commander got his intel." His gaze flicked nervously to Niko. Was he hiding something? If Niko suspected anything, he didn't react. The man continued. "I just know he came out this morning with a burr up his ass about breaking down the Wall and liberating the King." No sooner had the words left his mouth that the soldier blanched. "Apologies, again, my Prince. I forgot my place.

I shouldn't use such crass language in front of royalty or ladies. My mother would wash my mouth with soap if she heard me talk like that."

Quinn laughed darkly. "Of all the things to worry about, guarding your tongue shouldn't be one of them."

"When did he leave here?" Niko asked Mother.

"Moons ago. The *turmio* was still free when he departed. The frost season had only just begun." Mother seemed to be thinking back, trying to remember every detail of the King's last visit. "Actually," she continued, "he left on the same day as you three."

"You mean the day we escaped that tower you locked us up in?" Quinn pressed.

"Yes, Quinn," Mother answered dryly. "The very same day. Or the morning after."

"Wait, didn't we see some soldiers in the woods not long after that?" Elena attempted to lean forward and nearly fell over. Roska understood why she was sitting in the chair normally reserved for their mother. The arms of the chair kept her from falling entirely.

"You're right," Roska agreed, catching her arm and helping her back to a more upright position. "On the way to Aiden's with Castor."

"It was a decent size battalion," Lyra added. "We assumed they were preparing to attack the school, but it did seem odd that they had traveled so far north."

"Where was my father going when he left here?" Niko continued pacing, not directing his question at anyone in particular.

"I believe he was heading to Nexton. He mentioned meeting some traders there to negotiate tariffs." Mother slowly unclenched her hands from the edge of the table, massaging her palms as though she'd just realized how uncomfortable it was to have a prolonged death grip on the wood.

"Nexton. To the north of here." Niko froze in his steps. "She couldn't have. She *wouldn't* have." He turned quickly and knelt in front of Lyra, bringing himself eye-to-eye with the fox. "Do you recall exactly what the emblem on the soldiers' uniforms looked like? What *color* they were?"

It was an odd question, resulting in several raised eyebrows.

"It was the royal emblem," Lyra replied, a hint of confusion in her voice. "I don't see color though, so I couldn't tell you what color it was."

"Come here, little fox." Belladonna's voice sounded wrong. Dry, cracked, frail. Lyra hopped quickly down to the witch and jumped onto the table before her. "I would like to visit your memories, if that's all right. My magic ought to be able to filter color into your memories if I can view them through my own eyes." Lyra nodded and laid her head on Belladonna's open palm. The witch closed her eyes, and it seemed as though the sun faded from the sky. The light in the Great Hall dimmed, and the scent of pine, fir, and fresh snow wafted through the room. After a few moments, Belladonna slouched in her chair, resting her head awkwardly on the back of the wooden seat. Lyra lifted her head and gently licked the witch's palm. "The emblem was the same, but slightly off. Instead of the yellow sun and white rose, the sun was white and the rose was blood red."

"That's the emblem of the Queen's guard." The Commander looked to Niko, thoroughly confused and clearly failing to see the obvious truth.

"My mother," Niko seethed. "My godsdamned mother did this."

Roska looked from Niko to the Commander and back.

What the hells does that mean? Why would she kidnap her own husband?

31

BEATRICE

T HE QUEEN HAD KIDNAPPED the King. Beatrice couldn't stifle the cackle of laughter that bubbled over from within. Rosalina had truly lost her mind. Aside from her actions being wholly
treasonous and punishable by death, it was clear she'd gone insane if
she actually believed that *kidnapping* the King would win back his
favor.

Rosalina had always been a bit thick, but this was a whole new
level of depravity that Beatrice would never have expected from the
quiet, doting woman she'd met all those cycles ago.

"You can't really think your mother did this." Elena's shock at
the Queen's betrayal was sweet and surprising. After having been
kidnapped at the Queen's command, Beatrice would have expected
Elena to have a much lower opinion of Rosalina.

"You're joking, right?" Quinn said, rather harshly. "How can you
of all people be surprised by the crazy actions of the woman who had
you kidnapped just a few moons ago? Hells, the guards that took him
were probably the same ones that took you."

"Um, actually..." The new commander looked sheepishly at his
boots, shifting awkwardly on his feet.

"Actually what, Jamieson? Spit it out. "Niko snapped his fingers at the commander. "I'm really not in the mood."

"I'm sorry, Your Majesty." Jamieson stood at attention, although still quite tense. "Our battalion was sent to retrieve the young enchantress, at the Queen's command, although she claimed she was merely relaying the King's order."

"*Retrieve*? That's what you call attacking, drugging, and *kidnapping* me?" Elena's eyes glowed a brilliant—and terrifying—electric blue. Lightning danced under her skin and snaked from her fingers across the thick wooden table, leaving black scars in their wake. Jamieson had the decency to flinch and cower slightly at her rage.

Beatrice had never been so proud of Elena. She was clearly a force to be reckoned with, even in her weakened state.

"Elena," Roska warned quietly. He went to reach for her hand, but she jerked away from him.

"How *dare* you act like this was just a casual visit. Like I had *any* choice in the matter. You and your comrades kept me drugged for days, then locked me in a prison for *weeks*." Elena was on her feet now, unfazed by her diminished strength. Beatrice worried that Elena's rage was the only thing keeping her on her feet and she would likely pay for this outburst later. For now, though, she was the physical embodiment of lightning, and Beatrice beamed with pride.

Elena stiffly walked around the table, keeping her eyes trained on the young commander like a beast stalking its prey. Fists clenched tightly, her lightning emanated from her skin, small sparks flying off in all directions. Agon, who seemed equally enraged, chose to stay at the table, watching Elena as she prepared to unleash her fury on the guard.

In the back of her mind, Beatrice wondered if she should step in and stop Elena. Lashing out at this soldier wouldn't solve any of their problems. However, it would probably help Elena feel more in control of herself. She'd been taken, locked away, and lost in a demon dimension. And those were only the abuses that Beatrice knew about. Something else had happened to trigger Elena's powers all those moons ago. Needless to say, Elena had a lot pent up, and she needed a release. This soldier was as good a target as any.

You know Belladonna wouldn't agree with you. Zied's words interrupted Beatrice's backward attempt at justifying Elena's show of force.

I'm not saying she should kill *the man, just burn off some steam. And maybe part of his face. It would send a very clear message. No one would mux with her ever again.* Beatrice knew he was right though. Belladonna hated retaliation for retaliation's sake. "Violence only begets more violence, Bea," she'd say. Beatrice wouldn't vocalize it, but Belladonna was often right. It was safe to assume she'd be right on this topic too.

"Firefly," Niko's voice was calm and steady. None of the anxiety that filled Roska's warning tone. Nor did he have the angry, defensive attitude that resulted in Quinn charring a portion of the table before him. Niko was truly calm. Serene, even. It was entirely out of place and probably the only reason why Elena paused.

The Prince stepped between her and Jamieson. He kept his hands relaxed at his sides and his eyes locked on hers, utterly unaffected by the vision of vengeance she embodied.

For several tense moments, no one moved. The sound of Elena's crackling lightning echoed throughout the Great Hall. Her blue lights created an eerie light show, shadows flashing and dancing along the walls ominously.

"Firefly," Niko said again. He took slow steps toward her, his hands still at his sides and he closed the distance between them. "Attacking Jamieson won't undo what was done to you. It might feel good for a moment." Jamieson whimpered quietly but remained frozen behind the Prince. "But I promise you, it will only leave you feeling guilt at having caused someone else pain." Beatrice thought his words had a ring of experience in them. "Why don't we take a walk?" Niko offered Elena his hand, unworried about the lightning that flashed off of hers. "I hear Roska's been working wonders in the greenhouse. Maybe we could go see his handiwork? I know I could use some fresh air."

The last sentence seemed to be the one that broke through to her. Elena blinked, the glow in her eyes fading as she shifted her gaze from the Prince's eyes to his proffered hand. After an agonizing few moments, Elena seemed to make a decision. The lightning on her skin faded away, and she took the Prince's hand.

The second her power dissipated, the room seemed to sigh in relief. Jamieson nearly collapsed on the floor, catching himself at the last moment and returning to stand at attention.

"You're dismissed for now, Commander." Niko spoke without taking his eyes off Elena. "Return to the soldiers. Ensure that they are properly repairing all that they damaged in your attack this morning, then return to camp. I will come out to speak with you later this evening." Without another word, Niko wrapped Elena's hand around his arm—supporting her weight now that her fury had faded and her muscles remembered that they were still quite weak—and walked calmly from the room.

As the door closed behind them, Quinn turned back to them. "What the hells just happened?"

"That, my dear boy, was love." Belladonna spoke quietly, a reverent whisper, but her eyes were fixed on Beatrice. Love truly was the most magical thing of all.

32
QUINN

QUINN FLOPPED PETULANTLY ONTO the couch in their suite. "How the hells can she love him? She barely knows him."

At least you acknowledge that you're being childish, Lyra teased.

"I mean, seriously, how does that even make sense?" Quinn continued, refusing to take Lyra's bait.

"I don't think love is supposed to make sense," Roska added thoughtfully. Demoni slithered down Roska's arm and hopped over to her nest of blankets beside the empty hearth.

"Want a fire?" Lyra asked the ice dragon.

"I'm all right for now." Demoni smiled a toothy thanks and snuggled deeper into her nest of fleece and wool.

"Elena was ready to roast that soldier in the middle of the hall like it was nothing. I've never seen her like that." Quinn worried a loose thread on the hem of his tunic. "It was kinda terrifying, honestly."

Roska sat on the edge of the armchair closer to the fireplace. "I think she would have actually killed that soldier if Niko hadn't stopped her. She wasn't going to listen to us. It was like her mind had gone somewhere else entirely."

"I don't blame her for it, though. I wanna kill the people who hurt her too." Quinn paused for a moment, wondering if that was really a true statement. "I just don't think killing the messenger—or one random soldier, in this case—would really help."

"Look at you! Thinking more than one step ahead," Lyra praised him mockingly. "Killing, or even maiming, that soldier wouldn't have helped her at all. I'm all for meting out just punishment for crimes, and you both know I think physical pain is the best teacher." She flicked a red-hot ember at Roska as she spoke. Roska tossed a snowflake in response. "But the person who deserves Elena's rage and electric shock therapy is the Queen. Not some soldier who was "just following orders." Although we all know that's a bullshyt excuse to make terrible choices and avoid taking responsibility for them."

Roska and Quinn both nodded. Countless atrocities throughout the history of Waverly—and probably the whole world—could have been avoided if people had stopped to consider their actions instead of just doing what they were told.

Quinn closed his eyes. The day had started out so promising. He'd had a great lesson planned for his students. He was going to go on a hunt with some of the archers. He hadn't been out in the woods in nearly a week. Q was starting to feel trapped in the confines of the castle.

Then it had all gone to shyt. Quinn laid an arm over his eyes. Maybe if he laid here long enough, he'd be able to forget the look of disappointment in Minka's eyes or the electric death that had been hiding behind Elena's.

Gods. He was just so tired.

Quinn awoke to the setting sun burning behind his closed eyes. He hadn't meant to sleep, and waking up to the blinding rays of the late afternoon sun was not ideal. He grunted and shifted on the couch to hide his face behind the arm of the seat, shielding his eyes from the light.

"Wakey, wakey." Elena's singsong voice should have annoyed him, instead it triggered the biggest smile Q had worn in days.

He sat up slowly, wiping the sleep from his eyes, and grinned at her. She was seated in the chair Roska had been occupying when Quinn had first closed his eyes. He wasn't sure how long he'd actually been asleep, but it had been a few hours at least.

"Well, if it isn't Lady Vengeance herself," Q teased. "Finally get that rage under control? Or did you massacre Roska's plants instead? You know he'll be heartbroken if you hurt his herbs."

Elena's skin flushed a deep red, and she buried her face in her hands. "Gods, I can't believe I did that! I was seriously going to electrify that poor man."

"That *poor man* could do with a few justified shocks. He aided in your kidnapping and abuse." Quinn didn't bother hiding his anger, but he didn't let it control him either. He'd had plenty of time to learn the best ways to deal with his "big emotions," as Castor had called them.

"I agree, but killing him won't solve anything. And Niko is right; inflicting pain on that soldier will only cause me more guilt and pain in the long run."

Niko was right.

Mux that guy.

"What's up with you two anyway?" Quinn nudged Elena's knee with his own.

"What are you talking about?" Elena's blush deepened, and Q knew Roska had been right. She loved that Prince. Aiden had guessed from the start that Niko was in love with Elena, but seeing the deep red in her cheeks and watching her try to avoid eye contact with him, Q knew the feeling was mutual.

"He clearly cares for you." Quinn might not be happy about potentially having a Royal as a brother, but he also couldn't deny that the Prince was a good guy. And he'd been nothing but kind to Elena. "And I think it's pretty clear that you care for him too. I mean hells, you would *never* let anyone else call you a bug."

Elena swatted at his knee. "He doesn't call me a bug!" Then she seemed to realize what he meant and added, "Well, ok, he *does*, but he means it as a compliment... I think."

Quinn chuckled. Niko definitely meant it as a compliment. The Prince embraced their sister completely, accepting her exactly as she was. Magic and all. Which was especially impressive, considering his mother was clearly a magic-hating bigot.

His mother. The Queen.

"Do you really think the Queen kidnapped the King?" Quinn asked, gaze fixed on the fire blazing in their hearth.

"Niko does. From what I overheard when I was imprisoned there, she is absolutely insane. She blames Mother for the King leaving her bed. She thinks Mother bewitched him. Enchantresses can't even do that. Witches, maybe, but not Mother. I don't think the Queen even sees a difference between various magical creatures. She hates us all equally." Bitterness was heavy in Elena's voice.

Quinn had spent much of his childhood being hated and mistreated for a collection of bullshyt reasons. It was a feeling he was used to, and yet the Queen's blind bigotry still grated. She didn't know them. Hells, she didn't even understand their magic—not that Q really understood it—and she hated them to the point of wanting to massacre them all.

"What does your Prince want to do?" Quinn looked from the fire to the familiars curled up beside it. Agon slept draped across Lyra's back where she lay stretched out before the hearth. They looked ridiculous and impossibly comfortable.

Elena sighed, leaning her head back in the chair. "I have no idea." She closed her eyes, and Quinn wondered if all the excitement from the day was finally taking its toll on her. "He hates what she's doing, and he's stopped the soldiers, exerting his 'male dominance' bullshyt, but stopping her won't be that simple."

"Why not?" Q had been under the impression that the Prince was in charge of everything when the King was away. With the King now missing, that should mean that Niko was the top authority in the whole country.

"The military will listen to him, but the Queen's guard will be harder to stop. According to Niko, the Queen spent the last couple of decades building her relationships with each and every one of them and binding their loyalty to her over the ruling men." Opening her eyes, Elena sat up a little straighter and added with a grimace, "Honestly, it was a good plan. I feel bad for her, and I really hate that."

"You're kidding, right? How can you feel bad for the woman who *kidnapped* you and locked you in her timeless prison? She wants to kill you, El. Kill all of us." Q was certain he would never understand Elena's endless empathy. Especially for people who so clearly did *not* deserve it.

"She spent her whole life at the mercy of a man. First, her father, who married her off to the King the moment she was of-age. Then she was beholden to a husband she didn't choose and had his child regardless of her desire to do so. That child was a boy, so the moment he hit his sixteenth cycle, the soldiers started to defer to him. She never had her own authority. She never had any choice in life-altering decisions. They were all made for her." Elena paused for a moment, seeming to collect her thoughts. "I even understand why she resented Mother so much. Enchantresses live in a vastly different culture. Women are the only authority here. I imagine the Queen looked at the school—seeing all these young girls with more power, authority, and self-determination than she'd ever been given the chance to experience. My heart breaks for her. I don't forgive her actions, but I understand them."

Quinn openly stared at Elena. "You are an amazing person, El. The woman is easily the worst, most vile creature on the planet, and you still find a way to humanize her and relate to her. It's baffling, but also incredible."

Elena smiled weakly at him. "You don't think I'm being stupid or naive?"

Q rose from the couch and knelt before her, gently placing his hands on her shoulders. "El, you have never been stupid. You are the most compassionate person I've ever met. After everything you've been through, you should be a lot more hateful and vengeful. Instead, all the hells you've had to endure has made you so muxing kind." He pulled her into a tight hug. "This world doesn't deserve you. The Queen certainly doesn't deserve your kindness. You are too good for her. Hells, you are too good for all of us."

"I think it will make her a great queen though. What about you, Agon?" Lyra piped in, clearly having been awake and eavesdropping for a while.

Agon pulled himself across Lyra's back, stretching his lithe little body and yawning dramatically. "Oh, yes. Every great Queen has had compassion in spades. Elena will be the best Queen this country has ever seen."

Elena disconnected from Quinn long enough to throw a couple of sparks at the familiars. "Shut it. Both of you. I'm *not* going to be Queen."

"I mean... based on how Niko's been looking at you, it kinda seems inevitable." Q shrugged, then ducked just in time to avoid the small bolt of lightning Elena flicked at him.

He laughed as he helped Elena to her feet. "Come on, Your Majesty. We're missing dinner, and we need to figure out what the plan is for the current reigning nightmare."

33

AIDEN

IDEN HAD BEEN SLIGHTED yet again. He was beginning to think that Beatrice was ignoring him entirely in the hopes that he would just disappear. He wouldn't give up that easily though. He'd inherited god-like stubbornness from his father. No one could make Aiden do anything he didn't want to do.

No one? Aleerah asked pointedly.

Fine, you *can, but that's mostly because you're massive and have sharp teeth that you don't seem to mind using on my frail semi-mortal form.* Aiden eyed her suspiciously as she joined him on the balcony.

I only use force when it's absolutely necessary. She sat regally beside him, staring out at the deep purples and blues of the twilight sky.

I should have been a part of that meeting with the Prince and his Commander. I shouldn't have had to get second-hand information from Castor. When are they going to see that I'm here to stay? I'm here to help. It was beyond frustrating to be the most powerful being in the world and still be relegated to muxing guard duty. He wasn't even allowed in the school. Beatrice had restricted him to the Wall, the towers along the Wall, and the prison tower. It was offensive, honestly. He deserved better treatment. He was a muxing demi-god *and* the father of the most powerful children the world had ever known. Yet he was being treated like a fly in the kitchens: unwanted, dirty, annoying.

You have to earn their trust first, idiot. Aleerah flicked her tail in annoyance.

Why are you so unhappy with me? I haven't done anything to you in ages. He couldn't win. Everyone was blaming him for everything, and no one would give him the *chance* to earn their trust.

You are not the victim here, you self-important ass. You toyed with their lives, all of them. You can't expect them to just let that shyt go. You have to put in the work.

How do you propose I do that when they won't let me in on the important shyt? If there'd been a chair available, Aiden would have taken that moment to flop dramatically onto it.

I propose you start by not assuming everything is all about you, Aleerah snapped. She turned her massive wolf head, currently sitting level with his, and snapped her ferocious jaws at him. *I'm so sick of this pity party you've been throwing for weeks. Your children have been through hells and back—literally, in Elena's case—and all you want to do is sit around and whine and moan. "Poor me, no one invites me to things." If you want to get in their good graces and be involved in solving the world's problems, why don't you try being* useful *for a change?*

Aiden huffed and turned to walk away, but Aleerah jumped in front of him, blocking the door and forcing him to face her.

Castor told us the King was missing. If you want them to start trusting you, why not do a locator spell and see if you can find him?

That would go a long way in getting Niko to trust you. With Niko will come Elena. Then Quinn. Roska already trusts you, in case you missed that in all of your childish fit-throwing. Beatrice will thaw eventually. Belladonna may or may not, but you can't really blame her if she hates you for eternity. And knowing how long witches live, it might literally be an eternity.

Aiden glared at her for a long moment, turning over her—aggressive and condescending—advice. With another dramatic sigh, he nodded.

Fine, I'll try to locate that ass of a King. I can't promise it will work, though.

At least you can tell them you tried. Aleerah stepped to the side and Aiden strode into the bedroom in a huff of sullen determination. He'd do the damn spell. Then he'd interrupt their family meal—that no one had invited him to, *again*—and share whatever news he had. Maybe then they'd offer him a seat at the table.

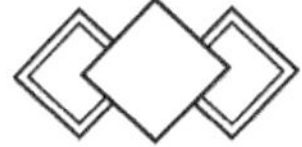

Unrolling a worn map of the kingdom, Aiden lit four taper candles, placing each at the cardinal points on the map. They served a dual purpose: calling forth the powers of the elements, each represented in their respective direction—air to the east, fire to the south, water to the west, and earth to the north—and also the considerably less magical purpose of holding the map down as it kept trying to roll back up.

Pouring a circle of black salt around the border of Waverly, Aiden began the spell. He felt safe in assuming the King hadn't left the country without telling any of his soldiers, so he kept his focus on the land within the kingdom's boundaries.

Aleerah curled up on the floor before their small fire. The tower Beatrice had allowed them to stay in was clearly not a space meant to host guests. At least not *welcome* guests.

Alee's exasperated sign caused their fire to dance, nearly putting out the flames of his candles, which would have forced him to start all over. Aiden grumbled in his mind but refocused on the spell before him. A small, bright light appeared on the map, indicating the location of the King.

That couldn't be right.

That was impossible.

Aiden blew out the candles one at a time, widdershins—counterclockwise—and reset the spell. He clearly had screwed something up and needed to try again. There was no way that locator spell was right.

It wasn't good news.

This was the kind of news that might get him kicked out of Harbor Ridge completely. Banished to his tower once more.

First of all, no one banished you to the tower the first time. That was a choice. The right choice, I might add, since it kept you from screwing up their destinies any more.

Just once, Aiden wished that Aleerah would sugarcoat things.

Sorry, not my style. She offered him a half-hearted grin that he thought was meant to convey regret, but he knew her too well. Aleerah never regretted her choices. She was of the mind that regrets were a waste of time and energy. While they both had an endless amount of time—what with being basically unkillable—Aleerah had decided that meant she had none to waste. Aiden had gone the other way. He had all the time in the world and was in no hurry to do much of anything.

Aiden walked confidently into the Great Hall, using the entrance farthest from the dais and making an excessive amount of noise upon entry. If he was going to make an unannounced visit, he might as well make a show of it.

He felt the heat of their respective glares the moment Beatrice and Belladonna caught sight of him. They weren't happy to see him. Unsurprising.

Silence flooded the room as Aiden strode down the main aisle between the long tables filled with enchantresses of all ages and specialties. Some of them gaped at him. Some looked on with curiosity. He tossed a few of the prettier young women shameless winks until Aleerah growled quietly behind him.

Spoilsport, he thought grumbly.

Petulant child, she volleyed back.

They reached the dais with every single pair of eyes fixated on Aiden. He'd never felt so important. He turned back to face the room and offered the enchantresses a bow with the flourish of his hand and a face-splitting grin. Some of the younger girls giggled until they were quickly hushed by the older women at their tables.

"What are you doing here?" Beatrice demanded.

"I have some information regarding the King's location," Aiden said, turning back to face the Headmistress. "I thought it would be best to tell the Prince straight away."

"What sort of information?" Beatrice glared at him, untrusting, as always.

"Spit it out then." Niko sat at the far end of the table, beside Elena. It wasn't typical for a Royal to dine at the edge of any table, but Niko wasn't an authority at Harbor Ridge. This was Beatrice's passive-aggressive way of ensuring the Prince knew his place in her school.

"It might be best if we do this in private," Aiden offered quietly, taking a couple of steps toward Niko.

"No," Niko snapped. "Tell me now."

"Well, Your Majesty, it would seem *you* are the King."

Niko stared at Aiden, seeming to not understand his words. Elena grasped the former Prince's hand, quickly searching his profile with anxious eyes.

"What the mux does that mean?" Quinn asked incredulously

"How can you be sure?" Niko didn't break eye contact with him, but Aiden could see his fingers twining and tightening around Elena's.

"I'm sorry to tell you, but I performed a locator spell, searching for the King, and the spell located you. The spell pinpointed the King of Waverly. Here, at this table. Because you are the King now. Which can only mean that your father has passed unto the Fade." Aiden was slightly surprised to find that he did truly feel sorry for being the one to break the news. He liked Niko. While Aiden didn't have any opinion of the former King, he cared for and respected Niko.

Even if they had already suspected it when they'd learned the Queen was the one who orchestrated his disappearance.

Aiden studied the young King as he absorbed the news. Something seemed to pass over his face, wiping away any emotion. He released his hold on Elena, quietly excused himself, and left without another word.

Elena turned to Aiden as soon as the door closed behind Niko. "Are you absolutely certain that the King is dead? Is it possible that your spell was wrong? Or perhaps it just misunderstood what you were asking?" Her voice was so hopeful. She was pleading with him to offer even a glimmer of possibility.

Aiden's heart broke a little. "I'm sorry, Elena," he said, shaking his head remorsefully. "I was very clear. The magic knew what I was asking, it just couldn't give me the information we were hoping for. The King is dead. It's likely he's been dead for moons and we just didn't know it."

"Why would the Queen kidnap her husband only to kill him? Doesn't that mean she'll be even more powerless now? At least when the King was alive, she could claim the orders she gave came from her husband. No one will want to take orders from the new King's mother." Roska had a surprisingly clear understanding of the political dynamics. Aiden looked at his son with quiet admiration.

"I imagine it wasn't her plan," Beatrice contended. "She most likely wanted to convince him to leave me, and when he didn't agree to her terms—whatever they might have been—she probably lost her temper. Rosalina has always been short-tempered and quick to lash out."

"What the hells are we supposed to do now?" Quinn groaned, letting his head fall back against the heavy wood of his chair. "This is such a shyt show."

34

ELENA

E LENA DESPERATELY WANTED TO respect Niko's privacy and give him the space he needed to process what his mother had done, what it meant for the country, and—more important- ly—what it meant for him to be the new King. She wanted to, but she also knew that if the situation had been reversed, she wouldn't want to be alone.

Dinner had ended not long after Niko had left the Great Hall, the enchantresses returning to their rooms or various chores. Roska had helped Belladonna—who was still feeling a bit weak—out to the greenhouse for some "plant therapy," as the witch called it. Mother and Aiden were actually speaking to each other. Not nicely, but they weren't fighting, and Mother wasn't threatening a myriad of creative physical tortures. It was progress.

Elena quietly excused herself and rose carefully from the table. She was improving every day, but this particular day had been ex- cruciatingly long, and Elena wasn't entirely sure her legs would carry her all the way to Niko's suite. Quinn perked up at her movement and jumped to his feet, offering her his arm.

"Thanks," she muttered, trying to hide her embarrassment.

"No problem. Where to?" Quinn let her set the pace as they stepped off the dais and exited the Great Hall.

"I think I just need to go to bed." Elena sighed. The day had started so suddenly, and she hadn't had much time to wrap her mind around the events of the day yet. First the attack on the Wall, with Niko carrying her out to speak with Mother and the soldiers. Then Elena had nearly electrified the new commander. She'd been all over the castle, and her body was fully drained from the endless excitement and physical exertion.

"Do you want to sleep in our room tonight? Or are you going back to Niko's suite?" The lack of judgment in his voice surprised Elena. She hadn't really expected him to be ok with her staying with the Prince.

You mean the King, Agon corrected.

Elena froze mid-step. Gods, Niko was the King now. That was going to be hard to wrap her mind around for a while. She couldn't even imagine how Niko must be feeling.

Quinn looked at her questioningly. Elena forced a smile and continued walking.

"I think I should at least check on him first. He may not want me to stay there anymore. It wouldn't be proper for the King to share a bed—or even a room—with an untitled enchantress." Elena flinched at her own words. She never really cared much for propriety or politics, but that was Niko's life. She needed to accept that whatever she felt for him—whatever he might feel for her—was ultimately irrelevant.

"First of all, if he kicks you out of his suite for something as pointless as 'appropriateness,' he may or may not wake up with his sheets on fire." Q winked as an evil grin spread across his face. "Secondly, you are more than welcome in our suite. We have a third bed just waiting for you, if you ever want it."

Elena smiled up at her brother as he helped her up the stairs to the royal wing. She hadn't spent a night with her brothers since she'd returned. She'd been rushed straight to Niko's bed and had spent every night there since. Elena wondered for a moment if her brothers felt neglected or pushed aside. She hated to think that she might have hurt them inadvertently.

"That's so sweet of you both. I might have to take you up on it." She debated voicing her concerns about offending them, but Lyra interrupted her thoughts.

"Just make sure it's a temporary thing, ok? I've enjoyed having a whole bed to myself. I'd hate to have to give that up."

Quinn's guffaw echoed through the stone stairway. "Mux, Lyra. You couldn't find a nicer way to put it?"

"Why? Elena knows I'm not nice. No need to try and convince her otherwise now." Lyra shrugged her little fox shoulders and hopped up the rest of the stairs with practiced ease.

Elena smiled at the little orange face that looked down at her from the landing. "I do appreciate your candor, Lyra. I wouldn't have you any other way."

Lyra gave Quinn a look that could only be interpreted as "told you." Elena giggled. She'd really missed this. The quiet, peaceful moments, when they weren't being hunted, chased, kidnapped, assaulted, or otherwise endangered. She wondered if they would ever get back to the simple lives they'd had in Andover with Amelia.

Elena's breath caught in her throat and she quickly turned to Q. "Oh, gods! Amelia! Have you heard from her? Is she doing ok? Was she harmed by the *turmio*?" Elena hated herself for not thinking to check on Amelia sooner. The woman had taken her in so freely when she'd had no one else, adopted her when her own mother had disowned her. Elena owed her life to that wonderful woman.

"She's fine, El," Quinn assured her. "I sent her a message as soon as we were released from the prison here. She's ok. Andover is fine. Amelia said she felt weak for a few days, but nothing more than if she'd had a bad cold." Quinn steadied Elena, leaning her against the cool stone wall, and began gently rubbing her arms. "Amelia is perfectly safe."

Elena took several deep breaths, trying to slow her racing heart.

"Does she know about me? About what happened to me?" Elena couldn't help but wonder if Amelia had asked about her. Elena loved the woman like a second mother. Honestly, Amelia had been more maternal and loving to Elena in the few moons that she'd known her than her actual mother had her whole life.

"She knows everything," Quinn promised. "I started to write it all out, but when I got to the third page my hand started cramping." Lyra barked a mocking laugh at that. "Shut it, smart ass." Quinn flicked a few sparks at the fox, who watched them fall on her fur, completely unfazed. "Castor ended up offering to deliver what I had and answer any of her questions. When he came back, his eyebrows had been singed off. Apparently, Amelia hadn't known about moonbirds and didn't react well to his transformation." A gleeful spark lit Quinn's eyes. Elena failed to stifle a small laugh at the thought of Amelia attacking Castor. "You know, Castor wouldn't speak to me for a week after that. It was muxing glorious."

Quinn's deep laugh reverberated in Elena's chest, filling her with a pleasant warmth she hadn't felt in quite some time. He offered her his arm again, and they continued on to Niko's suite.

"Roska wants to meet her, you know," Elena said after several quiet minutes. "Amelia. He hasn't said it outright, but I can tell he feels like he's missing out by not knowing her. I think he's afraid to, though."

"Afraid? Of Amelia?" Quinn looked thoroughly confused by that concept.

"Probably not scared of Amelia, specifically, but afraid of meeting someone who means so much to both of us. I imagine he worries that she won't like him." Elena kept her eyes on the ground before her. "I know I would be."

"Why wouldn't she like him? He's our brother. She'll love him simply because of that." Quinn didn't seem to understand what Elena was trying to imply.

"She means because he spent so long being told he was shyt." Lyra never did tolerate indirectness. "Seriously, Q. You should get that. We all know that feeling."

"But... it's Amelia." Quinn couldn't comprehend the idea of anyone being disliked by Amelia. It was sweet, really.

"Never mind," Elena said, patting his hand. "We'll take him there as soon as we get this shyt with the Queen settled."

"Well, then you'd better go check on your Prince. Oh, sorry. Your *King*." Quinn stopped outside a thick, wooden door with two guards standing at attention. "Here you are, milady." He dropped her hand and made the most dramatic and ridiculous bow. "Good luck," he added in a whisper, then pressed a kiss to her forehead and sauntered off down the hall. Lyra bound along beside him like they didn't have a care in the world.

They think they're funny, Agon smirked, but Elena could hear the amusement in his thoughts. She'd missed their playfulness.

She was eager for her body to finish its recovery so that she might be able to move around on her own again. It was nice being able to have one-on-one time with Q whenever he escorted her around, but she missed just being herself.

Elena turned to face the solid door before her. She had no idea what to expect from Niko, but she knew she'd have to open the door to find out.

She raised her fist, heart pounding, as she prepared to knock on the door.

Just as she was about to knock, the door jerked open.

Niko's eyes were wild and unfocused. "What the hells took you so long?"

35

BELLADONNA

WITH ALL THE DRAMA that had unfolded over the last two days, Belladonna couldn't help but feel like they were living in a drunken bard's song. Castor had offered to fly her back up to their bedroom, but Belladonna declined. She needed to be around plants after all the torment and abuse she'd experienced in the morning with the soldiers' attack. She needed to reconnect with nature. She needed to feel the dirt between her fingers and the roots beneath her bare feet.

Roska had kindly offered to escort her to the greenhouse. He was even thoughtful enough to word it like he was asking *her* for help. Roska had not-so-casually mentioned that he was struggling with some of the colder climate plants that he didn't have a lot of experience with. Belladonna knew it was a ruse, likely suggested to the boy by his mother who would know that the witch would need time surrounded by green in order to heal from the morning's trauma. Still, it was sweet of them both, and Belladonna happily took the offer.

She sat at a small wooden table, a collection of gardening tools spread out to her right, a large pile of dirt on the ground to her left, and a bag of various flower bulbs before her. She'd meant to start potting the plants so that they might bloom and flourish in the growing season. Instead, she'd been sitting there for twenty minutes, just holding the bulbs in her hands, feeling the weight of them, the life hibernating inside. Gently feeding her power into the bulbs, she watched their roots slowly sprout from the bulbs as they sat in her open palms. The small tendrils wrapped up her arms, feeding her soul with their essence. It was a moment of peace and symbiosis in a world overflowing with chaos.

Roska, who was seated at another table, looked over and dropped the trowel he'd been using. "Belladonna!" He rushed over, kneeling beside her and reaching for her hands as though he thought she was being eaten by the plants.

"It's ok," Belladonna soothed. "We're healing each other."

Roska eyed her curiously but didn't move to remove the bulbs or attempt to free her hands from the roots that were slowly twisting their way farther up her arms. He sat back on his haunches and gaped as the roots spread and grew with increasing speed.

The energy from the bulbs spread through the roots, soaking into her skin and spreading throughout her body. The green in her locks brightened to a vibrant, lush verdant. The flowers that had wilted and started to die off in her hair absorbed the life force shared by the bulbs, quickly reviving them. The beautiful scent of the flowers flooded her nose as the witch hastened her recovery with the blessed assistance of the bulbs. In return for their aid, Belladonna fed them with her own power. It was a thriving cycle of growing magic. By the time Belladonna was fully healed, the bulbs had transformed into massive, vivid, flourishing flowers.

"That was amazing." Roska's eyes glowed with admiration.

Belladonna beamed with pleasure. Roska was the only one of the triplets with whom she hadn't had much time to build a connection.

She and Elena had bonded immediately, drawn together by their love of magic. Quinn had been harder for Belladonna to relate to, but they'd built a solid—albeit still sometimes tense—relationship since the boys had arrived at Harbor Ridge. Roska had been hells-bent on bringing Elena home, to the point that he'd ignored and neglected most everything else. He'd spent weeks barricaded in the tallest tower, reading, researching, and preparing to bring their sister home. Castor was the only one Roska had ever invited into the tower, and that had stung a bit. The boy who resented and feared magic had bonded with a shape-shifting, magical moonbird. The hypocrisy of it definitely hurt, but Belladonna had kept that to herself. She couldn't really blame Roska for his reticence, nor was it fair of her to be upset that he felt a connection with Castor. She was happy that he was finding companionship; she'd just been jealous that Roska had still been so standoffish with her.

After they brought Elena home, Roska had seemed a bit lost. Unmoored. Belladonna had suggested to Castor that the boy might enjoy working in the greenhouse. She'd been secretly thrilled when Roska had taken Castor up on the idea. For weeks, she'd been looking for an excuse to join him and try to build their relationship within the safety and comfort of the plant nursery.

Belladonna winced a bit at the memory of that morning. This wasn't the ideal way to get herself invited into the greenhouse with Roska, but she was feeling much better now, and she was grateful to finally get some quiet time alone with him.

"It's really quite peaceful in here," she mused quietly. "I can see why you like it so much." She looked around the room. Taking in the sights and scents of all the beautiful, thriving plant life that filled the massive glass building. The sunlight filtered through the leaves of the ivy that grew along the eaves, creating a green tint with the light.

"Yes, I'm glad you recommended it."

Belladonna flashed her gaze to him. "What?"

"I knew it was your idea the second Castor said it. I wondered why you didn't suggest it to me yourself, but I assumed that it was easier this way. I know I make people uncomfortable." Roska refused to make eye contact with her as he spoke, clearly embarrassed.

Belladonna swiftly, but gently, untangled herself from the roots of the bulbs and sat them on the table. She turned on the bench, squaring her body with Roska's, and offered her hands to him. She wouldn't touch him if he didn't want it, but she needed to ensure that he heard and fully understood what she was about to say.

Much to her surprise and pleasure, he placed both of his hands in her upturned palms. Belladonna tenderly tightened her grasp, holding his gaze. "Roska, I have never been uncomfortable around you. I have kept my distance from you because *you* seemed uncomfortable with *me* and I didn't want to drive you away from your mother now that you finally have a chance to get to know her."

Roska studied her, likely trying to find any falsehoods in her statement. He would find none.

"When we first met, you seemed so anxious because of the lies you'd been raised to believe. About magic. About witches. About yourself. I never wanted to make you feel unwanted or unwelcome. The safest option seemed to be giving you plenty of space to find your own way." Belladonna blinked back emotions that threatened to leak from her bright eyes. "I can see now that it was the wrong path. I'm sorry, Roska." Her voice cracked when she whispered his name, but she held firmly to his hands and refused to drop her gaze. He *needed* to know she was telling the truth.

Roska blinked back tears of his own.

"I would like to hug you now, if that's all right?" Belladonna spoke quietly, afraid to break the moment that was passing between them. Roska said nothing but nodded. That was all the permission she needed. Belladonna rose to her feet, pulling Roska up with her, and enveloped him in the biggest hug she could. She poured every ounce of love and affection she had into that connection, impressing upon him that he was special, loved, and cherished. Belladonna knew that one hug wouldn't erase all the trauma that Roska had experienced at the hands of the Brotherhood. Nor would it magically conjure a flawless relationship between the two of them, but it was a step in the right direction.

Finally.

36

ELENA

ELENA STEPPED INTO THE room and quickly shut the door behind her. Niko was in a state and she didn't want the guards gossiping about him. She didn't want people to think that the new King had lost his mind.

He might have, El. Look at him. Agon's concern was justified, although his words seemed harsh.

Niko was pacing anxiously around the sitting room. His hair stuck out at odd angles, as though he'd been repeatedly pulling at it and running his hands through it. His normally warm coppery skin looked pale and clammy. Niko looked deranged. But he'd just learned that his mother killed his father and now he was King of Waverly. Elena assumed that sort of jarring news and paradigm-shifting revelations would have thrown even the strongest individual.

"Niko," she said, trying to conjure up the same calming tone he'd used with her just hours ago, when she'd wanted to murder that soldier.

Niko said nothing. He continued his wild pacing, as though he'd already forgotten she was there.

"Niko." She repeated his name a bit louder and more firmly. Elena took a few steps into the room, walking into the middle of his path and forcing him to either run into her or stop pacing. Thankfully, he chose the latter. Elena caught his face gently in her hands and drew his gaze down to hers. "Niko, you need to breathe."

His heart was racing. She could feel his rapid pulse beneath her hands where they rested on his neck, just below his jaw. His unfocused eyes seemed to stare off into nothingness.

What had he said in the stables...? Elena tried to remember the exact words he'd used when he'd helped to calm her from the state of panic she'd experienced after escaping the Queen's prison.

Elena tightened her grip ever-so-slightly, gently rubbing her thumbs up and down his racing artery. "Niko." She kept her voice mellow. "What do you smell?"

Her question seemed to confuse him, but Niko's eyes fixated on her for a moment as he took a deep breath.

"Wood smoke. Melting beeswax. Your lavender soap." He kept his eyes on her as he spoke. Elena smiled up at him.

"What can you hear?"

He blinked slowly, letting his eyes stay closed for a moment while he focused on her words. "My heart racing. Your steady breathing. The guards shuffling in the courtyard."

"You're doing great, Niko." Her thumbs stilled on his neck. "What do you see?"

Niko opened his eyes and looked down at her. "I see the most amazing, beautiful, thoughtful creature on the planet. And her rodent." His cocky grin spread back across his face, but he didn't move from her grasp.

Elena's face heated at his compliments. She knew she should look away, let go of him, and put a little space between them. But her body didn't listen to the logic of her mind. Instead, she took a step closer, closing the distance. Niko placed his hands gently on her hips, waiting to see if she'd object. She did not.

Elena felt a sudden coolness at her throat and realized that Agon had slipped away. He didn't want to be caught in the middle of this particular moment. Niko's grin shifted as he licked his lips and his gaze left her eyes to fixate on her mouth. He was asking for permission without words. Would she let him kiss her? Would she permit him to close the last of the space between them?

Elena froze. They'd spent a couple of weeks sharing a bed without touching. Niko had kept his distance, always respecting her space and staying on his side of the bed. He only moved to the bed after she'd snapped at him for sleeping on the couch. It had seemed so silly to her that two individuals couldn't share a massive bed. But now, they were looking at crossing a boundary that they'd been actively toeing since they'd met.

Nervously, she slid her tongue across her lips, pulling her lower lip between her teeth as she watched him.

Gods, yes. She wanted this. Elena had been trying to ignore her attraction to him since they'd met. She was tired of fighting this feeling. Being in his arms—feeling the warmth of his gaze and the heat coiling in her lower belly—she knew this was exactly where she was supposed to be.

Elena's hands moved from under his jaw to wrap around his neck, tangling her fingers in his dark curls and pulling his face down to meet hers.

"Are you sure?" His words were a whisper of warmth on her lips.

She didn't speak. Instead, she rose on her toes, brushing her lips lightly against his.

It was the barest of touches, but it felt as though the world caught fire around them. Niko's arms wrapped tightly around her, drawing her body firmly against his, her soft curves molding into the hardness of his chest and stomach.

A moan escaped her throat as he deepened their kiss. He consumed her. The heat of his body against hers, the feel of his tongue as it danced with hers... it was unlike anything she'd ever experienced. His hands roamed over her body. One hand moved farther up her back, gripping her hair to angle her head and enable him to deepen and control their kiss. The other drifted down. Elena gasped as the Prince—no King—grabbed hold of her ass and gently squeezed her flesh through the layers of her dress.

His touch emboldened her, pulling him down as she attempted to practically climb up his tall, lean frame. She needed to be closer. She moaned as his mouth moved from her now-swollen lips, kissing and teasing her neck with his skillful tongue. Elena nearly melted on the spot as he nipped her ear. A whimper escaped her lips and she leaned into him, encouraging him to do it again.

Niko chuckled against her skin, his breath tickling her neck. "Did you like that, Firefly?" Elena could feel the smug grin on his face against her skin.

"Shut up and keep kissing me," she whined. Elena knew she sounded needy and weak, but at that particular moment, she couldn't have cared less.

Niko kindly obliged, pressing more fervent kisses to her neck, nibbling her earlobes, and slowly untying the ribbons at the front of her dress. Impatient and irritated at the immense amount of fabric separating her from what she wanted, Elena tore at the buttons on Niko's shirt, desperate to get her hands on the warm, hard flesh beneath.

Niko shrugged out of the ruined fabric and had nearly finished undoing her dress when a pounding at the door shattered their passionate exchange and dragged them back to the cold reality of their lives.

Elena froze, suddenly realizing where their actions were taking them, and surprised by her rash choices. Niko's hands stilled, gripping the ribbons in frustration. Elena's heart was racing and Niko was dangerously close to her. His fingers teased the top of her dress, dipping slightly under the top of the fabric and grazing the sensitive skin beneath. Her breath hitched at the contact.

Another, more insistent, set of pounding knocks on the door. Niko cursed under his breath. He closed his eyes and pressed his forehead against hers.

"Mux everything," he muttered, his lips brushing her nose as he spoke. Niko placed a gentle, chaste kiss on her lips, pulled his ruined shirt back on as best he could, and waited for her to fix her dress before he went to the door. "What is it?" he asked curtly, clearly annoyed at having been interrupted.

Elena, however, wasn't quite as bothered by the interruption. She was honestly a little grateful for it. She had been ready to jump into bed with Niko after just a few—albeit quite magical and definitely better than she'd ever imagined—kisses. What was wrong with her?

The guard spoke quietly to Niko, relaying some message. Elena wasn't listening. She wandered across the room and out onto the balcony. Fresh air. She needed fresh air to figure out what the hells was wrong with her.

Nothing is wrong with you, Agon chided. *You are a normal, teenage enchantress with normal desires. Hells, half the girls from our class have already ventured out into the world to experience exactly what you and Niko were about to do.*

Elena's face was burning with embarrassment. If anyone else had said those things to her, Elena was certain she would have melted into a puddle of shame right on the spot.

You have nothing to be ashamed of. Agon joined her on the balcony, climbing up the baluster and sitting in front of her on the thick railing.

I know you're right, about the other girls, but it still feels like I've done something wrong. Dirty. Elena's mind flashed back to the men who'd attacked her in Amelia's inn. They'd been after the same thing she'd been more than willing to do with Niko. They wanted the same thing he wanted.

It's not the same. Agon flicked his tail, sending a small shower of sparks over the edge of the balcony. *Those bastards wanted to take from you. They didn't care about you. They intended to take what they wanted regardless of your feelings on the matter. They were human garbage who got exactly what they deserved.*

Elena flinched at the vehemence in Agon's tone. She agreed with him, of course, but the bluntness of his words was still startling.

Niko, Agon went on, *loves you. He hasn't said it yet, but everyone can see it. And you love him. I can* feel *that. What was about to happen between you was entirely natural. You deserve to feel that sort of happiness. We've been through hells, but Niko cares for you. He would never hurt you or do anything you didn't want.*

Elena sighed. Resting her elbows on the balcony, she looked out at the landscape before them. The snow had mostly melted, with only a few patches holding out in the shaded spots under the trees. Their room faced west, looking out over the Dark Woods, with the mountains visible to the north. It was a beautiful view. Agon twined his way beneath her elbow, taking up the space between her forearms on the railing. A cool breeze ruffled her hair as she pondered Agon's words.

She didn't know if his assessment of Niko's feelings was accurate, but she knew he was right about hers. Elena loved the new King. She had no idea what that would mean in the long run, but she knew she couldn't ignore it any longer.

They'd opened the floodgates with that first kiss.

There was no going back now.

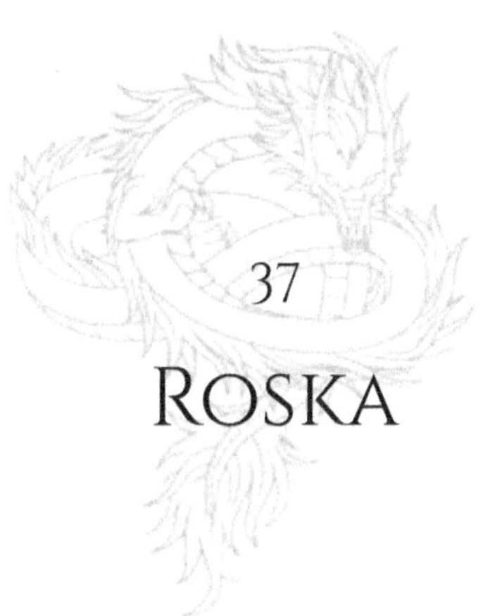

37

ROSKA

WITH BELLADONNA'S WORDS STILL echoing in his head, Roska meandered back to his room. It was late and they'd had a ridiculously long and trying day. He hadn't expected to connect with the witch as much as he had, but he should have realized much sooner that they had a great deal in common. Not just their love of plants, but the trauma and abuse they'd both suffered at the hands of the Brotherhood. It was the sort of bond Roska never wanted to share with someone else because it meant that person had been hurt too. But he was grateful for it at the same time. Someone else truly knew and understood the pain he'd suffered. Someone who could relate to his feelings on a visceral level.

The presence of the guards outside their suite doors told him that Quinn was already in their room. Roska offered a quick nod to the women and let himself in.

"I was wondering when you'd make it back here." Quinn was setting fresh wood on the glowing embers in the hearth. Night was falling and it would still be cold as the sun faded from the sky. Lyra flicked her tail and flames danced across the dry logs. "Want us to start a fire in your room?"

"Yes, please. That would be great." Roska removed his boots and placed them by the suite door. "Did Elena make it back to her rooms? She looked exhausted at dinner."

"Yeah, I walked her back. I told her she could sleep in here with us if Niko needed some alone time. She seemed nervous, like maybe as King, he wouldn't want to share a room with her anymore."

"Well, that's outrageous," Roska exclaimed. "The man is head over heels for her. She has to see that."

"Apparently she doesn't." Quinn shrugged. "Whatever. She'll see it eventually. Or he'll just come right out and say it. Either way, I told her she had the option of coming here. I doubt she'll take me up on it though."

"I'm glad you offered. It would be nice to have some time, just the three of us." Roska thought back to their time in the tower and their journey to Belladonna's after they'd escaped. It had been a hard, strained time, but it had also become some of Roska's fondest memories. Finally getting to spend time and connect with his siblings.

"El said the same thing." Quinn gathered some logs from the cast iron holder by the hearth. "Maybe we can all go hunting tomorrow. Well, I'll hunt, you two can gather plants, and we can have some time, just us."

Roska smiled. "That sounds perfect."

"Great. I'll send a formal invitation to our beloved sister through our ever-present guards." An amused smirk brightened Q's face.

Lyra huffed, clearly not as entertained by Quinn's teasing.

Roska couldn't help but chuckle at them both. He was so grateful for them. For all of them. Never in his life would he have dared to dream that he would one day have such a healthy and wonderful relationship with his family. His *family*. He never even thought he'd meet his parents and now here they were, his siblings and his parents—all three of them, because only a fool wouldn't consider Belladonna as much a mother to them as their biological mother—in the same home. Granted, that "home" was a massive castle that also served as a school for enchantresses.

Still, it was nice to finally be together with them all.

He couldn't wait to go hunting with his siblings. It had been too long.

Roska was just slipping on his boots when he heard a peppy knock on their suite door. Elena burst into the room before Quinn had a chance to reach the handle, practically knocking him over. Grinning sheepishly, Elena pushed some of her wavy brown hair behind her ears.

"Sorry, Q. I didn't mean to come in quite so aggressively." She tossed them both a couple of warm rolls from her enchanted cloak's pockets. "I'm just excited! We haven't hung out, just the three of us, in ages. It's gonna be great."

Roska thought he saw a hint of unease in her eyes, but it was gone in a blink. He must have imagined it. He took a bite of the roll, finished shoving his feet into the boots, and rose to give their sister a good morning hug. "I'm excited too, Elena. It's been too long."

Elena wrapped her arms around his middle, pulling him in for a tighter hug than he expected. Maybe he hadn't imagined her trepidation after all. When she didn't immediately let go, Roska gently rubbed a hand up and down her spine.

"You ok?" he asked quietly into her hair.

She didn't say anything, but shook her head and shrugged. Something was definitely bothering her, but she wasn't ready to talk about it. Roska could respect that. Instead, he changed the subject. "So where are we going, exactly? The Woods are still filled with soldiers."

"Yeah, but New King Niko's running the army now and he told them to back off." Quinn collected his bow and quiver, seeming oblivious to the way Elena had reacted at Niko's name. Roska hadn't missed it though. She was still holding tight to him; he'd felt her flinch against his body.

So, whatever was bothering her had to do with Niko. Roska's hands instantly tensed. Had Niko hurt her? Had he taken something from her that wasn't his? That she hadn't wanted to give?

Roska desperately wanted to sit Elena down and make her tell them everything that had happened, but he knew that wasn't the right tactic. If the situation were reversed, Elena would give him the space to open up when he was ready. He needed to give her the same courtesy.

"You two ready to go? Or are you planning on spending our first morning together hiding out in our suite, hugging awkwardly in the middle of the room?" Q teased.

"Doesn't feel awkward to me," Roska countered, rubbing Elena's back one last time before pulling back a bit to look her in the eye.

When he was certain she wasn't going to break down or cry, he asked, "What do you think? Are we awkward?"

"Psh, no. Q's just jealous that I hugged you first." She tossed a teasing look over her shoulder at him. "Don't worry, Q. You're still my favorite firestarter." Lyra barked indignantly. "Sorry, my favorite *human* firestarter."

Quinn laughed as Elena released Roska and scratched between Lyra's black-tipped ears. They all headed out of the suite, joking and teasing as they made their way from the castle and into the Dark Woods.

The last of the frost season's snow was still clinging to the shadows amongst the pine and fir trees of the Dark Woods. The sound of it crunching beneath their feet brought back memories of the last time the three of them had been leaving Harbor Ridge, stomping through fresh snow. They'd been on the run then, escaping their mother's misguided attempts to keep them safe by locking them away.

Misguided seems a little too kind. She threw us away. Demoni still harbored a great deal of justified resentment toward their mother.

Roska had let go of such anger. He didn't see the point of it. Holding a grudge against their mother wasn't going to help anyone and it would ultimately cause more harm than good. However, he didn't hold Demoni's resentment against her, nor did he try to persuade her to let it go. She was entitled to her opinions of their mother as much as he was.

"What are we looking for?" Elena asked, using her toe to knock some snow away from the base of a pine. "It's a little early in the season for harvesting wild herbs."

"Well, what do I know about plants?" Quinn shrugged and shifted the weight of his quiver. "I just know the deer are out and rutting like crazy right now. And the turkeys are just wandering around, waiting for my arrow to find their heart."

Roska cringed. Q was far too eager to kill things.

"Q, that's gruesome." Elena scrunched her nose, vocalizing her disgust and earning a nod of agreement from Roska.

"Maybe, but if not for hunters like me, you two would be hungry all the time." Entirely unaffected by their judgment, Quinn knelt in the melting snow, studying the tracks in the mud. "These look fresh." He pointed to some long, three-toed impressions. "Lyra and I will follow them and see what we can find. If you two don't want to see the death of some ugly ass bird, then you might wanna stay here." He smirked confidently at them.

Drawing from the power in his chest, Roska flung a handful of snowflakes at his cocky brother, icing over Q's sandy brown hair. Quinn quickly retaliated with a few harmless sparks of his own power, then shook the snow from his hair.

"We'll wander around here and see what sort of wild herbs we can forage while you go cut some poor creature's life short." Roska side-stepped the embers of Q's fire as they fell to the forest floor. The ground was so damp from the melting snow that they had no fear of accidentally starting a forest fire.

Quinn stuck his tongue out at them teasingly. "Let's go, Lyra. Leave these two to their plants." Lyra bound off ahead of Q, following the tracks as they went off in search of a turkey.

Roska and Elena meandered quietly through the woods, keeping within eyesight of each other, but studying the ground for fresh vegetation that they didn't have in the greenhouse. After several long, quiet moments, Roska started intentionally drifting closer to Elena. When he was a couple of paces from her, he looked up at her, trying to read her emotions based purely on her profile.

"You can just ask me," Elena said quietly. She didn't look up from the forest floor as she gently swiped her boot back and forth, searching for any plants hiding beneath the snow. Agon nosed around on the forest floor before her, pushing the snow around and uncovering small shoots of new plant growth.

"I don't want to push if you aren't ready to talk, but you seemed upset back in our suite. Did something happen with Niko after Q dropped you off?" He tried to keep his voice steady and non-judgmental, but his fists were clenched tightly at his sides, frosty air pouring from his skin. He liked Niko, but he wasn't above assaulting the man if he'd harmed their sister in any way.

Elena didn't speak for a while and Roska worried that he'd pushed too much. He shouldn't have brought it up. He should have let her come to him when she was—

"We had a... moment last night." Elena's cheeks were a brilliant shade of scarlet.

"What sort of moment?" He practically growled at her. Roska's fingernails were digging into the palms of his hands, but he couldn't relax. He *needed* to know what happened. Demoni's claws dug into his shoulder where she was perched around his neck. She was feeling the same sudden anger he was. If Niko had harmed their sister...

Elena's eyes flew to his, the flush draining from her face, seeming to realize the potential implications of her words and the direction his mind had run with them. "Oh, Roska, no." She tentatively placed her hands over his frosted fists, coaxing him to relax his grip. "It was nothing like that. We kissed." Her gaze drifted into the middle distance, the pink returned to her cheeks as she pulled her lower lip between her teeth again. "It was entirely consensual. I promise."

Roska forced himself to release the last of the tension in his hands, letting her small hands slip into his. He looked down at her, studying her face, trying to read her mind. "Are you sure? You seemed pretty upset in the suite."

"Yes, I'm very sure." Her eyes focused again, holding his stare to emphasize her words. "We were... interrupted before things got too... oh gods, this is so awkward. Before things got too intimate." She was clearly very uncomfortable with this conversation, but she kept talking, not breaking their eye contact or releasing his hands. "He was called away by the guards. Some issue with the soldiers. He never came back last night and now," she paused, looking away and worrying her lip again. "I'm afraid that he regrets kissing me." The words came out in a rush, as though she thought if she didn't spit them out now, she'd never give them voice.

Roska was stunned. His sister had kissed the Prince.

King.

Mux, that was going to take a while to wrap his mind around. All of this would. He and Q often teased Elena about one day being Queen. It hadn't occurred to him that it might happen sooner rather than later.

"I imagine the only thing he regrets is that you got interrupted." Quinn came stomping up behind them, a turkey carcass dangling by its feet over his shoulder. "What the hells took him so long anyway?"

38

QUINN

T RUTHFULLY, QUINN WAS A little surprised that Niko had picked *last night* to finally act on his painfully obvious feelings for their sister, but he supposed that grief could make people do impulsive things. Things they might otherwise put off for-mux-ing-ever.

"I thought you'd be unhappy with this development." Elena's expression was one of cautious curiosity.

"Why? Because some royal ass violated your face with his face?" Quinn grinned teasingly. "If it were another royal ass, I probably would be, but I actually kinda like Niko. Just don't tell *him* that." He repositioned the dead bird on his shoulder and nodded to their hands. "No luck with the herb harvest?"

Elena stared at him, confusion warring with wonder. Roska sniggered, tugging Elena at their joined hands. "Come on, El. Let's head back inside and continue this conversation with a proper meal." Roska turned to lead them back to the castle while Elena tossed suspicious looks over her shoulder at Q.

You've successfully confused the hells out of her. Nice going. Lyra padded silently beside him, avoiding the partially frozen patches of snow slush beneath the shade of the Dark Woods.

I didn't mean to, Quinn thought with a casual half-shrug, careful not to drop the turkey. *I've only ever wanted her to be happy. I think Niko is a good guy, for a spoiled royal. They'll be good for each other.*

I know that, but you've never shown him anything but contempt.

Quinn wanted to argue, but he knew Lyra was right. He teased the guy mercilessly for weeks. He didn't mean anything by it, not really, but Q could see how it might look from the outside. *I guess I'll have to make an effort to be nicer,* he pondered.

Not too nice though. He's still a royal and his mother is still the absolute worst human on the planet. Lyra hopped over a fallen log and ducked between some low branches. She was having fun running through the Woods. It had been so long since they'd been free to roam the Woods without being hunted.

He might ask her to be his Queen one day. That would make him our brother. I'm not sure I can treat him like Roska, but there's bound to be a middle option.

As long as I can still bite him when he's being an ass. Lyra winked at Quinn through the leaves of a holly bush.

Lyra, he chided, *you can't bite him* now. *You sure as hells aren't gonna be able to bite him if he's mated to Elena.*

Lyra ignored him, snapped her teeth, and hopped away to chase Agon through the brush.

Shuffling through the forest in companionable silence, the triplets took their time heading back to the school and the oppressive weight of their responsibilities. Lyra, who had managed to get to the edge of the Woods while the rest were still firmly in the shadows of the massive trees, suddenly froze, twitching her ears tensely.

Quinn whispered harshly for his siblings to stop moving as he lowered the bird carcass to the ground.

"What's going—" Elena started, but Q held up a hand, silencing her immediately.

Lyra's surefooted steps brought her silently back to him, her gaze fixed on something he couldn't see hidden deeper in the Woods.

Tension filled their hunting group as lightning crackled quietly in Elena's hands, icy mist poured from Roska's, and flames filled Q's palms.

We're being followed.

Can you tell by what? Q asked quickly. He couldn't see a damn thing in the shadows of the massive trees.

I can't be sure, but I think it might be wolves.

Wolves? This close to the school? What the hells? Wolves usually avoid populated areas. Why would they be hunting us? There's much easier prey out there. Turkey, for example. Quinn nudged the bird at his feet. He'd happily toss it to the wolves if it meant avoiding a fight with the predators.

I don't understand it either, but I can see nearly a dozen and they're working to encircle us.

None of this made any sense. Wolves didn't hunt humans, and they sure as shyt didn't hunt this close to a long-standing human settlement. They would have known this area was inhabited by humans and naturally avoided it.

What the hells was going on?

"Wolves." Q's voice was barely above a whisper, just loud enough to ensure his siblings would hear him. "We can't outrun them. We'll have to fight."

"Fight wolves?" Elena hit a painfully high octave. "You can't be serious. Why would they be hunting us?"

"I don't know, but they are and we won't be able to make it to the school before they attack."

Roska's icy mist took shape in his palms, transforming into two long, sharp ice weapons. Elena, still having a hard time accepting the truth of their situation, took a tentative step back toward the school.

As she moved, the wolves stepped into view. Lyra quickly positioned herself between the wolves and the triplets, fire blazing on her tail.

Don't do anything stupid, Lyra. Quinn knew she'd protect their siblings, regardless of the risk to herself. It was a quality he shared, but one that could easily get them both killed in this situation.

Her growl was low and barely audible, quickly drowned out by the snarls and growls of the charcoal gray wolves that circled around them. Quinn turned, keeping his back to his siblings and facing off with the three wolves closest to him. He could hear Elena and Roska following his lead, backing up against him, elements in their hands, prepared to fight off these unusually aggressive beasts.

They stood like that for what felt like ages. No one moved as the wolves seemed to freeze, savoring their trapped prey and seemingly superior position. Q couldn't take it anymore. He lashed out, unleashing a fireball aimed directly at the head of the wolf before him. His aim was true—unsurprising since the creatures were only twenty paces ahead of him. What was surprising was that none of the other wolves seemed bothered by their packmate's fiery death. If anything, they seemed energized by it. Reacting as though they'd been released from some invisible hold, the rest of the pack attacked.

Quinn let loose another fireball as the wolf to his right lunged for him. The fire missed the wolf's head, but scorched the creature's side, filling the air with the sounds and scents of sizzling meat. The wolf howled in agony as it attempted to continue its attack. Lyra jumped to Quinn's aid, snapping her viciously sharp teeth around the throat of the wounded wolf, pulling it away before it could reach him. A third wolf bounded into the air, tackling Q to the ground with its massive claws digging into his chest.

He cried out in pain, brashly grabbing the wolf's head and burning through the creature's skull. The animal collapsed on top of him, over a hundred pounds of dead weight trapping him on the forest floor.

To his left, Elena was fighting off two wolves. Q couldn't tell if she was holding back for some idiotic reason, or if her powers were still too weak. He managed to pull his arm free, shouted a warning to her, and blasted the closest of her two attackers with a fiery blast, reducing the creature to a flaming pile of flesh. She turned her full attention to the remaining wolf, panting as she fired a crackling bolt of lightning into the beast's chest. It collapsed on the ground, dead. Elena fell to her knees, gasping for breath as Agon took up a defensive position behind her.

Roska was to Q's right, backed up to a thick fir tree, two wolves before him and a third struggling to relieve itself of Demoni, who was coiled tightly around the wolf's throat. Roska shot bolts of ice at the wolves every time they attempted to close the distance between them. He didn't want to kill the animals, Q realized. Roska had never killed a creature in his life. Even when the soldiers had attacked, Roska had avoided any kill shots. While Q admired his brother's restraint, now *really* wasn't the time.

"Ros! You have to kill them. They will *eat* you if you don't!" Quinn struggled to move out from under the dead wolf, trying to position himself so that he could help Roska. He could barely see his brother beyond the wolf's body, but it was clear that Roska was grappling with the decision to end a life.

Lyra yelped and Quinn felt a sudden pain in his spine. Twisting, he could see that the wolf she'd been fighting had managed to throw her into a tree. She wasn't moving. The wolf stalked after her, likely intending to finish her off, but Elena was on her feet, blasting multiple small bolts of lightning at the beast until it fell to the ground, the stench of burning hair in the air. Agon bound across the forest floor, reaching Lyra in a moment. He nudged her face, trying to wake her. When she didn't move, Agon's gaze flicked to Q's for a moment, a warning to brace himself. Then the little electric weasel placed his nose to Lyra's and sent a small but powerful shock through her body. Quinn felt the lightning course through his own body, from the tip of his nose down to his toes and back again. It was horrible and invigorating. The power swept through him and he used the energy of it to throw the corpse from his chest into a tree a dozen paces away.

Turning on his heels, Quinn poised a fireball to blast one of the wolves who'd pinned Roska to the tree, only to find his brother standing over both beasts, bloody ice swords in his hands, tears streaming down his face.

Elena cried out in rage as she fired two final bolts of lightning into the wolf that Demoni was slowly choking out. The last wolf collapsed to the ground, smoke rising from its fur.

The silence that filled the forest sounded wrong after such a chaotic and violent scene. Panting heavily, Quinn recalled his flames and rushed to Roska's side.

"Are you hurt?" His gaze quickly assessed his brother's body, but the only blood was that of the wolves on his ice swords.

Elena stepped cautiously toward Roska, placing a gentle hand on his shoulder. "Roska, it's ok. You're safe. You didn't have a choice. They were going to kill you. You did exactly what you needed to do to stay alive."

Quinn couldn't help but think that those were the exact words he'd said to her after those bastards had attacked her in the inn. At what point was the world going to stop trying to tear them down?

Roska nodded slowly, dropping the bloody ice swords as Demoni climbed up the back of his clothes to settle on his shoulder.

"You didn't do anything wrong." Quinn positioned himself between Roska and the bloody scene, carefully placing his hands on his brother and turning him away from the sight of the wolves. "We need to get back. It's not safe out here."

Q let Elena guide Roska away from the gruesome remains of the wolves as he quickly scooped up the turkey carcass once more. No point in letting the bird go to waste simply because they'd had a more eventful expedition than they'd planned.

Eventful? Is that what we're calling this? Lyra didn't seem to appreciate his interpretation of events.

What would you like to call it?

I would call it a muxing shyt show. It seemed targeted. Like those wolves were hunting us. How could that even be possible?

Quinn didn't know how, but he couldn't disagree with her either. Those wolves had seemed very interested in them. Unnaturally interested.

We'll talk to Belladonna and Beatrice. Quinn didn't know if there could be some magical explanation for the wolves' uncharacteristic behavior, but if it was possible, he knew one of those women would know about it. Maybe the Brothers had some tool that allowed them to control wolves for some reason? It seemed outlandish, even as he thought it, but there was no *natural* reason for the wolves to have behaved that way.

Q exhaled a sigh of relief as they exited the Woods and returned to the safety of Harbor Ridge. Looking up at the ominous, imposing black Wall surrounding the school, Q couldn't imagine ever seeing it and thinking "home," but he also didn't feel the same sense of dread that he'd felt when they'd first arrived here with Aiden. The sharp juts of the towers at the cardinal points of the school were still violent and aggressive-looking, but Quinn didn't find them as unwelcoming now. Granted, they were by no means "welcoming" with their demonic gargoyles lining the rooftops, and vicious spikes along the peaks of each tower. At best, the school reminded him of a pissed off mother bear, defending her cubs from a violent world. Which, he supposed, was exactly the point of the school. To teach young, vulnerable enchantresses to wield their powers and defend themselves and others. He certainly wouldn't describe the view of the imposing, near-sinister castle as homey.

Quinn would *never* admit that the midnight black stone walls brought him a sense of calm and serenity that was almost as comforting as the thick wool blankets Amelia had knitted for him. The ones he'd bundled up with as a child, hiding under their warmth on stormy nights when his terror-stricken memories got the better of him.

Nope. He'd never admit that to *anyone*.

The school was a temporary safe house while they figured out what to do about the Queen and her alliance with the magic-hating Brotherhood.

After they dropped the turkey off in the kitchens and Elena spoke to the cooks about having a private dinner, featuring Q's kill, in the boys' suite, the triplets headed off to find their mother. They needed to figure out what insights—if any—she or Belladonna had regarding the wolf attack and see if they'd come up with a plan for dealing with the Queen.

They found Beatrice—Quinn still wasn't comfortable calling her "mom" or "mother" as his siblings did—in her office with Belladonna, Aiden, and New King Niko.

Niko jumped to his feet when they entered the room, making quick work of the distance between his chair and Elena. Q watched as Niko reached out for Elena, but then seemed to think better of it and dropped his hands before quickly apologizing for not returning to their room. He didn't offer any sort of explanation, but Q assumed it was just because they were in a small space and Niko knew everyone was listening and watching their exchange. Elena gave him a small smile that seemed to say, "I hear you, but we're not ok and we have shyt to discuss when we're alone."

Or maybe that was just Q's interpretation of the subtle hostility in his sister's eyes.

"Oh good! Maybe you three can make your vindictive mother see reason," Aiden exhaled, throwing his hands up dramatically in defeat. He clearly missed the interaction between El and Niko. Or he was trying to distract everyone from it. Quinn couldn't decide if their father was the cleverest person in the room, or the most oblivious.

"What do you mean?" Roska asked curiously.

"Your mother wants to take a more... aggressive stance with Queen Rosalina," Belladonna explained in her most diplomatic voice. Quinn had never pictured the witch as a peacekeeper, but clearly, she'd been thrust into the role of mediator by their headstrong parents. Based on the tension in her jaw and the vines wrapping tightly around the locks of her vibrant hair, Belladonna was incredibly uncomfortable in the position.

"She wants to attack," Aiden practically shouted. "Like a show of force would convince the Queen to back down and accept that the magical community as a whole isn't a threat." The irony in his statement was emphasized by the sparks that flared off his fingertips, singeing the rug beneath their feet.

"Aiden," Niko said in a calm tone rivaling Belladonna's. "I think you're misunderstanding Beatrice's intention." He turned to face the siblings, settling his gaze—unsurprisingly—on Elena. "Your mother isn't suggesting an attack on Riverayn. She wants to go after the Brotherhood."

Roska's hands instantly filled with razor-sharp shards of ice, his normally calm eyes glowing teal with rage. The temperature in the room dropped rapidly and Quinn felt compelled to call his own power to the surface just to counteract his brother's icy fury.

"Ros." Quinn stepped into his brother's eye line, mimicking Belladonna and Niko's calming tones. Roska didn't look up, his gaze unfocused as he stared off into the distance, trapped in some muxing nightmare of a memory most likely. Quinn tried again, reeling in the flames from his hands and placing them carefully on his brother's shoulders. "Hey, bro. I need you to take a few deep breaths and rein in that ice of yours. I can see my breath in here."

Roska seemed to register his words after a few moments. Blinking rapidly, he recalled his power. The light faded from his eyes as the temperature in the room began to rise again.

"Sorry," Roska muttered quietly. He rubbed his hands together and wandered over to stand in front of the fireplace.

Niko looked from Elena to Quinn, eyebrow raised questioningly. Quinn shook his head and motioned for the New King to continue.

"Aye, so your mum wants to attack the bastards who have been manipulating my mum into doing their dirty work."

"Manipulating?" Quinn scoffed incredulously. "You think they've been playing puppet master this whole time? That she didn't have any control of her actions or some shyt?"

"Q," Elena admonished.

"No, he's fine," Niko interjected. A fleeting moment of something passed between them, in which Quinn was certain the New King wanted to reach for Elena, but instead, he turned his gaze to Q. "I don't know if they'd been calling all the shots, but I know my mother isn't this diabolical. She's never been *this* good at long-term planning or strategy."

"What are you talking about?" Quinn asked.

"Did something happen? Is that why you were called away last night?" Elena glanced nervously between Niko and their mother.

"Aye, Firefly. Apparently, my mum installed a sort of fail-safe. If her commander wasn't able to breach the walls with the army, he was ordered to release a bioweapon of sorts on the school's food supplies."

Elena gasped at this revelation. "How could he do that?"

"Seems the Brotherhood abhors magic unless they can use it to their benefit." Niko scrubbed a hand roughly through his curls.

"Oh, yes." Roska chimed in, still staring blindly into the flames. "The Brotherhood has no problem using magic as a weapon to meet their ends."

Quinn could see the tension in his brother's shoulders. Cool mist poured from his clenched fists. The Brotherhood had spent sixteen solar cycles convincing Roska that his sole purpose in life was to destroy magic in order to "save the world."

"It seems the recently demoted commander unleashed some sort of magical plague on our crops and food stores." Beatrice's voice was tight with barely contained emotion. Quinn guessed it was anger.

"Oh, gods, no." Elena's breath caught in her throat.

"What does that mean?" Q's thoughts were a jumble. The wolves quickly forgotten as their mother explained that three-quarters of their food stores had been ruined in the magical blight, molded and turned to rubbish overnight. "Do we have any other stores, or supplies to keep everyone fed until the harvest season?" They'd only just started planting new seeds for the new cycle. It would be several moons before they had fresh food again.

Beatrice nodded. "We can hunt for meat, but produce will be a bit harder to replace. We can't exactly conjure new food from nothing."

Aiden raised his hand, indicating he wanted to speak. Clearly, he'd been spending too much time in a school environment. It was rubbing off on him. "Actually, I might be able to."

Elena spoke before their mother could vocalize whatever snide remark was waiting on the tip of her tongue. "Enough to feed everyone all season?"

"Not on my own, but if Belladonna and Roska are willing to help, I think we could work some magic," he winked at his own bad pun, "and conjure enough fresh food and thriving plants in the greenhouse to survive until the harvest. I'm not saying we can create a feast for the gods or anything, but it would be enough to keep everyone alive and healthy."

"Why didn't you mention this before?" Beatrice snapped, clearly irritated that a solution had been staring them in the face and refusing to speak up.

"Well, darling, you haven't really been all that interested in what I have to say these days." Aiden smiled brashly.

Beatrice's glare could have melted iron as she fixed her gaze on the back of Aiden's head.

"Then you, Roska, and Bella will take care of the food supplies." She turned away from their father, focusing her attention on Niko and her children. "Anyway, we need to decide how we're going to proceed. Do we go after the Queen? Or head straight to the source of all this and cut the heads off those bigoted, magic-hating snakes?"

Oddly, the Headmistress, the demi-god, and the centuries-old witch seemed to be waiting expectantly for the triplets to make the decision.

"What... what do you want from us?" Elena seemed to pick up on the same odd vibe from their parents.

Belladonna looked nervously from Beatrice to Aiden and back again. "Well, um..." she began awkwardly, but their mother cut her off.

"Your *father*," the word seemed to leave an acidic taste in her mouth, "informed us that you three have to lead the way. This is all a part of your prophecy; you three are the ones driving this ship."

"You can't be serious." The words fell from Q's lips before he had a chance to think them. This was stupid. Absolutely muxing *stupid*. They were kids. Well, technically Elena was an adult by enchantress standards, but they'd only been on this damned planet for sixteen solar cycles. Prophecy or no, they shouldn't be the ones deciding how to save the world from anyone.

"Honestly, Firefly, I'd rather have you three helping make this decision than those three." Niko tossed an irritated nod in the direction of their parents. Belladonna gave the New King a look of annoyance, Beatrice turned her fiery ire on him, and Aiden grunted disapprovingly. "At least you three will think this through and come to an agreement. Your parents have been bickering all morning. Hells, I bet they couldn't even agree on the color of the sky."

Quinn felt the weight of the world settle on his shoulders, yet again. He could see the heaviness of their options as it rested on Elena and Roska as well. They'd finally had an easy, peaceful morning—minus the wolf attack, which Q was trying to convince himself was just a fluke. And now they were being saddled with the weight of more world-altering decisions. All because of some damned prophecy.

Mux prophecy. Mux everything.

39

BEATRICE

MUX THAT MUXING DEMI-GOD. Why the hells would he keep a solution like that to himself? And then he had the gall to tell them that the triplets had to be the ones to make these impossible decisions? They were *children* for the Mother's sake. They weren't equipped to handle these sorts of world-altering choices.

Don't lie to yourself. Denial isn't helpful. Those three haven't been "children" in ages, possibly ever. They've been through too much shyt for you to discount them like that. Zied's intrusive—and annoyingly truthful—thoughts were not what she wanted to hear at that moment. *I'm not supposed to tell you what you want to hear. If you want that, go find a lackey.*

Beatrice ignored him, focusing her attention on her children instead.

"We have something else we need to discuss with you." Elena's serious tone and sudden proclamation raised the hairs on the back of Beatrice's neck. "We were attacked in the woods."

Ice flowed through her veins and Beatrice took a moment to regain her composure. Belladonna, Mother bless her, seemed to pick up on Beatrice's sudden mood shift and stepped closer, twining their fingers. Beatrice forced herself to take a slow deep breath. As she did, she assessed her children. They were dirtier than she'd expected, but she knew they had planned to venture into the Woods that morning, so muck was bound to happen. But now that she was studying them, she realized that Elena's hair was more chaotic than usual, strands sticking out at odd angles, and her knees were covered in mud. Roska looked pale, although that wasn't abnormal for him, but was that blood on his sleeves? Quinn's tunic, beneath his worn vest, was covered in what appeared to be large dog prints with what looked like claw marks on his chest.

"Attacked by my soldiers?" Niko stepped toward Elena, placing his hands on her shoulders while he inspected her for injuries.

"No." She covered his hands with hers. "Wolves." Beatrice thought she heard her daughter mutter something to the young King, but she couldn't tell what was said.

"Wolves? How far into the Woods did you venture? The packs don't come close to the school." Belladonna looked confused. "They say the smell of magic burns their sensitive noses. They avoid this place at all costs."

Beatrice had wondered about that before. She'd never once heard mention of her enchantresses having encounters with the local predators. Finding out that they thought she and her magical kin stank was mildly offensive. Still, if it kept the vicious creatures at bay, she wouldn't complain.

Although clearly, it hadn't kept them at bay this time.

Quinn quickly ran through the events of their encounter with the wolves. When he finished speaking, he looked from Beatrice to Belladonna expectantly.

"I've never heard of anything like that happening before." Belladonna stared out the window. "Castor found the bodies. He says it smells like magic, but he's having trouble determining if it's simply the magic you all used, or something else."

"*He* can smell magic too?" Q raised a curious eyebrow.

"Only when he's in the form of a wolf or fox. He doesn't like those shapes though. Too restrictive, he says."

Lyra scoffed, clearly miffed at the implication that her form was somehow less than, but didn't say anymore.

"I'll send Aleerah to join him. Maybe they can uncover what caused these wolves to act so unusually. Hunting and attacking humans so close to a human settlement... It's odd, to say the least." Aiden stroked his well-trimmed beard thoughtfully.

"I wonder if the Brotherhood had an agent nearby with some sort of talisman or spell to control the wolves," Beatrice offered.

"That's what I was thinking too," Quinn said. The rare moment of agreement between the two of them didn't go unnoticed. "But how did they even know we were out there?"

"They must have more spies in the Woods." Niko glared out the eastern window, toward where his soldiers were camped. "I'll speak with Jamieson again. Enforce the need to root out and remove all the Brotherhood's influence in our military." His eyes flicked back to Elena, concern for her clear on his face.

"What can we do?" Quinn asked, gesturing to himself and his siblings.

"We will look into the wolf attack. *You* need to focus on deciding our next steps in this fight with the Queen and Brotherhood. Are we going straight to the source?" Beatrice pressed. "Or are we taking care of that vile Queen first?"

Niko flinched at her words but didn't say anything.

"You can't seriously expect *us* to make this decision." Quinn's voice held a sharp edge. He looked ready to snap and Beatrice couldn't blame him for it. It was too much to ask of them, and yet it had to be their choice.

"I'm sorry, son," Aiden spoke up, genuine regret filling his voice. "It has to be up to you three."

Beatrice really hated that man and his endless, vague prophetic insights. Just once, she would like to get a straight answer out of him.

Her children deserved that, at least.

40

ELENA

"**I** NEED SOME AIR," Quinn mumbled as he turned and walked out the door.

Elena glanced to Roska, who offered her a curt nod and they both followed Q into the hall. She could hear Niko saying something to their parents as she strode briskly after Q. She couldn't understand his words, but she was more focused on catching up to Quinn than whatever Niko might be saying to the "adults" to placate them. They'd made it very clear that they weren't going to be of any use in this predicament.

Rein it in there, Sparky, Agon whispered in her mind.

Sparing a quick peek at her hands, Elena saw the sparks he'd been referring to. Bouncing off her fingertips, leaving tiny scars on the stone beneath their feet. She tried to calm herself down, taking dramatic deep breaths, but they needed to catch up to Q and she wasn't really worried about causing serious damage to the stones.

"Q," Roska called out as Quinn turned the corner well ahead of them.

"Please slow down," Elena panted.

233

Quinn seemed to hear the exhaustion—more like weakness—in her voice and slowed to a walk, allowing them to meet him at the bottom of the stairs that led to the royal suites.

"I don't get it. Why the mux would they do this to us, *again*?" Quinn huffed, flames dancing in his eyes.

"I don't know," Roska sighed. Leaning up against the stone wall, he brushed white blonde hair from his face and closed his eyes, looking up as though attempting to commune with the Mother Herself.

"Aiden must have seen something. It's the only thing that makes sense, although why the prophecy would insist on *us* dealing with this massive—potentially world-changing—issue, I have no idea." Elena leaned against the wall opposite Roska, casually glancing up and down the hall, attempting to look inconspicuously for a chair. Her body was still so damned weak and useless. Between their walk in the Woods, fighting off a pack of deranged wolves, and then climbing all those stairs to their mother's office, she was completely drained. She was, however, also incredibly stubborn and didn't want her brothers to see just how exhausted she truly was.

Footsteps echoed down the hall, moving quickly toward them. Elena groaned internally. Mother probably sent her guards to fetch them and bring them back. She hadn't dismissed them. She wouldn't have approved of their abrupt departure. Not that Elena much cared what bothered their mother these days.

Niko burst around the corner in an explosion of dark curls and the fresh scent of leather, wood smoke, and a hint of whisky. "Oh good! I found you. I thought I might have to chase you three all the way back to your suite."

Elena's face broke into a smile before she could stop it. Running her tongue softly over her lips, she could almost feel the tingles his kisses had left in their wake the night before.

"What the hells do you want, *Your Majesty*?" Quinn snapped, fire flaring in his eyes and casting a faint orange glow in the hall.

Niko tore his gaze from Elena's and nearly flinched at Q's harsh tone. "Hold on there, Q. I'm not the problem here. I'm trying to stop all of this before it goes any farther."

Roska stepped forward, placing himself between Niko and Q, forcing Quinn to break his rage-filled stare. Elena attempted to do the same, but the second she stepped away from the wall, she nearly collapsed. The weight of her body was just too much for her legs to carry for another moment. Much to her chagrin—and de-light—Niko's lightning-quick reflexes meant he caught her instant-ly, saving her from further injury. His strong arms wrapped tightly around her, capturing her in the warmth of his embrace. For several long seconds, Elena completely forgot about her brothers. Instead, she got lost in Niko. The feel of his muscular form all around her. The heady scent of him making her lightheaded.

Is it possible to get drunk on a person? she wondered idly.

I don't know, Agon chimed in, *but it is possible to thoroughly embarrass an entire hallway of creatures.*

Elena's face burned with the implications of his words, tearing her gaze from Niko to see that her brothers and their familiars were awkwardly trying to look anywhere but at her.

"Um, maybe we should get El to a chair before we continue this conversation," Roska suggested, still avoiding eye contact with her as Niko helped her stand again.

"Aye, that's a brilliant idea." He moved to pick her up, but Elena glared at him, raising one finger with lightning dancing across the tip.

"If you attempt to carry me, I will shock you, and I won't feel a single ounce of pity as you crumple to the ground, Your Highness."

"Right, well then," Niko tossed a furtive look to Roska and Quinn. "Would one of you gentlemen be so kind as to escort your delightful—and rather terrifying—sister to your rooms?"

Both Roska and Quinn had the decency to keep their chuckles *mostly* to themselves as they each moved to one of her sides, wrapped an arm around her, and carried her back to their suite.

They made it back to her brothers' suite just in time for lunch. Elena asked the guards to have the kitchen send for food as they entered the room. The boys got her settled on the couch while Lyra knocked a couple of fresh logs onto the smoldering embers in the fireplace, but didn't light them. It wasn't quite cold enough for a fire yet.

"Comfortable?" Niko tease in mock condescension as Roska brought her a pillow and situated it behind her back.

"Why, yes, I am." She beamed up at her brothers. "Thank you both. I truly appreciate your care and kindness."

Laying it on a bit thick, aren't you? Agon teased as he nosed a blanket into the perfect nest at her feet.

Ignoring him, she turned back to Niko. "So, what are our options?"

Niko grinned, taking an empty seat to her left. "That's what I like about you, Firefly. No nonsense. Straight to business."

Quinn and Roska said nothing as they settled into the remaining armchairs. Elena stared pointedly at Niko expectantly until he continued.

"Well, according to your father, the choice has to be yours. The three of you. Attacking my mother is an option, although as I've stated, it's not my favorite choice and it doesn't actually solve the bigger problem: The Brotherhood. I agree that my mother needs to be stopped and punished for her crimes." He clenched his jaw so tightly that for a moment, Elena was worried he might crack a tooth. She wanted to reach out to him, offer him whatever support she could, but Elena held back. She wasn't sure her support would be welcomed. Her family was the reason he was now at odds with his mother.

"Can we go directly after The Brotherhood and be successful?" Now, it seemed, it was Roska's turn to have hair-trigger powers. His eyes emitted a soft teal glow as he flexed his frost-covered fingers.

"It's possible," Niko began slowly, "but I'm not confident in that route either."

"Then what do you suggest, King Niko?"

Elena was a bit surprised by the hostility in Q's tone. He'd been kind to Niko lately, and even in the Woods, he'd been happy to hear that things had progressed between her and Niko. Why was he lashing out at Niko now?

Niko seemed unbothered by Q's antagonistic mood. "I think the safest option we have right now is to stay put and force my mother to come to us. This school is the most well-fortified castle I've ever been in. No one will be able to break in here without considerable magic, and everyone with that level of power is already here, fighting to keep this place and its inhabitants protected." His logic was sound, but Elena was still a little surprised to hear him say it.

Do you think he's pushing to stay here because you're still a bit weak? Agon didn't move his body, not wanting to call attention to his query, but Elena felt his gaze on her.

Gods, I hope not. That would be stupid. He can't make decisions about his kingdom based on me and my well-being. But even as she thought it, a small flame of hope lit in her heart. Maybe he was coming up with a reason to stay with her. She clearly wasn't in a position to travel or battle a hate-filled, murderous Queen.

"How do you propose we draw her out? I doubt she'd be likely to accept an invitation to parlay at Harbor Ridge." Roska didn't look up from his hands, but Elena noted that the ice had faded from his skin.

"Actually, that's exactly what I was thinking." Niko flashed her his most winning smile, that same arrogant smile he'd given her when he had suggested she simply walk out of prison. And damn him if it hadn't worked out exactly as he had planned.

Elena was starting to think that things always worked out according to plan for the former Princeling.

Gods, no wonder he's so damn cocky.

41
ROSKA

"So, we do nothing?" Roska asked incredulously. The New King had to be out of his mind if he expected them to just sit on their hands.

"No, not nothing," Niko replied coolly. "I will send a messenger from my army with a formal invitation for Mum to join us here. It will be an opportunity to discuss what she actually plans to accomplish. Think of it as a preemptive peace talk."

He sounded so self-assured, Roska wanted to believe him. But he knew the Brothers would never stand for peace. As far as they were concerned, peace could only be had once all the magical beings had been wiped from the planet. While Queen Rosalina might be amenable to some sort of agreement, The Brotherhood would never be. It was a waste of time.

"And you really think that will work?" Elena sounded so hopeful. Roska hated to disabuse her of her optimism, but even if this did work to solve things with the Queen, it was only a stopgap solution, not a cure to the real problem.

"I think it could." Niko turned to give Roska his full attention. "I know you have a history with The Brotherhood, and I have no doubt that you have the best insight into handling things with them. I imagine you think this plan for my mum is a waste of time, and you might be right. But I have to try. If we can get her on our side, it will make taking out the Brothers that much easier. Without her, they don't have an army or any real strength, right?"

"That's correct," Roska agreed. "The Brothers don't have weapons in their compound, outside of the kitchen knives and the garden tools." That didn't mean that they'd be easy to defeat though.

"Then I have to try this way." Niko was nearly pleading with Roska for his approval. It was surreal. Why would the New King need Roska's permission for anything?

He's not looking for your permission, Demoni interjected. *He wants your support. He's hoping you'll understand where he's coming from and give him the benefit of the doubt.*

I don't have any doubts about his motives or intentions. Roska looked away from Niko, staring off into the embers of the banked fire. *My concerns are with the time we'll be wasting, sitting around trying to reason with a close-minded bigot.*

I know that, but it's his mother. He can't see her the way we do. I think we should let him try things his way. Who knows? It might even work.

I doubt it. Roska hated being the glass-half-empty one in their group, but he was a realist. He knew how The Brotherhood operated. They'd let the Queen be the face of their war, but they were always pulling the strings, on stage and behind the curtain. For all they knew, The Brotherhood had three or four more plans in the works to annihilate magic after the *turmio* failed.

"What do you think?" Roska asked Q, who had been uncharacteristically quiet for a while.

"I think it's your call, bro. You know those bastards better than anyone. I'll follow your lead." Quinn looked passive, but Roska could see a hint of orange flame in the back of his eyes.

Roska's gaze shifted to Elena, but she didn't speak. She was letting him decide as well, unbiased by her input. This was his choice.

Well, mux him. They trusted his judgment so much that they were leaving this entire choice up to him.

Roska quickly brushed the wetness from his cheeks as it leaked from his eyes. "I guess we'll try it your way, Niko. If it doesn't work, at least we can say we *tried* to find a peaceful solution first."

42

BELLADONNA

BELLADONNA WOKE UP FEELING as though her flesh was on fire, melting from her bones as she writhed in agony.

Her cries of pain roused Beatrice violently from sleep.

The sky, which should have been black out their bedroom window, was glowing in vibrant oranges and reds.

"Bella!" Beatrice's voice was strained but Belladonna could barely focus as another wave of blazing heat washed through her. She couldn't even cry out anymore. Her throat was raw, like she'd been forced to swallow gallons of lava fresh from a volcano.

"Bella, please, talk to me."

Belladonna caught a glimpse of Bea's panicked face as her vision faded to black.

43

BEATRICE

"Guards!" Beatrice didn't attempt to keep the frantic tone from her voice. Belladonna was dying. Decorum be damned.

The guards rushed in instantly, spells at the ready, prepared to defend their headmistress from whatever had managed to sneak into her room.

"Fetch the healers. Now!" To their credit, the guards weren't fazed by her roared command. One stayed with them while the other tore off down the hall, her hawk familiar flying out the window, presumably to reach the infirmary quickly and warn the healers of their urgent need.

Beatrice shifted herself in their bed, pulling Belladonna's head onto her lap. The witch's skin was painfully hot. Beatrice could feel the heat burning through Bella and scorching her own thighs, but she refused to let Belladonna suffer alone. Calling on all the magics and spells she could think of, Beatrice did everything in her power to cool her beloved.

"Please." Her words barely a whisper through her emotion-clogged throat. "Please. You can't leave me. I've only just gotten you back."

Castor soared through the open window, shifting quickly into his man form and rushing to their bedside. "The forest is burning!"

Beatrice distantly wondered how the entire forest could burn. Maybe Castor was exaggerating. But the glow from their window confirmed that there must have been a massive fire nearby.

Roska rushed into the room. "I heard the guards racing to put out the fire and I thought, based on how Belladonna reacted to the soldiers cutting up her vines, I might be useful here." He paused awkwardly at the foot of their bed. Beatrice briefly wondered if he was second-guessing his decision to come here. Before she could speak, Castor waved Roska over.

"Yes, she needs you. Pour as much ice and frost into her as you possibly can. She's burning up from the inside. I can feel it. If we can't lower her temperature, she will die. Then I'll die."

Roska joined them, sitting carefully on the edge of the bed, and placed his frosted hands on either side of Belladonna's face. Beatrice kept muttering under her breath, casting her spells as her son worked to cool the mind of the woman she loved.

Demoni, seeming to appear out of nowhere, stretched herself along the length of Bella's sternum, resting her teal head on Belladonna's décolletage. With each exhale, the little frost dragon blew snowflakes onto Bella's scalding flesh.

The snowflakes melted instantly and quickly evaporated.

Healers dashed into the room and—having already been briefed on the situation by the guards and their fowl familiars—began preparing herbs to lower fevers, spells to draw the heat out of Belladonna's body, and decoctions to rehydrate her as her body burned through the water in her system.

Beatrice couldn't break from her spells to speak to anyone, for fear that even a single moment's pause in her casting might mean the death of her love. Instead, she closed her eyes, pressing her lips to Belladonna's searing brow, and prayed to the Mother that they would be able to save her.

44

QUINN

Q HAD WOKEN CONFUSED and disoriented. It had only been a couple of hours since he'd crawled into bed. It should have still been dark and near silent outside. Instead, there was a cacophony of yelling, racing booted footsteps, and something that sounded suspiciously like a wildfire reverberating throughout their suite.

Lyra jumped from his bed to the window, propping her feet up to see outside. "The forest is burning." She sounded just as confused as he felt, but they both bolted for the bedroom door. Quinn shoved his feet into his boots, hauled the suite door open, and was out in the courtyard in minutes.

The guards were fervently organizing themselves into a fire brigade. The tidal enchantresses were running out of the open gate as Quinn reached the Wall.

"How can I help?" he asked the first high-ranking guard he could find.

"Can you stop the flames?" She didn't look at him as she spoke, directing different groups of the brigade to try and quell the largest clusters of fire before they could spread.

"I don't think so..." Quinn had never tried *stopping* other fires before. He could control the flames he made without issue. Hells, last week he put on a muxing fire dance show for the class, shaping his flames into humanoids and having them put on a highly entertaining pageant. "I have an idea." Without waiting for the enchantress's permission, Quinn sprinted passed the fire brigade and into the heart of the fire.

What the hells are you doing? Lyra shouted in his mind, clearly not approving of his plan, but he had to try something. If they didn't stop this fire quickly, it would take over the whole castle and burn them all before the sun could rise.

Quinn stopped in the middle of the flames, raising his arms and calling his power, only this time, instead of pulling the fire from within, he demanded the fire around him bend to his will.

It was a strange sort of sensation. Whenever Q called on his fire, it felt familiar, comforting. It was a part of him and it recognized him as the ultimate authority. These wild flames didn't want to bow to him quite so easily.

Sweat beaded on his brow as he fought the flames for dominance. He could feel the heat of the fire licking his legs, but he refused to let it take hold of him. He was FlameBorn. Fire was his to command. Be it his own flames, or those created by nature. Q would take command of these flames. They were not permitted to rage any further and it was his job to contain them.

Lyra, sensing the internal struggle Q was fighting with the flames, began racing around him, spreading her own flames. At first, Quinn wanted to tell her to stop—although it was taking all of his mental energy to combat the wild fire—but he quickly realized that her flames were fighting *with* him. They were his loyal soldiers as he battled the wild fire.

As soon as the thought had left his mind, Q noticed Lyra's fire taking shape. The fire creatures started out small—little bodies with nothing more than single flames for arms and legs—but as they spread out from him, they absorbed the wild fire, growing with each step. In minutes, the fire around him was a fleet of flaming soldiers.

Lowering his arms, Quinn stared in awe at the magic he and Lyra had created.

Well, don't just stand there, Lyra snapped. *Let's finish this.*

Quinn sent a mental command to the fire soldiers. In an instant, they began to spread out, an ever-growing circle of flaming creatures, absorbing the wild fire with each step. Q panted at the effort of fighting for control and beamed at what they'd accomplished.

Slowly, they reclaimed the forest. With each step, his soldiers enveloped more of the wild fire, growing as they went until they were towering over the remaining trees. As they made their way farther into the forest, Quinn could see the damage wrought by the wild fire. The scorched trees were going to have a hells of a time recovering. He hoped Belladonna would be able to aid in their regrowth, once she healed herself.

The fire had spread suspiciously quickly, considering that much of the forest floor had still been supporting snow just yesterday.

I think this fire was the Brotherhood's handiwork, he thought to Lyra as they followed the fire soldiers out of the Woods.

No shyt, Lyra replied harshly.

How do you think they did it? Now that they had the fire under control, Q had a lot of burning questions.

Puns? Really? This seems like a punny time to you? Lyra clearly didn't appreciate his humor.

Why don't you run ahead and get Roska? Tell him we're gonna need a big snow hill to put these guys out in.

Without another word, his firefox bounded off.

Quinn directed the fire soldiers as they fought the wild fire into submission. By the time they were finished, the flaming creatures were taller than the Wall and Q was fairly certain he'd given several enchantresses heart attacks.

He stepped out of the charred Woods to find his flaming soldiers lined up calmly along the Wall, the tidal enchantresses standing at arms, prepared to fight the humanoid fire, and his students staring up at them in awe.

Quinn raised his hands, addressing the enchantresses. "Don't worry. These are mine. They won't hurt you."

At that, all eyes fell to him. Q had never felt more uncomfortable in his life.

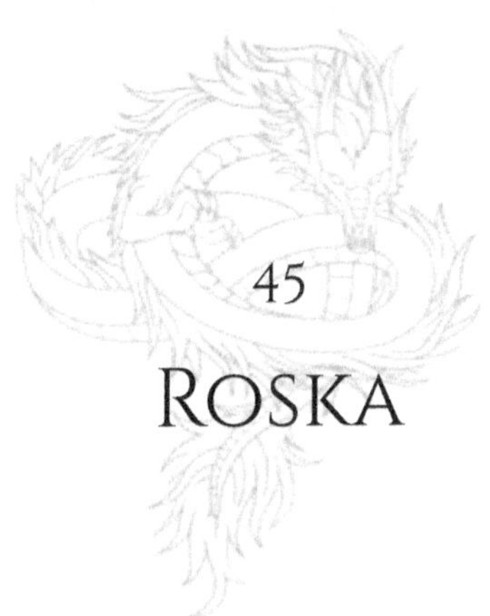

45

ROSKA

"WHAT THE HELLS...?" Roska swore under his breath, taking in the enormity of the flaming creatures before him.

"Um, hey, Ros. Wanna help me out with these guys?" Quinn looked a bit sheepish as he stepped toward Roska.

"What do you mean? How can I possibly help you with an army of flaming giants?" Roska was baffled by—and a little jealous of—the magical beings his brother had created.

"I was hoping you could make a few massive snow drifts or even some glaciers for these guys to put themselves out in. I don't think I can absorb all that fire without causing some serious damage to myself."

Roska thought Q was probably right. The amount of heat and power radiating off the fire soldiers was overwhelming, and Roska was still a few dozen paces away. He couldn't imagine how it would feel to have that sort of power tangibly close, much less absorbing it into his body.

"What in the name of the Mother happened?" Elena's exclamation was followed by a low whistle from Niko as they exited the main gate.

"I, uh, I stopped the forest fire?" Quinn didn't seem confident in his answer as he witnessed the matching looks of awe and confusion on his siblings' faces. "It seemed like a good idea at the time." He trailed off, shifting his eyes from their faces to the charred earth at his feet.

"Quinn," Elena exhaled his name, taking cautious steps toward the closest fire soldier.

"I didn't know what to do. I just wanted the fire to stop so I went into the Woods and tried to control it. When that didn't work, Lyra used her fire to make a barrier around me, then it kinda just... morphed into these little guys. Then they grew and grew, taking over the wild fire until we had these." Quinn's explanation of events was rushed. Like he thought he was in trouble and needed to explain his side of things quickly before someone decided he was the problem and punished him for it.

"Q, this is amazing!" Niko clapped Quinn on the back a little too enthusiastically, causing Q to stumble forward a step.

"Seriously, Quinn. I can't even imagine the amount of strength and mental control it would have taken to make these guys. You're incredible." Elena didn't take her eyes off the soldiers as she complimented their brother's magic.

Quinn's face was a brilliant shade of scarlet, clearly uncomfortable with their open praise and admiration. He side-stepped away from

Niko and turned back to Roska. "Do you think you can help me extinguish them?"

Roska leaned back, craning his head to take in the full height of the fiery creatures. He could probably make a snowdrift big enough for two of them, but there had to be at least a dozen flaming humanoids. "I think we might be better off with a glacier. Can you get them through the gate and over to the river without setting anything on fire? I think it would be easier for me to freeze the river and have them melt it, rather than trying to form a glacier from nothing."

"Won't that hurt the creatures who live in the water?" Concern flashed on Quinn's face.

"No, they should be fine," Elena answered. "The river regularly freezes in the frost season. The animals might be confused, but they'll just move along with the current, or swim farther down. As long as Roska doesn't freeze the *entire* river, the animals should be just fine."

"I won't freeze that much or even that deep. I just don't want these guys boiling the river either." He nodded to Q's creations as they began marching single-file through the gate. They had to duck to make it through the entry, but they fit.

The fire brigade now stood at attention on either side of the path the fire creatures were taking to reach the river. All of the enchantresses stared in open-mouthed awe at Q's fire mastery. The soldiers didn't even mar the stone as they stepped. They left no trace as they crossed the courtyard and reached the water's edge.

Roska jogged up ahead of them and began icing over the top of the river. It was a bit harder than he expected because the current was stronger during this time of the solar cycle, but he was able to freeze a thick layer of the river.

As the first soldier stepped onto Roska's ice, the frozen river hissed in response. Steam rose quickly as the flaming soldier seemed to melt into the ice. In a matter of moments, nothing was left of the creature but the mist that floated above the slush of river ice.

One by one, Quinn directed his soldiers onto the ice, melting the river almost as quickly as Roska could freeze it. The strength required to maintain his ice was draining. Roska couldn't imagine how Quinn handled all these flaming giants without even breaking a sweat. His brother looked completely at ease as he sent one after another to their dousing death.

Sweat dripped down Roska's back, following the path of his spine, as he struggled to keep his ice flowing. Demoni slithered down his body from her perch at his neck, reaching the riverside, and began feeding her power into the water.

Almost instantly, Roska felt as though a weight had been lifted. He took a deep breath and flexed his fingers, pouring more energy into his ice. He didn't understand it, but something about the way they worked together made the magic seem far more agreeable. It was as though the water in the river had been fighting him before, but now that Demoni was working with him, the water recognized their united front and submitted to their demands.

He could hear whispers from the enchantresses all around them as they worked to finish off the last of Q's soldiers, but he was too focused on the task at hand to spare them a second. This was unlike anything the enchantresses had ever seen before. Roska suspected it was something no living being had ever seen. Whatever magic flowed through their veins from their deity parentage, it was unique and baffling to these women who'd spent their whole lives believing men were incapable of any magic.

As the final soldier melted into the ice, Roska and Demoni cut off the flow of their magic, allowing the soldier to melt the remainder of the ice and return the river to its normal—albeit rather flooded—planting season current.

"Professor Quinn! That was muxing kick ass!" A young enchantress came rushing up to Q, flaming hand in the air as though she were trying to light the way.

Q's face flushed again, even brighter than before as he quickly knelt down to meet eyes with the girl. "Minka, you can't talk like that."

Roska was surprised to hear his brother chastise anyone's language. He would have bet everything he owned that the young girl had learned that sort of language *from* Q. Which would explain the very confused look on the girl's face. The flames on her hand faded, but Roska saw the glint of pride in his brother's eyes. Quinn brought his own flaming hand up and slapped it gently into the girl's palm just before her fire went out. The smile that lit up her face couldn't have been described as anything other than jubilant.

"Nice work, bro," Quinn said, rising from his clearly devoted pupil and clapping Roska on the back. "That was really cool," Q added with a dramatic wink.

"Gods, again with the puns? You're insufferable." With that, Lyra sauntered off, flicking embers from her tail as she made her way over to a collection of young girls. The girls were all wearing the black robes that denoted them as students, with bright red embroidery along the hems of their sleeves. Fire starters. Those must have been the other girls in Q's class. Some of the girls reached out to pet Lyra. Roska was impressed when the firefox actually stood still and let the girls run their flaming fingers through her burnt orange fur.

It shouldn't be that surprising, Demoni cut off his thoughts. *She is with him for nearly all of his classes.*

It made sense, he supposed. Roska had just never given it much thought.

"The Headmistress would like to see you." A guard announced. She looked from Quinn to Elena, and finally to Roska. "All of you. Now."

Mux. It sounded like they were in trouble. What could they have possibly done wrong?

46

AIDEN

AIDEN STOOD QUIETLY IN the shadowy corner of Beatrice's bedroom, half-listening as she drilled the kids with question after question, trying to understand what had happened and how Quinn had created those flaming soldiers. She'd never seen anything like it. Never heard of such a thing either.

Aiden had. About three hundred cycles ago, when the gods roamed the earth and demi-gods were more prevalent. Infernals weren't exactly "normal" but they were common enough to be a recognizable symbol of Lugh, God of War and Craftsman. His children were associated with fire, working as blacksmiths and glass craftsmen more often than not.

Seeing those creatures stepping out of the Woods shouldn't have shocked Aiden. It sure as shyt shouldn't have brought tears to his eyes, and yet he'd stood on the Wall, looking out at the flaming soldiers, feeling the cool trail of wetness that slipped from his eyes and down his cheeks. The sight brought on a myriad of emotions: pride, fear, nostalgia, love. Aiden had never expected to see those creatures again. Not since the Gods' War that had left most of his brethren dead on the battlefield.

Aiden himself had never been that adept at fire magics. He'd had plenty of half-siblings to fill that role, though.

They were all dead now.

He hadn't thought about them in ages. Hadn't *let* himself think of them. It was too painful. Unfortunately for Aiden and his avoidance mentality, Q's magic had forced the memories back to the surface.

"And what do you have to say for yourself?"

Aiden blinked, looking up to find all eyes fixed on him. "Sorry, what?"

Beatrice exhaled an annoyed sigh. "I said, what do you have to say for yourself? This is clearly a result of your biological influence."

"Aye, it is." Aiden raised a curious eyebrow. "Are you unhappy with how Quinn handled this? I would think you'd be pleased that he saved Belladonna from boiling to death from the inside."

"Of *course* I'm happy." Beatrice glared at him. "I already told them that, although you obviously weren't listening at all. I am quite proud of Quinn's quick action and the incredible skill it took to control and contain that wild fire. I'm equally proud of Roska for being able to freeze a river. That is no easy feat and they both accomplished these tasks with practiced ease." At this, she turned her glistening eyes to the boys.

Glistening? Gods, was Beatrice *about to cry?*

Don't be an ass. Aleerah snapped at him. *She nearly lost her mate today. It's been hells and she's doing her best to keep her emotions in check.* His dire wolf was out patrolling the Woods, but clearly, she was still eavesdropping through their shared connection.

I wasn't being an ass, Aiden argued. *I just didn't realize Beatrice knew* how *to cry.*

Before Aleerah could chastise him anymore, Aiden spoke. "Yes, those creatures are a result of my parentage. Many of my father's children had the power to raise such beings. The Infernals were a vital part of the Second Sun's War in the Age of Fire."

"The Infernals?" Quinn's eyebrow disappeared into his hairline. "They have a name?"

"Aye, of course they have a name! Everything has a name, my dear boy." Aiden strode to the window, looking out at the charred remains of the trees closest to the Wall. "It looks like your fire is the only thing that could have saved us from the so-called wild fire, too."

"What do you mean?" Elena asked nervously.

"Come see." Aiden took a step away from the window, giving the triplets and young King room to see what he'd just seen.

"What the mux?" Quinn muttered, staring out the open window.

"My damned mother," Niko swore.

Elena stared, confused, at the straight line of scarred and scorched trees that led directly from the army's camp to the Wall surrounding Harbor Ridge. "How...?"

Roska was the only one who seemed unsurprised by this discovery. Aiden suspected his youngest child had already assumed the fire was born of nefarious means. Roska shoved his frost-covered hands roughly into the pockets of his breeches.

"I imagine the Brotherhood enacted another of their fail-safes. Most likely through a third party, but I suppose it's possible that a Brother might be traveling with the soldiers." Aiden speculated that a younger Brother—or even a handful of Brothers—could have easily infiltrated the King's army, especially with the Queen on their side.

Niko took that moment to step out of the room and request the guards send for his new Commander. "I'll get to the bottom of this today. I won't allow these Brothers to wreak havoc on this place any longer. I will put a stop to this right muxing now."

Aiden admired the boy's moxie, but he knew it wouldn't be that simple. Rooting out traitors who blended in so seamlessly would be a hellsish feat under normal circumstances. Aiden suspected that these were far from normal circumstances, what with the young King's mother playing such a large role in the troubles that plagued them. And Elena, the woman he loved, being targeted by his mother. It was a shyt way to meet your soul mate, but Aiden decided it was no better than the way he'd met the mother of his children. Not that she was his soul mate.

No, Aiden had lost his mate many cycles ago.

Belladonna was struggling to sit upright in the bed beside Beatrice as Castor glided in through the opened window. "King Niko," the shifter said. "Your commander has arrived at the gate. The guards are escorting him to the Great Hall as we speak."

Niko seemed to flinch at the title, but offered a quick thanks, squeezed Elena's hand, and slipped out to meet his Commander and begin the needle-in-a-hay-stack style search.

"So... will I be able to do that again?" Quinn cast a furtive look at Aiden as he spoke, refusing to hold his gaze.

"Absolutely," Aiden cheered. "If you practice, I imagine you'll be able to do that and so much more. Hells, I had a brother who was able to quell an entire war with a fleet of Infernals. He avoided senseless death with his massive flaming army. The bloodthirsty rulers were quickly brought to see reason. You could easily be as powerful as he."

Quinn's face lit up at the prospect. Maybe he would finally be willing to give Aiden a chance. Spend some time with him and maybe—just maybe—they could finally bond and get passed the whole abandoning-them-at-conception thing.

Bit optimistic, but I'll agree that this is definitely a step in the right direction. Aleerah chuckled in his mind.

At this point, I'll take whatever I can get.

"I've spoken with Commander Jamieson," Niko announced as he strode purposefully toward their table on the dais in the Great Hall. The young King had moved his meeting with the Commander to a small, empty office closer to the gate so that the Great Hall might be available for lunch. He stopped beside Elena's chair, pausing as though he wanted to show her some sort of special attention in greeting, but thought better of it and took the empty seat to her left.

Aiden couldn't help the smile that slipped across his face as he witnessed the growing relationship between the two of them. He knew a lot of what they would face together, but thanks to the Fae curse, he had no idea when or in what order these events would take place. Elena was a strong woman, though, and he hoped she'd choose the path that led her to become an even stronger Queen. Assuming Niko ever got off his ass and made a move.

I heard a rumor that he did, in fact, make a move. Aleerah's voice echoed in his mind. She was still running the Woods, choosing to stand guard and search for any clues as to who set the fire, rather than being cooped up in the castle all day and night.

Where did you hear that?

A little bird told me. Well, actually he wasn't quite so little, and he was shaped like a hound at the time.

Castor always seemed to have the most interesting tidbits of information.

Aiden turned to view Niko and Elena anew, taking in this insight. It was clear they were fighting the urge to touch one another. Their hands sat so close on the tabletop that one would simply have to shift ever-so-slightly for them to make contact. Aiden wondered idly why they fought so hard to keep from touching. He'd never had that level of restraint with his mate.

They aren't mated yet, Aleerah reminded him.

Niko leaned forward, his shoulder brushing Elena's as he addressed the table, keeping his voice low so as to not be overheard. "Jamieson is putting together a small group of soldiers he grew up with and trusts. They will investigate the fire and hopefully we'll have some answers by morning. I've also told him to put the camp on lockdown. No one is to leave the campgrounds without explicit approval from the Commander himself."

Aiden nodded, impressed by Niko's command of the situation. The boy was barely into his eighteenth cycle and yet he was confidently commanding an entire army and preparing to go to war with his own mother. He was an impressive young man.

"That all sounds great," Roska interjected, "but it won't be enough. We need to go after the source of the problem."

Aiden was shocked by the vehemence in Roska's voice. He'd never heard the FrostBorn speak in anger, much less with the seething rage that laced his words now.

"We will, Ros." Elena placed a comforting hand on Roska's icy one. "But we can't just rush off. We need a plan."

Q presented his hand, revealing a dancing humanoid made of fire, swirling and twirling in his palm. "I've got a plan."

47

BELLADONNA

Q UINN'S PLAN WAS FOOL-HARDY, arrogant, and downright stupid. Which was why Belladonna felt confident that it could actually work. The Queen wouldn't expect it, which meant it had a much better chance than any of the ideas she, Bea, or Aiden had suggested the day before.

Still, it was muxing idiotic.

They finished their meal in the Great Hall, fleshing out the details of Q's plan. After lunch, Beatrice and Belladonna headed to the infirmary. None of the enchantresses had been injured while fighting the wild fire, but many were suffering from exhaustion due to the endless nights on watch, trying to defend against whatever evil schemes the Brotherhood and Queen Rosalina concocted next.

Several women had nearly collapsed over the last two days, and Beatrice had been forced to command them to bedrest, as well as instilling a very strict schedule, requiring all enchantresses to take at least one full day of rest for each three that they were on duty. The guards were especially unhappy with this new schedule, but they finally agreed when one of the guards nearly fell off the Wall while on her fourth straight day of sentry duty.

"You're looking much better, Marsali," Belladonna cooed to the young enchantress who'd been working as a healer in the infirmary since before the witch had come to Harbor Ridge.

"Thank you, Mistress," the girl attempted to offer her a bow, but Belladonna quickly caught her by the shoulders, forcing her to remain upright.

"We talked about this, Marsali. I'm just a witch. Not a mistress. Not a madame. And certainly not worthy of a bow."

"Apologies, ma'am. I'll try to do better." A small grin flashed across Marsali's face. Belladonna knew that grin meant that Marsali had no intention of "doing better" as she claimed. Chances were, the girl would drop into a full curtsey the next time they met.

Belladonna chuckled. "Yes, be sure that you do."

"How are the patients today?" Bea inquired.

"Most are recovering quickly, Headmistress. We have a couple," Marsali nodded indicating a pair of beds in the far corner, "that seem to have an underlying issue delaying their healing, but nothing too serious. Likely the result of malnourishment on top of their exhaustion."

Beatrice studied the two cots. "Damn them. It's Lillith and Seph, isn't it?" Marsali nodded. "I have never met two more stubborn, pigheaded enchantresses in my whole life. I imagine those two have refused breaks and meals in favor of standing guard. Not trusting anyone else to be as vigilant as they believe themselves to be."

Belladonna couldn't contain the guffaw that flew from her lips, echoing in the otherwise peaceful space. "You can't be serious."

Bea turned to face her, eyes wide and clearly scandalized by Belladonna's outburst.

"Oh, come on, Bea. You have to see the irony of *you* calling someone else stubborn and pigheaded."

"I most certainly do not." Beatrice clutched her hand to her collar indignantly. "I'm neither of those things. I just know what's best and I insist that others respect my choices for them."

Belladonna stifled another laugh. "All right, love. You're right. You've never been stubborn a day in your life."

Marsali's face turned bright red as she struggled to maintain her composure. After moons of seeing the two of them bicker like this, Belladonna had a sneaking suspicion that the girl enjoyed hearing Belladonna call Bea out on her bad habits.

Bea, naturally, hated it. Which was what made it so much fun.

Zied wandered through the rows of cots, sniffing heads and offering gentle, affectionate licks on the familiars of the younger enchantresses. Most of the children had recovered quickly after the *turmio* had been banished, but a handful of girls were still struggling to regain their strength. The healers assured them that the girls were recovering, just slower.

"It will take time," one of the healers had promised. "But these young girls were struggling before the *turmio*. Asthma, influenza, and one with some intestinal problems. Their bodies are fighting their preexisting issues, as well as rebuilding their magical reservoir. They should be back to normal by the growing season."

Something is happening in the camp. Castor's words invaded her mind.

Oh, for mux's sake. Couldn't they go one day without a crisis?

48

BEATRICE

STEPPING OUT ONTO THE Wall, Beatrice was overwhelmed by the cacophony of noise that greeted them. Based on the shouting, clashing of metal on metal, and the angry roars of battle, it sounded as though the soldiers were at war with themselves.

Castor cawed a single warning before nearly dropping the young King on top of her and Belladonna. Niko grunted as he landed hard on the stone beside her, but quickly righted himself and explained the situation they were witnessing.

"Jamieson's faction of investigators found a few traitors rather quickly." The King brushed his dark curls from his eyes, glaring out in the direction of Riverayn. "Unfortunately, the existence and accusation of betrayal quickly turned to madness. Soldiers accusing one another of treason, with little to no evidence to support such claims. Insults were hurled back and forth, and now they're fighting amongst themselves like children. With wickedly sharp blades and frayed nerves."

"What the hells are you going to do about it?" Beatrice demanded. He might be new to commanding an army, but Niko had to see that this was entirely unhelpful.

"I was actually hoping you might have a suggestion or two." His request for her advice floored her. The King had never once asked for her insights. She'd help shape his decisions over the cycles, of course, subtly steering him in the right direction. He would never have admitted that he needed or wanted her input. For Niko to come right out and ask for her opinion on how to handle things? It was astonishing.

Well, you do have considerably more experience with this sort of thing than he does. He would be a fool not to ask for your help. Zied nudged her thigh gently with his massive head.

I've never commanded an army before, she argued.

Maybe not, but you've been leading this school and its hundreds of occupants for decades. You know how to handle difficult situations and even more difficult personality types.

Belladonna caught her eye and offered a nearly imperceptible nod. She might not have known what Zied was saying, but Bella knew that Beatrice was the right person to help guide young King Niko.

"First thing's first, you need to stop the fighting before it gets any worse." She didn't wait for his response. Beatrice strode atop the Wall, getting as close to the soldiers' encampment as she could, then cast a freezing spell on them. In seconds, the soldiers were turned into statues. Still very much alive and healthy, but unable to move. Then she turned to Niko. "With your permission, I would like to spell your voice again so you might address your troops."

Beatrice could see the broad grin that split across Belladonna's face. She'd asked for Niko's permission before casting a spell on him. Weeks ago, Beatrice wouldn't have bothered to get his consent first, she would have just done what was necessary. All those debates about autonomy and consent with Belladonna were clearly leaving an impression.

Niko gave her a brisk nod and Beatrice spelled his voice once again.

"Soldiers, this is unacceptable. In-fighting and turning on each other is not going to accomplish anything but needless bloodshed. Commander Jamieson has been tasked with rooting out traitors, this is true. Our strong and enviable military has been infiltrated by bigoted zealots that want to weaponize us to fight their battles for them. We cannot allow them to do that! If you truly believe that someone you know has been turned against our beloved Waverly, then you must report your suspicions to Commander Jamieson. You will *not* take action without expressed orders from the Commander or myself. Anyone caught attempting to mete out justice on their own, will be court marshaled immediately. Am I understood?"

Beatrice removed her spell from the soldiers. Many stumbled to regain their balance as they had been frozen mid-stride, but they all quickly turned to face their king, standing at attention. As one, they saluted the King, and an echoing shout of agreement sounded throughout the camp.

"Return to your duties." Niko nodded to the soldiers. "Commander, I expect an update at dusk."

"Yes, Your Majesty." Jamieson's voice sounded small and pitiful compared to Niko's spelled command.

The King turned back to Beatrice and motioned to his throat. Undoing the spell, she smiled at the young man. "That was well done, Your Majesty."

Beatrice couldn't be certain, but she thought she saw a hint of a blush creep over the King's face.

49

QUINN

QUINN WAS BUSY SHOVING the last of his clothes in his pack when a knock sounded on their suite door.

Roska looked up from the book he'd borrowed from the school's library, eyebrow raised in question. "Are you expecting someone?"

Q shook his head, put down his bag, and walked over to open the door. He reached for the knob, but it opened on its own. Niko strode purposefully past him.

"Please, come in," Quinn muttered sarcastically, closing the door behind the New King.

"Sorry, but this couldn't wait." Niko looked flustered. Agitated. Quinn had never seen the man look anything but cool and confident. The drastic change in his manner was jarring.

"What's going on?" Roska sat up straighter on the couch.

"We can't take Elena to Riverayn."

"Come again?" There was an edge in Q's words that he hadn't intended but couldn't ignore. Niko couldn't really expect them to leave Elena behind. *Again*. They'd spent far too much time separated from her over the last several moons. Niko couldn't be serious.

"I know I'm asking a lot, but I also know she's not ready for the fight you're heading into. If she goes, she'll end up over-exerting herself, and I don't know what happens when an enchantress uses too much power, but I know it can't be good. She won't admit it, but she's still incredibly weak. Hells, she immediately went to sleep after I practically carried her back to our suite. She didn't even wake when I left out the damn window with Castor." Niko was pacing, running his hands anxiously through his hair. His normally perfectly styled curls were sticking up at odd angles. He looked deranged.

Out the window?

"Why are you going out windows?" Quinn couldn't imagine why anyone would go through an open window with the shifter.

"There was an issue with the soldiers and Castor offered to fly me out there. It was... a lot," Niko admitted.

"Is everything ok?" Roska asked, seemingly unfazed by the idea of the King catching a ride with the moonbird.

"Aye, I think it will be. But we need to address this issue with your sister."

"She seemed fine at lunch," Roska commented.

"Of course she did." Niko's jaw tensed. "She's putting all of her effort into being the strong, reliable person you all expect her to be."

Quinn flinched at Niko's words. He couldn't be right, could he? Elena wouldn't be putting up a front with them, just to keep them all happy. Would she?

You already know she would. That girl spent all of her life learning how to hide her true emotions, pretending to be something she's not.

Lyra's observation was blunt, but not as painful as the truth she spoke.

Q roughed his hand over the scruff that had been growing on his face.

If he admitted that he might actually agree with Niko—that Elena really was a lot weaker than she wanted them to see—then that meant he would have to accept that leaving her behind while they went to address the Queen might be the best thing for her. He'd have to *choose* to leave her. Q hadn't willingly made that choice since he'd set her up to live and work at Amelia's. Gods, that felt like ages ago. Things were so different and so much simpler back then.

Granted, glancing at Roska, Q knew he'd never wish to go back to how things were before. Still, he wished that things could finally be calm. Easy.

Life isn't easy, Lyra chided. *If it was, it wouldn't be any fun.* She gave him a sly wink from the chaise lounge she'd claimed as her afternoon nap space.

Another valid point.

Quinn looked at Roska. His brother seemed to be coming to the same realization. A subtle nod signified that they were in agreement.

"How do you propose we tell her?" Roska left the question up for either of them to answer.

Quinn chewed on his lower lip, trying to come up with the best way to explain to Elena that she wasn't fit for the battle they were facing and needed to stay put a while longer. It wasn't going to be easy. She would fight them tooth and nail and probably still try to sneak onboard their ships.

They could try convincing her that this was the best option. That she could join them once she'd fully recovered. She was a reasonable person. She'd see the undeniable truth. She wasn't ready for this confrontation. Not yet.

You have a lot of faith in her rationality, Lyra observed. *Or maybe this is just wishful thinking.*

It was definitely wishful thinking, but Q didn't know what else they could do.

"Leave now. While she's asleep. I'll stay here with her. The army will go where I go and stay where I stay. If I travel, even by ship, they'll know." Niko looked cautiously at the brothers.

"What do you mean "they'll know"? Sounds ominous and I'm really at my capacity for shyt news here." Quinn clenched his fists, trying to keep himself calm, and moved to sit beside Lyra on the chaise.

"Blood magic," Niko replied with a casual shrug. Those two words seemed to be his answer for everything and it was *really* muxing annoying.

"Yeah, gonna need more than that," he ground out between clenched teeth.

"It's one of the fancy new perks that comes with being King. My soldiers can sense my presence. It's not as creepy as it sounds," he added, seeing the look of disgust mirrored on Q and Roska's faces. "I just mean that they can tell when I'm nearby. They wouldn't be able to use it like your locator spells, but it works well enough that they are more aware of their surroundings when they can sense that I'm close."

"That's what the look was about." Roska studied the King.

"What look?" Quinn asked, thoroughly confused.

"The look," Roska explained. "The Commander looked like he was hiding something when he was here. Like he wanted to say more, about how they knew the King was supposed to be here."

"You saw that, huh? Aye, the soldiers felt that the King was suddenly nearby and jumped to the wrong conclusion." Niko admitted.

"Gods, you royals are the worst." Quinn sighed, rubbing his hands over his face.

"No, we're not." Niko looked thoroughly offended.

"Come on, man. Your soldiers can *feel* when you're close so that they'll be on their best behavior? It's like you're encouraging them to be muxing stalkers."

"It's not like that." It was Niko's turn to exhale a sound of annoyance. "I'm not making them stalkers. The gods know I would happily remove this magic if I could."

"We're getting off-topic," Roska interjected. "How do you propose we confront your mother without you? You're the New King, are you not? You are the supreme authority in this country. You could just tell her to stop and she'd have to obey."

Niko sat down hard on the couch beside Roska. "You'd think so, but I doubt it. My mother still sees me as a child and she won't bow to my authority. Not to mention, if Aiden's conclusion is right, my mum is the one who killed my father. She's lost any semblance of self-control or rational thinking."

Quinn huffed in agreement. The Queen was definitely insane if she thought killing her husband was how she would win him back.

Don't forget her plans of mass murder and magical genocide, Lyra added.

No, of course not. Can't forget those flawless and perfectly rational plans. Quinn absentmindedly reached over, scratching Lyra between her ears. "You think we're gonna kill your mom?"

"I hope not, but if it comes to that, it will be a lot easier for you to take her down if my army is as far away from the capital as possible."

It wasn't a terrible plan. It wasn't a good one by any stretch of the imagination, but at least it would guarantee that Elena stayed safe. And with Niko and his army here to protect her, the Queen wouldn't be able to get her hands on Elena again. Although Q doubted she'd try that a second time.

The Brotherhood would still be a problem, but they could address that after they got the Queen and her rogue soldiers under control.

"Ideally, you won't have to hurt her. A show of force will *hopefully* be enough to get her to back down. Then you can put her in one of the blood magic prisons until Elena and I arrive." Niko stretched his arms over his head, causing a series of loud pops to escape his joints.

"Why would the blood magic prisons hold her? She's still the Queen. I thought the blood magic was tied to the royals." Baffled, Roska looked at the New King.

"Aye, it's tied to royal blood, but through my father's side. My mum married into royalty. The blood magic only worked for her while she was pregnant. Once I left her body, my royal blood left with me and she was back to needing my father to manage all the blood magic items in and around Riverayn." Niko grimaced. "She often complained to me about it. Feeling as though the castle never really accepted her as its Queen."

Q could understand that. He still didn't like the woman, and he'd be more than happy to be the one who threw her in one of those fancy prison cells, but he could relate to always feeling like an outsider.

They sat in silence for several minutes, each man stewing in his own thoughts about royalty, feelings of being outsiders, and concerns for Elena.

Niko sat up, placing his elbows on his knees as he looked first at Roska then Q. "So, you'll do it? Leave soon, while she's still asleep?"

"You don't mind dealing with the fallout?" Quinn asked, surprised that the New King would willingly place himself in the way of Elena's electric wrath.

"If it means she'll remain safe, I'll do anything." The strength in his voice made Quinn believe that Niko meant every word. The New King would put himself between Elena and any danger. It was an interesting observation, but not one Q had time to delve into. Especially if they were meant to be gone before she awoke.

"All right, then we'd better get packed and head out." Quinn stood up from the chaise and turned to Lyra. "Run ahead and tell the *adults*," he said, the last word dripping with irony, "about the change in plans. Tell them we'll meet them at the docks in thirty minutes."

With a quick nod, Lyra hopped off the chaise, pawed the door open, and disappeared in search of Beatrice, Belladonna, and Aiden.

Niko rose and offered Q his hand in gratitude. "Thank you. I wasn't sure how this would go and I truly appreciate your trust. I won't let anything happen to her. We will join you at Riverayn as soon as she's fit to travel."

Quinn firmly grasped the New King's hand, allowing some of the heat from his power to seep into his palm. Niko's eyebrows shot up as the warmth quickly grew from soothing to mild discomfort, pushing into painful. Quinn held fast as Niko tried to extract his hand. When the New King's eyes flew to Q's, he said, "If anything happens to her, *anything*, it won't be your hand I scorch. Those royal jewels of yours will be a melted sack of useless flesh when I'm done. Am I clear?"

For a split second, Q thought he saw a flash of begrudging admiration—or possibly amusement—pass over the New King's face before he nodded. "Crystal."

Q released his grasp, strode into his bedroom, grabbed his pack, and said over his shoulder to Roska. "I'll meet you by the boats. Gonna let the guards know the new plan. See you out there."

He spared Niko one last—mildly threatening—passing glance, and then he was out the door.

50

ELENA

NIKO WAS BEING INSUFFERABLE. Again.

"You can't keep me from going with my brothers to stop your insane mother!" Elena couldn't help but yell. She'd spent ages—at least that's what it felt like—trapped in that gods-forsaken hells. She would not be trapped here, now, by this arrogant prince. King. Whatever.

"Then you'll have to walk, because I'm not taking you." Niko stood at the stern of the longship, arms crossed stubbornly over his chest.

"Fine, then I'll drive the damn ship myself," Elena huffed, pushing past him to reach the steering oar.

"Ha! Good luck, Firefly." Niko stepped aside with a flourish of his hands, inviting her to try for herself.

Angrily, Elena grabbed hold of the steering oar and tried to direct the ship. Nothing happened. She pulled, twisted, and silently pleaded with the gods to make the damn ship work. Nothing.

"How's it going, Firefly?"

Mux everything. Mux that damned man and his muxing blood magic. Mux her father and his cryptic prophecies. Mux her mother. Mux her brothers. Mux everyone.

Elena collapsed in a heap on the deck beside the steering oar. Angry tears filled her eyes.

How could they have left her behind?

Niko knelt before her, concern etched on his face. He placed a gentle hand on her knee, squeezing lightly. "They didn't want to leave you," he said quietly. "You haven't fully recovered yet. We don't know how long it will take for you to regain your full strength, and the wild fire was proof that my mother isn't going to stop. They had to go stop her. Quinn made me swear that I wouldn't let you run headlong into a fight until you were fully recovered. He threatened... some very important body parts, and I'd rather like to carry on my family lineage one day." Niko offered her a small grin and a wink.

Elena sighed. She felt so useless. Defeated. All those moons in The Nothing had drained her of so much life. It had taken all of her energy to race out of the school and climb into the royal longship. She didn't want to admit it, but they had been right to keep her from the fight. She was utterly exhausted and she hadn't even left the harbor.

Niko lifted his hand from her knee and offered it to her, helping her stand and lean against the side of his ship.

"I feel so useless," Elena admitted finally.

"I know that feeling well, Firefly. I spent moons watching your family try to bring you home. I couldn't do anything to help. I was useless and it was the worst thing I've ever felt in my life." He still held her hand. Twining his fingers between hers, he held on tightly. Elena got the feeling that he would hold on to her forever if she let him. And she was starting to believe she wanted that too.

"I'm sor-" she started, but he quickly—albeit gently—placed his free hand over her mouth.

"Don't you dare apologize. Firefly, you are amazing. Powerful, brilliant, and impossibly stubborn. It's why I lo—like you so much. But I swear to the Mother, if you apologize for saving the world, I will throw you over the side of this ship and make you swim back to the harbor." Niko's eyes pinned her in a hard stare before he slowly removed his hand from her lips.

Elena smiled but didn't say anything else.

Instead, she turned to face the river, watching the fleet as the enchantresses prepared for war, loading their ships with supplies and weapons as quickly as possible. Once prepared, each ship set off to join her family in their journey to Riverayn to stop the Queen's endless aggression and finally bring peace back to Waverly.

Elena held on to Niko's hand, refusing to acknowledge the warmth that spread from their contact all the way to her heart.

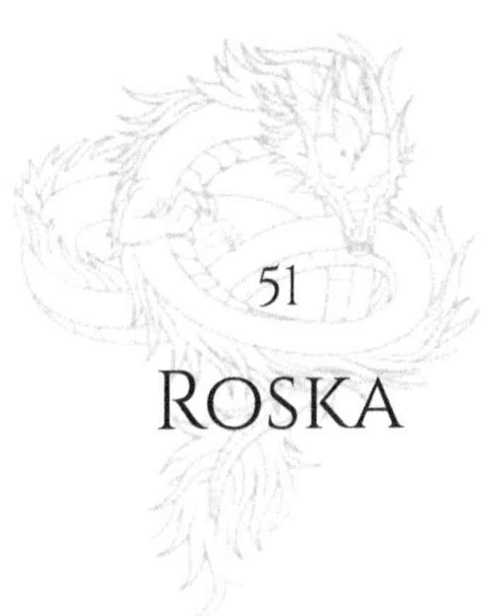

51

ROSKA

W AR. THEY WERE GOING to war with the Queen.

Roska hoped that Q's show of force would be enough to avoid any bloodshed, but he wasn't optimistic. The Queen had already shown herself to be quick to violence and indifferent about inflicting needless pain.

Ever since he'd learned that Queen Rosalina was the one who'd turned him over to the Brotherhood, Roska had been harboring a growing rage against the heartless woman.

Castor had let it slip one night when they'd been working in the greenhouse after yet another failed day of research when they were still trying to bring Elena home. Their mother had been friends with the Queen, back when she was just an enchantress and Rosalina was the daughter of a lord. When Mother had given birth, she'd sent the boys away. Roska had been sent to live with Rosalina, the new Queen of Waverly. Mother had trusted the woman to care for and raise him as though he were her own. Unfortunately, and unbeknownst to their mother, Rosalina hated all things magic, including infants. She passed him off to the Brotherhood, who spent the next sixteen cycles abusing him and training him to bring about the *turmio* and the end of all magic.

She let her hate fill her and guide her to selfish choices. Demoni shifted on his neck. *We can't let that same hate fill us and ruin our future.*

What future? We have nothing before us but misery and murder. Roska leaned over the rail of the longship, resting his forearms on the sunbaked wood. Flicking his fingers in annoyance, he rained sparkling snowflakes into the rushing river current.

Nothing? What about Brigit? Demoni slid from his neck, down his sleeve to sit curled between his arms. She held his gaze, giving him her most incredulous stare.

What about her? She's likely forgotten us already. And even if she hasn't, she doesn't know who we really are. She deserves better than a rejected, broken, son of a half-mad demi-god and an arrogant enchantress. Roska moved to walk away, but Demoni spat ice over his hands, freezing him in place at the railing.

She may not know the whole *truth of our parentage, but she was interested in you. She cared for you. When this shyt is over, we are going to find her. Even if it means I have to enlist Q and Elena to force your hand.* Her tone and her icy glare broke no argument.

Roska was about to argue when Q waltzed over, clapping a cocky hand on his back. "What's going on here?" He gestured to Roska's frozen hands. "Having trouble controlling your powers?" Q looked genuinely concerned.

"No," Roska said, wrenching his hands free of the ice. "Just a bit of a disagreement, that's all." He shook the last of the ice from his sleeves. He could still feel Demoni's glare on his face, but he chose to ignore her instead. "How are things going? Did the captain have any idea how long it will take us to arrive at Riverayn?"

Quinn looked curiously between Roska and Demoni for a second, like he considered asking a few probing questions. Thankfully, he thought better of it and said, "Cap says it should take about three days. The current is strong and pushing us along much faster than they'd originally anticipated. Plus, the tidal enchantresses have promised to take shifts and make sure we get there as quickly as possible without causing any damage to the river banks or marine life."

Roska spun around, leaning casually against the ship's railing, watching the women as they moved about the ship adjusting sails, organizing supplies, and generally operating as though this was a normal day for them. Roska wondered if it was. He'd been surprised when Mother had suggested taking Harbor Ridge's fleet of ships. He would never have suspected that the school even *had* ships. Roska had assumed that all of their travel was on foot or horseback. It was ignorant, really. The entire western side of the school was bordered by the river. Of course they had ships. They had a harbor, didn't they?

Still, it had been a shock when the seismitists had combined their powers to unearth the hidden warships. According to Mother, the ships hadn't seen much use in an age, but they were still well maintained.

The warships weren't that different from Niko's longship. Slightly wider, to accommodate approximately fifty enchantresses. The hull was thicker and heavier, with higher railings to allow for cover if they were attacked from either side. Instead of benches lining the rails, like on Niko's ship, the decks of the warships were left mostly bare. There was seating below decks, as well as sleeping quarters filled with a couple dozen hammocks. The intent was for half of the crew to be sleeping while the other half managed the ship. There was a small kitchen, as well as the captain's quarters. Quinn and Roska would be bunking with the rest of the crew. The captain of their ship, a severe older tidal enchantress named Kate—or One-Eyed Kate, when she was out of earshot—had made it very clear that there would be no "funny business," as she called it. Not that Q or Roska had any intention of misbehaving on a ship filled with war-ready enchantresses.

Quinn watched the crew with rapt attention. He was clearly enjoying this experience.

Roska, on the other hand, was starting to feel quite nauseated. He'd been mildly seasick on Niko's longship, but not unbearably so. He had hoped it was a one-time occurrence, but obviously, that was not the case.

"Hey, Ros." Quinn placed a steady hand gently onto Roska's shoulder. "You doin' ok? You look a little green."

Roska tried to answer, but when he went to speak the only thing that came out of his mouth was his lunch.

The sway of the hammock only intensified his nausea. Roska was in hells. There was no other explanation for the immeasurable misery that consumed him.

He spent the majority of the next three days drifting in and out of consciousness, drinking broth that Q practically force-fed him, and praying for the end. Either the end of the journey or the end of his life. He no longer cared.

Demoni draped herself across his brow, working to keep him cool and combat the clamminess that coated his skin. Lyra seemed to be keeping close as well. Roska had faint memories of her laying beneath his hammock, her tail flaming, presumably to ensure that he and Demoni didn't lose too much heat.

It was literal hells.

Roska would never look fondly on his time with the Brothers, but while he was fighting to keep his intestines from revolting, he would have happily been laying back on the cold, packed earthen floor of their cellar.

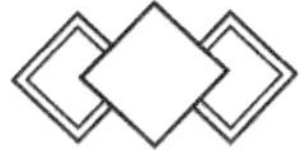

"Hey, Ros." Quinn's voice floated through Roska's mind, smoothly and calmly, entirely unlike the actual ship that was slowly killing him.

Roska squinted against the morning light as it filtered through the small, circular windows.

"Hey, bro." Quinn placed a gentle hand on Roska's shoulder. "We're approaching Riverayn. The captain says it should be smoother and slower now, as they navigate the marina, and then we'll be on solid land. Just a bit longer." Quinn glanced out the window, frowning at something. "An hour tops."

"What's wrong?" Roska's throat was raw, his voice sounding more like a croak than actual words.

"Nothing," Quinn said, a little too quickly. "You just rest. I'll come get you once we're docked." He patted Roska lightly, careful not to jostle him.

Roska thought he saw a meaningful look exchanged between Lyra and Q before his brother turned on his heel and quickly left the cabin.

"What's going on?" Demoni asked.

"Nothing to worry about." Her words projected calm, but the irritated flick of Lyra's tail betrayed her true feelings.

"Liar," Roska muttered.

Lyra glared at him, seeming to debate how much she should say. After several long moments, she sighed grumpily and confessed. "It looks like the army outside Harbor Ridge wasn't the *entire* military force, as Niko had assumed. There are about a hundred guards waiting for us at the harbor."

52

BELLADONNA

BELLADONNA HADN'T HAD MUCH experience with the royals of Waverly during the century she'd spent living in the Dark Woods. She'd heard stories about them, but they didn't know of her existence and she'd been intentional in keeping it that way. It hadn't really been a conscious decision at first. In the beginning, she'd been running for her life, then literally falling into Beatrice, then building their cottage in the Dark Woods.

However, after Beatrice had left, Belladonna had grown more reclusive, isolating herself in the heart of the Woods and rarely leaving the clearing. Castor had kept her abreast of the goings on in Waverly and even traded some of their wares in smaller hamlets around the Woods. He was quite the adept gossip, which made him uniquely qualified to serve as her eyes and ears.

I'm not a gossip! Why do people keep accusing me of such nonsense? Castor ruffled his feathers from his perch on the Crow's Nest. He was either immune to irony or thriving on it as he flapped his midnight-black wings in the air.

What would you call it then? When someone eavesdrops, shares secrets that aren't their own, and is generally a busybody? Belladonna gathered her vibrant green locks over her shoulder, picking out the wilting leaves that marred her otherwise flawless, otherworldly aesthetic.

I'm simply a very friendly creature. I like to know things and share that insight with parties that might appreciate it. Castor cawed out in annoyance. *If you don't want to hear my information, then I'll stop telling you. But of all the creatures on this planet, you have benefitted most from my "gossip."*

Belladonna chuckled, looking up at her familiar. *Castor, my darling, you know* I *appreciate all of your insights. I'm not sure everyone does, though. Perhaps it's time we discuss those things called "boundaries" again?*

If he were physically able to roll his eyes in his moonbird form, Belladonna was certain he would have. *Boundaries are for strangers and people who have no tact. I am neither of those.*

Well, sweet Castor, despite your best efforts, you don't actually know every being in the world. There are still some *strangers in the world, yet. As for tact, I'm not even sure you know what that word means.*

Castor spread his wings, allowing the wind to lift him from the rail of the Crow's Nest. He glided down, making slow, lazy circles down to her as though he hadn't a care in the world. Just as he was about to land beside her, he shifted into his human form.

"I know exactly what it means." His long, thin fingers pulled a wilting flower from the crown of her hair. "It was because of my tact that I informed Roska of Beatrice's ties to Rosalina and the Brotherhood. You and Bea were content to avoid that topic forever. I, quite *tactfully*, explained the history there."

"Yes, you were so tactful and sensitive that you blurted it out in the middle of the greenhouse. It took me two days to revive all of the plants that were lost under his snow when he exploded from your *judicious* insights."

"Well, if you two hadn't been so hells-bent on sidestepping the issue—" Castor never finished his argument. They were both promptly silenced by the view that greeted them as their ship rounded the bend.

On the riverside and all along the harbor, dozens of soldiers waited, weapons at the ready. Belladonna blinked rapidly, trying to comprehend the sight before her.

Niko had assured them that the majority of the royal army was camped out in the Dark Woods, awaiting his orders. He was clearly mistaken. Either that, or the Queen had recruited quite a few new members since the army had left.

Without a word, Castor leapt into the air, shifting back into the moonbird, and flew off to get a closer look.

Belladonna gripped the ship's railing, closing her eyes and opening herself further to the connection she shared with her familiar.

Beside her, Belladonna felt the warmth of another's presence.

"What can you see?" Bea whispered in her ear. Keeping her voice as low as possible so as to not alarm the enchantresses on their ship.

"These aren't normal royal soldiers. They have the same emblem that Lyra saw on those soldiers in the woods. The ones who likely captured the King."

"Mux. Rosalina. What the hells is she trying to do? She has to know she can't beat us in a fight. Not like this." Beatrice exhaled roughly. "What the hells is she planning?"

53

QUINN

Castor's warning caw sent Quinn racing up the stairs and onto the deck.

"It looks like the Queen has expanded her guard," the shifter said as he transformed into a tall, imposing—and unsettlingly thin—man.

"No shyt." Quinn reached the prow of the ship, studying the rows of armed men and women lining the shore and standing guard on the docks. "How the hells are we supposed to have any sort of peace talks with that damned woman if this is how she greets us? We won't even make it on land with all of those antagonistic soldiers in the way."

Castor eyed him curiously. "Antagonistic?" He raised a single eyebrow.

"What? I can't learn new words?" Q looked away as a blush warmed his cheeks. He'd been spending more time in the library of Harbor Ridge. He hadn't told anyone, but he'd been hoping to learn more about their heritage and his powers by reading history books about their grandfather.

"Oh, sure. Professor." Castor smirked.

"Shut it." Quinn grimaced. He would never hear the end of this. "Let's stay on point, please. What the hells are we supposed to do now?"

Castor stared at the ship ahead of them, the ship their mother and Belladonna were on. They'd chosen to spread out rather than all ride on one warship. Belladonna and Beatrice took the lead ship. Q and Roska were in one of the middle ships, and Aiden was riding with Aleerah on the last ship.

"Your mother wants to know if you can build your Infernals from here or if you need to be on land to manifest them."

"What?" Quinn's eyes flashed frantically from Castor to the soldiers along the water's edge, then to their mother's ship, and back to the shifter. "She can't be serious, right? We were gambling that I'd be able to make them again on purpose in the first place! It's not like I've had a lot of practice creating massive, flaming giants."

"This was your idea," Castor reminded him coolly.

Quinn threw his hands up in exasperation. "I know it was my idea, but I never claimed it was a *good* idea. And now she wants me to do it from the middle of the damned *river*?" He'd mostly been hoping that showing up at the capital with a fleet of warships and a couple hundred enchantresses would be enough to make the Queen rethink her alliance with the Brotherhood. Q wasn't sure he'd be able to recreate those Infernal things on purpose. He'd been under a hells of a lot of stress last time. Not to mention, he'd been standing in the middle of an inferno and his little fire guys had grown so big because they'd absorbed *that* fire. He didn't actually make them that big. There's no way in hells he'd be able to—

"He can do it." Lyra spoke with such confidence, she shattered his internal spiral.

"The hells I can." Quinn gaped at her. She'd lost her damned mind.

You don't have to create a massive army like before. Just one or two to show off. You've always been good at showing off.

Quinn glared at her for a moment. "Fine," he grunted through his teeth. "I'll try, but I can't promise this will work."

"Give me a couple of minutes to let Aiden know what's going on. If you need help, send up a flare." With a cocky wink, the shifter transformed back into a moonbird and took off toward the last ship in their fleet.

Quinn stood at the railing, gripping tight to the worn wood of the warship. What would happen if he failed? They didn't really have a backup plan. They hadn't been planning on encountering an army in the first place.

You can do this. Lyra's calm voice soothed some of the edges of his ragged nerves.

How can you be so sure? He looked down at her where she sat beside him, flicking her smoking tail back and forth anxiously.

Because we thrive under pressure. All of our most impressive magical feats have come in the middle of a shyt show. It's what we do. Lyra shrugged her fox shoulders at him.

Quinn sighed, releasing the tension that was causing his shoulders to bunch nearly to his ears. They could do this. Because they were fighting to protect the ones they loved. Because they were strong.

Because they were the most powerful fire creatures on the planet. Because he was FlameBorn. He was born for this shyt.

Quinn glared irritatedly at the small flaming figure dancing in his palms. No matter how hard he tried, he couldn't make the creature grow any bigger than a sapling, and the minute he turned from it to create another, the first one would wither and die.

"I can't muxing do this," he muttered under his breath.

"Sure you can," Castor cheered, overly optimistically. "You already have. You just have to do it again."

"Oh, sure. Like it's that simple, huh? Snap my fingers and make a whole army of flaming giants appear?" Quinn flicked the flaming dancer at the shifter. "If it were really that easy, I would have done it ages ago. It wouldn't have taken a wild muxing forest fire to motivate me."

"Maybe that's the difference," Roska proposed. He'd managed to climb out onto the deck when the warship had stopped moving. They'd anchored themselves in the middle of the river, guards keeping watch on the Queen's soldiers along the riverbank. Roska's face was still unusually pale as he sat cross-legged on the deck, leaning back against the railing.

"What are you talking about?" Q snapped. He didn't mean to, but with everything riding on him, he'd lost all patience. Roska flinched subtly at Quinn's harsh tone and he immediately felt guilty. "Shyt. I'm sorry, Ros. I didn't mean to lash out at you."

Roska blinked and shrugged. "It's fine. I understand."

It wasn't fine, but Q didn't push it. He needed to get control of his magic, but more importantly, he needed to rein in his temper. "What were you saying? About the difference?"

"I was just thinking. Last time, you felt your life was in danger, but more than that, you were working to protect the school, the staff, your students. Your protective instincts have always been stronger than most. I think the wild fire triggered that instinct at a much higher level and that enabled you to tap into stronger magic."

Quinn stared blankly at his brother. Maybe he was right. That fire had threatened everyone he loved. Stopping it had been life or death. Failure hadn't been an option.

Failure isn't exactly a viable option here either, Lyra noted.

It really wasn't.

Quinn's legs gave out as he leaned against the railing beside Roska. He slid down the side of the thick wood until he was seated, legs stretched out before him, defeated. Q let his head fall against the railing with a loud thunk. Maybe knocking his brain around a bit would help loosen his magic up.

Not likely. Lyra padded over and laid her head on his lap, looking at him with a surprising level of concern in her soulful brown eyes.

The instant their gazes connected, something clicked in Q's memory. "Hang on a second. Last time, I didn't create the Infernals from scratch. I built them from *your* fire."

"Oh, that's interesting." Castor stroked his chin. "I wonder how that might affect things. One second…" He didn't get up to leave, but his gaze left their warship and drifted over to lock in on Belladonna. He stared quietly into the distance for several moments, before bringing his focus back to them. "Belladonna thinks that might be the trick to it. Working together magnifies your powers exponentially."

"Say that again?"

"He means you are stronger together," Demoni explained from her perch around Roska's neck. "Just like we were when we had to freeze the river."

Roska nodded in agreement. "It was much easier when I felt her powers intermingle with mine."

Quinn raised an eyebrow in question at Lyra. *Wanna give it a shot, girl?*

Lyra gave him a little foxy nod, then stood up and moved to the far side of the ship. If they were going to combine their powers to create a flaming creature, they should definitely be as far away from the others as possible. Considering they were all stuck on the ship together in the middle of a rapidly flowing river.

Castor signaled to the tidal enchantresses, calling them back to attention, in case things went badly.

Ready? Quinn thought nervously.

Always. Lyra winked confidently. With a flick of her tail, a small fire started on the deck of the ship.

Quinn scooped it into his hands before it could damage the wood and began feeding it with his flames. At first, it seemed like nothing was happening. The little ball of fire didn't even take shape as it sat flickering in his open hand. Then it began to grow, slowly stretching itself into a humanoid shape. Thin, spindle-like limbs grew from the middle of the ball, spreading out into strong, almost muscular arms and legs. Its head took shape, including an intimidating scowl. Well, intimidating for being the size of a pumpkin.

But then it just kept growing. The tidal enchantresses sprayed a mist over the deck, to keep the wood from burning as Q placed the Infernal on the floor. It had grown too big for him to continue holding, and still, it grew. When it began to weigh down one side of the ship, Quinn directed it to the middle, maintaining balance while keeping it away from the masts or rigging.

When the creature stood face to face with the enchantress in the Crow's Nest, Q stopped feeding it. Everyone on deck stood silent, collectively holding their breath in awe or fear of the creature. Quinn waited. He fully expected the creature to dissolve the moment he pulled his power away, but it stayed. Standing at attention in the middle of the ship. Awaiting orders. Awaiting *his* orders.

Castor clapped him on the back enthusiastically. "You did it!" He stared up at the Infernal with pride. "Now do it again. Beatrice says we need at least a dozen to put the fear of the gods—more like the fear of magic—into those soldiers and their demented Queen."

"Are we sure making them fear magic is the best solution?" Roska wondered from his seat on the deck. "It just seems like a fear and misunderstanding of magic is what got us in this mess in the first place."

Quinn agreed. If the Queen and The Brotherhood weren't so damn afraid of magic, the *turmio* would never have been released, Harbor Ridge would never have needed to build a cemetery, and Roska would have had a posh life in royal luxury.

"I'm just the messenger." Castor raised his hands in mock surrender, but there was a glint of mischief in his eyes. "You two are the ones calling the shots here, aren't you? Wasn't that what your parents said? The three of you are the ones prophesized to end this whole shyt show. Seems to me, that makes this your call."

54

AIDEN

"IT'S HAPPENING." AIDEN SHIFTED awkwardly at the prow of the ship. He could see Quinn's Infernal standing proudly in the middle of their ship.

A pain built suddenly behind his eyes, causing Aiden to squeeze them closed, hoping to block out the onslaught of visions that were sure to crash through his mind at any moment.

"What's happening, sir?" One of the guards moved to join him.

The guard strained to see beyond their ships, but she couldn't see what Aiden was witnessing. The physical world quickly faded from view as mental images overwhelmed the demi-god's mind. The Fae and their cursed prophecy. Things were changing, something was happening with the boys and it was shifting the path they'd been traveling on.

Scenes of what could be flashed in his head. Potential paths being moved, replaced, rearranged. Aiden's hands flew to his temples as the visions continued swarming. He stumbled backward, falling into something large, warm, and soft. Aleerah. She'd caught him before he landed ass-first on the deck. She slowly laid down, taking him down with her as carefully as possible.

All around him, Aiden could hear angry cries, shouts for aid, cheering, crying, laughing. He couldn't tell what was real and what was in his head.

An image sharpened in his mind. Elena. Older, bits of white streaked through her dark auburn hair. Niko looking down lovingly at her. Children running around behind them. A small babe cradled in her arms.

Another flash and he saw Quinn. A deep scar cut through his eyebrow but a proud grin made his whole face glow. Wind blew through his hair as the scent of salt water flooded Aiden's nose.

Another flash. Roska. Wiping down tables. Was he at a bar? No, an inn. A plump woman tossed a roll to him and Roska caught it casually. There was a girl there. The girl from Nexton? Possibly. She looked older.

Another flash and blackness consumed him.

"We've come to negotiate peace with the Queen as representatives of the King." Beatrice's voice echoed off the stone walls surrounding Riverayn, rousing Aiden from his impromptu nap. Squinting against the bright sun, Aiden shielded his eyes as he worked to stand.

Are you all right? It's been a while since something like that has happened. Aleerah eyed him nervously. She was right. The last time he'd had visions like that had been the night he'd met and impregnated Beatrice.

Could go for a stiff drink, but otherwise, I'm fine. He brushed the hair from his brow, finding the skin clammy and cool. He really hated the Fae.

You can't blame them for your own stupid actions.

Sure I can. He tossed her a smirk, taking slow steps back to the prow to get a better sense of what was going on.

The ships were moving. Q's Infernals—there were at least half a dozen of them now—were standing guard at the prow of their ship, serving as a bold warning to anyone who might attempt to stop their entry. He hadn't created a mass of flaming soldiers, although Aiden couldn't be sure if that was intentional or simply because they lacked the room to form an army while on the ship.

Castor circled overhead and perched beside him on the railing. Aiden studied the moonbird's face, waiting for his friend to shift back into his human form.

"What's the plan? I get the sense that things have changed." He motioned to his ears as the ringing began to subside from Beatrice's spelled and exceptionally loud voice. Aiden kept his tone casual even as a migraine threatened behind his eyes. Damned visions always took such a toll on his body.

Castor seemed to be studying him as well, head tilting from side to side. His keen eyes missed nothing. Aiden had long since given up on trying to keep secrets from the shifter. It was a waste of time and energy.

After several long moments, Castor hopped down from the railing and transformed. "What did you see?"

"Nothing bad," Aiden promised. And it was the truth. The visions he'd had were of the not-too-distant future. All of his children were alive and mostly unharmed, although that scar he'd seen on Q had looked rather deep. Aiden wasn't sure if Q was even able to see properly through that eye.

"But you did see something. Something new." It was a statement, not a question. Castor knew that whatever Aiden had foreseen, it was brand new. Brand new was always a bit unsettling. The paths were written by the Fates. If the Fates were creating new stories, it meant big things were coming.

"We're entering the harbor?" Aiden asked, changing the subject abruptly. They had more pressing issues to address right now. Talk of new prophecy could wait.

Castor stared at Aiden a moment longer, then nodded. "Q and Roska have decided to take a more... diplomatic approach to dealing with the Queen. Beatrice has announced our arrival and requested an audience with Her Haughtiness. She agreed, after we saw her gawking out a window at his small army of Infernals." A mischievous grin split across the shifter's face. Aiden chuckled in amusement at the mental image that presented itself. Arrogant Queen Rosalina hearing Beatrice's spelled voice, preparing to blow them off, then looking out her window to find a small collection of massive flaming warriors waiting to greet her.

It was a show of force, but a much gentler one than Beatrice had hoped for. Beatrice wanted to instill fear in the magept who had attacked and killed her enchantresses. She'd been *abundantly* clear on that front.

Which was why Aiden was so relieved when the triplets agreed to take over the decision-making when it came to dealing with that bigoted, power-mad Queen.

Beatrice couldn't think clearly or unbiasedly. Understandably, of course, but her way would have thrown them into a war that would have cost hundreds of lives and irrevocably changed Waverly. And not for the better. She was too emotional. A sentence Aiden had never thought he'd utter about Beatrice, but clearly, there were still things in this world that could surprise him.

"She sent a guard down to negotiate the terms of a meeting," Castor continued. "No guards. No soldiers. Just the boys and their parents."

"I doubt the Queen will adhere to those rules. She'll have her pet soldiers lying in wait, if not openly armed and aggressively greeting us at the gate."

"Probably, but that's why Q insisted on bringing one of his big flaming friends." Castor's smile grew even wider. "He said it was 'non-negotiable.' The Queen didn't have an option. It was *fantastic.*"

Aiden's gleeful face mirrored Castor's. He wished he'd been in the room when the Queen had gotten that message. He could only imagine how hilarious it would have been to see her rage at such a demand.

"Gods, that boy really is amazing." Aiden chuckled, crossing his arms over his chest. "What about you? Zied? Aleerah?"

"We'll be accompanying you. Queen Rosalina doesn't know that Aleerah and I can venture farther away, so she'll assume that our presence is necessary. Plus, I think she'll be too distracted by that guy." He nodded toward the Infernal as it stepped off the ship and onto the dock Q and Roska's ship had moored alongside. The creature had skillfully avoided setting any of the ship's rigging alight, and it now walked calmly and confidently ahead of Quinn toward the castle gate.

Aiden was continuously impressed by Q's control. The creature didn't leave a single scorch mark on the dock, the cobblestone, or the grass.

The crew guided their ship into the harbor, mooring alongside the others, and Aiden and Aleerah quickly hopped over the railing to join the boys at the gate.

Castor flew ahead of him, perching on Belladonna's shoulder as she, Beatrice, and Zied strode up to the wrought iron gate.

"We have agreed to your terms, Rosalina," Beatrice called out, annoyance lacing her words. "Open this gate so that we might discuss this like adults."

Ah, patronizing the Queen. There's no way that will end badly.

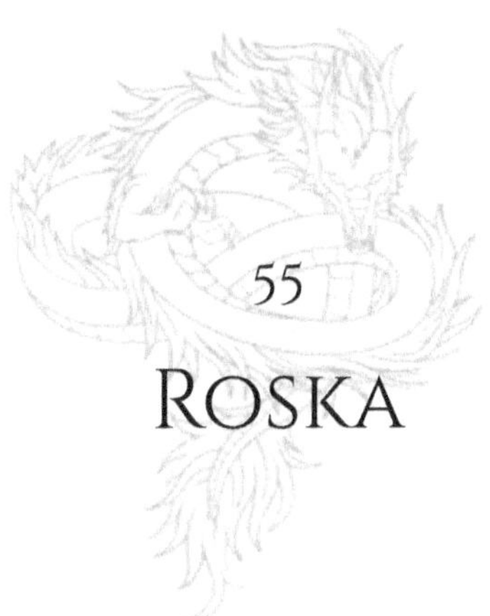

55

ROSKA

ROSKA GLANCED BACK OVER his shoulder as the gate closed behind them. Five of Quinn's Infernals stood guard around their ships, protecting the enchantresses they'd left behind as part of the negotiations.

His skin prickled, anxiety manifesting physically on top of the nausea that had only just subsided. There was no way this would go as smoothly as they hoped. The Queen would fight back. She probably already had her guards lying in wait to attack them as soon as they were out of reach of the enchantresses.

Roska cast furtive glances over his shoulder and into the shadows of every corner and alleyway as they passed through the cobblestone streets to the castle. Soldiers lined both sides of the street, marking the path the Queen intended for them to take. It felt like a death march. Icy mist flowed from his fingertips as they followed the path, led by the one Infernal who had been permitted to accompany them.

"Feels a bit ominous," Quinn commented, leaning close to Roska to ensure they wouldn't be overheard. Roska didn't risk responding, not trusting his voice to not betray him and reveal the fear that was growing stronger with each step. Instead, he offered a subtle nod.

They were ready for a fight, but it would be a bloody one. They were effectively surrounded in an unknown area. If the soldiers decided to attack, it wouldn't end well for anyone.

Thankfully, the soldiers didn't seem intent on attacking. Not yet, anyway.

Aiden and Aleerah followed closely behind Quinn and Roska, with Belladonna, Beatrice, and Zied bringing up the rear. Castor circled overhead, disappearing at times only to pop back up on a rooftop or store sign a few paces ahead of them.

The castle entrance was blocked by four guards and an iron portcullis. When they reached the gate, Roska wondered if this was the end. They'd been escorted to a dead end, if that gate didn't open, this would be a perfect place to attack them.

For several long, tense seconds, they stood at the gate, awaiting their fate. Roska exhaled a sigh of relief when he heard the grinding of gears and saw the portcullis begin to rise slowly.

Quinn's Infernal ducked beneath the stone archway, leading them into the castle proper. Roska couldn't help but stare in awe of the stained glass windows that seemed to tell the story of their kingdom's history.

Images of kings and queens reigning from their ornate thrones. Scenes of battles fought long ago. Magic versus sword-wielding soldiers. Women tied to stakes, surrounded by blazing fires.

"Quite the welcoming scene, isn't it?" Belladonna asked bitterly. Her gaze was fixed on a series of windows depicting the witch hunts. Roska couldn't even imagine the painful memories such images must have evoked in her. Beatrice wrapped a comforting arm around the witch's shoulder as Castor dove through the closing gate and cawed his annoyance. "Well, if you would stop flying off, you wouldn't be at risk of being left behind."

The Infernal barely fit in the expansive hallway, ducking under chandeliers filled with unlit candles before practically crawling through the doorway into what appeared to be the throne room.

The Queen was waiting for them on her throne, perched on a dais at the far end of the massive room. She looked about as happy to see them as they were to see her.

There's no way this ends well.

56

BELLADONNA

"**Y**OU SELF-RIGHTEOUS, PITIFUL EXCUSE for a queen. I never had to bewitch your twit of a husband. He came running to my bed chambers. The arrogant fool convinced himself that he was in love with me. I would have happily never seen him again. He was a means to an end. Access to power I was otherwise barred from. I never cared for him. If anything, I found him dreadfully boring and entirely incompetent, both in my bed and out. I never wanted your husband, and I can't fathom why you did."

Belladonna stepped between Bea and the Queen. "Darling," she said in a quiet, measured tone. "I'm not sure this line of communication will be helpful."

Once they'd been escorted into the throne room and the doors had been firmly closed behind them, Beatrice had dropped all pretense of decorum and laid into the Queen with a ferocity that was inadvisable at best.

More like incredibly idiotic. She knows we're surrounded, right? I mean, sure we're powerful and all that, but if she starts a war right here and now, we will not all make it out alive.

Belladonna tossed a quick glare to Castor where he circled around the head of Q's Infernal. Despite the high ceilings, the Infernal had been directed to sit, after nearly setting the ceiling alight. Refocusing on Bea, Belladonna placed a calming hand on the headmistress, drawing her attention away from the Queen. She offered Beatrice a small smile and a gentle squeeze. Beatrice needed to remember that they came here to make *peace,* not start an all-out war in the middle of the throne room.

Beatrice's hostile glower flicked from the Queen to the witch. For a moment, Belladonna wondered if she *could* reach Bea long enough to get her to take a step back. Zied took a step closer to Beatrice, nudging her thigh with his massive, snowy head. Beatrice blinked slowly. Something shifted in her face. Whatever rage had been building within her seemed to abate. Belladonna watched the fury drain from her beloved's face and gave her an almost imperceptible nod.

Thank the gods.

Belladonna ignored Castor as she stepped aside and turned to face the Queen. Rosalina was eyeing them shrewdly, analyzing the way she and Beatrice interacted. A look of disgust passed over her face as she realized the full nature of their relationship.

Looks like Her Haughtiness has found another reason to hate you. Goody.

"Rosalina," Beatrice began again, but the Queen raised her hand, cutting her off.

"You will address me as Queen Rosalina or Your Majesty. We are not friends, Enchantress. You will not address me as though we are." There was nothing but cold contempt in her voice.

Beatrice flexed her fingers, clenching and unclenching her fists before she attempted to speak again. "*Queen* Rosalina, we are here to discuss peace and ending this pointless fight you've started."

Belladonna winced at "pointless." It was accurate, but demeaning the Queen's actions wasn't going to win her favor. The witch looked over at Quinn and Roska. She needed one of them to step up and take over the negotiations before Beatrice could make things any worse.

"*Pointless*," the Queen bit out through clenched teeth. "Saving the world from the scourge of your vile magic isn't pointless. It is the noblest thing I can do for this godsforsaken world."

Belladonna felt the heat from Quinn's magic before she saw the flames lash out from his hands. The Infernal began to rise, moving slowly toward the Queen. This was *not* going well. Castor flew down, directly across Q's line of sight, causing the boy to blink and break his focus. Roska stepped closer to him and whispered something in his brother's ear. Q's flames and the Infernal vanished.

Belladonna offered the FrostBorn a small smile of encouragement. Maybe he would be the most level-headed, cool-tempered option for this meeting.

Seeming unsure of himself, Roska took a step forward, addressing the Queen while keeping his eyes downcast. "Your Majesty, we didn't come here to fight." Rosalina barked a very unqueen-like laugh at that statement, but Roska continued. "We are here to negotiate peace, at the request of the King."

That caught her attention. Rosalina's hawk-like gaze honed in on Roska as she scrutinized him. "The King? You honestly expect me to believe that my husband sent you lot to negotiate anything?" The incredulity in her tone made Belladonna want to peel the skin from the woman's face. The Queen was the epitome of arrogance.

"Not your husband," Quinn interjected. "Your son. The New King. After you killed his father." Belladonna could still feel the heat radiating from Q, but thankfully he kept his flames under his skin.

"My... my *son* sent monsters to negotiate with me?" Disbelief marred her cruel features. This was a betrayal of the highest order, as far as she was concerned. One she clearly hadn't been expecting. Belladonna noted that she didn't deny killing the King. Interesting.

"Lady, I swear to the Mother—" Quinn took a couple of threatening steps forward, but Roska placed himself between his brother and the Queen, resting a clearly frosty hand on Quinn's near-flaming shoulder. He shook his head once, discouraging further action, and turned back to the Queen.

"Regardless of what you think of us, your son, King Niko, has asked us to come here and resolve this issue with you." Roska's voice didn't shake or stutter. He'd found his confidence now and he wasn't backing down. Belladonna's heart swelled with pride.

Rosalina moved to speak, but to everyone's surprise, Roska cut her off. "With all due respect, Your Majesty, you no longer have the authority here. King Niko is the rightful ruler of this land now that his father has passed unto the Fade. That means that you are to defer to his rule. We have been instructed to make peace with you—if we are able—and imprison you if we are not."

Rosalina blanched at his words. "Lies. My son would never imprison me." Her voice wavered as she spoke, doubting her own words.

"You killed his dad, lady. You attacked the school while he was inside. Hells, you tried to kill the woman he loves." The vehemence in Quinn's voice shocked the room.

"The woman he *what*?" Rosalina shrieked in outrage. "That little bitch who nearly took out half my army?"

In an instant, every single magical creature was poised for violence. Fire blasted from Q's hands, scorching the thick rug they stood upon. Jagged shards of ice flew across the room, spearing either side of the Queen's throne, narrowly missing her shoulders. Vines bound her to the chair, a particularly thick one wrapping around her mouth, effectively silencing her. Aleerah and Lyra snarled as Zied pounced onto the throne, nearly toppling it in an effort to shut the idiot woman up permanently.

"You will *not* speak of my daughter in such a way ever again." Beatrice stalked toward the incapacitated Queen. "I trusted you once, believing that you would care for my son, raise him with your own, and show him the love and affection I'd always shown you. I will not make the mistake of putting my faith in you again. If it weren't for your son, I would have killed you the instant I set eyes on you. Don't make me regret not following through with my instincts."

A moment too late, the Queen's guards rushed the room, swords and spears at the ready. Roska and Demoni coated the floor with ice, causing the guards to slip and fall. Aleerah crossed the room in two massive leaps, baring her sharp fangs and daring any of the soldiers to try and get up. None of them did.

"Castor, dear," Beatrice said in a surprisingly sweet voice. "Would you be so kind as to fetch the enchantresses? We need to clean up in here." She never took her eyes off the Queen as she spoke. Castor took off through an open window as Beatrice closed the remaining distance between herself and Rosalina. "Out of respect for your son, I will try and keep this as painless as possible. But if you fight me, you will bleed."

The Queen's eyes widened with fear.

"I *really* hope you fight. I would love to see that pretty white dress of yours turn to red."

57

QUINN

QUINN HAD NEVER REALLY been afraid of their mother. Infuriated by? Often. Distrustful of? Of course. But it wasn't until that moment—hearing her steady voice as she threatened such bloody violence—that he felt truly afraid of her power. Not for himself, obviously. And he didn't really worry about the safety of the Queen. Mux that bitch. But the idea that their mother was capable of any level of violence was unsettling.

They all sat at a table in a sitting room off the throne room, one of the endless, excessively luxurious rooms in the expansive castle. The Queen and her guards had been placed in various cells. The Queen herself had been moved to one of the "special" cells that could only be opened with blood magic. Apparently, anyone could put someone *in* one of those cells, but they had to have royal blood to let someone out. Clever and muxing confusing.

What happens when the royal line dies out? Lyra asked curiously.

I guess they wall off that part of the castle? Or people wander in and die of starvation? It was an interesting thing to wonder about, but they really didn't have the time for it at the moment.

Much to their mother's disappointment, the Queen hadn't fought them as the enchantresses moved her to the blood magic cell. Q assumed it was probably because she physically couldn't move. Belladonna didn't reel her vines back in until the bitch Queen was tossed—literally—into a cell.

Castor had been sent to fetch Elena and Niko, although Quinn suspected that they were already on their way. He knew Niko wouldn't be able to keep Elena away for long, but he was grateful that they hadn't been in the throne room. He never wanted Elena to hear anyone talk about her the way the Queen had.

"Castor says Elena and Niko are already halfway here. Apparently, they only waited a day before departing," Belladonna announced. Then she paused, seeming to listen to something in the distance, and laughed. "It seems our dear girl didn't take kindly to being left behind."

"Well, we all expected that." Aiden stretched out in the chair across from Q.

"Yes, but I don't think we expected her to assault poor Niko." A sly smile lit up the witch's face.

"She attacked him?" Roska sat forward in his chair, clearly thrown by their sister's violent acts.

"Not exactly." Belladonna laughed. "She set his clothes on fire on their balcony. She told Castor it was an accident but Niko seems to think otherwise."

Quinn couldn't help the mirthful laugh that escaped his lips. He could picture it perfectly. Elena collecting all of the guy's clothing, throwing it into a massive pile on their balcony. and "accidentally" lighting it up with her electric shocks until the whole pile was nothing but ash.

"Don't look so proud," Roska chided him.

"Why not? We knew she'd be pissed. At least now we also know that her powers are coming back stronger than ever." He chuckled, catching their mother's eye to find her beaming with just as much pride as he was. Elena was a force to be reckoned with. It was probably good that the New King figured that out sooner rather than later.

"The Young King says they should arrive by sunset tomorrow," Belladonna continued, as though she hadn't even heard Q praise Elena or seen Beatrice's prideful smile.

"Well, tell him to shift into a giant fish and push them along. We've got a lot of shyt to get settled and I don't wanna spend any more time here than we need to." Quinn never felt comfortable around so many people. Harbor Ridge was crowded, but they were all magical, most were kids, and he felt comfortable there.

You didn't always, Lyra reminded him.

It was true. In the beginning, he'd been stressed about getting Elena back and on edge around so many people that didn't even believe he could exist. A magical male was unheard of, so he'd been forced to pretend he was someone else whenever he was around the enchantresses. It had been exhausting.

When their mother had openly claimed them—*You mean after you saved their asses?* Lyra sniped—things had changed. He'd been able to lower his guard some. Then he'd become an instructor and they got Elena back. He wouldn't go so far as to say Harbor Ridge felt like home, but it was definitely home-adjacent.

He still wanted to get back to their home in the woods, and then visit Amelia. So much had happened since he last saw her. He missed her terribly, and he wanted to talk to her about all the things that had happened. Then he wanted to show off his magic. His fire. His Infernals.

Riverayn was crawling with people. Not just soldiers and royal guards. Civilians. Thousands of them. Bakers. Blacksmiths. Maids. Cooks. The dock master and his dozens of dock workers. Traveling merchants and their employees. Shop owners. Farmers. Families. There were more people on the docks when they arrived than in the entirety of Andover. Quinn had never felt claustrophobic before, but inside the castle, listening to all the footsteps as dozens of people crept about doing their various jobs, it felt as though the walls were closing in.

Q rose from the table and strode to the window. The expansive view helped to alleviate some of his mounting tension. The river below forked into two at the tip of the castle. It's how Riverayn had gotten its name. *The land between two rivers.* It wasn't exactly accurate, but it suited the place and no one complained. In the distance to the north, Q could see mountains alongside the river. Harbor Ridge was nestled beside those mountains. If he turned to the east, following the river to its source, he could just make out a hint of the Dragon's Teeth. Staring off into the distance, he let his mind wander. What would things have been like if he'd decided to just go home that night? The night he'd found Elena and Agon curled against the elements on the side of the road. If he'd decided to wait and check his traps in the morning? He and Lyra would have come upon two corpses—like they'd been expecting—instead of a couple of shocking, *living* creatures.

Quinn imagined that their life would have continued on much as it had. Hiding out in their hut, ignoring the world as much as possible. Never knowing the truth about their parents or discovering his own magic.

Things would have been a lot simpler, sure. But they also would have been depressingly boring. Quinn said a silent prayer of thanks to the Mother for reuniting him with his family. As muxed up as things had been, Q couldn't imagine going back to his life before. He didn't even want to picture a life without his family.

They were just sitting down to breakfast the next morning when a servant announced the impending arrival of Elena and Niko. According to the boy, their ship had been sighted and they would be docking within the hour.

Finally. Quinn exhaled a sigh of relief. Once they handled things with the Queen, then they could make a plan for the Brotherhood and finally be done with all this shyt.

Quinn finished his breakfast quickly and excused himself from the table. He couldn't sit still a moment longer. He'd wait for them at the docks.

58

ELENA

ELENA HAD NEVER SEEN this side of Riverayn before. The only time she'd been brought into its walls, she'd been unconscious and imprisoned. During her departure, she had been so fixated on reaching her brothers in time that she'd never once looked back.

It was a stunning view. The morning sunlight reflected brightly against the pale gray stone of the castle walls. She was surprised—and disappointed—to see there wasn't a single bit of greenery on the stones. At Harbor Ridge, the stones were so slick and smooth, nothing could climb it. As if in an effort to differentiate itself entirely, Belladonna's cottage in the Dark Woods had been *covered* in vines. It almost looked as though the plants had formed the house for the witch. The stone walls of Riverayn were pristine, giving it an almost sterile feeling. It existed in nature—being the city between two rivers—but it did not coexist *with* nature. This close to the river, the entire capital was shielded by the thick, intimidating walls making it seem more like a fortress than a thriving trade center. Niko informed her that the other side of the city was far more welcoming. A wide main road allowed for heavy traffic in and out of the city proper each day. Merchants and vendors passed beneath a wide drawbridge each morning to sell their wares, then traversed back each evening to their homes in the larger neighborhoods outside the walls.

There were plenty of living quarters within the city walls, Niko had explained, but those were held by the wealthier merchants, visiting royals—lords, ladies, dukes, duchesses, etc. Elena had frowned at the clear distinction between the wealthy and the working class. A literal wall separated them. In the event of an invasion, the drawbridge would be raised and those in the smaller homes and hamlets surrounding Riverayn would be left to fend for themselves. It was cruel, heartless even.

Niko had been taken aback by her accusation of favoring the wealthy when she'd pointed it out to him at first. He seemed to take personal offense. But their lengthy boat ride had given them time to talk and he'd come to see that there was truth to her observations. There was a harsh division between those with and those without. He'd been stewing quietly at the stern of the longship ever since. Not ignoring her, exactly, but lost in his own thoughts.

Elena had spent the trip testing out her magic, seeing how far she could push herself before it became too much and she had to rest. She was still weaker than she'd been before the Nothing, but only slightly. Hells, she'd managed to burn every single article of Niko's clothing, which was really saying something. He traveled with more clothes than Elena had ever owned in her entire life.

He really doesn't travel light, does he? Agon mused.

Elena's shoulders shook with silent laughter. She stood at the prow of the ship, watching with fascination as the dock workers guided merchant ships into port.

"What's so funny?" Niko asked. He'd managed to sneak up behind her while she'd been distracted by the workers. His words were a warm breath on the back of her neck. Elena startled at his closeness. She hadn't even heard him move.

Turning to face him, warmth flushed her cheeks when he caught her staring at his lips a second too long.

"See something you like, Firefly?" His voice was low, barely a whisper, but she felt every word like a lightning bolt to her core. She wet her lips, her eyes falling back to focus on his, wondering what would happen if he kissed her right now.

They'd never gotten back to that moment in his suite days ago. Neither of them had said a word about it. It was as though it never even happened, except for the awkward moments and tense glances they shot each other when they thought the other wasn't looking. But being this close to him, feeling the heat of his body mere inches from hers, Elena couldn't help but want more. She leaned in slowly, subtly, creating the invitation and giving him the option to accept or decline.

He watched her for a second longer, heat flaring in his eyes, opening his mouth slightly and leaning in to meet her.

The blare of trumpets broke the spell surrounding them. They jumped apart as if they'd been caught doing something inappropriate. They had been.

There is nothing wrong with what you were doing or feeling, Agon interrupted her thoughts. *You are two consenting adults.*

Yes, but he is the King. He can't just go around kissing random enchantresses. He will be mated. To a royal. Someone who can help him run the country. Elena stared up at the impossibly high walls surrounding the city. Trumpeters sounded again, heralding their arrival. *I'm not that person, and I'm not sure I even want to get mated.*

Agon scoffed but didn't argue with her. She scooped him up off the longship's deck and sat him on her shoulder.

It didn't matter now anyway. They had more pressing concerns.

Like a Queen who wanted to kill them all, and a rogue sect of soldiers aligned with her.

Not to mention the ever-present threat of the Brotherhood and whatever vile things they had planned next.

Her desires for the New King were nothing in comparison. She would just have to ignore those feelings. Let them—let *him*—go so that she could focus on fixing all that was currently wrong with their world and get back to her normal life.

What is that exactly? Living in Harbor Ridge and feeling un-wanted? Like an outcast every day? Or living in Andover and hiding our magic from everyone for fear that they might discover us and harm us?

Elena flinched at Agon's bluntness. He was right, of course, but he didn't have to be so brutal about it.

Elena stared openly, mouth agape in awe, as Niko led her through the castle gates, flanked on all sides by a small cadre of personal guards. Commander Jamieson had insisted on sending his most trusted soldiers along with them to Riverayn. Elena wasn't entirely sure it was necessary. She felt confident that she could have protected both herself and Niko from any threat they might face, but she didn't argue. It wasn't her place to step in and tell the King or his soldiers how to handle their business. Besides, Niko wasn't *hers* to protect.

The guards came in quite handy as they walked the streets of Riverayn, from the Harbor to the castle proper. Elena was too engrossed in taking in every single detail. Stained glass windows served as stunning store signs—a fish monger's shop identified by a beautiful scene of a flowing river with several large salmon swimming upstream; a butcher's sign showed a scene of a fat, happy pig in a field of lush green grass; a tailor's was a long, skinny depiction of a formal gown draped artfully over a mannequin. It was unlike anything she'd ever seen before and Elena was enthralled. If they weren't on such a time-sensitive mission, she would have happily spent the day wandering around the merchant shops, admiring their wares as much as their architecture.

Niko squeezed her hand and Elena realized she'd come to a complete stop, halting their party, in front of an herbalist's shop. The stained glass window at the front of the shop looked alarmingly similar to Belladonna's cottage in the woods. Elena felt an inexplicable pull toward the shop. She *needed* to go inside, although she couldn't pinpoint why she felt that way.

"Everything ok, Firefly?" Concern laced his voice and Niko followed her gaze toward the shop. "Do you need some herbs at the moment?"

Elena blinked, forcing her eyes to leave the shop and find his. "No," she said slowly. "There's something about this place though." Her voice trailed off as her eyes sought out the storefront again.

"Do we need to go inside?"

"No." Elena shook her head. "It can wait."

Niko nodded, squeezed her hand once more, and led her back up the cobblestone road that led to the castle. His thumb rubbed back and forth over the back of her hand as he escorted her to his home.

His *home*. The castle that loomed ahead of them. It wasn't exactly "threatening," but it wasn't welcoming either. Large, spiked turrets lined the inner walls that separated the castle from Riverayn's markets and neighborhoods. It was a sight to behold. Flawless, near-blinding stone walls, iron and crystal clear glass windows, brilliant red stone shingles on the roofs of all the watch towers and the castle itself. It painted a picture of power and intimidation. One that let any onlooker know that the power residing in that castle could either make or break a person's life.

Elena stared up at it in awe. Niko failed to hide a chuckle as she slowed to a stop again, unabashedly staring up at the fortress that served as his home and the center of all political authority in Waverly.

"Firefly, I promise I will give you a thorough tour of everything Riverayn has to offer, *after* we get this shyt settled with my mum. But we have to make it inside the castle to do that." He tugged on her hand and Elena had to remind her feet to keep moving.

"I'm sorry," she whispered. "I've just never seen anything like this. It's amazing and a bit terrifying."

"There's nothing to be afraid of here." Niko tossed her a cocky grin over his shoulder. "No one would be stupid enough to attack you. Even without my guards surrounding us, you are a force. My clothes could attest to that if they hadn't all been reduced to ash."

Elena fought back the laugh that threatened. "I wouldn't have had to do that if you'd just listened to me in the first place. I told you I was ready to leave. You claimed you needed more time to pack. I was merely helping speed up that process."

Niko's deep laugh vibrated through her chest, spreading a calming warmth throughout her body. "I'll never make that mistake again, I swear, Firefly. From now on, I'll pack as light as you do."

Elena sent a small shock through their joined hands, causing Niko to jump. It was an argument they'd been having since they left Harbor Ridge. Elena didn't "pack light", as he implied. She simply didn't own very much. Three chemises, two bodices—one blue and one green—and two skirts to match the bodices. One pair of leather boots. Three pairs of fleece leggings. It all fit perfectly in her enchanted cloak. She never needed to bother with actual luggage. Everything she owned was comfortably wrapped around her shoulders.

Castor's caw from above distracted Niko from whatever snarky remark he was preparing. The shifter circled overhead twice before diving down and seamlessly transforming into a man, landing casually beside them.

"Having a nice stroll through the city, are we?" He raised a mocking eyebrow at them. "Because the rest of us have been listening to your mother shrieking like a banshee through stone walls all morning. It would be lovely if you two could move it along so we might shut her up."

Shattering whatever peaceful, playful energy they'd been basking in over the last few days, Niko's hand reflexively tightened around hers at Castor's words. It was Elena's turn to comfortingly rub her thumb across the back of his hand.

"Yes, of course," Elena replied firmly.

"Let's get this shyt over with." Niko squared his shoulders and strode purposefully into the castle, leading her through the endless halls and off to finally confront his mother.

"Do you—do you want me to go in with you?" Elena watched Niko as he paced back and forth in front of the stone wall. They could hear his mother shouting to be released through the thick, cold bricks. Elena vividly remembered her time trapped in one of those cells. She didn't really want to revisit that place, but she would if he needed her to.

Niko brushed the curls from his forehead, glaring at the stone that stood between him and his father's—probable—murderer. No one should have to face such burdens alone. She reached out and tentatively placed a hand on his tense shoulder. He jerked in surprise at the contact. Had he forgotten she was there?

"Sorry," he said quickly, grasping her hand and slipping his fingers between hers. "I appreciate the sentiment, Firefly, but I can't ask you to do that. Go back in the cell she threw you into, after planning to murder you, and force you to face her? It's too much to ask of anyone. I would never put you through that."

Elena tightened her grip on his hand. He had been listening, and clearly, he'd read her thoughts. "You didn't ask. I offered. Besides," she added with a grin, trying to seem more confident than she actually felt, "it might be good for me. Seeing how far she's fallen. Cathartic."

A single eyebrow shot up, disappearing into his near-black curls. His eyes searched her face, looking for any sign that she wasn't comfortable or didn't want to follow through on her offer. Elena kept her face calm and open, ensuring he wouldn't find a single shred of doubt.

While Elena certainly didn't enjoy the idea of being trapped in a blood magic prison cell again, she trusted that Niko wouldn't leave her there, and she knew the Queen posed no threat to her. Without her royal lackeys—sorry, *guards*—she was entirely harmless. Elena could easily shock the vile woman into submission if need be.

Niko studied her a moment longer, seeming to find her more than willing and able to accompany him, and nodded his consent. Elena could see some of the tension leave his body as he adjusted his fingers where they wrapped around hers, tightening and steeling himself for the emotional attacks he would almost certainly face. The New King turned and led her through the wall to the cell that held his villainous mother.

It was pitch black in the cell. The Queen raged on, her cries echoing off the bare stone walls. Elena was surprised that the Queen didn't try to attack them and liberate herself from the room.

"Would you mind sparking this one up for me, Firefly?" Niko spoke quietly, but his voice seemed to scare the Queen.

"Who's there?" There was fear laced in her words. She tried to project power, but missed the mark.

Niko nudged Elena's free hand with something hard. A torch. She drew her lightning to the tip of her finger and sparked the torch to life. The red-orange flame illuminated the depressing prison cell. The Queen whirled on them with unfettered aggression, raising her hands, fingers splayed as though she intended to claw their eyes out with her nails. In a split second, recognition passed through her heated gaze. She fixated on Niko first, emotions racing across her face. Rage. Hurt. Betrayal. Then her eyes flicked to Elena. It seemed to take her a few moments to place Elena's face, but it was perfectly clear the instant the Queen realized who had accompanied her son into her cell.

"*You,*" she snarled accusingly. "You are the reason I'm in here." She advanced on Elena, hatred in her eyes as she quickly closed the distance between them.

Elena took a step back, unsure how to handle the deranged Queen. Niko stepped in front of her, blocking her from his mother's view. "No, Mother, she's not." His voice was hard, but not entirely unkind. "You are here as a direct result of your actions. Mum, you committed *treason* and tried to start a war you had no hope of winning. All in the twisted name of love."

The Queen stared at Niko, baffled. Elena wondered if the woman really had lost her mind. She didn't seem to comprehend his words. "I was trying to *save* our kingdom from those wicked women."

"Mum," Niko said calmly, "you have to see that your actions were wrong."

Elena flexed her fingers around Niko's, reassuring him with her touch. He was practically begging his mother to admit her wrong-doings. Elena wondered if he was hoping to redeem her. If she admitted she'd made mistakes, it wouldn't undo the pain she'd inflicted, the lives she'd stolen by aiding in the release of the *turmio*, but perhaps it would mean she wasn't beyond saving.

He can't really plan to forgive her, right? Agon questioned, disbelief filling his thoughts.

She's still his mother. He loves her. He wants to save her. It's hard to accept that your mother is the villain in your story. Elena understood his motivation perfectly. She had tolerated her mother's indifference and constant reminders that she was a disappointment her whole life. Always striving to finally make her mother happy. Always struggling to accept that her mother would never accept her. It wasn't until her sixteenth birthday, when her mother kicked them out, that she realized the depth of her mother's distaste for her. Then, it had taken the unexpected truth of her conception, birth, and siblings for Elena to see that her mother didn't hate her. Elena served as a constant reminder of the other children their mother had lost. Madame LaBelle—headmistress and seemingly heartless mother—was, in fact, heartbroken. Elena was like a wound that wouldn't heal, festering and causing her mother endless pain.

It didn't make her actions acceptable, but now that she knew the full story, Elena could understand them. Possibly even forgive their mother. Eventually. It also made Elena uniquely qualified to understand Niko's desire to save his mother from herself.

The Queen shifted her gaze from Niko, over his shoulder to Elena. The rage filled her eyes again, back with a vengeance as she spoke through gritted teeth. "The only thing I regret is not killing that little harlot when I had the chance."

Agon hissed, bright blue sparks flying off his furry body. Niko took a large step forward, handing Elena the torch and forcing his mother to take several steps back. "You will not speak to her that way, Mother." He released Elena's hand as he continued to advance on his mother, driving her to the far side of the cell.

The Queen backed into the corner and let out a malevolent cackle. "She's bewitched you too then? She's an evil temptress, Niko. You've let her pull you under and now you're her willing slave." She looked past Niko, pinning Elena with a look of pure loathing. "Just like her whore of a mother did to your father." The Queen spat on the ground at Elena.

"Mother, you will stop this now or you will spend the rest of your life in this muxing cell."

"Why?" She glowered at him. "Why would you imprison the only person in this world who has always loved you? I'm trying to *save* you from making the same mistakes your foolish father made."

"Where is he, Mum? Where is my father?"

The Queen looked away at his question. Her eyes flicked around the cell, trying to avoid Niko's arraigning stare.

Elena's heart broke for Niko as the truth hit him once more. His father was dead. Most likely at the Queen's hands.

"Mother." He growled her name, demanding answers. Elena fought a flinch at the anger in his voice.

The Queen glared up at him like a petulant child. "He's gone."

"What does that mean?"

"It means he's never coming back." The Queen actually had the gall to sound annoyed with Niko for asking about his father at all.

"What did you do?" Niko pressed.

"Why do you assume I did something? How do you know he didn't die at the hands of those wicked women?"

Niko's fist clenched tightly at his side. Elena could see the mounting tension in his body as he tried to control his anger. He didn't want to lash out, but the Queen was pushing him, gaslighting him, and he was losing patience. "I will not ask again." His voice strained with the effort to keep his emotions in check.

Elena balked as the Queen rolled her eyes at him. As though *he* was being unreasonable and she was being forced to cater to a bratty child.

Can I shock her? Just once. Agon's lightning flashed throughout the room. *It would make everyone feel better, and it might even make her behave like a muxing adult.*

That wouldn't be helpful. Despite how badly she too wanted to strike the Queen, Elena knew violence wouldn't solve anything.

"Fine, if you really want to know. He died." The Queen was so callous and matter-of-fact as she made that announcement. As though the death of her husband—the man she claimed to love so much she attempted to start a *war*—didn't matter.

Niko's shoulders slumped, his head falling forward as a small gasp escaped his lips. Elena crossed the cell quickly, reaching out and gently placing her hand on his back. He looked so defeated, so broken.

The Queen scowled at Elena but didn't move toward her. Elena assumed Agon's bared teeth and lightning was likely the reason the Queen kept her distance.

"How?" Emotion tightened his voice as Niko stared unseeingly at the cell floor.

"He fell."

"Queen Rosalina," Elena spoke quickly, with a threat of rage in her own voice. A blue light created a soft glow in the room, informing Elena that lightning danced in her eyes. "The whole story, now. Or I will escort your son from this room and you will not see him again." Elena was shocked by the authority in her own voice, but she refused to back down as the Queen gawked at her. Clearly, Queen Rosalina hadn't expected Elena to talk back to her.

When she didn't speak, Elena started to guide Niko away from the Queen. He seemed oblivious to the world around him. Letting her gently tug his shirt, turn him and lead him to the wall they'd entered through.

"Stop." The Queen tried to speak with the air of power, but it was now clear who had the control in this cell. "I will tell him. But only if he agrees to spare me."

Niko looked up at her words. "Why do you deserve to be spared? After everything you've done. You've killed dozens. You are the reason there are grave markers for *children* at Harbor Ridge now. You have done nothing to show remorse or regret for the cost of your actions. Why the hells should I spare *you*?"

"Because I'm your mother." As though that meant she was above the law. Free to do as much harm as she pleased without any thought to the consequences.

"Tell me the whole truth and I will decide if you deserve my mercy." There was no cruelty in his words. He was utterly numb, and that scared Elena far more.

The Queen studied him for a long moment, seeming to weigh her options. When she finally spoke, it was in a rushed voice, as though speaking quickly might soften the blow and win her his favor and mercy. "I had my guards find your father and bring him home. He wasn't happy about being forced to return home and was very vocal about it. He said such cruel and thoughtless things to me, Niko." Her voice cracked as she spoke, tears clinging to her eyelashes. When Niko didn't respond, she continued. "We were in my chambers, discussing his relationship with that bitch—" Niko took a threatening step toward her and she quickly changed her wording. "The headmistress. I pleaded with him to leave her and stay only in my bed. I was more than willing to cater to his every whim and devious desire."

Niko's face twisted in disgust, but the Queen either didn't notice or chose to ignore it. "I offered myself to him then, but he laughed at me. He *laughed* at me, as though I was ridiculous for expecting my *husband* to warm *my* bed, and no one else's." Anger started seeping into her words as she spoke. The Queen began pacing along the far wall of the cell, the story spilling from her lips. "He had the gall to look at me with disdain. He stepped out onto my balcony, laughing and going on about how he had no interest in my bed. I'd served my purpose, he told me. I'd born him a son. He didn't need me anymore. I was enraged. He didn't *need* me? I'm his Queen. I'm supposed to rule at his side. Not that enchantress whore. How dare he brush me aside so carelessly?

"I followed him out to the balcony, demanding his attention and respect. He just laughed. I slapped him." She stopped her pacing and turned to face Niko. "I didn't mean to hit him so hard; I was just so upset. He fell backward, lost his balance, and went over the railing. It was an accident, my love. You have to see that." The Queen took a few tentative steps toward Niko, raising her hands and reaching out to touch his face. Something in his eyes deterred her, and she lowered her hands dejectedly. "You must know that I never meant to hurt him. I just wanted him to love me again. Like he did before he met *her*."

Niko glared down at his mother. The lightning in Elena's eyes had faded, leaving the torch as the only source of light in the room. It flickered softly, the crackle of the flames the only sound.

Without a word, Niko grasped Elena's hand, turned, and led her out of the cell, leaving his mother behind, calling out his name. The

Queen begged for forgiveness, but the tightness in Niko's grip told Elena that she would find none.

59

ROSKA

They were all waiting as patiently as possible in the throne room while Elena and Niko were in with the Queen. Roska wasn't sure what Niko hoped to accomplish by interrogating his mother, but he understood the compulsion to address one's demons in person. He fully intended to do the same with the Brotherhood. Sooner, rather than later.

"What sort of lies do you think she's telling him?" Quinn asked, staring intently down the hall that led to the blood magic cells.

"Anything that makes her sound like a victim, if I know Rosalina at all." Mother sounded unusually bitter. She had ever since they'd left for Riverayn. Roska wondered if it was a manifestation of her guilt for having placed him in the Mad Queen's care.

"She always was a bit of a silver-tongued devil. I imagine she's spinning the tale to make it all seem like either she was brainwashed by the Brotherhood, or she was acting out of heartbreak and therefore not responsible for her actions." Aiden lounged on the King's throne, leg thrown casually over the arm of the massive chair. He was the picture of nonchalance, which was how Roska knew their father was nervous. He'd spent enough time with the demi-god over the last few moons to be able to recognize his moods. The man was anxious, possibly even scared. Aiden knew something was coming, Roska could see it in the way their father tried to project cool indifference. He knew better than to ask though. If Aiden had *seen* something that was about to happen, he steadfastly refused to speak on it. He'd explained once that it was because he didn't want to sway the outcomes of things. Aiden believed that he wasn't meant to have the visions he'd stolen from the Fae, so any time he sensed a fork in the metaphorical road, he refused to intervene.

Something big was coming.

Roska just hoped that it wasn't something of the deadly sort.

Roska bolted upright in his chair when Elena and Niko entered the throne room. Niko was pale as he strode mindlessly to the long table in the center of the room. He nearly collapsed into an empty chair, Elena grasped his hand tightly as she sat beside him.

"What happened?" Roska asked, concern etched in his tone.

"She confessed." Niko's voice sounded utterly disconnected, monotone, and emotionless.

Roska fell back in his chair, mouth wide with shock. "Confessed?"

"Confessed to what?" Quinn wasn't shocked so much as suspicious.

"To killing my father." The New King stared blankly at the highly polished table before him. Roska worried that he might not make it through the day. The Queen was a bigoted, evil woman, but she was still his mother. To hear her confess to killing his father had to be devastating.

"She said it was an accident, Niko." Elena gripped his hand tighter, rubbing her other hand comfortingly across his shoulders. "She didn't mean to kill him." Elena turned to her brothers. "The Queen explained that she and the King had been fighting on her balcony and she slapped him. He lost his balance and went over the railing."

A heavy silence descended on the throne room. No one could fully comprehend the Queen's confession. If the Queen had told them the truth, then maybe she didn't deserve the blood magic cell after all. Killing the King was still a crime, but doing so by accident? Roska didn't envy Niko for the decisions he would have to make regarding his mother. The people of Waverly would demand an explanation for the sudden death of their otherwise healthy King. They would want to know how Niko had become King and they would have many questions about the Queen's actions.

Being royal sounds miserable, Demoni observed. Roska couldn't disagree.

"Do you believe her?" Mother asked. She seemed to be trying to keep her judgments to herself, but Roska thought he heard doubt in her voice. She didn't trust the Queen. Truthfully, none of them did, but Niko was her son. If anyone would be able to read that woman, it would be him.

When Niko didn't answer and continued to stare blankly at the table, Elena answered for him. "We don't know. All we have is the Queen's story. It would be easy to take her at her word, but she's proven to be deceitful and self-serving." Niko flinched subtly at her words, but he didn't contradict her. He knew his mother was the villain of this story. "I think we should speak with the staff. Maybe someone saw or heard something to confirm her version of events." Elena addressed the room but kept her gaze fixed on Niko. Waiting for him to disagree with her, maybe? Niko offered an almost imperceptible nod. Roska was impressed that Elena was stepping up, making these hard choices, and leading when it was clear Niko wasn't in a position to do so. He didn't know much about her upbringing, but he knew being a leader didn't come naturally to her. She clearly cared deeply for Niko if she was willing to step forward—so far out of her comfort zone—and make these hard decisions for him.

"I'll take the house staff." Quinn rose from his chair. "No one ever notices them. If anyone saw anything, I'll bet it was one of the maids."

Elena nodded and Quinn quickly left the room.

"I can revisit her memories," Belladonna offered, coming to take a seat across the table from Niko. "I can use my magic to join my mind with hers and see what happened for myself."

Niko's head jerked up to face her. "You can?"

Belladonna nodded solemnly. "I've done it with Quinn a couple of times, helping him work through some of his darker memories. It's not painful, I promise," she added quickly when it seemed Niko was disturbed by the thought. "I just use my magic to meld my mind with someone else's. I guide them back to a specific moment or feeling, and I can witness their memories unfold as if I were there with them."

Beatrice stepped behind Belladonna's chair, placing a supportive hand on the back of the witch's neck. Roska wondered if Beatrice and Belladonna had ever shared memories like that. What sort of memories would they want to revisit together?

Probably not any you want to witness, Demoni teased. Roska shuddered at the implications. No child ever wanted to witness the romantic exploits of their parents.

Niko's body had gone rigid as he gaped at Belladonna.

"Maybe we'll save that as a last resort," Elena answered for him. "If we can't find anyone to corroborate her story."

Belladonna nodded, unoffended.

"What can we do to help you right now, Niko?" Aiden spoke softly. Roska was surprised to hear an almost paternal affection in his voice. He'd never really considered Aiden to be much of a *father*. Roska recognized that the demi-god was *their* father, but the man acted more like a big brother than a parent most of the time. He'd assumed it was simply because Aiden had no experience as a parent. He didn't know how to be a father because he'd never had the chance to learn.

"Why don't we have some food? We haven't eaten since breakfast, Niko. I'm sure you're hungry." When Niko didn't move or react, Elena tacked on, "I know I am."

Her admission of hunger seemed to snap Niko out of his numbed mental state, at least a little. His eyes cleared as he turned to her. "I'm so sorry, Firefly. I should have asked the cooks to bring us food as soon as we'd arrived."

"I'll go speak to the cooks and have some food brought up. Would you like to eat in here? Maybe you should try and get a little sleep too? You both look exhausted." Roska pushed up from the table as he spoke.

"That's a great idea, Ros. Can you ask the kitchen staff to make something hearty but not too heavy?" Elena turned to Niko, gently pulling him up from his chair. "We can eat in your room and take a nap. I'm so tired. I know you have to be, too."

Niko nodded, pulling her hand into the crook of his arm. "That's a good idea. Food and sleep."

Roska admired the way Elena was handling things. Handling Niko. He was certain that if Elena had suggested Niko needed to eat and sleep, he would have declined. Probably make some argument about being King and having responsibilities. He would have been right, but he wasn't in the right mindset for making major decisions right now. The New King looked as though he might pass out at any minute. With Elena wording it as though *she* were the one who needed food and sleep, she appealed to his need—more like compulsion—to take care of her. He would eat and rest *with* her because he believed that *she* needed it. It was quite clever, honestly.

Roska jogged down the hall, heading for the kitchens while Niko guided Elena to his chambers—apparently, he had an entire wing of the castle to himself.

When he reached the kitchens, Roska relayed Elena's requests to the head cook and took a seat on one of the barstools in front of a flour-covered table.

"Can I get something for you, sir?" one of the cooks asked. "We just took some rolls from the ovens. Maybe a bit of fresh butter or jam to go with it?"

Roska was about to decline when his stomach let loose the loudest—and most embarrassing—grumble. Cheeks flushing, Roska simply nodded as the young man chuckled and placed a couple of steaming rolls on a plate. He set the plate before Roska, then brought him a small bowl of blackberry jam and another bowl of butter. Roska muttered a quick thanks while he sliced open a roll and slathered a large helping of jam on one side.

The moan that escaped his mouth as he tasted the bread was borderline pornographic. Roska had eaten well at Harbor Ridge, but the food there had been purely sustenance. The food that sat before him now was decadent. It was rich, full of vibrant flavor, and unlike anything he'd ever tasted in his life.

"That good, huh?" The young cook smiled as he brought over a glass of milk. "I'm glad you like it. The jam is my personal recipe. More honey, less sugar, and just a hint of cinnamon. It's what gives it that extra something."

"It's magnificent." Roska praised the cook through a mouthful of bread. He took a long drink from the milk and smiled sheepishly at the young man. He couldn't have been much older than Roska. Honey brown eyes, light brown skin, and flour in his short black hair.

"Thanks." He smiled and Roska felt something electric zing through him. Similar to Elena's lightning, but less powerful and more warming.

"I'm Roska, by the way." He offered the cook his hand. When their skin connected, it was as though that shock magnified and lit up his whole body.

"Miguel."

60

QUINN

S*O, WHAT'S THE PLAN?* Lyra asked silently as she trotted along beside Quinn down the long hallway.

I'm going to ask the maids what they saw. Q had thought he'd been pretty clear about that when they'd been in the throne room.

You're just going to ask them, "Hey, did you see the Queen kill the King?" And you expect them to answer honestly?

I thought I'd start by figuring out which maid or maids service the Queen's chambers, then asking them directly, yeah.

Lyra's bark of laughter echoed off the stone walls. *Gods, you're naive. You expect them to betray her so easily?*

Quinn stopped in the middle of the hall. He hadn't thought of it like that. They knew the Queen was rotten to her core, but it was possible the staff didn't see her that way. It was possible they actually liked her, felt *loyal* to her, and wouldn't give her up too quickly.

What do you think we should do, then? Quinn asked. Clearly, Lyra had some sort of plan, or she wouldn't be so cocky in dismissing his.

I think we should talk to the chambermaids.

Quinn stared at her incredulously. *That's literally* exactly *what I was going to do.*

No, not the maids who take care of the Queen and her rooms. The chambermaids. The ones who clean out the chamber pots for the whole castle.

Quinn's nose scrunched in disgust. Chamber pots. Those fancy ass pots that rich people used because they were too good to use an outhouse, or just piss in the woods.

Why would we want to talk to them? Q raised an eyebrow speculatively. *What would they know that the others wouldn't?*

Your face should be reason enough. Q thought she was making a dig at him, but she continued. *You look down on them.* Quinn wanted to argue, but he knew his face already confirmed her accusation. *Everyone does. No one wants to talk to them, and everyone goes out of their way to ignore them.*

The truth of her words struck him like a slap to the face. Everyone ignores them. No one would notice if a chambermaid was in the room when they committed regicide—or was it mariticide? Chambermaids were practically invisible.

The sheer brilliance of her plan made Q as close to giddy as he'd ever been in his life. *Where do we find chambermaids?*

Mux if I know, Lyra snapped, flicking her tail in annoyance. *Am I supposed to do everything for you?*

Quinn chuckled and started down the hall once more. They'd find the servants' quarters, and then just keep asking for chambermaids until they found one. It might take some time, but of all the servants who might admit to seeing the Queen kill the King, an invisible girl was their best bet.

It was clear when they'd reached the servants' quarters. The thick, soft rugs that had lined each stone hall quickly shifted to thin, threadbare carpets. There were no windows in the servants' halls, only oil sconces that left thick, black smoke hanging in the air. The ornate doors that marked each room on the main floors were replaced by chipped, unvarnished wood and iron doors.

It was bleak and a bit depressing.

The servants were appalled to find him and Lyra in their halls, several offering to escort him back to the "castle proper", as they called it. When he asked to speak with a chambermaid, every single one of them made a look of disgust and tried to deter him. Even the servants avoided and neglected these invisible girls.

After insisting—rather aggressively—one of the haughty butlers finally directed him to the space where the chambermaids slept. It was the most depressing sight Q had ever seen. And he'd slept in the gutters in the alley behind the butcher's shop in Andover.

The room was underground, in the basement beneath the kitchens. Q could see the shuffling feet above him through the cracks in the floorboards as the cooks went about preparing for dinner. Hot grease dripped through the floor, landing on his shoulder. Quinn bit his lip to keep from cursing. He didn't want to startle anyone, but muxing hells. That hurt.

On the hard-packed earth floor, there were three makeshift pallets. They looked to be old, empty grain and flour sacks.

These poor kids, Quinn thought. *No one should be forced to sleep in a place like this.*

You can tell them that. Lyra motioned to the maids looking down their noses at him as he stood in that godsforsaken room.

"Where are the chambermaids?" he demanded. The cocky maids quickly lost their self-righteous looks. They didn't answer, but one of the maid's eyes flew to a small wardrobe across the room. Quinn glared at her for a moment, then strode across the room. He pulled the door, but it wouldn't budge. He looked over his shoulder at the maids, but they had all fled.

Quinn put an ear to the wardrobe. "Is anyone in there?"

A muffled cry came from inside.

Mux those assholes. "I'll get you out. Just hold on."

Quinn scowled at the wardrobe door. He couldn't use his fire to break it open. He might burn one of the girls that way. He couldn't pull it open. It was either locked or stuck. Either way, sheer brute force wouldn't do it without risking harm to the girls trapped inside.

Too bad you don't travel with lock picks anymore. They'd be handy right about now.

Lyra was right. He didn't have lock picks anymore, but he had a dagger and he could make that work. He was out of practice—picking any locks with a blade was a unique challenge—but he'd been damn good at it for many cycles. Thank the gods for muscle memory. It took him longer than he would have liked, but Quinn was able to finagle the tumblers in the wardrobe lock with the thin blade of his boot dagger.

He wrenched the door open, revealing three terrified pairs of eyes staring wildly up at him.

They were children. Hells, the oldest couldn't have been more than ten cycles old. The youngest looked to be about six. The oldest girl put herself between Quinn and the others, using her body to block his view of them as best she could. Q saw the look of abject terror on all three faces, but the oldest girl's eyes held a look he was all too familiar with. Resignation. She'd been beaten down for so long, she expected it. She didn't intend to fight back against whatever she expected him to do to her. She only wanted to protect the younger girls.

Quinn sat back hard on the floor, dropping his dagger and tightening his hands into painful fists.

These poor kids. Lyra stepped cautiously closer, keeping her head down.

"We aren't going to hurt you." Quinn kept his voice low and calm, keeping a tight grip on the rage that flooded his system. It wouldn't do any good to loosen his grip; he'd lose control of his fire and terrify the girls even more. They'd clearly been through hells. "My name is Quinn. This is my friend, Lyra. We'd like to take you out of here, if that's ok? We could go up to the kitchens for a snack. Would you like that?"

The younger girls kept their faces hidden behind filthy hands, whimpering quietly behind their protector. The older girl glared heatedly at him. Quinn took a deep breath and released his fists. He sat up, crossing his legs and laying his hands calmly on his knees.

He needed these girls to trust him. He wouldn't force them to go anywhere with him, but he couldn't leave them down here.

Lyra crawled over to the wardrobe. Filth and muck darkened the light orange and white fur that covered her belly. The tip of her tail flared gently, offering light without projecting any sort of aggression. When she reached the threshold of the wardrobe, she laid her head down on the worn wood. Her nose was mere inches from the oldest girl's bare foot. Close enough for the girl to reach out and touch, if she wanted.

"You can do whatever you want to me." The girl's voice was harsh, blunt. "Just leave my sisters alone."

Sisters. Mux every godsdamned one of those shyt servants.

"We aren't going to hurt you. Any of you. I just want to talk to you. I was hoping you could help me with a problem."

The girl's hate-filled glare didn't waver, but behind her, the youngest girl seemed to take an interest in Lyra. She peeked under her sister's arm, green eyes alight with curiosity.

Lyra noticed her gaze and shifted ever-so-slightly, giving the girl access to her back, without moving her head. She was letting the little girl touch her, without making her feel threatened by Lyra's sharp teeth or the fire glowing on her tail.

The older sister's eyes flicked from Quinn's to Lyra and back again. She didn't trust them, but maybe she wanted to. Quinn didn't move. He'd been where this girl was. He knew the overwhelming urge to protect the ones she loved would drive her to do pretty much anything. He needed answers about the Queen, but he could wait. The Queen was in prison. She wasn't going anywhere anytime soon.

These girls, though? They'd been through gods only knew what kinds of torture. It would take time to earn their trust. He could wait.

A tentative hand slipped passed the oldest sister's outstretched arms, fingers gently brushing through Lyra's thick, burnt orange coat. Lyra sat frozen. When nothing bad happened, a second hand—Quinn suspected it belonged to the middle sister—reached out and touched Lyra as well.

The older sister didn't take her eyes off Quinn, but he could tell she was aware of her sisters' actions and cautiously weighed their options. Q sat perfectly still, hands on his knees, dagger out of reach. He wanted to project as much peace and safety for these girls as Amelia had given him. He didn't know the situation surrounding their lives or how they came to be chambermaids, but he wouldn't let them come back to this hells hole. When they left with him today, they would be going to a safer, happier home. Even if it meant taking them all the way to Andover and Amelia.

"What do you want from us?" the oldest asked. The defeat in her voice broke his heart. She was so accustomed to people taking from her, using her and her sisters. He didn't want to imagine the things that had been done to them. He couldn't let his mind go down that path. He'd end up slaughtering the entire kingdom.

"I just want to talk." Quinn held her gaze, keeping his eyes as soft and impassive as possible.

The younger sisters seemed emboldened by Lyra's calm, scooting closer and burying their hands in her soft fur. The oldest flicked her eyes nervously between her sisters and the fox. She seemed to expect Lyra to snap at any moment.

"About what?" she asked, her wary eyes now fixed on where her sisters' hands disappeared into Lyra's fur. To her credit, Lyra didn't even seem to breathe. She was statuesque in her stillness.

"The Queen."

All three pairs of eyes flew to his face. Steel seemed to form under the oldest girl's skin as her sisters pulled their hands back and cowered behind her. "Why?"

"Because I think she killed the King, and I want to know if any of you saw anything."

Don't sugarcoat it or anything. Not like there are three terrified kids here. Lyra chided without moving a muscle.

These kids have been through enough. They don't need me lying to them or trying to make light of shyt.

"Why would you believe anything we have to say?" the oldest pressed. She didn't deny his claims. Interesting.

"I'm a friend of the New King. King Niko."

Friend, huh? We're claiming him as a friend now?

"He wants to know what happened to his father. My sister, brother, and I are trying to find the truth." The girl seemed to light up a bit at the mention of his sister. Maybe she'd be willing to talk to Elena. "If you'd like, I can bring you three to see my sister. She's just upstairs with King Niko. I know she'd love to meet the three of you."

The youngest peeked out from under her sister's arm again. "You have a sister?" Her voice was tiny, weak, like she didn't use it very often.

"I do. Her name is Elena. She's an enchantress." The girl's eyes grew wide. "Can I tell you a secret?" He was speaking to the littlest girl now, but he could see he had the unfettered attention of all three. The little girl nodded enthusiastically. Quinn smiled, leaned forward, and spoke in a stage whisper. "I think she's in love with King Niko." The little girl giggled, a smile lighting up her tiny face. "Would you like to meet her?"

The little girl looked cautiously up at her big sister, who chewed on her lip nervously.

"I won't let anyone hurt you," Quinn said, locking eyes with the oldest. "*Ever* again."

The vehemence in his tone must have convinced her. The oldest gave a subtle nod of agreement and cautiously reached out to touch Lyra. Unlike her sisters, she didn't reach for the firefox's back. Instead, she placed her hand right between Lyra's eyes. Giving the canine a chance to betray her. It was a test, but one Quinn would have done as well. The girl didn't trust them, but she was willing to take a risk, putting herself in harm's way. When Lyra didn't move, the girl scratched between her ears and slowly climbed out of the wardrobe.

Lyra took slow, deliberate steps away from the wardrobe, keeping her tail down and her face as nonthreatening as possible.

The youngest climbed out of the wardrobe and bounded over to Quinn before her sister could stop her.

"I'm Lilly." She smiled at him. "I like your dog."

Lyra huffed indignantly. Quinn chuckled. "Thank you. She's actually a firefox. She has magic, just like me and my siblings." To demonstrate, Lyra padded over to the single candle on the floor by the girls' pallets. With a careful touch of her tail, she lit the wick.

Gasps escaped all three girls. Excitement, awe, and fear.

Quinn stayed on the ground, unmoved from his cross-legged position, as the girls crept closer to Lyra. The oldest hung back, watching him closely. She took a tentative step forward, looking down at him from her position standing over him. "Why are you being nice to us?"

Quinn didn't think his heart could break anymore, but he'd been wrong. It shattered at the dejectedness in her question. No one had ever been nice to them before, so why would he? "Because you're a person. All people should be treated with kindness," he explained, but then he paused, thinking of his foster parents, the Queen, the Brotherhood, and all the people who had abused these innocent little girls. "Well, all people should be treated with kindness until they show their true colors. Some people deserve to burn."

He worried for a second that his violent words might scare the young girl, but she seemed to appreciate his candor and nodded solemnly. She offered him her hand. "I'm Delilah. These are my sisters, Ivy and Lilly."

Quinn shook Delilah's hand. "It's an honor to meet you." And he truly meant it. "Would you like some food before we go to meet my sister?"

Delilah contemplated their options for a moment, watching her sisters play with Lyra's ears and examine her glowing tail. "Yes, I think my sisters would appreciate a snack. It's been a couple of days since we last ate." Her statement was so casual, Quinn felt the rage in him build. *Days. No one had fed these girls in days.*

"Let's get moving then. I think I smell fresh rolls. If we're quick, I bet they'll still be warm." Quinn kept his voice light as he stood. If he let the girls hear the anger that flowed within him, they'd be too scared to go anywhere. Better to wait and unleash his ire on those who truly deserved it. He just needed to figure out who that was first.

Quinn led the way out of the servants' quarters and into the kitchens. Several of the servants looked disgusted and uncomfortable as Quinn passed by with the girls following along behind him, but the flames burning in his eyes drove their gazes away and kept their mouths shut tight. Lyra followed behind the youngest girl, snapping her sharp teeth at anyone who dared to make a comment as they passed.

Roska was still in the kitchens when they arrived, chatting with a flour-covered cook. The young cook jumped when he saw Quinn with the chambermaids, but instead of chastising the girls for being dirty in the kitchens, or being in the kitchens at all, he knelt down before them and asked if they'd like some food. He brought them plates of rolls, jams, freshly washed fruits and vegetables, and set them up at a table that was clearly his workstation.

Roska caught Quinn's eye and motioned for him to follow. They stepped away from the kitchen bustle, although Q made sure to stay within eyesight of the girls and Lyra stayed beside them. "Who are they?" Roska asked curiously.

"They're the chambermaids. Ros, I found them locked in a muxing wardrobe. The oldest says they haven't eaten in days. I don't know who the hells is running the staff around here, but I swear to the Mother, I will kill them for what they've put those girls through." Fire danced on his arms as he vented to his brother. Quinn had kept such a tight grip on his powers since finding the girls, he needed to burn off some of his rage before he exploded.

Roska placed his icy hands on Quinn's arms, cooling the fire within him. "They will never have to go back there. We will take care of them." Roska understood and shared Q's rage instantly. "How did you find them? I thought you were going to talk to someone about the Queen."

Q nodded. "That's why I went to find the chambermaids. No one pays attention to them. They can see and hear everything and no one even notices that they're there. I think they know something. But I have to convince them to trust me first."

Roska gave him a knowing look. "So you brought them to the kitchens for food. Smart. They probably haven't eaten this well in ages. Maybe ever. Miguel will take good care of them."

Quinn raised an incredulous eyebrow. "Miguel?"

Roska's face immediately flushed as he pulled his arms back and crossed them over his chest. "Yes. Miguel."

"What about Brigit?" Q asked. There was no judgment in his words, just curiosity.

"What about her? I haven't seen her in moons. She probably doesn't even remember me."

"Ros, we both know you aren't that easy to forget. But we can deal with that later. I'm taking the girls to see Elena once they get their fill. Maybe then they can tell us what—if anything—they saw and we can finally finish this bullshyt with the Queen."

"Mind if I join? I'd like to hear what they have to say, too." Roska looked past Quinn to the girls as they finished their relatively simple meals.

"Of course, bro. Maybe you can help me build some trust with them too." Quinn knew he was going to need all the help he could get.

61

ELENA

A KNOCK AT THE door roused Elena from where she'd been dozing in an armchair beside the bed. She'd insisted that Niko sleep in the bed but had steadfastly refused to join him. She promised to stay close by, but insisted she wasn't that tired after all. It was a lie, of course, but she knew he needed sleep. She pretended to read a book in the sitting area until she heard the steady rhythm of his breathing, then she'd allowed herself a respite, dropping all pretense of reading and succumbing to the exhaustion that plagued her.

She rose from the chair, stretching and releasing the most delicious pops in her spine. "I'm coming, I'm coming," she muttered quietly as the knock came again, more insistent this time. She gingerly closed the bedroom door and stepped quietly to the suite door. "Yes?" she asked, pulling the door open slightly.

"El, I have some people you need to meet." Quinn, Roska, and three small girls in threadbare rags that barely passed for clothing stood in the hallway outside their door.

Elena pulled the door open wider and welcomed them into the space. The girls looked around the room, mouths and eyes agape as they took in the luxurious space. A chandelier with dozens of candles hung from the high ceiling. A thick, elegantly detailed rug covered the polished stone floor. Three massive couches created a semicircle around a low table, facing the massive fireplace. Elena smiled at the awe on the girls' young faces.

Quinn looked around the room, attempting to hide his own awe. Clearing his throat he said, "Elena, I would like you to meet Delilah, Ivy, and Lilly." At hearing their names, the girls quickly closed their mouths and dropped their eyes, staring nervously at their bare feet.

Elena knelt down before them, meeting their eyes individually. "It's lovely to meet you, ladies. How can I help you?"

The youngest girl, Lilly, beamed up at Elena. "Gods, you're pretty," she whispered. Instantly, the girl seemed to regret her words, clamped her mouth shut, and stared, embarrassed, at the floor.

Elena grinned at the girl, reaching out slowly, and offering Lilly her hand. When Lilly tentatively took it and glanced back up, Elena's grin widened. "Thank you, sweetheart. You are very pretty too." Tears sprang to the girl's eyes as she shook her head in disagreement, but Elena wouldn't hear anything to the contrary. "All three of you are absolutely beautiful. I don't know where they've been hiding you here, but I think you should stay in one of the guest suites for a while." She glanced up at Q and Roska, "We should invite their parents to join us."

The oldest girl spoke at this. "We don't have parents." She wasn't embarrassed. She spoke matter-of-factly.

"In that case, Delilah, that would put you in charge. No wonder these two are so strong. I would be so grateful if you would be my guides here. I'm new to the castle and I don't really know my way around here." The girl stood a bit straighter at Elena's praise, lifting her jaw with pride.

"We would be happy to, milady."

"Oh, Elena, please. I'm no lady. Just an enchantress who failed out of magic school." She offered Delilah a small, self-deprecating smile.

"We actually came here to talk to you about the Queen," Quinn said, guiding the conversation to his intended purpose. "These girls are the chambermaids. Well, I suppose they *were* the chambermaids." Delilah blanched at Q's words. "Now they are the royal guides." A proud smile split across the young girl's face. "As chambermaids, though, they were given the run of the castle and no one noticed them. I think they might have some information about what happened to the King."

Delilah shut down at the mention of the King. Elena worried what that reaction could mean. She knew the King had a proclivity for straying from his marital bed, but she desperately hoped that didn't mean he ventured into the rooms of children.

"What do you know about my mother?" Niko spoke from the bedroom doorway.

Elena jumped to her feet and closed the distance between them quickly. "Niko," she said in a quiet voice. "I thought you were still sleeping."

"I need to know what they have to say." Niko attempted to take a step forward, but Elena blocked his path. He was clearly angry and she didn't want him to scare the girls.

"Niko, wait." She placed a firm hand in the middle of his chest, forcing him to stall and look at her. "They're children. Scared and abused by the look of it." She kept her voice low so they wouldn't be overheard. "If you go in there demanding answers, they will shut down and refuse to say anything. You need to calm down first." She could feel his heart racing under her palm. He studied her for a moment, then nodded. He took several slow, deep breaths before he spoke again.

"I apologize, ladies," Niko spoke calmly and kindly. Taking Elena's hand in his, he twined their fingers and walked into the room, stopping in front of Delilah. "I didn't mean to startle you. I'm deeply sorry, and I hope you can forgive me."

The younger siblings kept their eyes downcast, but Delilah stared up—way up—at her King while she debated his words. Elena was surprised by the girl's moxie. She didn't cower in the presence of royalty. She nodded an acceptance of his apology and that was that.

"The Queen killed him."

"That's what we heard," Elena replied as Niko tightened his grasp on her hand. "We were told that they got in a fight, she slapped him, and he lost his balance, falling off the balcony and dying."

Delilah chewed her lip, contemplating her next words. She looked nervously from Niko to Elena.

"If that's not the whole story, we need to know." Niko spoke quietly, keeping his tone neutral even as his fingers dug into Elena's hand. "The truth is the most important thing. You will not be punished for telling me the whole truth."

Delilah studied him a moment longer. "That is kinda what happened, Your Majesty. But he didn't really *fall*."

"She pushed him." Ivy piped in.

"They were fighting, and she slapped him, that's true, Your Majesty," Delilah added quickly, "but he didn't lose his balance and fall. The Queen screamed at him and pushed him over the edge."

"She called him all sorts of bad words," Lilly added.

"It was really weird." Delilah's voice sounded off. Distant. "Like the air around the King moved and pushed him over the edge." The girl shook her head, realizing the words she'd spoken and blushing at them. "Apologies, Your Majesty. I'm not sure why I said that."

Elena studied the girl for a moment, wanting to ask more about this revelation, but Niko's hand went slack. She knew this was what he'd feared and prayed wouldn't be true, but she could also tell that he knew it was the whole truth, without a doubt.

The Queen had willfully and intentionally killed the King. She'd committed treason. Mariticide. Regicide. And now Niko had to determine how to deal with her.

"Thank you for your honesty, ladies." He spoke without emotion. "Elena, can you get them settled? I need to attend to some things." Without waiting for her response, he dropped her hand and strode from the room.

62

BELLADONNA

AN AGGRESSIVE POUNDING ON the door jarred Belladonna from her meditative state. She was still recovering from the onslaught of pain she experienced when the wild fire had burned through the Dark Woods. Meditating with the plants in their bedroom was helping, but the incessant pounding on their door was not.

She wrenched the door open angrily, prepared to bite the head off whatever idiot thought banging on a door was an appropriate way to request entry into a space. She stopped cold when she saw the pale, tight-lipped King beyond the threshold.

Belladonna stepped aside and Niko marched into the suite.

"What's happened? Oh gods, Elena?"

Niko shook his head quickly. "She's fine. I need you to interrogate my mother."

Belladonna gawked at him. He couldn't be serious. After the visceral reaction he'd had at the mere suggestion, there was no way he'd suddenly changed his mind. Unless...

"Quinn found a witness who tells a different story, didn't he?"

"He found three."

"Three? Three witnesses?"

Niko nodded. "Three little girls who have no reason to lie. They all tell the same story. Murder. She pushed him over the balcony on purpose. She *killed* my father." Niko clenched his fists and gritted his teeth so hard, Belladonna was certain his jaw and hands would be sore by the end of this.

"Are you sure this is what you want? Once you know the truth, the whole truth, you can't undo it."

Niko didn't hesitate. "I need to know what really happened."

Standing in the throne room, with Niko seated in his father's chair, he glared down at his mother. Elena stood beside him, her hand resting supportively on his shoulder as she looked on at the Queen with quiet disappointment.

She'd been restrained and brought to be interrogated before the King, with the assistance of Belladonna's magic. They would get the whole story from Rosalina. Whether she liked it or not.

"Bring her to me." Belladonna's voice sounded distant and disconnected.

The guards hauled the disgraced Queen from the chair and dragged her across the room to kneel before the witch.

Belladonna glared down at the woman as she placed her hands on either side of her cornsilk hair, closed her eyes, and dove into the Queen's memories.

Images flew through her mind in a blur. Snippets of conversations and glimpses of scenes passed in and out of her mind's eye. Belladonna tried to direct the memories, but it was considerably harder with an unwilling host.

After what felt like ages, Belladonna's mind caught on a very recent image of the King. Hints of silver flashed through his hair and a small collection of wrinkles gathered by his eyes. He was yelling something. Calling the Queen unreasonable. They appeared to be on the Queen's balcony.

This must be it! Belladonna latched on to that memory and pulled herself into it. She watched from the shadows as the Queen berated the King for his philandering ways. He laughed at her, genuinely amused by her outrage.

"I got what I needed from you. I have an heir. I don't need you anymore. I could have gotten rid of you ages ago, just like my father did with my mother. I didn't. You should be grateful." The King looked down on the Queen, disinterest and boredom etched on his face.

The Queen, however, was not so calm. She raged against the man, running up to him and slapping him across the face so hard Belladonna could feel the pain in her own palm. "You arrogant, selfish bastard. How dare you talk to me that way. How dare you talk to the *Queen* that way!"

To Belladonna's surprise, the King laughed again. He wiped the back of his hand on his lip, finding blood, and began to cackle like a deranged beast. He actually found it amusing that the Queen had made him bleed?

Gods, the world would truly be a better place without these two, she thought. Almost immediately, Belladonna regretted the thought. Wishing someone ill, or death, wasn't like her. This man was a wretched human, and the Queen was considerably worse, but Belladonna wouldn't let herself stoop to their level.

The Queen advanced upon the King, raising her hand to slap him again. He swatted her away as though she meant nothing to him. Belladonna supposed that she did.

The King turned to walk away, muttering something about female hysterics. His words were quickly drowned out by the rage-filled shriek of the Queen as she charged and shoved him with all her might. The sheer force she used seemed to warp the very air around him. The King stumbled backward, closer to the railing, losing his balance as he went. Rosalina screamed, putting every ounce of her anger and feelings of betrayal into her rage-filled cry. The air itself cowed to her fury, whirling around her and lashing out at the King, knocking him over the edge.

What the hells?

His screams of terror were cut short by a sickening crunch.

As she was pulling out of the Queen's mind, another memory caught Belladonna's attention. One that Rosalina couldn't possibly *remember*, but it was part of her past and therefore existed in her mind.

Her birth.

The Queen's mother, a round-faced, pale-haired woman was straining and crying out in the birth bed, surrounded by her maids and midwives. Her husband, a lord of some kind, was nowhere to be seen.

Typical. Men are always happy to create a child but never present when that child is brought into the world.

Belladonna was about to remove herself from the Queen's mind entirely when she saw something impossible. Improbable, rather. Newborn Rosalina exited her mother's body, but she wasn't alone. An animal was wrapped in the newborn's arms.

Not just any animal.

A moonbird.

Belladonna would have recognized a witch's familiar anywhere, and yet, witnessing Rosalina's birth, and the babe clutching the moonbird to her tiny body, Belladonna's mind couldn't comprehend what she was seeing.

The Queen had a witch's familiar?

Rosalina was a witch.

Belladonna watched the scene unfold before her, thoroughly befuddled. The midwives seemed just as shocked. One woman held Rosalina while the second stared in pure shock at the bird in the babe's grasp.

"Give her to me," Rosalina's mother rasped.

The midwife passed her the child, a look of utter confusion on her face. The Lady was unfazed. She waved over a guard Belladonna hadn't noticed, taking the frail moonbird from her child and handing it to the guard. "Get it out of the castle. As far away as you can, and leave it."

Belladonna didn't understand what she was seeing. Separating a newborn from their familiar was like severing a magept from their soul, their conscience.

Without question, the guard took the moonbird and disappeared from the room. Within seconds, newborn Rosalina began to cry in agony. Belladonna could only imagine the pain the child was in. As a witch aged, the tether that connected her to her familiar expanded, allowing them to travel farther and farther apart. But as a newborn? Being more than a few paces apart would have been torture.

"Hush, darling," her mother cooed, wiping the babe's brow with a moist cloth. "This is for your own good." Her mother waved again and a handful of guards entered the room, surrounding the maids and midwives and herding them into the corner of the room.

"Milady, what is going on?" One of the maids demanded as the guards pulled their swords.

"I'm protecting my daughter." Her voice was calm, completely detached from the scene beyond the birthing bed. "Your sacrifice will not go unnoticed and your families will be well compensated for their losses." With that, the guards made quick work of slaughtering all of them. The guards then turned to the Lady, bowed, and carried the corpses from the room, closing the door firmly behind them.

The Lady rocked newborn Rosalina back and forth in the bed, cooing and shushing the child. With a wave of her hand, she summoned an altar cloth, candles, and garden shears to the middle of the bed. It settled in the afterbirth between her legs. The Lady placed baby Rosalina on the altar cloth, lit the candles, and began casting a spell.

Oh, gods. It wasn't just any spell. It was the banishing spell that kept a familiar from its witch. The Lady was banishing Rosalina's familiar. By the looks of the map and herbs she had laid out beside her, she was banishing Rosalina's familiar from Waverly entirely.

Belladonna couldn't bear to watch anymore. She closed her eyes and removed herself from the Queen's mind.

The Queen sat in a chair in front of Belladonna, her head lolled to the side, slow to wake from the memories Belladonna had forced her to relive.

"Well?" Niko demanded.

Belladonna kept her answer simple and succinct. The New King had been through enough as it was, she didn't need to drag it out by giving him all the gory details. Not to mention she had no idea how to process everything she'd seen. "What the witnesses told you is true. Your mother willfully and intentionally pushed the King from her balcony." She would keep the further revelations to herself for the time being, until she had a chance to discuss things with Beatrice.

Belladonna was surprised to see there wasn't an ounce of shock or surprise in Niko's reaction. He'd known his mother had been lying. He had wanted to believe her, but he knew better.

How utterly heartbreaking. To learn that your mother killed your father and to not even be caught off guard by the revelation.

"Niko," the Queen moaned pathetically, "my darling boy. You have to believe me. I was doing this for you. For us. For Waverly. He was being controlled by that whore." At that, Rosalina cut her eyes viciously to Beatrice.

Beatrice, however, looked on with nothing but pity. She'd moved passed her anger toward Rosalina and now only had pity for the wretched woman.

She's a better woman than I, Belladonna mused.

No argument here, Castor chimed in from his perch on the high ceiling's chandelier.

Belladonna wondered if the Queen realized who she was. Had she known her mother was a witch?

Niko ignored his mother's pleas, ordering the guards to take her back to her cell.

"What will you do with her?" Elena asked quietly, watching the guards haul the shrieking, disgraced murderer away.

"The punishment for treason is death by hanging." Niko answered automatically.

Elena stepped in front of him, taking both of his hands in hers and drawing his focus to her. "Yes, but what will you do with her?"

Niko blinked, tears glistening in his bloodshot eyes. "I have no idea."

63

ELENA

THEY SPENT THE NEXT week debating and discussing all possible options for how to handle the Queen's violent betrayal. Life in prison in a blood magic cell. Public hanging. Indentured servitude. The latter was the one that got the most interest. Niko couldn't bear to execute his mother, but he couldn't let her go unpunished either. Life in prison was an option, but Niko worried that his mother might somehow escape or needle her way into his mind and manipulate him into releasing her. Surprisingly, it was Beatrice who had offered the idea of servitude.

"She could serve out her life sentence as a servant at Harbor Ridge."

Elena had been utterly floored by the suggestion.

"Humor me, for a moment," their mother had said. "She's taken from all of us. She's taken your father from you, but she's taken children from us. There's a godsdamned cemetery at the school now that never should have existed. You deserve your pound of flesh, but so do we." Beatrice had gone on to explain that the Queen wouldn't be treated unkindly, but she would serve as she had treated her lowliest of servants. Quinn had appreciated that comment, having been the one to witness firsthand just how the Queen allowed her lowest servants to be treated.

It had taken Niko a few days of stewing on the concept, and conferring with some of his—newly appointed—trusted advisors, but he'd agreed to the idea.

Elena was dreading the moment when he informed his mother of her sentencing.

"Queen Rosalina, you have been found guilty of treason, regicide, mariticide, freeing a demon from its prison to commit mass murder, kidnapping the King and an enchantress, and conspiring to overthrow the crown—namely, me. The traditional punishment for even one of those crimes is death by hanging."

The Queen nearly collapsed at Niko's words. She hadn't expected him to find her guilty of anything and she clearly wasn't prepared to pay the price for her actions.

"That being said, I cannot execute my own mother."

Rosalina visibly relaxed, releasing the tension that had been keeping her upright. "Thank you for your mercy, my darling son. You will not regret it." She bowed and turned to leave the throne room when Niko spoke again.

"I wasn't finished."

Rosalina flinched at his tone, but thankfully kept her mouth shut.

"As this was an unusual case of malice and murderous intent, in which you aided in unleashing a demon that resulted in the mass murder of dozens, your punishment needed to be equal to the pain you wrought in your misguided attempts to reclaim something that was never yours."

Something that was never yours. Harsh, considering the Queen was trying to win back the love of the King, but it was likely true. The King never really loved anyone but himself.

"As penance for your heinous actions, you will serve out a life sentence in servitude at Harbor Ridge, where you will be under the direct authority of Madame LaBelle."

Hatred clouded her face as Rosalina turned her glare from her son to Elena. "You," she hissed. "You have corrupted my son. Just like your whore of a mother corrupted my beloved husband."

The Queen thrust her hand into her skirts, emerging with a tight fist clenched around a wickedly sharp dagger. She lunged for Elena. Elena barely had time to react. As the tip of the weapon came slashing down toward her, Elena raised her arms in defense, lightning flashing like a shield down both of her arms. Suddenly, Niko was in front of her, blocking Elena from the death blow his mother intended for her.

Time stood still as Niko grunted. The dagger had been truly wicked, slicing right through his sternum and plunging itself into his heart with a horrid, wet thump. He fell back into her, knocking them both to the floor as Elena tried to cushion his fall.

"No!" Rosalina shrieked. "You idiot child! Why did you do that?" The Queen rushed to his side, but Elena reacted first. Throwing her hands into the air, she unleashed all the rage and fear that filled her. Blinding blue lightning exploded off her fingertips, scoring the oak ceiling, shattering the stained glass windows, and sending the Queen flying across the expansive room. She landed with a thud on the unforgiving stone floor.

To everyone's surprise, the Queen rose quickly, fire burning in her eyes as she raised her hands. Elena gasped in utter disbelief as she saw the wind warp around the Queen, as though Rosalina was controlling it. The vile woman twisted her fingers in odd and complicated motions, causing the wind to twist as well.

Mother Goddess. The Queen was a witch?

Elena didn't have time to comprehend this turn of events, as the Queen had created a tornado in the middle of the throne room.

Belladonna and Mother seemed unfazed, quickly leaping into action and calling forth their own magics. Roska and Quinn positioned themselves between the Queen and Elena and Niko. Quinn conjured an Infernal, guiding it toward the Queen and her wicked cyclone.

Aleerah jumped before Elena, nudging Niko with her nose. "We need to move him. He can't stay here. He could be killed."

Elena couldn't help but think that he was already well on his way unto the Fade, but she didn't argue with the dire wolf. Aiden appeared by her side, helping to lift the King from her lap and throwing one of Niko's arms over his shoulders. Elena quickly lifted the other arm, wrapping it across her shoulders as well as they half carried, half dragged Niko to the edge of the throne room.

"You cannot stop me, you fools!" The Queen's deranged voice echoed off the stone walls of the throne room, distorted by the howling of the wind from her cyclone. "I have spent my entire life hiding who I am and cowering to inferior beings. I will *not* cower a second longer. I spent my life watching men rule the world simply because they could. Enchantresses showing off their magics like they didn't have a care in the world! Whereas I was forced to hide my true self from the world. Why? Because enchantresses are revered but witches are evil? I thought having my wolves kill you like the vermin that you are would be poetic, but doing it myself with be so much more cathartic!"

Her wolves? She sent those wolves to attack us in the Dark Woods? Agon's thoughts echoed in her head, but she couldn't focus on them.

The Queen's wicked tornado surged across the room, heading straight for Quinn and Roska. Elena gently laid Niko down on the floor as Aiden threw up a shield around the three of them. She watched in horror as shards of glass from the shattered windows whipped around the room. Mother and Belladonna held hands, chanting something Elena couldn't hope to hear, while Quinn's Infernal lunged toward the Queen. Roska built an ice wall around himself and Quinn, shielding them from flying debris as Quinn focused on controlling his Infernal. It was clear the tornado was affecting Q's ability to direct the flaming creature.

"Give me a window!" Elena shouted at Aiden.

"What?" Aiden looked at her as though she'd lost her mind.

"Give me a *window* in this shield. If I can blast her with a bolt of lightning from here, it will break her concentration on that damned tornado and give them the chance they need to stop her."

Aiden didn't look convinced, but he nodded. With a wave of his hands and a few words muttered in a language Elena had never heard before, a small hole appeared in the shield, directly in front of her. She had a clear shot, assuming her brothers didn't move and the tornado's powerful winds didn't pull her lightning off course. She had one chance at this. If she missed, the Queen could easily tear the entire castle down on top of them.

Don't think about that. Agon's voice echoed in her mind. *Just focus on the task at hand. Remember when we were living in that tower at the start of the frost season?*

Elena didn't particularly like thinking about the time their mother had imprisoned them "for their own good," but she knew why Agon had brought it up. They had spent days honing their magics. Target practice had been one of her favorite things to do. She'd gotten pretty good at it, too.

She took a deep, steadying breath. Her eyes locked on her target: the Queen's chest. At this point, she didn't even care if she killed the woman. Niko was unconscious on the ground beside her, his mother's blade still sticking out of his chest.

Mux the Queen.

Elena raised her right arm. Looking down the length of her arm, pointing a single finger, and taking aim.

One heartbeat.

Two heartbeats.

Three.

She let her lightning fly.

Blinded by the light of her electric bolt, it took several seconds for Elena's vision to clear, when it did, she saw her brothers dragging the Queen's limp—but unfortunately still conscious—body from the room and back down the hall that contained the blood magic cells.

Elena could hear the Queen's cries echoing down the hall as they forced her back into her cell. She couldn't focus on that hateful woman. Not when Niko was bleeding to death.

She sat down beside him, shifting his weight and laying his head in her lap while she took a closer look at the wound. The wound he'd sustained to save her. "You idiot," she choked out as tears flowed freely down her cheeks. "Why did you do that?"

"Had to... couldn't let her... hurt my Firefly." Niko started coughing violently, blood splattering his lips as his life force drained into his lungs.

Elena clutched his head to her chest, sobs wracking her body. She couldn't lose him. Not after everything. They still had so much left to do.

Aiden lowered his shield as her mothers crept quietly closer to where she sat with Niko against the throne room wall.

Her gaze flew to her mother, silently pleading with the woman to do something, *anything*, to save him. Mother said nothing, but shook her head nearly imperceptibly. Elena looked to Belladonna next. Surely the witch had access to other magics. Something that could heal him. When Belladonna only stared back, tears racing down her face, Elena knew there was nothing she could do.

Elena shifted, turning to see their father as he stared out the throne room window, watching the sunset as though the world wasn't falling apart behind him.

"Help him," Elena cried, her voice rough and strained. "Please, you have to be able to do something. You're a *god*."

Aiden turned to face her, walking slowly over to kneel beside her. "Demi-god, actually."

"Does that muxing matter?" Quinn snapped. Her brothers had returned. Elena hadn't even noticed.

"It does, actually. If I were a god, I could just snap my fingers, and he'd be good as new." Aiden spoke to Quinn, but he kept his eyes fixed on Elena. "As a demi-god, I can help him, but there is a cost."

"Anything. I'll pay *any* cost, just save him." Elena struggled to get the words out around the emotion that clogged her throat.

"I believe you, darling, but it's not that simple. It has to be his decision too."

Niko's breath was labored and ragged. He slowly opened his eyes, staring up at Elena. "Whatever it is, if it means I get to stay here with you, I'll pay it."

"If I do this, your life force will be forever intertwined with his. If he gets cut, you'll bleed, and vice versa." Elena was nodding and agreeing before Aiden even finished his sentence. "Think first, darling. If one of you dies, so will the other. There will be no way to undo this. Once it's done, it will bind you until death."

"There's nothing to think about. My heart has been tied to his since I met him." As the words left her mouth, Elena realized the weight and the truth of them. As much as she'd despised him when they first met, she'd known then that there was something about him that she needed.

Niko's eyes never left hers. She could see the love he had for her glowing in his eyes, even as his light faded. "Muxing do it already," she snapped at her father.

Aiden gingerly pulled the knife from Niko's chest. It made a sickening squelching sound as the blood started flowing rapidly. Quick as lightning, Aiden firmly pressed one hand over the wound and placed his other hand on the same spot on Elena's chest. Niko groaned, blood rushing around Aiden's hand as he tried to quell the bleeding while also muttering an incantation under his breath.

Elena thought she felt a hint of warmth spread through her chest, but then it seemed to flicker out.

Mother Goddess, please let this work, Elena prayed, grabbing hold of Niko's hands and squeezing as though she could save him through sheer force of will.

A sudden, blinding light radiated from beneath Aiden's hands as a searing pain bored through her chest. Elena's mouth hung open in a silent cry as Aiden's magic bound her to Niko. Her lightning flared, ricocheting off the stone floors and walls of the throne room.

Darkness danced around the periphery of her vision as the pain in her chest crested and finally began to fade.

Aiden removed his hands from their respective chests and sat back on the floor beside them, panting slightly. "How do you feel?"

Niko freed one of his hands from her vice-like grip and rubbed his fist on his sternum, massaging the spot that had been a gaping hole only moments before. "Surprisingly good," he said with a smile, looking up at Elena from where his head still rested on her lap. "How about you, Firefly?"

Elena closed her eyes. She felt... different, but not in a bad way. It was like her body had been split open and now a part of her resided elsewhere.

Because it does, dummy. Agon teased, licking the remainder of the tears from her cheeks.

Elena leaned into her familiar, pushing him just a little too far so that he nearly fell off her shoulder and onto Niko's face. Agon's claws tightened on her blouse, but he kept any more snide remarks to himself.

"I feel ok. I can tell that something is different, but it feels good. Warm. Tingly." Elena brushed a stray curl from Niko's sweat-slick brow. She felt the heat of his gaze as his eyes trailed down her face, latching on to her lips. The tingling warmth quickly spread from her extremities to pool in her low belly as a blush spread over her cheeks.

"Maybe we should give you two a few minutes," Aiden chuckled. Rising to his feet, he herded the others from the room, closing the door to the throne room as they departed.

Niko's soft lips tipped up into a sly grin as she stroked his hair absentmindedly. "I guess you're stuck with me now."

Elena broke into a broad grin of her own as she leaned forward and pressed her lips lightly against his. It wasn't quite a kiss, feather-light and chaste.

Quicker than she would have thought possible—especially considering he'd been mortally wounded only moments before—Niko was on his knees before her, wrapping his arms around her and kissing her with the passion of a formerly dying man.

Elena's fingers tangled deep in his curls, pulling him closer, and rising to her knees she pressed her body against his. She had a vague sense of Agon slipping from her shoulders and slinking from the room.

Niko groaned as she pulled his hair, dragging him down to lay on top of her on the cold stone floor. Deepening their kiss, his legs wedged themselves between hers. Elena practically purred as her hands roamed the muscular plains of his chest and arms.

"Something you like, Firefly?" His voice was a harsh whisper in her ear as his tongue teased that most sensitive spot where her earlobe met her neck.

All coherent thought fled from her mind as Elena lost herself in the overwhelming pleasure he wrought from her. Tightening her grip on his hair, Elena pulled his lips back to hers. Losing herself in the heat of the moment and releasing all the fear that had plagued her just moments before.

Later that evening, as they were sitting down to dinner with her family, Elena couldn't deny the weightlessness she felt. So much had happened in the last cycle. Losing her home. Discovering who she truly was. Finding her family. Reconciling with her mother. Finding the man she loved and binding herself to him. It was all so overwhelming.

"Firefly." Niko's whispered concern drew her focus.

His face was blurry. Oh, no, she was crying. Gods, why was she crying now? Everything was *finally* ok.

"Are you all right? What's wrong?" He stroked a strong hand up and down the length of her spine.

"I'm ok." Her voice was a watery laugh. "It's just been a really long time since I sat down to a meal and the world *wasn't* ending."

Quiet laughter filled the room as her family joined in.

"I can't remember the last time we had a meal that wasn't centered around making some kinda plan to stop someone from doing something diabolical," Quinn remarked, stabbing his steak with extra enthusiasm.

"I believe it was the night before Elena turned those bastards to dust," Lyra added thoughtfully.

Niko turned back to Elena, eyebrows raised in question.

"It's a long story. I'll tell you later." Casting her eyes down, attempting to focus on her food, warmth flooded Elena's cheeks.

"It's really not." Agon climbed into her lap. "A group of drunken brutes tried to take something that didn't belong to them. Elena stopped them. They'll never do it again."

"I guess it wasn't a long story after all." Elena's cheeks were on fire with every pair of eyes focused on her. "Let's talk about something else. *Anything* else, please."

"I've got some ideas to help reform this shyt show of servants you've got here, Your Majesty." Quinn flicked his gaze from Niko to the three young girls they'd adopted into their family. The girls weren't listening though. They were too enthralled watching Demoni as she created snow and ice sculptures.

"And I would love to hear them. Tomorrow." Niko sighed, stretching his arms high above his head and rolling his neck. "I just sentenced my mother to life as a servant, then nearly died, and was magically tethered to your enchanting sister for the rest of my life. I'm pretty sure that's all I can handle for today."

The doors of the Great Hall opened and a fleet of servants entered the room carrying dozens of small cakes in various colors and flavors. They set down platter after platter of cakes before Roska and Quinn. Her brothers looked around the table, thoroughly confused. Elena beamed at them.

"It occurred to me that neither of you ever knew our birthday and likely never got to have a proper birthday celebration. I took it upon myself to remedy that." Elena gestured to the cakes. "One for each cycle we've been on this planet. Sixteen in total, each. And next week, we'll have a big celebration to honor the completion of our seventeenth trip around the sun."

"Wait, next week?"

"Our birthday is next week?"

"Yes, boys." Mother smiled at them. A genuine smile. Elena was still getting used to seeing their mother genuinely happy. "On the twenty-fourth day of the planting season, I gave birth to three, perfect, magical creatures."

Roska and Quinn looked at each other, then to all the cakes piled high before them. Confusion faded as other emotions quickly passed across their faces. Quinn's face settled on excitement, while Roska's seemed a bit more reserved. Elena knew it was just because he felt overwhelmed by it all. He would come to her later, with questions or things he wanted to talk about. She would be waiting.

"Which cake should I start with? I'm not sure I can eat all this by myself." Q waggled his eyebrows at the girls. "I wonder if there's anyone here who would be willing to help me eat all these cakes."

The girls' shrieks of excitement as they volunteered to help left a ringing in Elena's ears, but she wouldn't have had it any other way.

EPILOGUE

*T*HREE SOLAR CYCLES LATER

Growing season in the Age of Sun and Storm

They were celebrating their twentieth solar cycle today. The castle was bustling with guests from all over the country, come to celebrate the birthday of the magical triplets. Harbor Ridge had sent its finest enchantresses to put on a show at sunset, and Amelia had brought along her newest foster children, a quartet of rambunctious boys that reminded Quinn unsettlingly of himself at that age. Thankfully, none of these boys seemed to have his affinity for fire.

Elena was pacing in her rooms after banishing the glamorists her mother had sent to help her prepare for the night's festivities. Belladonna tried to talk Beatrice out of it, of course, but Mother had been convinced that this was a special night and it deserved special treatment.

Roska wandered the halls, Demoni curled around his neck, as they silently discussed how they would take down the Brotherhood. They'd managed to eradicate all of the Brotherhood's influence in Riverayn *and the surrounding major cities. The remaining Brothers had fled to their compound to the east. Roska had been working with King Niko, Aiden, and the royal guards to plan an attack and finally rid the world of the Brotherhood's hateful bigotry. They were just waiting for the perfect time to strike.*

Quinn bumped into Roska in the hall outside Elena's room. Things had finally settled and he was adapting to this new normal. He had rooms in the capital and a suite to himself at Harbor Ridge, where he still taught occasionally. Amelia also kept a bed warm for him at the inn, where he spent most of the frost season, keeping her company and helping to wrangle the children she continued to house and raise until a family could be found for them. He also kept his home in the woods. He and Lyra would sneak off for days at a time when they needed the quiet time to reset and recharge.

Beatrice and Belladonna had taken to spending the majority of their time at Harbor Ridge, raising, training, and educating young magical people. No longer was Harbor Ridge exclusive to enchantresses. Once word had gotten out that witches were safe in Waverly—when Niko had formally banned the hunt and persecution of them—more and more had started showing up at the gates. The school now hosted dozens of witches in classes alongside the enchantresses, as well as the odd Fae looking to expand their knowledge. It was truly a magical safe haven for any creature hoping to learn more about their power.

Aiden had even taken up teaching history lessons at the school. He also assisted King Niko in navigating political challenges. Having lived through so many failed rulers, he knew which paths were likely to end violently and which paths would find peace and prosperity.

The girls—Delilah, Ivy, and Lilly—served as Elena's personal confidants and guides as she learned to navigate the tense political waters of Riverayn. Elena adopted them as her sisters, and the girls thrived under her patience and guidance.

Tonight was a big night for them all, but it was an especially important night for Niko. Tonight was the night he would finally ask Elena the most important question a person could ask another. He prayed to the Mother she'd say yes.

The sun had set. The enchantresses had put on the most magical show. Niko and Elena stood hand in hand on the balcony overlooking the courtyard, the citizens of Riverayn waiting below. It was time for his annual speech. It was a tradition he'd started the first cycle they'd celebrated the triplets' birthday in the capital. This cycle was special, though. As the enchantresses amplified his voice, he turned to face Elena, smiling down at her as she beamed at him with all the happiness in the world glowing through her eyes.

"Elena, my beloved Firefly," he began, his voice echoing throughout the capital. He took both of her hands in his, knelt before her, and asked, "Will you be my Queen?"

Tears flooded her eyes in seconds. Unable to speak, she nodded vigorously, pulling him to stand and throwing her arms around his neck.

Cheers reverberated off the castle walls, growing louder with each passing moment. Roska and Quinn clapped the loudest, calling on their magics to shower them in warm—but utterly harmless—embers and snowflakes. Beatrice and Belladonna held each other tight, tears reflecting in their own eyes. Aiden laughed heartily. He'd seen this image before, ages ago. He was thrilled to finally see it come to fruition.

So much had changed in the last four cycles. He couldn't wait to see what was in store for them next.

Acknowledgments

This book was a labor of love and a personal challenge. When I started drafting it in June of 2022, I challenged myself to get the first draft finished by the end of November. 6 months. It seemed crazy at the time, and honestly, it probably was. I definitely won't be pushing myself to publish 3 books in 6 months ever again. That being said, it was a lot of fun and I'm really proud of the finished product.

When I first started writing Storm and Flame all those years ago, I had no idea what I was doing or what to expect. I'm so grateful for all the ladies in the Moms Who Write group on Facebook, especially Arielle Hadfield. She is the first person "in the biz" who read my book and her praise and kind words of encouragement were what gave me to confidence to seriously consider self-publishing. If she hadn't offered to take a look at my first chapter and give me her insights, I probably would still be in the query trenches, bitterly hoping some magical agent would show an interest and manage to hook an even more magical publisher. Instead, thanks to Arielle's confidence in my writing, I started looking into doing it myself, and here we are! Three books in the world. Arielle, thank you. I couldn't have done this without you.

Have you noticed the covers? I happened upon Joli's Instagram feed while I was researching cover artists. She had several stunning premade covers, so I messaged her to see if she worked on commission as well. She has a magical way of taking my word-vomit descriptions and turning them into perfect pieces of art. I give her a theme and a few elements I want to keep or change, and she makes the most beautiful covers. It's like she's in my head. People always say "don't judge a book by its cover" and I agree that is true when it comes to everything, except books. The cover is the first thing people see. If they don't find the cover interesting, they aren't going to pick up the book. Joli does amazing work and that art grabs people's attention to reel them in. I wouldn't have the success I've had without her beautiful work. Thank you, Joli! I can't wait to see what you come up with for the next book!

I know I already thanked him in my first book, but my husband deserves a second (and third, and fourth, and millionth) shout-out for being such an amazingly supportive human. He's been so wonderful throughout this whole process. He doesn't have opinions often, but he voices them when he does and they tend to be spot-on. He's my favorite sounding board. The person I dump all my nonsense thoughts on while I'm trying to figure out what I need or want to say. Just for him, I will include his one suggestion every time I ask for a word. Here's the word he always offers, no matter what I'm looking for. You ready, honey? This one's for you!

Penis.

There, I put it in the book.

Oh, and here's one for Melissa. Fallopian Tube.

I think that about covers it! I'll see you in the next one. And yes, there will be a next one, don't worry!

ABOUT AUTHOR

Mallory lives in Texas with her husband and their two young boys. She spends her days homeschooling and full-time parenting. Her nights, and any free time she manages to carve out during the day, are devoted to reading and writing.

If you enjoy my stories, please make sure to leave a review on your favorite sites. That's the absolute best way to help me spread the word about Elena, Quinn, and Roska. Thank you so much! I'll see you in the next one.